THE FOOTBALL GAME

BY

SCOTT SAMAIN

EPILOGUE

FIRST HALF

CHAPTER I
KICK OFF

**CORRIDOR OF SAINT BARTHOLOMEW'S
HOSPITAL MATERNITY WARD**

SATURDAY 30TH JULY 1966

CITY OF LONDON

The double doors of the corridor entrance flew open. Albert Gorman had to walk briskly to keep up with the hospital bed being wheeled swiftly along the dimly light corridor. Albert's wife Liz was lying in pain on the bed, which was being pushed by an Orderly towards the delivery room. A midwife and a nurse were walking along on the other side of the bed opposite Albert, who was holding Liz's right hand. His left hand was holding a white earpiece to his left ear that was attached to a personal transistor radio, which he had bought when they had first come out in nineteen sixty-one. He had used the money he had received from his first pay packet from the Daily Orbit printworks on River Street in the City of London. This is where he had first set eyes on Elizabeth Calie Kerry from the accounts department above the print floor. Albert had to go up there once and from the moment he saw her it was love at first sight. He had charmed her and she had fell in love with him too. The transistor radios had become all the rage and drew lots of complaints from the older generation. Young adults had the crackling tinny sound from pirate radio stations blaring out in the parks and streets. Postmen even had to be banned from using them on their rounds but Albert had looked after his which was still in mint condition. He had hurriedly stuffed it into his trouser pocket as they left the flat to get to the hospital when Liz's waters had broken.

"You still listening to that bloody radio?" Asked a heavily breathing Liz.

"Eh? Er...Yeah... You've rumbled me then... You don't miss a trick do ya!" Albert looked at Liz a bit sheepishly.

"You might as well take that stupid bloody thing out your lughole and let us all bleedin hear it properly!"

The Nurse and the Orderly laughed. The Midwife frowned at them both.

Glancing at Albert, Liz asked breathlessly. "Well? How they getting... ARRGH!" Liz cried out in pain as another painful contraction pulsed through her body.

Liz squeezed Albert's hand causing him to wince.

"Alright alright! You nearly broke me bloody fingers!" Albert shook his hand and gave Liz a painful look.

The midwife looked at her watch that was hanging neatly upside down from her upper left chest area.

"That's every three minutes Mrs Gorman, it won't be long now." The midwife said sternly.

"Well... How they getting on then?" Asked a breathless Liz again. She had no choice but to have an interest in football since she and Albert had started courting. He played for his local team and often turned up to their dates in his muddy training kit.

"Two two. And we're in extra time now. Anyway, I've got the earpiece in cause the doctor ain't gonna wanna hear Ken Wolstenholme rabbiting on about how we're stuffing the jerries while he's trying to pull the baby out is he? Them posh doctors don't like football, do they? They like Rugby or polo or summink. What do you reckon Nurse? What's our doctor like?" Albert gave the nurse a cheeky look.

"I think..." The Midwife interrupted before the nurse could say anymore.

"Well, I know that he won't like the radio in the delivery room and nor will we! Anyway, I don't know what all the fuss is about, grown men chasing a ball around for heaven's sake." The midwife shook her head and threw a look to the nurse who in turn looked straight to the ground.

"It's the world cup final for crying out loud! Us versus the jerries... At the home of football!" Albert raised his hands above his head in exasperation.

"Bleedin football! I'm having a baby here!" Liz shouted as they all entered the bright white delivery room.

Doctor Parsons was preparing himself for the task of delivering Baby Gorman. The orderly pushed the bed into position and walked straight out of the delivery room without acknowledging anybody. Doctor Parsons walked over towards the bed.

"Ah, Mrs Gorman. How are you feeling? He asked cheerily.

Liz was trying to get comfortable on the bed.

"I'm really in pain doctor. I just want it over with now." Liz, as hard as she tried, could not get comfortable

"That's quite normal Mrs Gorman. Nurse, contractions?"

"Every three minutes at last count doctor."

Liz moved and winced in pain.

"And here comes another one!" Liz shrieked as the pain of the contraction coursed through her body.

The midwife and the nurse set the stirrups into position and then helped Liz to settle as the contraction subsided.

"Let us move your legs and get them into the stirrups please Mrs Gorman."

Albert watched intently as the nurses prepared his wife for the delivery of their first child. The earpiece still in his right ear, connected by the thin white cable that ran down to the radio in his right trouser pocket. Albert had been secretly praying earlier for a boy. Albert wasn't a religious man but as a child, when he once asked his parents what his religion was, he always remembered his dad telling him "C of E boy, Church of England!" He could hear his father's voice in his mind before he prayed for a son.

"Come on girl, you can do it... GOAL!!!" Albert's sudden shout startled everybody in the room, and everybody suddenly focused on Albert.

"Three two! Geoff Hurst!" Albert punched the air.

Liz threw Albert a dirty look. Her normally coiffured, bouffant ginger hair was wet and straggly from the sweat of the tough labour. Her face was pale and sweaty.

"Bloody hell Alb... Aarrrrgghh!" Another painful contraction quickly returned to Liz, causing her to grip the side rails of the hospital bed.

"Mr Gorman! What did I tell you about that bloody radio?" The midwife scolded Albert.

"Radio?" Doctor Parsons looked at Albert.

"You see. I told you he wouldn't like it!" Snapped the midwife with a sarcastic smile.

Albert looked pleadingly into the Doctors eyes.

"It is the world cup final doc..." Pleaded Albert, like a small child shuffling on his feet. His head was slightly bowed but his eyes were still fixed on the doctor's eyes.

All eyes apart from Liz's were on the doctor.

"Mr Gorman I'm quite aware it is the world cup final! You've brought a radio? In here?" The doctor couldn't believe it.

Albert looked guilty.

"Well…" Albert felt uncomfortable.

"Yes, he's got a bloody radio!" Liz barked as Doctor Parsons swung his head back and forth from Liz to Albert.

"Well get it out man!" Doctor Parsons pointed to his surgical instrument table.

"Sweet as a nut Doc!" Albert took the earpiece out from his ear and put the radio on the edge instrument table.

He pulled the earpiece jack out of the radio and turned the sound up. The radio crackled in the background.

"Jolly good move Mr Gorman!" He gave Albert the thumbs up.

The Midwife interrupted their moment of camaraderie.

"Doctor. With all due respect, I do not think we should have a radio in the delivery room." The midwife stared at Doctor Parsons.

Doctor Parsons' face turned red. He gave the midwife a scowl.

"This is my delivery room and if I want the radio on, I shall bloody well have the radio on!"

The Nurse sniggered. The Midwife scowled at her. Doctor Parsons felt between Liz's legs.

"The head is coming. Now push Mrs Gorman. Nurse, forceps?"

The nurse took the forceps from the row of neatly placed instruments on the tool table which now had the transistor radio on it. She thought about knocking the radio off. She was about to pass the forceps to the doctor's hand that was waiting in the air to receive them.

"That's it Mrs Gorman." Encouraged the doctor.

The hand that was waiting in the air disappeared.

"Don't worry about the forceps, its coming now." The doctors voice quickened.

The raised voice of Kenneth Wolstenholme broke the moment.

"And here comes Hurst. He's got... Some people are on the pitch... They think it's all over. It is now! Its four!"

Everybody except the Midwife and Liz cheered as Liz gave another painful push.

"Aarrrgghh!" the pain was etched on Liz's face.

"That's it babe! Come on darling push! Push! We just won the bloody world cup!"

"One more big push Mrs Gorman." Said the nurse.

The nurse, midwife and doctor had their eyes focused on the miracle that was occurring.

The midwife and doctor both had their arms under the sheet gently coaxing the baby out, ready to pull.

"That's it Mrs Gorman." The nurse moved around and picked up a clean towel and rubbed down Liz's forehead and face.

"Nearly there. You're doing just fine." The nurse said softly.

"AAAAARRRRRRGGGHHHH!" Screamed Liz.

"Here it comes. Nurse, towel." Demanded the midwife.

The nurse darted back around and handed the midwife a clean towel. The baby's cries could be heard. The midwife pulled a bloody, mucus covered crying baby, from under the sheet. She wiped the baby and wrapped it in the towel.

"Here we are Mrs Gorman. A boy." The midwife handed Liz the baby boy.

"Yeeeessss get in, a little boy. A boy!" Albert had tears in his eyes.

Liz was tearful.

"He's beautiful..." admired Liz.

"Would you like to cut the cord Mr Gorman? The nurse offered Albert the cord cutting scissors.

Albert took them and examined them, curiously tilting his head, looking at the right-angled metal shaft that led to the rectangular, saw-like blades, which gleamed in the bright light of the delivery room. Albert leant in and started to cut the cord that the nurse was holding up. Albert struggled to cut but persevered.

"There you go." Albert looked pleased with himself.

"Let's hold him then." Albert couldn't wait to hold his son.

Liz went to hand him their baby son but winced in pain.

The midwife took over.

"Let me take him." The midwife scooped up Baby Gorman and handed him to Albert.

Albert was shuffling a bit, clearly not knowing what to do.

"It's OK Mr Gorman. He won't bite!" Chuckled the midwife. Her hard-nosed demeanour had softened now that the baby was delivered. She wasn't a horrible person but took her job very seriously and liked everything in order. She knew how things could go wrong very easily during a delivery after having been involved in the delivery of over five hundred babies as a nurse and then a midwife. The memories of each delivery that did not have a happy outcome always haunted her now and then and always as the delivery process started each time.

Albert took his son into his hands for the first time and held him aloft as he had just won the greatest trophy in his world, just as his England idols were doing the same in their world, with the Jules Rimet trophy at Wembley on that fateful, sunny Saturday afternoon of the thirtieth of July nineteen sixty-six.

The day England won the World Cup. The day Bobby Gorman was born.

CHAPTER II

HOME

HACKNEY MARSHES NOVEMBER 1975

Nine years had passed. It was a cold and slightly misty, Saturday morning, over Hackney marshes pitches. Albert and John were standing on the touchline on one of the many pitches watching their sons playing football. They both had their hands in the pockets of their sheepskin coats. John's was black, Albert's was camel brown.

"You see that shit the other night, John?" Albert almost spat the words out.

"I know mate, they were fucking awful!" John replied with a sneer.

"Lucky they never had to qualify in sixty-six eh Alb?"

"Too right! They never qualified for the seventy-four-world cup and now they've fucked it up for the Euros next year! I might get me track suit out and show them how it's done!" Albert replied.

"Fuck me Alb, you'd have no one left in the team!" John chuckled.

"Don't worry mate, I'd give you a run out!" Albert put his left arm around John then took his arm back again quickly.

"I'd do a better job than most of that lot. My boy definitely would!" Albert pointed towards his son Bobby, out on the pitch.

"He's doing really well mate." Acknowledged John.

Albert pointed toward a group of men wearing overcoats and trilby hats.

"See that lot over there John..."

John turned slightly and looked towards where Albert's finger was pointing to.

"They're all scouts... I've heard a couple of them are here to look at my boy." Albert said proudly.

"You must be well proud John. My one's got no fucking chance. He knows it and I know it. But he loves it. Know what I mean?" John grimaced.

"That's it mate. If you both enjoy it, then so what? But he's better than most of them." Albert said reassuringly.

"You know what I mean, but anyway, what about these scouts mate?" John asked enthusiastically.

"Well, I've heard there's one from Hotboots." Albert pulled a face as if he could smell gas.

"One from Pulham. And there's only one from the Artillery!" Albert could not contain his excitement.

"Blimey Alb!" "Well, I've heard they're here to look at a few of the boys but I've had the nod they're definitely looking at my boy, so fingers crossed, eh?" Albert crossed his fingers as Bobby glided past two opposition defenders with ease which caused the scouts to hurriedly take notes.

451 FELLOWSHIP COURT HOXTON

Bobby and Albert were sitting down at the kitchen table while Liz was cooking breakfast. She turned her head away from the gas cooker where the bacon sizzled, emanating Albert's favourite smell around the whole of the two bedroomed Maisonette. It was situated on the fifteenth floor of the new sixteen floor tower block, which was part of the newly built Fellowship Court council estate. They had been holding out on the waiting list for the new block and were recently moved by the council from an older one-bedroom flat in a block on the older Jefferson Court estate just around the corner. They had been holding out on the wating list for this block. Things were so cramped at the old flat with Bobby having to sleep in with his mum and dad once he outgrew his cot. Once he started school, Albert had bought a Zed bed which Bobby slept on in the front room. Liz would fold the bed away each day. They were all enjoying the space of the new place, especially Bobby, now that he had his own bedroom, which was adorned with newspaper cuttings of his Artillery idols, especially some very yellow and tatty ones, from the seventy-one double winning side. These had been on the wall of the kitchen at the old flat as he had nowhere else to put them up. Liz wouldn't let him put them up in the small front room which had doubled up as Bobby's bedroom for so long

"You looking forward to it mate?" Liz asked her only child enthusiastically.

"Yeah, can't wait mum." Beamed Bobby.

"We're gonna stuff 'em ain't we son!" Enthused Albert as he clenched his fist and shook it towards Bobby across the table.

Bobby clenched his fist and shook it back towards Albert's direction. "Yeah, dad we are!"

Albert leant across the table and proudly ruffled his son's dark brown hair.

"That's it son."

Liz turned fully to face them both and looked on affectionately at her two boys as she often called them. Albert and Liz had wanted more children, but Liz had miscarried badly two years after bobby was born. There were some complications which meant that Liz would not be able to conceive again. They were both devasted but had made the decision to accept the situation and move on.

"Don't encourage him in all that aggressiveness Alb..." Liz looked pleadingly at her beloved husband.

"He's alright Liz, he needs a bit of that in his game don't ya son!" Albert ruffled Bobby's hair more forcefully this time.

"Yeah mum. The big clubs won't take you if your too soft." Bobby was trying to reassure his mother.

He shrugged his shoulders.

"The Artillery never won the double by being soft did they boy?" Chipped in Albert.

Liz served two plates of sausages, eggs, bacon and baked beans. Albert and Bobby's eyes lit up at the sight and gleefully accepted the plates of steaming hot food.

"Here are, get this down you." Liz beamed feeling pleased with herself for her efforts, which were always well received.

"Thanks babe, that looks lovely!" Albert smiled at the plate of food and then at Liz.

"Cor thanks mum! I love your fry ups!"

Liz leant down and kissed Bobby on the forehead.

"Make sure you give your kit to Jean after the game, she's going to pop in. I told her you're out all day. John's taking Tommy over the Hotboots, so me and Jean are going to have a nice quiet afternoon out on the balcony." Liz was looking forward to some rest, relaxation and a good old natter with her mate.

"Well, we hope they get stuffed, don't we son! Albert sniffed as he finished chewing his mouthful of sausage and beans.

He looked out of the kitchen window. It was a spectacular view across East London from their vantage point on the fifteenth floor and was what Albert wanted. From Bobby's room the view was of the City of London and West End and the British Telecom tower that Bobby marvelled at some nights.

"Yeah dad!" Bobby replied through a mouthful of egg and bacon.

"Bobby! Don't talk with your mouthful! I've told you before! And you Alb, where's you're bleedin manners?" Liz scolded her two boys.

Albert and Bobby both looked at each other.

"Sorry mum."

"Yeah, sorry love...Any chance of a bit of bread and butter?"

THE CLOCKTOWER END LOWER TERRACES AT ARTILLERY STADIUM

"Not to worry mate. You can't win every game. Besides, they were a good little team. I mean that little winger was something else, weren't he?" Albert looked across at Bobby who was looking straight ahead, sulking.

Bobby hated losing when playing with his team. He was trying to forget by watching his Artillery heroes playing at his beloved Artillery Stadium. But he had to endure the usual wind up from his dad whenever they lost. Albert would dissect the game and let bobby know where he had made wrong decisions. Albert was Bobby's harshest critic. Albert always assured his son that it was tough love to help him. Bobby also hated the smell of the Old Clerkenwell tobacco smoke that was wafting around his place amongst the throng of the men around him who smoked the roll ups like their life depended on them.

"No he weren't!" Bobby snapped back.

Albert burst out laughing.

"Don't worry about it son. Anyway, let's hope these lot do us a favour eh?"

"Come on Artillery!" Bobby shouted at the top of his young voice.

The supporters around them all chuckled. Albert put his arm around Bobby and chuckled.

"That's better son! Get it out your system! That's what it's all about."

At that very moment, Artillery scored. The whole crowd went wild with celebration. Bobby was cheering and got carried along with the crowd.

THE BRITISH LION PUBLIC HOUSE

Albert and Bobby walked into a busy British Lion or The Lion as it was known by the locals.

"Artillery two, Pulham one!" Albert bellowed.

Most of the pub turned and acknowledged Albert. He shook hands with a few of them and patted some of them on the back. This was an eclectic mix of predominantly Artillery supporters, with a sprinkling of Haringey Hotboots & East Ham fans and one lone Manchester Football Club supporter who was a bit of a glory hunter due to Manchester FC winning the European Cup and because he loved George Good the famous Manchester FC winger. Albert got to the bar.

"He's alright while I have couple ain't he Len?" Albert asked out of respect to Len, who was the licenced victualler of the establishment.

Len looked toward Bobby then looked at Albert, who was one of Len's most regular customers.

"I ain't seem him Alb. Anyway, how'd he get on today?" Len winked at Bobby.

"They lost one nil. He's got the right hump. But they had some little winger who weren't half good." Albert tilted his head and raised his eyebrows as he gave Len the look as if to say, you know what I mean.

Bobby scowled at Albert.

"Were there any scouts there today, Alb?" Len asked enthusiastically

"Yeah, but who knows eh Len?" Replied Albert, shrugging his shoulders.

"Just got to keep going though ain't he. Here are Alb, give him a bottle of pop. On me." In one swift movement, Len pulled a small glass bottle of lemonade from under the bar, popped the cap off on the bottle opener on edge of the bar then placed the bottle on the bar.

"Nice one Len." Albert smiled.

Bobby was staring around in wonder, looking pleased to be in the pub.

ARTILLERY FOOTBALL CLUB YOUTH TRAINING ACADEMY MAY 4th 1982

It was a sunny afternoon at the Artillery youth training academy. The grass had recently been cut and the smell of freshly cut grass filled the warm air. One of the youth coaches, Philip Green, cupped his hands to his mouth.

"Gather round please boys!" Phillip gestured with his arms for all the youth team players to come towards him.

Phillip Green was an older man from another generation. His hair was slicked back with Brylcreem with a slight parting. He had served in the Korean war and had been bayoneted during a battle where his battalion were storming a Korean stronghold. He had miraculously survived thanks to the battalion medic and the field doctors. He had once shown the young men the long scar, which ran from his solar plexus down to his belly button, to remind them all how lucky they were to be training to be professional footballers and not being sent off to war.

"This is it now, this is where we find out." Bobby whispered to his best mate Tommy Eden.

"Now some of you will be taking the next step with us, some of you will not. If you are not taking the next step with us, I wish you all the best for the future. There is a notice on the board outside my office, which tells you which room to go to. When you are changed, form a queue outside the room you are allocated to and wait to be called in with your parents. That will be all. Good luck boys." Phillip gestured towards the changing rooms. They all started to move.

"I thought they would tell us now Tommy." Bobby said nervously.

"I don't know, but I'm off to get changed. Quick! Don't want to be last in the queue!" Tommy ran off excitedly.

Bobby stood still for a few seconds then chased after Tommy.

ARTILLERY YOUTH DEVELOPMENT MANAGER'S OFFICE

"Now Mr and Mrs Gorman. Bobby has done very well with us and has improved well this season but I'm afraid we will not be taking him on..." The Youth Development Manager Edward Cunningham said in a stern, but sympathetic voice. He was sat at his desk opposite the already seated Gorman family.

Edward Cunningham had also served his country, during the second world war, as an officer during the D-Day landings. He had led from the front and landed with his battalion and stormed onto Sword Beach. Half of his battalion were cut down almost instantly by heavy machine gun fire that rained down from the machine gun nests above them on the cliffs.

After they had got off of the beach that they had all named Hell, he had led what was left of his men and a mixture of other battalions right into Paris and liberate the French people. Bobby had once asked Edward what it was like, but he would not tell Bobby anything other than it was horrific and that he would not wish it anyone. Edward had echoed Phillip Green's sentiment that all the young boys were lucky these days. Edward was of a stern nature and Bobby had told his father how Edward was hard on the boys. Albert knew these kinds of authoritarian men from his two years national service with the Royal Electrical and Mechanical Engineers. These men had made some of the national service men feel very inadequate, Albert included, due to not having seen any action nor experienced the horrors of the war. Albert didn't like them then and he certainly did not like this one sat in front of him, dictating his boy's future.

"You what? Not taking him on?" Sneered Albert.

"Albert..." Liz said softly as she grabbed Albert's arm.

"No Liz, hang on a minute, what about all them goals he scored and all the clean sheets he helped keep?" Albert almost spat the words out. He pulled his arm from Liz's grasp.

"Mr Gorman, as I said, we will not be taking him on. There are lots of factors we look at..."

"Like what?" growled Albert, his face contorted with rage.

"Well, if you'd let me finish Mr Gorman, there are many factors we take into consideration, like size..."

Albert interrupted again.

"Size? Size? He's got plenty of growing still to do! He's only just turned sixteen for Christ's sake!"

Liz interjected.

"Albert let the man finish! Sorry, you were saying?" She smiled nervously.

"Yes. As I was saying... Many factors, such as size and temperament, are taken into consideration. His temperament is a concern sometimes." Edward looked sternly at Albert.

"That's just him being young though. Come on, can't you have another look at him?" Albert looked pleadingly at the man who held his sons Artillery career in his hands.

"Mr Gorman, believe me, we have looked at this enough. This has been one of the hardest decisions this club has had to make, considering your son's talent, but it is not over for him at all. Other clubs have shown interest in Robert. One with very strong interest, who wish to speak with you both immediately." Edward said encouragingly. He had always referred to Bobby as Robert even though Bobby was not a nickname as Albert had named his son after Bobby Moore, for his exploits captaining England to World Cup glory, despite him being a West Ham player. This was coupled with the fact that Albert had met Bobby Moore a few times in various pubs in the City and West End of London. A lot of Londoners, some of whom Albert knew, had moved out to Chigwell and Hainault after the war and used to go to a pub called The Retreat in Chigwell Row. Bobby, Liz, John and Jean Eden had ventured over there a couple of times before the sixty-six world cup to meet old friends and both times Bobby Moore had been in the pub, and they had all chatted to him. Bobby Moore had moved out that way as it was near West Ham's training ground.

Albert slammed his fist down on the desk which made Liz and Edward jump. Bobby didn't even flinch. He just sat, staring at the floor.

"I don't want him at any other club. I... This is..." Albert's world was caving in. His wife and Edward were both staring at him in disbelief.

"Albert! What clubs have looked at him? What club is it that wants to talk to us?" Liz asked as she tried to calm the situation.

"Here is a list of interested clubs." Edward passed a sheet of paper across the desk towards the Gormans.

"The one highlighted is the club who wants to speak to you right away. This is very positive as most of the players whom we are releasing have either little or no interest in them at all. That is a credit to Robert." Edward looked towards Bobby.

"Thank you. Will that be all sir?" Bobby was trying so hard to hold himself together and fight off the tears.

"Yes Robert. I wish you all the very best for the future." He stood and walked around his desk to where Bobby was seated. Bobby stood and shook hands with the man who had just ended his lifelong dream.

Bobby turned to his parents.

"Can we go now please?" Bobby's tear ducts were beginning to overflow.

"Yes darling. Let's go Albert, there's lots more people for him to see yet." Liz said defiantly. Her eyes were welling with emotion. She stood and ushered her only child away.

Albert was still seated, staring at the man who had just ended his own lifelong dream of having a son that played for the club he had supported, along with all the generations of men in his family before him that had supported The Artillery. He slowly stood and shook the hand of the man before him, whom he now hated more than anything or anyone he had hated prior to this devastating day for the Gorman family.

"Yeah, let's go!" Albert looked Edward square in the eyes and then released his foes hand from his tight grip and turned and ushered his family out of the office. Alberts feet shuffled as he made his way out.

KINGS CROSS STATION JULY 1982

The Gorman family were walking towards the platforms on a busy afternoon. Rush hour was approaching. The sun was shining through the high roof skylights, illuminating the station.

"Now listen son, if you don't like it, or anyone gives you any grief up there, you get on that train and come straight back home... D'you hear me? We can talk to a club nearer home!" Albert was pointing at Bobby as he spoke.

"Yes dad." Bobby nodded and walked on in front of his mother and father.

"Fuck the money! I'll get you a job on the print if I have to." Albert reassured his son.

"No thanks Dad!" Bobby laughed. "I don't think I could do the early starts!"

Liz started to cry.

"Yes, my little darling. You get on the first train home..."

Bobby stopped walking, turned and hugged his mother.

"It's alright Mum. I'm not a baby! I'll sort them Northerners out! I've seen enough Coronation Street. I might even have a pint down the Rovers!" Bobby remarked, trying hard to be cheerful.

"There's your train boy." Albert pointed towards platform twelve where an Intercity one two five was resting against the buffers.

"I better go then..." Bobby broke off from the tight embrace of his loving mother and acknowledged his father.

Albert had tears in his eyes too which was unheard of.

"You take care Son." Albert hugged his son tightly, which was also a bit of a rarity.

Liz hugged both her boys.

"And you ring us as soon as you get there!" The generator of the train starting up interrupted them.

"I better go then." Bobby broke away and started to walk towards the train.

He stopped then turned around to face his parents who both looked as sad as he could ever remember seeing them. Bobby raised his hand to wave at them, but his hand hardly moved. His arm fell back by his side. He turned and boarded the train. The train conductor's whistle could be heard as he blew to signal departure. Bobby got to a seat and put his case up on the luggage rack on the platform side of the train. He sat down and took the seat by the window. Liz and Albert walked towards the window. They were waving. They both blew kisses at him. This was something Bobby had never seen his father do. Bobby waved at his parents. This time he waved properly and then harder than he had ever waved before as the train pulled away. As he arched his head to keep his parents in view, they slowly disappeared into the distance. Bobby straightened himself then took his seat. He sat bolt upright for a second. Tears started to roll down Bobby's cheeks. He slumped back onto the rough fabric of the seat then held his head in his hands.

CHAPTER III
MAGGIE'S DEN

MAGGIE BRAITHWAITE'S HOUSE PORTHAM
GREATER MANCHESTER

"This is your room, there's the bathroom, that's the spare room and that's my room. You're free to use the house as you please as it's your home now too, but no coming in at all hours. That's all I ask. I'll do your breakfast, you get dinner at the club and tea will be around 6 o'clock every night."

Maggie Braithwaite was a dark-haired woman with shoulder length wavy hair. She was proud of her home even though she knew it was a bit dated. Bobby was thinking that she looked pretty for an older woman and that she was dressed smartly. He couldn't work out how old she was. He wasn't sure if she was younger or older than his mum. Thirties, early forties or fifties? He couldn't be sure. She was showing Bobby around the digs that his new club had provided for him to live in. She spoke with an accent that sounded similar to the people on Coronation Street. He had watched it with his Mum since he could remember. They walked back downstairs. It was a tidy upstairs but Bobby though it looked old fashioned.

"I forgot to mention that there's a phone there." Maggie pointed to a grey rotary phone which was hung on the wall between the front door and living room door. It had a box next to it to put money in, similar to the red phone boxes in London. Bobby and his mates used to go in the phone boxes now and again to make prank calls to random people in the telephone directories, local bossiness and their friends. There was a small table directly under the payphone with an old, tatty looking, Manchester telephone directory, a new Yellow Pages, phone book and a Bic ball point pen neatly arranged. Bobby suddenly remembered that this payphone set up was identical to the one in The British Lion.

"It's a pay phone so make sure you have plenty of change. I'll show you how to use it later. Maggie had wrongly assumed that Bobby had never seen or used one before.

You know where the bus stop is now. It takes about fifteen minutes to get into town. If you need anything, just ask, and I'm sure between me and the club we can sort it out. Any questions?" Maggie looked at Bobby. She was smiling. Bobby wasn't

"No." Bobby looked at her then looked around the hallway. It was nice enough, quite plain. He noticed that the carpet was quite thin by the front door. He wondered how many boys had lived here before him.

"Come on lad cheer up. Some boys don't get another chance like you have. You've got to make the most of it kidder. Come on, cheer up now... Give your parents a ring and let them know you're here now... So they don't get worried about T' boy oop north!" Maggie comically wobbled her body and head really laid her northern accent on thickly as she spoke.

"Can we go down the Rovers later then?" Bobby smiled for the first time since he arrived in the Greater Manchester suburb of Portham.

"Go on, you cheeky beggar!"

They both cracked up laughing.

"That's better. Now I'll start making us something for us tea, that's probably dinner where you're from, so why don't you give your parents a call and then go and unpack. Tea will be ready in about an hour. Bangers and mash, OK?"

Bobby's eyes lit up. He had noticed the smell of something cooking but his senses had been overwhelmed by his new surroundings.

"Yeah! That's one of my favourites!" Memories started to flood into Bobby's mind of his mum's sausage and mash with thick gravy. He remembered how he used to help make the mash and clear the saucepan with his fingers and would then lick of the smooth, heavily buttered mash. He stared into the distance for a few seconds.

"Ok then. Chop chop!" Maggie clapped her hands which brought Bobby back from his malaise. He did not know that the Portham FC parent liaison officer had asked Liz what meals Bobby liked. Sausage and mash was on the list that had been sent to Maggie.

He reached into his pocket and pulled out two five pence pieces. Maggie came over. He'd used telephone boxes so many times. Especially whenever he had a girlfriend. He would get scolded by his dad about the phone bill whenever he used the phone at home.

"Now just dial your number." Maggie said happily as she turned and walked off to the kitchen.

Bobby put his finger into the zero first as he remembered his mum telling him that the dialling code was zero one for London. He then turned the dial fast on the grey telephone. Zero, one, seven, nine, three, five, six, two, two. He still couldn't dial as fast as his mum. As the dial returned back for the last time, there was a short silence, then Bobby could hear the deep dialling noise. Brrrp brrrp.

"Hello" his mums voice cheerily answered.

"Hello mum it's me. I'm here."

"Oh, thank gawd for that I've been worried sick!" Liz's tone had changed dramatically.

"Alb! He's there!" Bobby imagined his mother standing at the phone in the hallway, calling to his dad, who would almost certainly be sitting in his chair in the front room, watching the telly with the Evening Standard in his lap doing the crossword.

"Is he alright?" Bobby heard his dad's voice in the background and heard the shuffling as Albert made his way into the hallway towards the phone.

"How are you my little soldier? What's it like?" Liz asked with a big hint of concern in her voice

"It's alright. Maggie's nice." Bobby smiled as he replied, playing the scene out in his mind, that his mother and father were playing out down the other end of the phone.

"You alright boy?"

"Yeah, I'm alright dad." Bobby raised his eyes with a smile. Bobby was imagining Albert standing next to Liz by the phone.

"How was the journey?" asked Albert.

The pips started to go.

"Dad the pips are going and I ain't got anymore change.

"Ok darling love you lots! Ring me tomorrow after training." Liz said affectionately.

"They got a bloody payphone! Tight northern..." Albert was cut off as the phone went dead.

Bobby laughed and put the phone down. Maggie popped her head out from the kitchen.

"Everything alright love?"

"Yes thanks."

"Your mum and dad happy that your here safe?"

"Yes thanks. Very happy." Bobby went red.

"That's good. They seem a lovely couple." Maggie looked at a picture on the wall in the hallway. It was a picture of a younger looking Maggie on her wedding day with her husband.

"Why don't you go and unpack and get settled eh?" Maggie said softly.

Bobby nodded.

As he walked up the stairs, he noticed Maggie gazing at her wedding picture. Bobby got to the top of the stairs. Straight ahead was the bathroom. The door adjacent to the right was Maggie's room. There was a smaller door next to that. Bobby turned to the right at the top of the stairs and opened the smaller door. It was an airing cupboard similar to the one at home. There was a floor standing copper cylinder for hot water and a shelf above it. There were neatly folded towels on one side of the shelf to the right and a mixture of black and white bras and knickers on the other side to the left. The bras were bigger than any that he had had the luck of seeing or unhooking. Bigger than his mums even, he thought to himself. He reached in and felt an upturned cup of one of the black bras. It was silky. He felt the strap which was lacey. He heard what sounded like a pan dropping on the floor in the kitchen below which startled Bobby. He quickly pulled his hand out of the cupboard and closed the airing cupboard door and quickly opened the door to the right which opened into his room. He walked in and closed the door behind him. He looked at his case which was on the bed. He didn't really register his room when Maggie showed him around the house earlier on. The room was painted all white with a brown carpet. He had a single bed which had a white blanket, a white pillow and a cream looking sheet folded back over the blanket. There was small wardrobe in the corner of the room to the front of the door and a chest of four draws to the right of the door. Both matching brown oak wood. Bobby walked towards the window. There were net curtains and brown drapes either side. He looked out of the window. The houses looked different to Bobby compared to the houses he had seen in London. He looked at his suitcase case on the bed. The case had seen better days. It was a grey case. The one his mum took on holiday to Spain last year. It was always used when they went to the caravan that his nan and grandad owned down in the seaside village of St Swithen on the Essex coast. Bobby smiled. He unzipped the case. He then pushed it to the right as he couldn't deal with unpacking it at that point. He laid down and curled up on the space that was left on the bed and stared into space.

PORTHAM ATHLETIC FOOTBALL CLUB TRAINING GROUND

"Right, you lot gather round, gather round! Barked the Portham manager Neil Glover in his thick Yorkshire accent.

Neil was a thin man in his late fifties with combed back, light brown hair that was interwoven with strands of grey. His hairline had receded quite far back. He was dressed in a light blue tracksuit and white trainers. Bobby knew that Neil was a former pro but couldn't remember what position he had played. The players jogged over.

"Right. I want to introduce you all to our new signing, Robert Gorman. He is a Left Back and has come from the Artillery youth set up. He is joining us in the senior squad to train with us for now and then go on from there. I want you all to help him settle in and make him feel comfortable. Robert, Carl Pilford is our captain. I will leave it to him to introduce you to everybody. I'm off to see the chairman so I will see you all tomorrow. Neil walked away towards the ramshackle training headquarters where Bobby had visited with his parents a few weeks earlier. It contained some offices, a canteen and changing rooms. The Portham FC captain, Carl Pilford, came across and shook Bobby's hand.

"Pleased to meet you kid. Don't worry about this lot, there an horrible looking bunch of fuckers but they're all pussycats really, Ain't that right boys?" Shouted Carl.

They all shouted various expletives in agreement.

Carl took him around the assembled team and Bobby shook hands with all of them.

"Now Bobby's still a bit young so we need to take care of him and not lead him astray! After speaking to the gaffer, he won't go straight into the team but will be back up to the old pair of legs we've got at Left Back at the moment..." Carl looked towards Billy Thorpe, the veteran left back who had played for Portham for most of his career.

Neil Glover had spoken to Bobby about him. Billy was not as tall as Bobby imagined. He certainly looked old to Bobby. Billy's hair was like Bobby Charlton's in the nineteen sixty-six world cup. What was left of his hair was black and he had a thick black moustache. Bobby thought that he looked like a barrel. Billy was a complete contrast to Carl Pilford. Carl was tall. Taller than Bobby. Carl was lean, clean shaven and had his dark brown hair swept back.

"Fuck off! There's plenty to come from me yet! You'll have a long wait, boy, before you get a game before me let me tell thee. But you show me you're up for it and I'll teach you how to be a proper Left Back. Forget what you've learnt down pansy South..."

"Fuck off I ain't no pansy!" Bobby cut Billy short and stared straight at him.

The rest of the team laughed. Billy stared at Bobby for a while. Everyone fell silent. Bobby was staring back at Billy. The rest of the team looked back and forth at them both, looking like lions, trying to psyche each other out. Billy walked towards

Bobby and stood right in front of him and looked him up and down. Bobby stood still, looking down at Billy, who was a good four or five inches shorter or so Bobby thought.

"Well, you've got some balls son, I admire that, but you interrupt me again, I'll kick you all round this field and back down to London again. You understand?" Bobby carried on looking down at Billy. He looked a bit scared, but he wasn't going to back down.

"Alright." Bobby didn't really know what else to say.

Billy and all the others started laughing and Bobby eventually started laughing. Billy winked at Bobby.

"Stick with me lad, I'll make you a star!" Billy ruffled Bobby's hair and walked back to where he was standing.

"Right, that's enough of this bollocks! Bobby, collect up the cones and let's get changed and have some lunch. Then it's time for a song Bobby boy!" Carl chuckled.

Bobby was bewildered.

The rest of the team sniggered and laughed.

PORTHAM FC CANTEEN

The players were all just about seated after grabbing their trays of food. Chicken and asparagus with a banana and a cup of water. The canteen was a portacabin and smelt a bit like Bobby's local chip shop back home. Rather like the one at Bobby's primary school. Bobby was last in line. He was having the food scooped onto his plate.

"Do you know what they're on a about." The jolly, rotund, canteen lady Doris Evans laughed.

"All new signings have to sing a song in front of the team. We've been looking forward to this. The highlight of our day!"

Bobby grabbed the plate of food and moved along to the next

dinner lady, Betty Billinghurst.

"Hello love." Betty replied in her thick Lancastrian accent.

This took Bobby completely by surprise as she looked like she was from Jamaica or Barbados. He expected her to speak in the same patois as his friends' parents from school, who had come over from the from the West Indies to work and then settled. Betty spooned on the asparagus.

"What you going to sing?" She asked with a big smile on her face.

Betty turned and put Bobby's plate of food onto the large cooker and put a plate over the top of the food. She turned around and faced Bobby who was looking bewildered.

"I'll keep it warm for you love. Go on, your audience awaits." Bobby slowly turned and faced the seating area of the canteen. The whole squad was eagerly awaiting Bobby.

"So, Bobby, can you stand up on the chair and sing your song please." Ordered Carl Pilford, who was sitting at one of the four large tables nearest the serving area. Carl stood up and pulled an empty chair out and did a presenting motion toward the chair.

"Do I have to?" Pleaded Bobby.

The whole squad and canteen ladies were shouting and goading him on.

"I don't know what to sing. I didn't know I had to do this!" Bobby was embarrassed and annoyed.

Carl put his finger to his lips and turned and gestured with his hands to all those in the room to quieten down.

"You don't have to, but you have to perform a forfeit if you don't." Carl informed Bobby.

"A forfeit? What's that then?" Bobby asked inquisitively.

"You have to wash all of our cars for six months for nothing, plus anything else we can think of during those six months." Carl folded his arms and smiled and tilted his head slightly.

"Fuck that!" Bobby walked over to the chair then jumped up on to it.

He bowed three times in everybody's direction. Doris and Betty both smiled and gave him a thumbs up.

"Alright, here we go then." Bobby started singing 'Too much too young' by The Specials.

Some of the younger players appreciated it, a few older players were looking a bit confused. Some were laughing. Doris and Betty were doing a little dance.

"You done too much, much too young!" Bobby belted out the song that he loved so much and started bopping about as his confidence grew.

"Now you're married with a kid, when you should be having fun with me..."

NOKE CITY FC TOUCHLINE

Neil Glover and his assistant Dave Jenkins were standing side by side in front of the away dug out at Noke City's ground.

"Billy's struggling a bit after that challenge. I don't think he's going to make it through the game." Neil Glover was looking extremely concerned for his veteran left back.

"What do you reckon then? Give him another ten minutes, and see?" Replied Dave, who didn't seem as concerned as Neil as he had seen Billy run off a lot worse a tackle.

"No. He's hurt. Get Bobby to warm up right now please." Neil replied curtly.

"You sure he's ready boss?" Dave was concerned now. He turned around and looked at Bobby, who was watching the game intently.

"I wouldn't say he's quite ready, but he's all we've got and besides, he's going to have to make his debut at some point so get him warmed up please." Neil Glover was looking straight at the pitch, surveying the game as he spoke.

"Right you are boss." Dave turned towards the bench and took a few quick strides towards Bobby.

"Bobby, time to get warmed up lad." Dave couldn't help smiling as he knew how badly Bobby had wanted to make his debut since he joined.

Bobby had been an unused substitute in the last two games since getting picked for the squad. Billy looked shocked for a second but got straight up then started running down the touchline.

NOKE CITY COMMENTARY BOX

"Thorpe has looked like he's been struggling for a while and now young Bobby Gorman, the left back who was released by Artillery in the summer and signed by Portham in preseason, is warming up and will probably replace Thorpe, who has been struggling since making a goal stopping challenge on the Noke striker and colliding with the goalpost." The radio commentator Tony Court, who was wearing a brown sheepskin coat, was sitting up in the gantry next to his regular pundit Sam Wellesley.

"Yes, he's in trouble and he's no spring chicken. Rumour has it the boy Gorman has been signed as his eventual replacement, but it looks like he is replacing him right now. Young Gorman is pulling his tracksuit off. What a wonderful moment for the Left Back. The ref has blown for the substitution and Thorpe looks very unhappy but gives Gorman a hug and says a few words of encouragement as the Assistant Manager Dave Jenkins is giving him tactics." Explained Sam, who wore a black sheepskin coat.

"So young Bobby Gorman replaces veteran Billy Thorpe with the game still up for grabs with Portham one nil up at the moment." Tony informed the radio audience.

NOKE CITY PITCH

"Right lad, just keep calm and enjoy every moment. It don't last long this career and I'm nearly at the end of mine, so you enjoy it son. You deserve your chance. Now go and take it!" Billy hugged Bobby who couldn't quite believe Billy was hugging him, let alone that he was about to make his debut.

Billy went and sat down as the crowd cheered and chanted his name. Dave Jenkins appeared at Bobby's side.

"Bobby, keep tight to their winger as he is a danger. Just keep calm and alert and don't get caught too high up the pitch as this lot are good on the counter. You got it?" Bobby was just looking straight ahead at the referee, waiting for the signal to come on. He nodded in acknowledgement.

NOKE CITY COMMENTARY BOX

"Well, there's a bit of a mixed reception from the away fans as Gorman comes on." Remarked Tony Court as Bobby ran onto the pitch.

"Thorpe is such a legend, but the home fans seem happy that such a youngster has come on. Maybe they think they have more of a chance now the veteran has gone off." Tony chuckled at his own summation of the events taking place below him.

"Well, most of them are clapping and cheering but it's probably a mixture of him being so young and the fact he has come up from Artillery. These fans are hard to please and perhaps he needs to prove himself. But the older players will be there for him and encourage him. I remember making my debut and I can tell you, it's such a mix of emotions. I hear he is a good player and has impressed in training so far." Sam informed the listening audience through the microphone that he was holding against his top lip. The curved metal guard prevented the black sponge ball from making contact with his skin and left a gap of around two inches. He also had on large grey earphones, or cans, as they were known as in the commentary industry.

"And here come Noke on the counter and young Gorman has been caught in possession too high up the pitch and has lost out to their tricky young winger John Kennedy." Explained Tony with an air of concern for the young player making his debut. Tony was also wearing the same audio equipment as Sam, but his kit was black.

"Kennedy puts in a cross and... Goal!!!! Edwards gets on the end of a beautiful cross from Kennedy! Peter Edwards rose majestically above the Portham defence and powers in the header! One one!" Cried Tony.

"And young Gorman has just had a nightmare getting caught out there. He has just been taught a harsh lesson. The away fans are not happy. I really feel for the young boy but what a great bit of skill from Kennedy and the header from big Peter Edwards was magnificent but that's what they're good at Noke, hitting teams on the counter. Gorman has got to keep his head up and he seems furious with himself shaking his head and shouting expletives that I cannot repeat over the airwaves." Commented Sam forlornly.

Bobby was shaking his head, swearing and rubbing his head.

"He knows he's messed up, but his captain is straight over there gesticulating to Bobby to keep his head up." Said Tony.

Carl Pilford jogged over to Bobby.

"Come on mate forget it now. Just stay focused and hold your position. Don't come past the halfway line. We can't lose this game." Carl patted Bobby on the back.

"Sorry Carl. I'm really sorry, he was so quick!" Bobby was looking down at the green turf.

"Don't worry. Come on!" Encouraged Carl.

NOKE CITY COMMENTARY BOX

"Just three minutes remaining now. Can Portham hold on. They're on the backfoot now, as they have been most of the game, even though they were one nil up, their goal was very much against the run of play. Tony remarked.

"Portham have shut up shop now, with only their front men high up the pitch waiting for any long balls that might come their way. Glover is shouting at them to defend now." Sam informed the thousands of fans up and down the country tuned into their commentary from Greater Manchester Platinum 967 MW.

The radio station had dedicated it's Saturday afternoons to the English football leagues. The station had built up a cult following up and down the country, in some nearby foreign countries, on cargo ships at sea and anywhere else that that could pick up the medium wave frequencies. Tony and Sam had been in a large part responsible for this, due to their excellent and oftentimes emotional commentary, which was unheard of at the main radio stations. They also had a great rapport and sense of humour between themselves and the listeners, which gave them a great connection to all of their fans. They always made a point of responding to fan mail and also made appearances as guest DJs in clubs around the country and sometimes abroad.

Neil Glover was shouting and gesticulating to his players.

"And there's the final whistle, Noke one, Portham one." Tony exhaled the comment.

NOKE CITY AWAY DRESSING ROOM

The whole team were despondent. Dave Jenkins the assistant manager was talking to Bobby.

"Bobby, I don't want you to worry about it but that's why we give you instructions. I clearly told you what to do and then look what happened." Neil walked over to them both. His face was red.

"Ok Robert, we understand it was your debut and you weren't really expecting to come on, but you need to listen lad. We cannot afford any more slip ups or dropped points. If things go wrong, you mustn't get too frustrated or let your head go down. We were lucky not to lose that game. You need to put it behind you now lad. We've got that lot up the road at home next and you're going to be playing as it's not looking good for Billy. He has had to go to the hospital. It's his knee...."

" Boss I'm sorry about the goal and I've said sorry to all the boys. I'm gutted about Billy..."

"He is a fine defender. I know he has high hopes for you lad and so do we. Don't worry about Billy he'll be chatting those nurses up about now. Let's get going." Neil clapped his hands but could not hide his disappointment behind the positivity he was trying to emanate.

MAGGIE'S HOUSE

Bobby was struggling with the pay phone.

"Hello Mum."

"Hello darling how are you?" replied an exciting sounding, Liz.

"I come on as sub today!"

"Oh, darling well done. Alb... here are Alb, he only got on as sub!" Bobby could hear his dad approaching the telephone.

"Hello mate what happened then? Tell me all about it." Albert sounded excited too.

"Well, Thorpey got injured and they told me to warm up while they see if he could carry on, but he couldn't. Then I come on about ten minutes from time and we were one nil up, but I got caught in possession and their winger put in a blinder of a cross and their big striker headed it in. I was gutted. It was my fault. I'm sure I recognise that winger from somewhere..." Bobby's mind drifted off to when a young winger from a team that Bobby's junior team lost to, ran past him and scored. His memory failed him as to what team the kid played for or what he looked like, but the memory still hurt Bobby. Now he had a similar memory to deal with for the foreseeable future. His father's voice jarred him back to reality.

"Don't worry son. What was the score in the end?"

"It finished one all in the end. Everyone was alright with me, but I could tell they had the hump. And the crowd were pissed off!" Bobby was very dejected.

"Oi! Language boy! Come on son, don't worry... It's probably happened to all of them at some point and don't worry about that crowd... You graft hard and they'll like you. Anyway, at least you didn't lose. You playing the next game?" Albert was trying his best to cheer his son up.

"Yeah, it looks like it as it don't look good for Thorpey. The boss said he'll probably be out for a while. It's at home next against Boldham, our local derby. It don't get much bigger than that for Portham. It's like Artillery v Boots round here! Are you going to come?" Bobby asked hopefully.

"You try and stop me mate! Here are Liz, he's only playing at home in the local derby next week. Our star Left Back is playing in his first derby, oop north!"

CHAPTER IV
BUILDING SANDCASTLES

PORTHAM ATHLETIC FC HOME CHANGING ROOM

The team and coaching staff are sitting down while Neil Glover is giving his pre-match talk.

"Right lads I don't need to say much, you all know the importance of this game to those fans out there and to this club. Bobby, this is it for you lad, the chance for you to win this crowd over. You work hard and they will forgive you anything. Just stay sharp at all times! Remember your position at set pieces and play your game. That's all I ask of you. The rest of you know the drill. Look after Bobby. You lot, and me for that matter, have all been in his position before. So, you know what it's like and you know what to do. I have great vision for this club, but we need to win these games to realise that vision. I trust you. All I ask is that you trust me to get you all to where you belong." The team were all visibly enamoured by that last comment.

"Alright, let's do this." Shouted Neil.

The team all cheered and shouted as they all started moving out of the door towards the tunnel.

PORTHAM ATHLETIC FC PITCH

The home fans were shouting, cheering and singing. The away

fans were shouting, jeering and booing. The Portham fans started chanting. "P. A. F. C! P. A. F. C! P. A. F. C!"

An Boldham fan in the away end shouted. "What do you think of Portham?"

A section of his fellow fans responded. "Shit!"

The Boldham fan responded back. "What do you think of Shit?"

The fans responded back. "Portham!"

"Thank you!" Another response returned from the solitary fan.

The final response was. "That's Alright!"

All the Boldham fans in the general vicinity laughed.

PORTHAM COMMENTARY BOX

"And here they come now, the home side, Portham Athletic, The Wasps, in their home strip of yellow and black stripes. The away side, Boldham, are in their blue and white strip." Announced Tony Court broadcasting with his partner Sam Wellesley, as always, for Great Manchester Platinum 967 Medium Wave.

"Yep, the big local derby in this division. A massive game for the players but most of all, for the fans. This means so much to them. Who has the bragging rights in the pub, or at work on Monday morning. It's going to be interesting with Billy Thorpe still out. I hear he could be out for a while. Young Gorman, who didn't have the greatest of debuts, is set to deputise today and make his full home debut. It's going to be one hell of a game and with both teams chasing promotion, there's a lot at stake." Sam commented in his smooth, Recital Pronunciation brogue, that always had a hint of Lancastrian sprinkled into his almost always perfect commentary.

PORTHAM ATHLETIC EXECUTIVE BOX

Liz and Albert were standing in the Executive box having some food and drinks while looking out onto the pitch.

"Can you see him? What numbers he wearing?" Liz's head was bobbing and weaving trying to catch a glimpse of her beloved son.

"Hopefully they've give him the number three. That's a Left Back's number. Oh, they have an all! There he is Liz, look, our little boy. Alberts voice was raised in excitement.

"Where, where? Oh yeah! Oh, look at him Alb." Liz eyes moistened.

"I know I just hope he concentrates and keeps calm." Albert said hopefully.

The Chairman, Dickie Godstone, walked in and greeted some people he didn't recognise. He saw Liz and Albert then walked straight over to them., chugging on a large cigar as he walked.

"Hello Mr and Mrs Gorman, so glad you could make it. Have they been looking after you?" Dickie had a slight look of concern. Hoping his staff had not let him down.

"Hello Dickie!" Albert stood up and shook hands with Dickie.

"Call me Albert! Don't worry about the Mr and Mrs. Yes, they have mate and thanks for the tickets and the hospitality, very nice!" Albert was well pleased with this situation and was smiling broadly as he was when he had relayed the situation to his cronies down the British Lion after Bobby had told him.

"Yes, thanks Dickie it's lovely and the hotels really nice!" Liz gushed.

"Not a problem. We are very happy with Bobby. He's a good lad. He has had a lot to deal with lately but he's doing well. He is a credit to you both. Anytime you want to come up here it's on me, hotels, the lot!" Dickie was proud of his new signing and loved it that he was dealing with nice people from London as he had not had any dealings with Londoners before, especially true cockneys. He had hated cockneys just because they were from London, but meeting Liz, Albert and Bobby had made him realise that working class people were generally the same, wherever they came from. Dickie was very much working class and had made good but had never forgotten his working-class roots.

"Much appreciated Dickie. Nice one!" Beamed Albert as he too liked Dickie knew even though that dickie had made good, he had not betrayed his working-class roots.

"Yes, thanks so much and thanks for looking after Bobby, we met Maggie earlier, she's lovely." Replied Liz, who now felt some comfort that her little soldier was being looked after by nice people, so far from his home.

"Yes, she really is. Between us, she couldn't have children and she lost her husband Derek quite young to cancer. It all happened so quickly. Not long after being diagnosed, he passed away. They both used to come to games together. Derek was an apprentice here. He got injured badly during a game. His knee went. Cut short his playing career. After he recovered it was clear he couldn't play at a decent level, so he got a job delivering car parts and started coaching the youth team here. Then they started taking apprentices in who didn't live locally, just like your Bobby. So, it kind of made up for them not having their own kids you know? Maggie had a bit of break from it all after Derek passed but carried it on once she was ready." Dickie informed them.

"Yes, we had a chat about it. She's got all the pictures up of the apprentices that have lived there. I love her. Bobby couldn't be in better hands." Liz enthused.

"She's an angel!" Gushed Dickie.

"And a bit of a looker an all eh Dickie?" Albert nudged Dickie and winked.

"I can't argue with that Albert!" Dickie chuckled and blushed a little.

"Oi you two!" Liz dug Albert in the ribs.

"On that note I better get to my seat. I'll be seeing you at half time no doubt." Dickie shook Albert's hand.

"Cheers Dickie. See you later mate."

"Thanks Dickie." Liz looked at Albert scornfully.

"You always have to lower the tone don't you!" she whispered.

"I'm only having a laugh with him! I bet he's been sniffing round it though, the old dog!" They both look back out onto the pitch as both teams are on the pitch warming up waiting for the whistle.

"There he is Liz!" Albert was pointing down towards the pitch where Bobby was jogging on the spot and stretching out.

"Oh yeah! Look at him Albert I'm so proud of him."

"I always knew he'd make it… Although I didn't expect him to end up oop north lass!" Albert smiled at his wife, proud of his attempt at a northern accent. He noticed a waitress and waved her over.

"I'm gonna get her to get the drinks in." Albert was locked onto the waitress, making sure she didn't get called over to anyone else.

A petite young waitress with brown, shoulder length hair, walked towards them.

"Can you ask her to get us a bag of nuts please Alb?" asked Liz, nonchalantly.

"I've got a bag of nuts you can have later, back at the hotel, nudge nudge wink wink!" Albert gently nudged his wife with a knowing glint in his eye.

"Go on, get out of it you!" Liz replied, smiling bashfully.

PORTHAM ATHLETIC TOUCHLINE

The referee blew his whistle. Portham Athletic kicked off. The home and away crowds were singing their hearts out.

"This is what it's all about Dave. Listen to those lot out there… We must win today!" Neil Glover knew what derby games meant to football fans, having played in many a steel city derby during his playing career whilst at Heffield United.

"He's gone three at the back today, so we'll have to get down the flanks and pass it in, rather than put crosses in. Those three lumps of theirs will get up and head them away." Remarked Dave Jenkins who was very much a disciple of the beautiful game. He could work out a team's game plan faster than most. Neil Glover knew this from his time managing him as a player and was one of the reasons why Dave Jenkins was stood by his side.

"Agreed. The wide boys will have to do it for us today both offensively and defensively. We need to keep our eye on young Bobby today." Neil briefly turned his head towards Dave for a split second and then immediately fixed his gaze back to the game.

"Definitely! I've had a quiet word with them all individually about that situation." Dave assured his boss.

"Well done Dave.

PORTHAM ATHLETIC PITCH

Carl Pilford cupped his hands to his mouth. "Come on lads keep it tight and don't give them Fuck all!"

"You won't get a chance to give us fuck all son." The opposition centre half, Norman Hardcastle, looked intimidatingly towards Carl.

"Fuck off Softcastle!" Carl almost spat the words out.

Hardcastle laughed. "Very original!"

PORTHAM COMMENTRY BOX

"I can see lots of shouting going on down there as this match promises to be a lively encounter with the home side kicking from right to left." Explained Tony Court through his microphone.

"This is such a great derby up here in the North-West. It's all about bragging rights for the fans but these two teams have aspirations of achieving bigger and better things and to do that they both need to win these types of games." Responded Sam Wellesley.

"This is the one hundred and twentieth league derby between these two sides with both teams having had their fair share of success and failure over the years. This is the first time in six seasons that they have competed in the same league, with Portham returning to the second division after getting promoted as third division runners-up. They narrowly missed out on the championship under Neil Glover, who was brought in midway through last season after the sacking of Gerald MacArthur. That decision by Dickie Godstone raised a lot of eyebrows at the time but it paid off in the end. And the whistle blows. Boldham, on the attack now." Tony informed the listeners.

PORTHAM ATHLETIC HOME STAND

The Portham crowd were loud. Two home fans were being very vociferous. Mark and Sammo were lifelong fans and had been friends since they first met at an away game thirty years ago.

Mark was short and portly, Sammo was tall and thin. They were both decked out in club shirts, hats and scarves. Mark had various Portham FC pin badges on his scarf, which had seen better days.

"Come on you lot get a grip will you, there pissing all over us already!" Shouted Mark towards his beloved Portham players.

"Alright Mark, calm down they've only just kicked off! Give them a chance." Retorted Sammo, in his calm, soft voice.

Mark ignored his best mate and shouted. "Come on Portham!" In his high pitched shrill.

MAGGIE'S HOUSE

Maggie rushed in through the front door carrying three shopping bags in each hand. She back kicked the front door which slammed shut behind her as rushed straight into the kitchen. As she got into the kitchen, she gently dropped the bags down minding not to crush anything. She switched on the radio that was next to the empty fruit bowl on the worktop, adjacent to the sink.

"As we approach the halfway mark of this tense affair at the Portham versus Boldham local derby, neither side has managed to break the deadlock. Nil nil." The familiar voice of Tony Court sounded tinny on the small radio which was a present to Maggie from her late husband Derek, just before he lost his sudden, but short, brave battle against a brain tumour.

Maggie smiled as she remembered the day that Derek had given the radio to her. He was so excited that they could listen to their beloved Portham on the day that one of their former guest apprentices had made their debut away to Everton in an FA cup game. Just as Bobby was making his debut then. Maggie started to put the weekly shopping away.

Sam Wellesley's voice cut through Maggie's reminiscence.

"Yes, it's been a bit fiery as you would expect with the fierce rivalry between these two sides but as you say, neither team has managed a goal and you have to say that both teams have defended well especially Portham, but I would say that Boldham have had the better chances and are shading it slightly for me."

"And the whistles gone for half time. Some of the players are arguing as they come of the pitch... It looks like Portham's young Bobby Gorman is involved in an altercation with the big Boldham defender Norman Hardcastle. Who I have to say, should know better?" Tony scornfully reported.

With her eyes closed, as if to imagine talking to Bobby face to face, Maggie said quietly to herself. "Bobby... Calm down love, calm yourself down."

PORTHAM TOUCHLINE

"Go and sort them out please Dave. Tell them all to calm down and get back to the changing rooms... Sharp! I'll see you in there." Neil looked Dave squarely in the eyes.

Neil was very annoyed at his players behaviour as they were leaving the field of play.

"Righto boss." Dave started gesticulating at the Portham team to get off the pitch quickly.

"Get in the dressing room! Now!" Dave hollered.

The players all reacted as Dave Jenkins very rarely raised his voice. They all jogged away from their antagonists.

Bobby was pulled away from Norman Hardcastle by his captain, Carl Pilford.

PORTHAM DIRECTORS LOUNGE

Albert and Liz were standing in the director's lounge, looking slightly out of place.

"You see him getting stuck in Liz? He ain't having none of it off that big Sandcastle bloke! That's my boy! That definitely calls for a drink!" Albert chuckled.

"Leave off Alb, my nerves are shattered! Mind you, if I see that bleeding Sandcastle he'll get a kick in the you know what's!" Liz did a slight kicking motion and spoke with a mean look on her face and an even meaner streak in her voice.

This caused Albert's chuckling to erupt into laughter.

"Calm down love it's only a game! I wonder where he gets it from?"

Liz was shaking her head and still had the mean grimace on her face. Liz was not afraid to stick up for her family, as she did regularly at the resident's association monthly meetings, regarding the block of flats that the Gorman family previously lived in and the new block that they currently resided in. Liz was a kind natured lady but had a fiery temper at times.

Dickie Godstone approached.

"Ah Liz, Albert, how are you? Let me get you both a drink." Dickie signalled to one of the waitresses to bring drinks over, but Vicky reacted quicker. She darted over towards Dickie and as she did so, nodded at the other waitress, to let her know that she had the order covered.

"I'm loving it Dickie, but Liz is getting a bit hot under the collar though!" Albert nodded towards his wife.

"Well, he's still my little soldier!" Liz put on a bit of a mock sad face which broke into a smile that said she knew that she may have been a bit overprotective.

"Don't worry Liz, the boys are looking after him out there on the pitch and Neil knows exactly how to protect him. Not that he really needs it, did you see him out there? I was so proud of him! He is just what we need! The crowd love him for it!" Enthused Dickie.

"I hope so. I don't like the way some of them were with him last time. Bobby told me about it." Liz looked at Dickie, letting him know that she was not happy about the situation.

"That's just some of the more, shall we say, less educated of our fans. We would never let any harm come to Bobby." Dickie reassured the concerned mother.

"Like it Dickie!" Grinned Albert, as he could see that Dickie's reassuring manner, was calming his wife down. Sometimes, once Liz went, there was no calming her down.

Vicky brought over a tray of drinks for them all.

"Thank you darling." Liz took her gin and tonic from the silver drinks tray.

"Cheers love." Albert took a pint glass which was half filled with bitter with one hand, then took a bottle of light ale with his other hand.

"We got it in especially for you Albert. Thank you, Vicky. Keep Mr and Mrs Gorman in drinks please." Dickie made sure that Vicky understood him. He wanted to keep the parents of what he thought, after what he had witnessed from Bobby during the game, could be the best signing that the club had ever made, which meant bums on seats and cash being spent at his club. Underneath the charming exterior, there was an underlay of ruthless businessman

"Yes Mr Godstone." Vicky nodded and looked straight at dickie to let him know that she understood. Vicky was already onto this vibe anyway as there was a buzz about Bobby and his family plus, she had taken a shine to both Bobby and his family, as well as the fact the Dickie had told her to look after the Gormans about five times already.

"Thank you, Vicky," Liz smiled at Vicky.

"No problem, Mrs Gorman, it's my pleasure." Vicky smiled broadly.

Albert pulled a one pound note out of his pocket and placed it on the silver drinks tray.

"Cheers Vick." He said with a big smile. Happy to look after someone who was looking after him.

"Thank you, Mr Gorman, very generous." Vicky blushed slightly.

She was not used to receiving tips. Mr Godstone did occasionally tip the waitress, but not often enough, as they had all moaned about at some point, regularly, during break times together. Not to be outdone, Dickie pulled out a wad of cash and placed another pound note on Vicky's tray. Vicky blushed even more.

"Thank you, Mr Godstone, much appreciated." Vicky walked off back towards the bar.

As Dickie scanned away from Vicky his eyes caught onto a couple walking through the lounge doors. "Oh no!" Dickie gasped aloud to himself.

"What's up Dickie?" Albert could see Dickie was concerned.

"It's Peter Barbour, the Chairman of Boldham... With his latest bit of stuff!" Dickie exclaimed.

They all looked towards the entrance door to the director's lounge.

"Bloody hell! That is a bit of stuff an all!" Albert was transfixed.

"Albert!" Liz grabbed her husband's arm, sensing a threat, as woman did in these kinds of situations.

"Blimey he looks old enough to be her father, talk about bleedin sugar daddy!" Liz said with an air of disgust.

Peter Barbour and Stella Ingham walked over and joined the clearly aghast party.

"Ah Dickie, how the devil are you old chap?" Peter Barbour boomed in his well-educated accent, that belied his

Lancastrian roots.

"Very good Peter, and you?" Dickie enquired falsely, not giving a damn how his rival was.

Dickie's accent was well and truly Lancastrian, which he was proud of. He came from a family of Butchers. Peter Barbour was very much old money, which dated right back to the horrific, dark satanic cotton mills of Blackburn, Lancashire. A place not too far from where they were.

"Not too bad. I'll feel a lot better after we have beaten you lot! Have you met my girlfriend, Stella?" Peter said proudly of his latest trophy girlfriend.

"I don't believe I've had the pleasure. Good afternoon, Stella, pleased to meet you." Dickie smiled through gritted teeth as he introduced himself.

"Good afternoon, Dickie, I've heard a lot about you." Stella beamed a knowing smile. Her pearly white teeth almost dazzled. She had an Ocelot fur coat on, which was purposely undone to show off her ample cleavage for all to see, in an expensive, low-cut white dress.

"All good I'm hoping?" Dickie replied slightly nervous and a touch agitated.

Stella giggled.

"Not really!" she broke out into a braying laugh.

"Don't you just love her!" Peter nervously interjected.

"Not really!" Dickie retorted.

After a slight pause, Peter laughed in a relieved, nervous kind of way.

"Anyways, let me introduce you to Mr and Mrs Gorman. Our Bobby's parents." Dickie proudly motioned his arms in an offering gesture.

"Ah the young hothead! Pleased to meet you both. Someone probably needs to have a word with him, to quiet him down a bit." Peter said the words in a very condescending manner.

"And someone needs to have a word with most of your team! The way they were trying to kick my Bobby and wind him up... They ought to be ashamed of themselves!" Liz retorted, sticking up for her little soldier.

Albert cut in before Liz went any further.

"Well, he's certainly given your lot a run for their money." Albert was very quick and smug with his retort.

"Can't argue there! Anyway, we shall see Mr Gorman, we shall see. Anyway, I'm off to get us a drink. When you come to our place, I will have seats for you in our director's box and you shall have some proper hospitality!" Peter looked around the director's lounge. It had seen better days.

"Toodle Pip!" Peter Barbour held his hand out to Stella. She took his hand and they almost waltzed off. Dickie was incensed by Peter's derogatory remark but held it together.

"Yes, toodle pip Peter. We can't wait for your proper hospitality when we beat you at your place!" Dickie was again smiling through gritted teeth. His front teeth were long and slightly uneven. His front left molar had been crowned. It was whiter and slightly wider, but not as long as his right molar. His left incisor was missing.

Peter Barbour turned and shot them all a sarcastic smile. Peter's teeth were just as dazzling as Stella's. A stark contrast to his counterparts set of gnashers. Peter often remarked to others that Dickie's teeth looked like the East end of London after the war. A reference to when London was bombed to its knees during the blitz of World War two.

Stella Ingham laughed, throwing her head back as she walked off. Peter tugged her away.

"What an arsehole! Oops excuse my French Dickie" Liz chuckled.

"My thoughts exactly Elizabeth!" Dickie laughed out loud.

"I'll be all over his hospitality when we're over their place. But yeah, what an arsehole! A right pair of tits!" Albert snarled.

"Indeed, they were Albert, indeed they were my man! Anyway, talking of hospitality, let me get you both another drink as they will be out again soon." Dickie's remark had tickled Albert and he chuckled as he spoke.

"Nice one Dickie, you're a gentleman!" Albert beamed a knowing smile to Dickie and winked.

"You two are a right pair of tits!" Scolded Liz.

"What?" Albert held his hands out in mock surprise trying not to laugh.

PORTHAM ATHLETIC HOME CHANGING ROOMS

"Right then lads, I want to go three at the back now and I want the backs to push up with more emphasis on the right, and Bobby, I still want you to push up, but you need to be the cover at the back if we get caught in possession. If they break quick, you have the pace to get back. Ok?"

"Yes boss." Bobby was very focused and was listening intently to his manager.

"I also want you on the posts if they get any free kicks, Ok?" Neil stared intently at Bobby.

"Ok boss." Bobby acknowledged Neil's instructions.

Neil turned his attention to the rest of his team

"Now remember, we are playing a high line. I want crosses coming in with the big lads coming in to attack them. Talk to each other out there. We can beat these lot! Just keep calm, stick to the plan, remember our training ground drills and most importantly, enjoy the occasion. Now let's have this lot and give our punters something to brag about when they go to work on Monday and do a job they probably hate. Let's give them all something to smile about." The whole team started cheering, shouting and pepping each other up.

They started to move out of the changing room ready to go out into the tunnel.

PORTHAM COMMENTARY BOX

The referee blew his whistle while the crowd were cheering loudly.

"And Portham kick off for the second forty-five as the crowd are really singing their hearts out. I have to say the away crowd are certainly giving the home crowd a run for their money at this local derby today. Second versus fourth in the league. Boldham gain possession. Archer shoots and hits the bar!" Tony's voice rose to a crescendo as the ball hit the bar.

"That was close! Ooh that was close. We know Archer has a good long range shot in him having scored a similar goal against Crystal Rovers last week. I think we're going to see a lot of shots and balls over the top as both of these teams go for it." Sam was excited with what he had just seen.

Tony interjected. "The ball comes back into the Boldham half after that long kick up the field from Max Prior, the long serving Portham Goalkeeper."

PORTHAM ATHLETIC PITCH

"Carl's up!" Carl jumps for the airborne ball that was coming his way.

Norman Hardcastle jumped up with Carl and elbowed Carl in the left side of his head. Norman made contact with the ball with the top of his head. They both landed back on the turf.

"Aarrrgghh! Ref?" Carl appealed to the referee for a foul whilst holding his head. Hardcastle had caught Carl but not too hard.

"Play on, play on!" The referee shouted.

PORTHAM COMMENTARY BOX

"Hardcastle really went in with his elbow there. Carl Pilford expected a free kick, but the ref waves play on. Pilford remonstrating with the referee, but he is having none of it! Play on says the ref." Tony explained.

PORTHAM PITCH

Carl was running alongside the referee.

"Ref come on. He did me with his elbow for fuck's sake!" Shouted an enraged Carl.

The referee turned his head towards Carl.

"Your no angel Pilford now get on with it man. I'm not spoiling this game with loads of cards. You're all as bad as each other. Any more lip and I'll card you! Now fuck off!" shouted the ref.

Carl ran away.

"Wanker!"

Without turning back, the referee acknowledged the aggrieved Portham captain.

"I heard that!"

PORTHAM FC HOME STAND

"Is he blind or what this ref?" Sammo was angry with the referee's decision.

"Come on Portham get stuck in will ya!" Shouted Mark.

"Give us a P." Mark raised his voice even louder.

"P." Shouted some of the nearby fans in reply.

"Give me an O." Mark and Sammo shouted in unison.

"O." Replied the nearer fans.

"Give me an R." Mark and Sammo were getting louder

"R." More and more fans joined in the chant.

"Give me a T."

"T."

"Give me an H."

"H."

"Give me an A."

"A."

"Give me an M"

"M."

"What have you got?" Spittle flew out of Mark's mouth as he was gripped by the veracity of the situation that he had created.

"Portham!" The fans sang in unison.

"Thank you!" Shouted both Mark and Sammo.

"That's alright!" Shouted the rest of the fans.

Mark and Sammo laughed and the crowd around them laughed with them.

PORTHAM FC DIRECTORS BOX

"The ref's letting it run on... Just how it should be." Albert observed.

"As long as he doesn't let them hurt Bobby, that's all I'm

worried about." Liz was looking frightened.

"He ain't a little boy any more Liz, he's a professional footballer. He's holding his own out there with hard nuts who are nearly twice his age. I'm proud of him. If he was a softie, he wouldn't be here now." Albert was trying to reassure his worried wife.

"Maybe if he weren't such a little hot head he might still be at Artillery, and we wouldn't have to come all this way up north... And he might still be living at home with us!" Liz was upset.

Albert put his hand to his forehead. "Not this again Liz. Bloody hell! This will do him the world of good, trust me. Let's not spoil it eh?" Albert leaned over and kissed Liz softly on the forehead.

"I know. I just miss him at home that's all." Liz said forlornly.

PORTHAM PITCH

Bobby was in possession and was about to pass the ball when he got taken down by a tackle from behind by Norman Hardcastle.

"Aarrrgghh! Fucking hell!" Bobby winced in pain as he hit the turf. The crowd roared in absolute rage at Hardcastle.

"Come on son, up you get." Hardcastle said sarcastically as he stood over Bobby.

The young left back got up and shoved Hardcastle causing him to stumble backwards and fall over. The crowd roared even louder, this time in appreciation. Hardcastle got back up to his feet and they both butted their heads together. The other players rushed over. A melee erupted.

"You think your tough you little fucker? Eh! Eh!" Hardcastle growled.

"Well, I just put you on your arse didn't I old man. I'll fucking have it with you any time!" Bobby's eyes were bulging. He was enjoying the situation.

The referee rushed over as the melee was broken up by other more sensible players. The referee gave both Hardcastle and Gorman a yellow card, as the home and away crowds were shouting for each player to be sent off. The electric atmosphere within the stadium built even more.

"OFF OFF OFF OFF OFF!" Shouted both the home and away crowds

PORTHAM HOME STAND

"Fucking get that Sandcastle cunt off will ya ref!" Screamed Mark. His eyes were bulging and the veins in his forehead were popping to the surface of his pale skin.

"There's no place in the game for all that. That boys got more skill in his little toe than Hardcastle will ever have the old bastard!" Sammo said in a slightly louder voice than normal.

PORTHAM PITCH

"Hardcastle! You should know better. I should send you off! And you young man, need to calm it down a bit! Now let this be a lesson to you. Any more of this and you'll both be off. Now get on with it... And shake hands." The ref was stern, almost telling them off like a schoolteacher.

They both shook hands reluctantly. Hardcastle ruffled Bobby's hair. Bobby pushed his hand away as the crowd laughed and shouted.

"Touch me again and I'll knock you out." Spat Bobby.

"Now now son! You're getting a bit ratty, but don't worry boy, it'll soon be bedtime." Norman Hardcastle blew Bobby a kiss.

PORTHAM COMMENTARY BOX

"That's the third yellow of the season for Hardcastle and the first of his professional career for Gorman." Tony explained.

"I'm sure he'll be getting a few more in his career if he carries on like that but this is par for the course for Hardcastle." Chuckled Sam.

PORTHAM DIRECTORS BOX

"If I see that bleeding Hardcastle arsehole I'll swing for him I tell you!" Liz was furious with what she had just witnessed.

Albert was laughing.

"Your poor little soldier! If he was hurt, it would be a different matter but he ain't. He put the geezer on his arse! And look at this crowd love, they're loving him." Albert was looking around the stadium with the biggest, proudest smile on his face.

Some sections of the crowd were singing and clapping Bobby's name to the theme tune of the children's television programme WE ARE THE CHAMPIONS.

PORTHAM HOME STAND

"Bobby Gorman... Bobby Gorman... Bobby Gorman..." Mark was clapping and singing his heart out.

"I like this kid Mart. He's got a bit of pace and skill. And he's tough an all. Just what we've been crying out for." Sammo happily commented.

"He is something ain't he? See him put old Sandcastle on his arse. That was worth the ticket money alone." Mark chuckled as he spoke proudly of his latest, favourite Portham player.

PORTHAM COMMENTARY BOX

"Jack Crater puts it in... Goal! Carl Pilford heads it home. One nil Portham with five minutes to go! The home crowd are going wild and down on the pitch the Portham players are relieved with the goal. Some of the Boldham players remonstrating with each other." Said Sam.

"Oh, what a goal! A bullet header from a lovely cross put in from the right by Jack Crater and Pilford somehow got on the end of it to head the ball into the Boldham goal. The question is, can Portham hold on now, as that goal came very much against the run of play." Explained Tony.

"We shall see with just under five minutes remaining now." Replied Sam.

PORTHAM PITCH

Neil Glover had his hands cupped to his mouth to amplify the instructions he was about to pass to his players.

"Calm down you lot! Keep your shape, keep your shape. Sit deep, sit deep! We'll get them on the counter. Carl! Carl talk to them! Talk to them!" Shouted Neil.

"Now Portham have a free kick on the edge of the area to be taken by their free kick specialist and captain, Carl Pilford. Explained Sam.

Neil still had his hands cupped to his mouth.

"Push up now you lot lets attack this one and finish them off. Bobby, Bobby stay back now lad you know the drill." Bobby gave his manager the thumbs up, and Neil gave him the thumbs up back.

"Bobby, you stay back and cover. Stay back!" Shouted Carl, pointing to where Bobby needed to stay. The last match was still in his mind.

PORTHAM COMMENTARY BOX

"He's lining it up now and... Oh, I don't believe it. He's hit the upright! Shouted Sam.

"Pilford took the free kick which beat the wall, but it cannoned off the crossbar and come back into play. Portham were trying to get the second goal but now Boldham defender Hardcastle has headed the ball into the path of John Drydesdale who is on his own with only the keeper to beat but young Gorman, who stayed back this time, is running as fast as he can to intercept the nippy Drydesdale. Gorman is catching him with unbelievable pace. I can't believe it! Screamed Tony.

"Gorman slides in and takes out Drydesdale but did he get the ball first?" Sam asked rhetorically as he couldn't be sure from his view.

"The home crowd are going wild with relief and excitement as Gorman has intercepted what was surely going to be a goal!" Tony was animated.

"The away crowd are not happy!" Interjected Sam.

" Off! Off1 Off! Off! Off!" The away crowd chanted, apoplectic with rage.

"The away fans are incensed and are calling for Gorman to be sent off. The referee is having to consult his linesman as Gorman is already on a yellow card. It looked like he took the player before he got the ball to me." Tony explained from his point of view.

"Gorman is protesting his innocence and is gesturing that he got the ball. This is in danger of erupting again as players from both sets of players surround the referee as he tries waving them all away." Said Sam.

PORTHAM PITCH

"Ref, I got the ball I swear." Bobby protested

"I know son. Linos just confirmed it. The referee reassured Bobby.

"Now you lot get away! It's a corner." The referee turned and waved the rest of the players away and pointed to the corner flag to the right of the goal and blew his whistle.

PORTHAM COMMENTARY BOX

"The referee has blown for a corner and the Boldham players are furious." Shouted Sam.

Tony started to chuckle.

"The Boldham bench are going crazy and there seems to be a bit of arguing going on down there between the two assistants who are being pulled back by their respective managers."

PORTHAM PITCH

"You lot have been getting at him all game, now Fuck off." Dave Glover rarely lost his temper. Neil Glover was trying to drag Dave back to the dugout.

"Come on Dave! Don't worry they've blown for a corner. Sod that lot for now. He is still on the pitch that's all we need to know."

The Portham Goalie, Max Prior, hugged Bobby as they set up for the corner to be taken.

PORTHAM COMMENTARY BOX

"Boldham take the corner and... Oh, what a save but its back out as the keeper Max Prior could only parry the ball...

Hardcastle and Prior have collided... Both players falling over the ball has come back in from a shot from the Boldham striker, but young Gorman has stood firm on the line, but it has bounced off of his outstretched right foot... Parker has scrambled across the ground for it. He finally has it in his hands. He is curled up in a ball, protecting the ball with his life." Tony said excitedly.

"Unbelievable stuff here as there can only be seconds left on the clock as the Portham keeper slowly gets to his feet and takes his time as the Boldham players and bench gesture for him to take the kick." Tony explained.

"He launches the ball high up field... And that's it! The whistle blows and Portham have won this by the slenderest of margins at this heated local derby! Portham One, Boldham nil." Exclaimed Sam.

The crowd were going wild. The Portham players and a few hundred fans that had ran onto the pitch, all mobbed Bobby Gorman. The home crowd were singing Bobby's name. Some of the away crowd also invaded the pitch. Pockets of fighting broke out between the rival supporters on the pitch and in the stands. Both sets of players ran from the pitch, back down the tunnel to safety.

PORTHAM HOME DRESSING ROOM

The players were running into their dressing room. Neil Glover was patting them all on the back as they filtered in. Dave Jenkins was handing cans of beers out to the players as they all came in buzzing from the result. Neil and Dave had agreed to let them celebrate or commiserate in the changing room. Bobby, who had managed to break free from the throng of human beings out on the pitch, by slipping, sliding, bobbing and weaving his way through by giving a handshake here and a hug there, went to take a beer from Dave.

"Hold on a minute! Gaffer! Young Bobby wants a beer. What do you reckon?" Dave said in a mock well-spoken voice.

"Well, he is too young... But I would say he has bloody well-earned it... Go on then! And while you're at it, I'll have one an all!" Boomed Neil.

The changing room erupted with cheers and laughter. Some of the players shook their cans up and sprayed beer all over Bobby. Some of the beer foam hit Dave.

"Here watch it you lot!" Dave handed Bobby a beer.

"Here you go son, you did bloody earn it today. And do you know what? The boss hardly ever has a drink." Dave turned his head to face Bobby side on and wagged his finger at Bobby.

Bobby gleefully accepted the beer.

"Nice one Dave. I listened this time!" Bobby beamed a knowing smile at Dave then cracked open the cold white can, emblazoned with the red S of Skrel.

Neil Glover walked to them both. Dave handed him a Beer. Neil took it from Dave's outstretched hand. He opened it then touched Bobby's can with his can.

"Cheers Bobby!" Neil raised his can to Bobby.

"Cheers boss." Bobby smiled from ear to ear.

They both took a mouthful of their beer.

"You did well today, you kept your composure... Most of the time!" Neil ruffled Bobby's sweaty hair.

"You must not let it go that far. Other refs may have sent you off, but that idiot should know better. I like your aggression lad, but you must channel it in the right way. We shall have to work on that won't we Dave..." Dave was taking a sip of his beer.

"Yes boss. I'll work with him on that."

"I think you might have won the crowd over a bit, especially with putting Hardcastle on his arse. It's good you can look after yourself. I understand you did a bit of boxing?" Neil had found this out from Albert, who was only too happy to let Neil Glover know this juicy bit of information, knowing that Neil Glover would appreciate it.

"I did boss but had to give it up to concentrate on football." Bobby replied.

"Well, you made the right choice. Although the fans have let themselves down with all that fighting. It's no wonder the game has got such a bad name. There will be someone killed before long… But anyway, well done lad. And don't tell anyone about the beer. Anything that happens in this dressing room, stays in this dressing room. Ok lad. Anything!" Neil gave Bobby a menacing look.

"Yes Boss." Replied a slightly taken aback Bobby.

"Good lad. I'll see you upstairs. I bet your parents can't wait to see you. And by the way, you're the sponsor's man of the match." Neil's face softened as he informed Bobby of the news that he had been told by one of the one of the club's administrators, just before he had walked into the dressing room. He turned and walked away, knowing he had just dropped a lovely bombshell.

"Really? Thanks boss!" Bobby could not believe his ears.

Neil Glover did not turn back to Bobby but acknowledged him by raising his arm up above his head, giving a thumbs up as he exited the dressing room.

Carl Pilford walked over to Bobby with a big smile on his face.

"Man, of the match, eh? Well done out there mate, I was well impressed and so were all the lads! The crowd were going mental, especially at the end. That hasn't happened for a long time!" Carl hugged Bobby.

"Thanks mate. Yeah, I couldn't believe it! They were all grabbing and hugging me... A few even kissed me but the fighting was a bit naughty though."

"I know. That does spoil it a bit. Anyway, I suppose the gaffer told you the golden rule, did he?" Carl gave a look as if to say he already knew the answer to his question.

"What happens in the dressing room stays in the dressing room. Ok lad. Anything!" Bobby replied in his best impression of Neil Glovers voice.

Carl burst out laughing.

"That was pretty good. He says the same to us all. An old player of his at another club apparently spoke to the papers about something that happened and that was it. He never played again... Right, let's get ready and get upstairs."

PORTHAM DIRECTORS LOUNGE

Bobby strode into the director's lounge, excitedly looking for his mum and dad. He spotted his mum's ginger hair immediately and darted towards her, almost knocking one of the waitresses trays out of her hand. Bobby was oblivious to this, but the young brown-haired waitress, skilfully weaved her tray to the right, then over Bobby's head. She took it in her stride and smiled. She knew who this young, handsome footballer was, but their paths had not yet crossed. She saw Bobby get to Liz.

"Alright mum. Alright Dad. "

Liz spun around, nearly spilling her gin and tonic.

"Hello darling! Oh, come here." Liz pulled Bobby towards her for a kiss and a cuddle.

"Alright Mum!" Bobby hugged his mother and gave her kiss on the cheek.

"Come here son." Albert hugged his son proudly and patted him on the back.

"You done so well mate, we're so proud of ya son!"

"Alright Dad! Bobby pulled away.

"There's the gaffer, he's coming over." Bobby looked nervous.

"Don't worry son!" Albert ruffled his son's hair.

Neil Glover approached the Gorman family.

"Mr and Mrs Gorman. Lovely to see you again. How are you both?"

"Hello Neil, good to see you too mate. We're alright now that's bleedin over!" The two men shook hands firmly.

"Hello Neil. Yeah, my nerves are shattered after that." Liz put her right hand to her forehead and exhaled.

"So are mine, don't you worry about that Mr and Mrs Gorman!" Neil exhaled.

They all laughed.

"No, he did very well. A few things still need to be worked on with his game but overall, a great performance in one hell of a game. He was our man of the match!" enthused Neil.

"It was Neil. It was some game out there! I wanted to get me boots on and get down there with you all! We heard he got man of the match... We were so proud of him". Albert wishfully thought about getting his boots on and playing in the same side as his son and also thought back to his playing days at school and then for his local club on a Saturday over Hackney marshes.

Dickie Godstone was schmoozing the various VIP's that were gathered in the director's area but stopped in his tracks when he saw his manager with the Gormans. He politely broke off his conversation with a successful local builder, who had been a sponsor of the club for a few years, then strode over towards them.

"Bobby! Shake my hand son, shake my bloody hand." Dickie's hand was outstretched.

Bobby's hand connected with Dickie's large hand and Dickie shook it vigorously, stretching Bobby's shoulder and pulling him slightly off balance.

"Well done lad!" Boomed Dickie.

"Thanks Mr Chairman." Bobby got his hand back and straightened himself out.

"Careful Mr Chairman, we don't need young Bobby injured... He did do well Mr Chairman, but he did get a bit carried away." Neil gave Dickie a look. His eyebrows were raised accentuating the already deep furrows in his leather football and weather-beaten brow.

"Neil's right Bobby... It was a big fiery game, but we have a reputation as a good family club... Not like that lot running onto the pitch and fighting with our fans. We cannot have that, so calm it down a bit please... You understand me, right?" Dickie wagged his finger at Bobby.

"Yes, Mr Chairman." Bobby looked to the ground.

"You listen to them Bobby." Liz put an arm around her dejected looking son.

Albert cut in.

"He's got to have bit of it in his game though gentlemen... He was getting slaughtered out there by some of that lot." Albert felt he had to make a point and defend his son. He put his arm around his son too. Mother and father both protecting their son.

"I agree Mr Gorman. I don't want to take it out of him completely, but he just needs to channel it better. I know he can do it. Dave and I will work with him on it. Don't worry about that. But anyway, what a bloody game eh?" Neil's smiling face broke the brief impasse and lifted the mood. Something he often had to do during team talks. He did not want to upset the Gorman team that were stood in front of him.

"Yes, indeed Neil I'm very proud of what you and the team did today." Smiled Dickie.

Carl Pilford walked over toward them. Bobby noticed and wriggled out of his parents' arms before his Captain saw.

"And here's our captain, Mr Pilford. Well done today lad you did well, and you certainly earned your win bonus today." Dickie said with a wry smile.

Something told Albert that Dickie didn't quite enjoy giving out bonuses for people doing their jobs. He smiled to himself.

"Thanks Mr Chairman." Carl acknowledged the Gormans.

"Hello. You must be Bobby's mum and dad. I'm Carl." Carl and Albert shook hands.

"Good game today, Carl!" Albert patted Carl's back.

"Yeah, well done mate. I see you were looking after my Bobby." Liz smiled as she looked at her son.

"Excuse us please. The chairman and I need to have a chat in his office. I'll leave you all to get acquainted… Mr Chairman?" Neil moved his head in the polite fashion that meant let's go.

"Yes, excuse us, we always have our little chats after the games, so we'll see you all later." Dickie smiled at the Gormans.

Dickie and Neil walked off towards the boardroom.

"Mate well done today, you played a blinder."

"Thanks Mr Gorman. Your Bobby played a blinder too."

"He did mate… And call me Albert. He got a bit hot under the collar though, didn't you son."

"Alright leave him alone now Alb." Liz scowled at Albert.

"Leave it out will ya! Right, I want a pint! Get us a beer please captain." Bobby clapped his hands together.

"I don't think so sonny Jim!" Liz scolded Bobby.

Carl laughed. "Sonny Jim! He can have a shandy, can't he?"

"Course he can have a shandy! And you can get me another light and bitter while you're at it Captain!" Albert did the same clapping motion that Bobby had just did.

Bobby had got this action from his dad who always did this whenever he was excited about something.

"Oh, go on then." Said Liz, rolling her eyes at them all.

"I'll get them in then. Where's young Vicky? She's a lovely lass. You wait till you see her Bobby." Carl leant in towards Bobby's ear.

"A few of the lads have been sniffing round her but she won't have none of it..." Carl leant back and looked around for Vicky.

"She's a lovely girl. She's been looking after us all afternoon." Liz said, with a big smile on her face, as she too looked around for Vicky.

"She's a right little sort Bobby! I think she's about your age an all! Get in there son!" Albert nudged his son.

"Albert!" Liz dug her husband in the ribs.

"ARRGH Liz! Albert winced.

"He could do with a bird to keep him company up her eh Carl?" albert winked at Carl.

"A few of the boys have tried asking her out but she won't have none of it. She's a good girl. She's studying hairdressing at college. She works in the hairdressers on day release and works here for extra money." Carl informed them all.

"I knew she was a good girl! Now keep schtum you lot, here she comes. And no more of your stupid comments Albert or you'll feel my knee in your bollocks!" Liz said very seriously.

Carl leant into Bobby.

"I love your parents' mate!"

"So, do I... Sometimes!"

Vicky walked over.

"Hello Mr and Mrs Gorman... Hello Carl... You must be Bobby. Everyone's talking about you!" Gushed Vicky.

"Oh hello." Bobby felt a bit uncomfortable. He thought Vicky was beautiful.

"Hello darling. Yes, that's my Bobby, the one I was telling you about." Beamed Liz.

"I've heard all about you Bobby." Replied Vicky with a wry smile.

Bobby looked horrified and scowled at his mum.

"What you been saying mum? You're so embarrassing!"

"Don't worry son. I don't think she told her you've only just stopped wetting the bed." Albert winked at Vicky.

"So, I think you're in the clear son."

Vicky giggled. "Don't worry I won't tell anyone!"

"Classic Albert, classic!" Carl Pilford couldn't help but laugh.

"Yeah, very funny dad!" Bobby was not pleased with his parents at all.

"So, it'll be the usual for you three, but what can I get you Bobby?" Vicky was grinning knowing full well he was underage.

"Well, I want a pint, but this lot will only let me have shandy..." Bobby looked around in the vain hope someone would relent and let him have a proper pint of lager.

"Bobby will have a pint of shandy please Vicky." Liz soon killed off any hope Bobby had of getting his pint.

Carl, Liz and Albert all started laughing to each other. Vicky looked right into Bobby's eyes and smiled broadly. Bobby thought he saw something in Vicky's eyes that told him that all hope may not be lost just yet. Or was he just hoping? He wasn't entirely sure.

"Ok I won't be long." Vicky broke off her gaze into Bobby's eyes, turned and glided off towards the bar. Bobby's gaze followed her.

"Told you, didn't I?" Carl whispered in Bobby's ear.

"You were right about her dad!" Bobby gushed. His face had gone red.

"I ain't saying nothing mate." Albert replied with a big grin on his face knowing that nobody, even his wife, could argue with him about being right about how beautiful Vicky was.

"Lovely girl." Liz followed Vicky with her eyes then looked at Bobby and grinned.

Dickie and Neil walked back out of the boardroom towards them.

"Hello again everyone. We have had our chat and Neil would like to have a quick word, seeing that the relevant parties are here. Neil?" Dickie motioned for Neil to take over.

Neil started to address them all.

'It has unfortunately been confirmed that Billy Thorpe's playing career is over due to his injury. He will remain with the club in a coaching capacity but as one door closes, another one opens. The door has opened for you Bobby. I want you to be my first choice left-back. The chairman would like to sit down with you and your parents to re-negotiate your current short-term contract and improve it a bit. Hopefully tie you to the club longer and give you better wages rather than the YTS wages you are on. After today's performance it was an easy decision to make for us to offer you this opportunity but believe me, we have a lot of hard work to do and a long way to go before you are the finished article. So, do you think you are up to it?" Neil was looking at Bobby with his eyebrows raised and brow furrowed.

"I am up for it boss! I don't need to think about it!"

"Good lad Bobby." Replied Neil.

"That's wonderful news young Bobby!" Dickie was beaming.

"I ain't got a problem with it Neil. Dickie, perhaps we can get it sorted while we're up here." Albert enthused.

"Well perhaps we can think it over first..." Liz looked sad.

Neil noticed and cut in.

"Mr and Mrs Gorman let's have a good night tonight then you can have a think about it for as long as you want. You can get back to us when it is convenient for you both, whether that be this weekend or maybe the next home game. I'm sure the chairman will happily take care of getting you here and putting you up again. Mr Chairman?"

"Yes of course, of course. Neil's right. No rush but you can see how keen I am!" Enthused a smiling Dickie.

He had not seen the home crowd as excited as he had during the game for as long as he could remember. He knew Bobby's passion would put bums on seats as he had told Neil Glover during their catch up. Neil had been reluctant to put Bobby straight in despite Billy Thorpe's career being over and he had floated the idea of changing formation, so that Bobby would not have to start every game, but Dickie had a way of persuading Neil sometimes. Neil agreed, as he had no doubt of Bobby's ability, it was just his lack of experience that worried him, but he knew his coaching team and players well enough that they would all help Bobby's development. He knew changing the formation would hinder the team more as a whole, compared to keeping things as they were and slotting Bobby in at left back.

Vicky walked over with a tray of drinks.

"Ah Vicky! Right on cue!" Dickie clapped his hands and rubbed them together.

"I saw you and Mr Glover walk over so I've got you both a drink too."

Vicky was as efficient as ever. She had quickly become a favourite of everyone at the club soon after she joined. One of the clients at the hairdressers where she was doing her YTS was head waitress at the club. Vicky had mentioned that she was looking for extra work to supplement her low wages as she was saving to buy a car. The head waitress offered her a trial and soon took her on for match day hospitality.

"That's my girl! There you go!" Dickie placed a one-pound note on the tray.

"Thank you, Mr Godstone. That's very nice of you." Vicky was very happy with Dickie and Albert trying to outdo each other in the tip stakes. Along with this and the other tips she was getting, she was raking in the cash.

"That's alright love. Keep up the good work." Dickie winked at Vicky as he knew she was taking the business of keeping the Gormans happy very seriously. A little more seriously than Dickie knew.

Vicky put the tray down on the table and started to hand out the drinks.

"Here's your shandy Bobby. We don't want it getting mixed up with the proper drinks, do we?" Vicky smiled at Bobby.

"Shandy? Good lad Bobby!" Dickie chuckled.

"See Bobby!" Liz pointed her finger at her son.

"I wouldn't have minded if he had one. It's probably best you stick to shandy though." Neil smiled at Liz.

"I think so." Liz replied to Neil, enamoured by Neil's support.

Vicky finished giving the drinks out then picked the tray up and walked past Bobby. She whispered in his ear while the others were chatting.

"It's lager with only a tiny splash of lemonade." Vicky said without so much as giving him a glance as she moved off.

Bobby looked on smiling at her. He took a big swig of his pint.

"Thanks Vicky."

"That's OK Bobby. Just let me know if you want another shandy." Vicky said loudly as she walked away, not looking back at Bobby, smiling to herself.

The rest of them heard Vicky and all laughed apart from Bobby, who was just staring in disbelief at Vicky as she walked off. She took a drinks order from a group of some of the other players. He watched with a pang of jealousy as they were all chatting her up and flirting with her. She cast a quick glance back to Bobby and winked at him with a wry smile. She turned back to start taking the order from his rowdy teammates.

LATER IN A TAXI

"He's pissed!" Sneered Albert, who was drunk too.

"But he's only been drinking shandy!" Liz exclaimed. Always sticking up for her little soldier.

Bobby slurred his reply. "Yeah, I've only been drinking... SHANDY!" Bobby shook his head as he wobbled in the back.

"Well, he had enough of 'em to be pissed! He ain't used to it is he." Moaned Albert.

"If you start feeling sick let us know and he can pull over." Liz shouted.

The taxi driver eyeballed his rear-view mirror, seeing the young, inebriated Bobby.

"You puke up in here lad and you'll be paying for it to be cleaned! I've had enough of your lot puking in my cab!" He hated picking up from Portham after a game.

Bobby did his best to focus on the rear-view mirror. "I'm alright, I'm alright! Leave me alone will ya!"

The taxi driver focused back on the road.

"Open the bloody window and get some fresh air. Were nearly there now."

"Good shout driver. Sorry about this." Albert was shaking his head.

Liz wound down her window quickly.

"Remember we're having Sunday dinner at the hotel tomorrow so make sure you get there nice and early as were getting on the train back straight after. First class an all!" Gushed Liz.

The taxi pulled over outside Maggie's house.

"Here we go!" The taxi driver said loudly, relieved that they had made it without any mishaps.

"Come on son. I'll help you out." Albert faced his son then turned to get out of the cab.

"I'm alright dad honestly." Bobby kissed his mother on the cheek then opened the door and got out.

Bobby was a bit unsteady on his feet.

"I'll see you tomorrow." He waved and turned around towards his digs.

"Goodnight babe, see you tomorrow." Liz shouted out of the window.

"Goodnight son. And well done today."

Bobby shouted back without turning back. "Thanks daddy!"

"Alright driver, The Hotel please." Chuckled Albert.

"Hang on! Let's wait till he gets in." Liz was worried as she saw Bobby struggling with getting his keys in the door but managed the simple task eventually and staggered in.

"Alright we can go now, he's in." Liz smiled now that she knew her boy was safe indoors.

CHAPTER V
AND HERES TO YOU MRS BRAITHWAITE

Bobby staggered into payphone and knocked the phone receiver off. Maggie appeared at the living room doorway and switched the hallway light on to reveal herself, startling Bobby.

"Good evening young man! Have a few drinks after the game, did we?"

"Good evening young lady! Yes, I had a couple of shandy's..." Bobby replied cockily to a very different looking landlady.

"That's OK as I've had a few me self tonight! Come on let's have a nightcap! You can tell me all about today!"

Maggie led a slightly shocked Bobby into the living room. She was wearing a black silk nightgown. Her hair was done and hanging down very wavy. She had full make up on and had painted her long fingernails red as he had noticed as her hand lent against the architrave of the doorway. He also noticed that her toenails were painted red as she was wearing a pair of black, fluffy kitten heeled slippers which showed her toes through the front. Bobby had never seen her so done up.

"You look all dressed up Maggie..." Bobby said with a big grin and a glint in his eye as his wobbled.

He thought Maggie looked a like one of the readers wives in the carrier bag full of porno magazines that he and his mate Tommy had found behind a bush over the park one day, which had been dumped as a pornographic oasis. Probably left by an unknown man, who was trying to rid himself of his guilty secret, who had perhaps finally got lucky with a woman who had wanted to move in with him. Who knows why these carrier bags full of pornographic magazines often turned up at the side of a road or behind bushes on a regular basis all over the UK and probably all over the western world, during the late 70's and early 80's.

"I was Bobby love. I was supposed to be going out earlier but got stood up." Maggie said sadly. She was wobbling and clearly drunk.

Maggie walked into the front room. Bobby followed.

"Stood up?" Bobby wasn't sure what she meant.

"Yes Bobby, stood up! Or blown out as you might say!" Maggie giggled.

"I didn't know you had a boyfriend, Maggie!" Bobby was shocked.

"He's not my boyfriend Bobby, just a man I've known for a while who said he would take me out for a drink. The bastard didn't turn up, so I stayed in and had a drink on my own." Maggie walked over to the small cabinet that Bobby had already previously investigated, which contained drinks paraphernalia.

There was a bottle of R Whites Lemonade and a bottle of Smirnoff vodka, but it had a blue label rather than red. Maggie started pouring them both a large measure from the bottle of vodka then poured in a dash of the lemonade. She then used a what looked like small a pair of tongues to grab some slices of lemon from a plate and then dropped a slice of lemon into each of the glasses.

"Get that down you. And don't be telling anyone we had a drink, will you?" Maggie said with a wry smile

"No don't worry, it can be our little secret. Anyway, I didn't know they did Blue Smirnoff!"

"Good lad! Its proper vodka this is! It's stronger than the red stuff. So, I listened to the second half on the radio this afternoon. Sounds like you had some game love."

"Oh Maggie, it was like being in a dream, I'm so happy! The crowd seemed to love me, and I played well, much better than the last game… And we won in the end." Bobby slurred his words as he enthused after remembering the previous game for a split second

"I hear you got into a bit of a kerfuffle… It's no good if you get sent off." Maggie gave Bobby a scolding look then smiled.

"I know… They've all had a word with me, but they were kicking me, so I just give a bit back."

Maggie laughed.

"The chairman and manager want to sign me on a better contract right now, but my mum and dad are going to think it over."

Maggie got up a bit unsteady. Her gown fell open to reveal most of her breasts that were almost overflowing out of the black lacy bra that she was wearing. She looked at Bobby, who was gawping at her, and stood up straight to adjust her gown. She then leant over and gave Bobby a kiss on the lips then gently whispered into his ear.

"Well done Bobby…" Maggie turned towards the door and looked back at Bobby.

"Now pour us another drink. I'm off to the little girl's room." Maggie left the room.

Bobby was just staring ahead not sure of what just happened.

THE GORMAN'S HOTEL ROOM

Liz and Albert were lying in bed. The bedside lights were on.

"What do you reckon then love?" Liz snuggled up to her husband.

"I reckon we need to make the most of it for Bobby. I mean, they seem to love him, but he's only played two games so far. I think this'll be the best place for him for now, at least for a couple or three seasons. Let's get as much as we can out of them to get some money for Bobby and get them to pay for us to get down here and pay for our hotels. Who knows how long it will all last?"

"That sounds good to me love. Now I suppose we might as well make use of this hotel room then." Said Liz with a grin.

Liz pounced on Albert.

"Now that sounds good to me love!" Albert's face was alight.

"Switch the lights off then." Liz commanded.

Albert leant across to his left and switched off the bedside lights.

MAGGIE'S HOUSE

Maggie came back into the living room.

Bobby stood up slightly unsteadily.

"Here's your drink." Bobby said proudly.

"Good lad." Maggie took the drink, sat down on the sofa and took a sip. She winced.

"That's a bit strong love, are you trying to get me drunk young man?"

Bobby sat down on the armchair and turned to face her.

"You already are! Your perfume smells nice…"

"Careful Bobby, flattery will get you everywhere!"

They both started giggling. Bobby took a sip of his drink and he winced even more than Maggie just had.

"Bloody hell that is strong! It's like firewater this stuff!" Bobby pursed his lips and exhaled.

"Told you its proper stuff. Come and sit over here, you look all uncomfortable over there." Maggie tilted her head to entice him over.

Bobby stared at her for a few seconds.

"Alright then."

Bobby downed the rest of his drink. He got up and walked unsteadily over to the settee. He sat down next to Maggie as she downed her drink.

"That's better." She said reassuringly.

Maggie stroked the inside of Bobby's thigh. He started to kiss her and immediately slipped his hand through the gaping silk gown and started fondling her right breast as Maggie groaned in appreciation. She suddenly pulled away.

"Ooh you little fucker! Why did you do that?"

"Because I wanted to." Bobby was a bit unsure of himself all the same.

"Good!" Maggie snapped back. She started kissing Bobby. He put his hand between her legs. Maggie pushed him away. She stood up and slipped off her gown to reveal herself. She stood in front of Bobby slightly unsteady from standing up so quickly.

"Do you like what you see Bobby?"

"Yeah!" Bobby smiled but still seemed a bit unsure at this sudden turn of events.

Maggie leant down and started undoing Bobby's trousers. She struggled to get the belt undone at first but soon prevailed. She then unbuttoned the waist and unzipped the fly then pulled his trousers down. Bobby's penis was filling with extra blood as it fast became erect. Maggie pulled his pants down, but they got caught on his erect cock, causing it to flick back against his belly as Maggie almost ripped the pants off at the second attempt.

"You do look pleased with what you see!" Maggie was talking to Bobby's now fully erect penis.

Maggie pulled his pants further down his legs to get them out of the way and then started to perform oral sex on him for a few seconds.

She stood up "Right, let's get upstairs then!" Maggie demanded of Bobby who was sitting there with his trousers and pants around his ankles with his shoes and socks still on. He was wondering how he was going to get upstairs in his current state of half undress.

MAGGIE'S BEDROOM

Maggie was lying on the bed naked. Bobby undressed his top half in a hurry and almost fell onto the bed. He climbed on top of Maggie and kissed her, but she pushed his head down towards her vagina.

"Lick me, Bobby!" commanded Maggie.

Bobby started licking at Maggie's vagina. Maggie groaned with enjoyment. He tried to move upward but Maggie held his head down there, forcing him to carry on.

"Not yet Bobby, not yet!" Maggie groaned.

Bobby gripped the back off Maggie's thighs and pushed them upwards. Bobby parted Maggie's hairy bush with his fingers, almost like Moses had done with the Red Sea, then lapped at her like a dog drinking from a bowl of water. Bobby pushed his tongue deeper into Maggie's vulva. Maggie groaned more and more in ecstasy.

"Now Bobby, now." She shouted as she released her grip from Bobby's head.

Bobby moved up and slid his bulging penis into Maggie's sopping fanny. The slight squidge and squelch could be heard as they engaged in fast intercourse. They were both moaning in ecstasy. Bobby was already losing control as the heat of Maggie's passion transferred to Bobby's Glans. If in doubt, pull out as his dad used to say jokingly, when he had often spoken to Bobby drunkenly, about not wanting grandchildren just yet. Bobby thrust his cock into Maggie hard and fast a few more times before pulling out and ejaculating. His hot white cum shot out hard and far. It was illuminated by the green light of Maggie's bedside digital alarm clock. The rope of semen arced over Maggie. The front end of the long jet hit the headboard of the bed. The rest of it landed on Maggie's hair, right cheek, right breast and her stomach. The rest of Bobby's load landed on her lower stomach and pubic hair as it pulsed out weaker and weaker. After Bobby had finished, he laid down on his back beside Maggie. They were both breathless.

"I've never seen that before!" Maggie giggled.

Bobby kind of sniggered but was already falling to sleep.

BOBBY'S ROOM THE DAY AFTER THE NIGHT BEFORE

Bobby was woken by the sound of the phone ringing. He was very groggy and unsure of where he was for a moment. He looked around and realized he was in his room at Maggie's. He could hear Maggie's voice.

"He's still asleep, I think. He seemed a bit worse for wear when he got in... Ha ha... Ok if he's not up soon I'll give him a knock... Ok I'll see you this afternoon love. Bye"

Bobby could hear Maggie walking up the stairs and then

heard the familiar floorboard creaks as she walked onto the passageway and towards his bedroom. Maggie walked in and sat down at the end of the bed. She looked more like the Maggie that Bobby was used to. Rather plain looking and tidy. She had removed all her make-up and nail varnish. Her hair was wet so she must have had a bath Bobby thought.

"That was your mum. We're all meeting for Sunday lunch at their hotel. They're meeting with the Chairman first, quite soon actually, to sort your future out! We'll meet them at one o'clock." Maggie smiled.

Bobby wasn't sure what to say.

"Ok. I feel really hungover! You coming as well?" Bobby wasn't sure what was going on.

"Yes. Last night stays between us ok!" Maggie snapped the words out and pointed her finger at Bobby.

"Don't ever mention it to anybody ok… We both shouldn't have drunk so much and ending up… you know…" Maggie raised her eyebrows and nodded her head to towards the bedroom wall.

"That's alright with me… I really enjoyed it! Bobby beamed. His hair a mess.

"Good, so did I but that's enough of that now. Up you get! This is an important day for you. I'll make you a bacon butty and a cup of tea. You can have it while I get ready."

"Thanks Maggie, I won't say anything if you don't."

"I won't be saying anything, trust me. I ought to be ashamed of myself!"

Maggie closed the door behind her. Bobby laid back looking very pleased with himself.

HOTEL RESTAURANT WHERE BOBBY'S MUM AND DAD WERE STAYING

Dickie, Albert and Liz were already seated as Maggie and Bobby walked over to them.

"Maggie, Bobby. Glad you're here! Boomed a very sharply dressed Dickie Godstone.

Dickie got up and shook Bobby's hand. Dickie moved towards Maggie and gave her a peck on the cheek.

"Where were you last night?" Maggie whispered almost spitting the words out as she struggled to keep her audibility to a bare minimum. She moved her head so that she could hear the inevitable response that she knew was coming, but still doing her best to maintain their secrecy.

"I couldn't get away!" Dickie hissed into her ear.

Dickie could smell the nice scent on Maggie, caused by the expensive perfume he had brought her recently.

Maggie jerked her head to the opposite ear of Dickie. She always thought his large ears resembled rashers of bacon on each side of his large cranium.

"You could've bloody phoned you bastard!" Maggie hissed the words and jerked her head back with a smile, to keep up the charade that she was happy, to everybody else.

Bobby caught a look at them both. He thought that they looked a bit suspicious. He carried on looking at them as his father whispered into his ear.

"We've sorted everything mate and got you a bloody good deal. You can sign tomorrow. We can talk about it later. You'll be well looked after, and they will pay for us to come and visit you." Albert pulled away from his son's ear and looked him in the eyes for a reaction.

Bobby looked toward Maggie and Dickie who still seemed to be in a secret conversation as far as he could see, but he was also trying to take in what his father had just conveyed to him. He looked away from Dickie and Maggie. He looked at his father, who was looking at him with moist eyes and the biggest beaming grin he may have seen from his old man yet. He looked back at Albert and then just hugged him tight and was beaming himself.

"Hello darling!" shrieked his mother.

Liz grabbed her son from her husband and hugged him tight. Bobby rested his shoulder on his mother's shoulder and caught sight of Dickie, who was showing Maggie to her seat.

"Hello Mum! Thanks for sorting things for me." Bobby squeezed his mum.

"That's alright love. Come on, let's sit down and have a bit of Sunday dinner." Liz released her son from her grip and made for her seat.

With that, the whole party started to sit down at the table.

"Now Bobby, we have sat down together and sorted all of the terms out for a three-year contract for you..." Dickie proudly announced but was abruptly interrupted.

"Three years?" Bobby enquired, with a confused look on his face.

"Don't interrupt love, what have I told you about that." Scolded Liz.

"I didn't expect that. It seems like a long time..." Bobby replied wistfully and frightened at the same time.

"What I will say lad is not many clubs would tear up a youth contract and offer a three-year full contract on the strength of two games now." Dickie stated with an air of confidence and surety as he was a little miffed at Bobby's reaction, but was trying to filter his emotions, as he had learned to do over the years. His face had reddened.

It's OK Dickie, I don't think he's really thought about it properly yet." Albert interjected, worried that his son was about to mess up the biggest opportunity that may ever befall him in his life.

"No, I haven't really. I am really pleased though. Thanks Mr Chairman." Bobby suddenly felt that this situation was right.

"You had me worried for a bit there lad." Dickie laughed nervously.

The whole group chuckled.

Dickie didn't normally act on instinct alone as he would always like to see a youth player who steps up to the first team play at least five games, but he felt this was the right thing to do.

"It doesn't happen often Bobby. Most of the lads that have stayed with me never made the grade. They get released and never find new clubs." Maggie said with a reassuring look.

Suddenly, Bobby thought of all the young players that had stayed with Maggie and wondered if she had shagged the life out of each of them and caused them to be released. He was snapped out of this horrifying thought by the sound of his father's louder than usual voice.

"Bobby? D'you hear what Maggie said?" Albert chirped, having no idea what his son was just thinking.

"Yeah, yeah. No, thanks again dickie and thanks for looking after me Maggie..." Bobby struggled to get the thought of Maggie in her outfit that she had on last night, out of his head.

His thoughts turned to the long line of apprentices faces that he was recalling in his head that Maggie had pictures up of, on the walls of her tidy little semi-detached house that had been all but paid for by the club. All those young fresh faces, failing, falling, one by one, in the battle between shagging Maggie every night and the daily Portham training regime. Bobby was once again snapped out of his thoughts. This time by Dickie Godstone's voice.

"You will get a decent wage of one hundred pounds a week, playing bonuses if you play a certain number of games, goal bonuses and win bonuses. The bonus amount depends on gate receipts over the course of each month. We will also pay all your expenses at Maggie's and your Mum and Dad's expenses whenever they want to come up. I'll even throw in tickets for other grounds for your parents and for one or two of your friends from back home whenever we play away. How does that sound?" Dickie was trying not to grit his teeth as had been driven to a hard bargain by Albert. He had never agreed terms like this before with any player.

"Bloody hell!" Bobby could not believe what he was hearing.

"Young man!" Liz stared hard at her son.

"Sorry mum! I'm well happy with that. Can we have dinner now please?"

"Yes, come on let's order lunch. Your mother and father have a train to catch." Dickie took control of the situation.

"Yeah, I'm starving!" Bobby rubbed his hands together.

"You probably need it to get over that hangover!" Albert gave his son a stern look then couldn't help but smile.

Bobby looked a bit sheepish.

"He was quite entertaining banging about all over the place when he got in." Maggie giggled

Bobby looks embarrassed as they all laughed. He looked at Maggie who gave him a knowing smile that nobody else noticed.

"I reckon that Vicky must have been getting her drinks mixed up." Liz remarked innocently.

Bobby started thinking about Vicky.

"Roasts all round then?" Dickie took control again. He was hungry and had no time for small talk.

"Lovely Dickie!" Albert was hungry too.

"Yes, please Dickie." Agreed Liz.

Dickie looked at Maggie who just nodded and didn't really acknowledge him. Nobody else noticed this except Bobby.

Across the foyer from the restaurant was the hotel bar which was a bar open to the public as well as hotel guests. This was a favourite haunt of Mark and Sammo's as it sold their favourite ale, and they could get a nice Sunday roast. Due to them both living alone, this was a Sunday ritual for them unless Portham were playing. They were stood side by side at the bar. The restaurant toward the right of them. They were both supping on their pints. Sammo put his drink down and casually gazed around the place. He thought that he had noticed someone familiar.

"Here Mark, is that Godstone over there in the restaurant?" Asked Sammo who was peering over toward the restaurant

"Where?" Mark craned his neck so that he could see around Sammo. He looked over towards the restaurant. Mark struggled to see long distances through his thick lensed glasses.

Sammo pointed towards the table where Dickie Godstone was sitting with the rest of the party.

"Oh yeah! So it is! And it looks like young Bobby Gorman is over there as well." Mark couldn't believe what he was seeing.

"I think it is you know. That must be his family with them, down from London. Probably having lunch together before they head back." Sammo surmised.

"Shall we pop over there and say hello?" suggested Mark.

"I dunno. It looks like a nice family lunch going on." Sammo was unsure. Mark always did things like this. He was never comfortable going along with his ideas.

"Well, they ain't got their grub yet. Come on mate, let's have a quick chat with them, just to say hello like."

Sammo thought for a second.

"Ok... Why not."

They both downed the rest of their pints in unison and walked over towards the restaurant area.

Dickie Godstone happened to look over towards the bar area. He looked straight at the oncoming pair of Portham Football Club fanatics.

"Oh, here we go!" Dickie sighed as he looked back at his guests.

He knew they had seen him. It was too late. There was no hiding from them.

"What's up Dickie?" Albert enquired. He clocked that something was troubling Dickie.

"These two on their way over to us... They're a couple of die hards of ours. There OK... A bit annoying at times." Dickie explained.

Mark and Sammo approached the table. Dickie got up and shook them both by the hand.

"Hello Mr Godstone, hope you don't mind us popping over and saying hello?" Mart was excited.

"No problem boys." Dickie said through slightly gritted teeth.

"And is this young Bobby Gorman we see before us." Mark enquired in faux shock.

"Yes, this is our new signing!" Dickie said proudly.

Mark and Sammo both moved round. Bobby stood up and they all shook hands.

"Great game yesterday lad, I was really impressed. You're just what we needed." Sammo remarked, almost breaking into a smile.

Mark nudged Bobby lightly with his elbow.

"Ere, and our Sammo ain't easily impressed you know. But yeah, you played a blinder yesterday." Mark said proudly.

"Thanks a lot, I really appreciate it. I'm just trying to do my best." Bobby was slightly embarrassed.

"Champion! Is this your mum and dad?" asked Mark enthusiastically.

Albert stood up.

"Yes mate."

Albert shook both their hands. Albert was feeling proud that the superfans of his son's first professional club were so impressed.

"I'm Albert and that's my beautiful wife Liz." Albert said jokingly.

Liz waved at them.

"Albert! Hello boys. I hope you weren't booing him a couple of weeks back." Liz asked with a bit of a scowl on her face.

"No no" Mark and Sammo both replied at the same time.

"And this is Maggie, who looks after my Bobby at her house." Liz informed them.

Bobby thought about how Maggie looked after him last night.

"Hello love. You've looked after a few of our apprentices in the past. Is that right?" Mark knew of Maggie.

"You looked after young Archie Law for a while. Dunno what happened to him as he looked a right good prospect." Sammo looked off into the ether, remembering a move and a sublime pass that young Archie Law had made that led to a goal for Portham.

"That's right love." Maggie answered matter of factly.

"He seemed to lose interest in the end. We had to let him go." Dickie responded with an air of defeatism.

"Funny one that... Anyway, I hope your signing him up on a long-term contract..." Mark enquired firmly.

"Don't you worry lads. We'll have some news to announce very shortly. We're really going for it in the next couple of seasons so bear with us as we are trying get it right, to take the club forward. Spread the word and get the crowd behind us please lads." Dickie looked at them both, knowing that they would only be too pleased to spread the word of the chairman and owner.

"Thanks for letting us know. Here Bobby, any chance of your autograph?" asked Mark.

"Mark!" Sammo was embarrassed.

"Here are son, they want your autograph!" Albert said proudly.

"Ooh I say!" Liz couldn't believe what was going on as she looked at her son proudly.

Liz looked at the two Portham supporters who were clearly so happy to see a player who they already regarded as a hero. She noticed one of them looking a bit uncomfortable.

"Yeah, that's alright boys, no problem. What shall I write it on though?" Bobby was a bit lost.

"I've got a pen." Mark started scrambling about in his pockets.

"Here son, use the napkins." Albert took two napkins from his and Liz's part of the table and passed them to Bobby.

"Yeah, that'll do nicely Mr Gorman." Mark chuckled. He was quoting the American Express advert that was currently airing as he handed the small blue pen that he got from the bookmakers.

Bobby was about to sign the napkins then realised he didn't know their names.

"What's your name mate?"

"I'm Mark and he's Dave but we call him Sammo. You might as well do him one as well."

Booby signed one napkin and gave it to Mark.

"Well, if you don't mind Bobby." Sammo was still feeling a bit uncomfortable with the whole situation.

"Nah that's alright Sammo!" Bobby encouraged Sammo that it was all OK as he signed his signature for the second time and then handed the signed napkin back.

Mark and Sammo were both smiling proudly studying and admiring the signatures on the napkins.

"It looks like our lunch is on its way over now chaps." Dickie interrupted the love in as he wanted them gone now. He was politely trying to tell them both to fuck off.

They both snapped out of their very temporary trance.

"We'll be off now then. Thanks for talking to us." As much as Sammo was happy, he was also relieved that they had to be on their way.

"Yeah, thanks ever so much and nice to meet you all." Mark waved to them all and turned towards Dickie.

"Come on Mr Godstone, get us out of this league." Pleaded Mark.

"Aye lad, I'll do my best. You can be assured of that. Good day gentleman." Dickie ushered them both away from the table. His hunger was now getting the better of him.

"Mart and Sammo walked off back towards the bar as the waitress brought the food over.

OUTSIDE THE HOTEL AFTER LUNCH

It was drizzling. They were all stood outside trying to avoid the rain.

"Bobby, Maggie, can I give you lift home?" asked Dickie.

"I'm going to stay here and see my mum and dad off at the station." Said Bobby. He was already starting to feel upset.

"You don't have to love." Reassured Liz.

"No, I want to." Bobby didn't want them to go.

"Ok lad. You coming Maggie?" Dickie almost demanded Maggie came with him.

"Alright. See you later Bobby." Maggie turned to Liz and Albert.

"And good to see you both. See you next time."

Liz and Albert both gave Maggie a hug.

"Thanks for looking after him Maggie. We'll see you all again soon." Liz and Maggie broke their embrace.

Albert shook Dickie's hand.

"It's been a lovely weekend, look forward to seeing you both again soon." Dickie gave Liz a kiss on the cheek.

"Cheers Dickie. Right let's go and get our bags." Albert was ready to get home now.

Bobby, Liz and Albert headed back into the hotel. Maggie and Dickie walked off up the road, deep in conversation.

PORTHAM TRAINING GROUND

It was a sunny day at the training ground. The team were being put through their paces by Dave Jenkins as Neil Glover kept a watchful eye on proceedings from the side lines.

"Come on lads we need to be super-fit now for these last few games. You need to watch what you eat and drink very carefully. We have the chance to get promoted. I do not want us to fail." Shouted Dave.

"You listen to him! You all have the ability, but fitness has been my concern lately. Some of you need to look at your re-fuelling habits." Bellowed Neil.

Re-fuelling boss? We're not bloody cars!" Replied Tony Cook. His reply raised a few laughs from some of the other players. This infuriated Neil Glover.

"Right, stop! The lot of you! Come over here right now!" Neil shouted at the top of his voice.

All the players stopped in their tracks. They looked surprised for a second but jogged straight over to where Neil Glover was standing.

"You're right Tony. You're not cars. You are athletes." Neil was clearly enraged but he was trying not to lose his composure.

"What I mean by re-fuelling is what you eat and drink. And I have to say you are a case in point. I've noticed in the last couple of games you have been blowing out of your arse at around the sixty-minute mark and not being effective enough. I know you smoke, I know you drink to excess and I'm sure you're eating habits are not great. Now, for example, would you put two-star petrol in that nice Granada of yours?" Neil Glover asked a rhetorical question with a knowing look. His brow furrowed, revealing the lines in his forehead.

"Not if I wanted it to run like shit I wouldn't, no way boss!" Replied Tony, who was clearly feeling the heat.

"That's my point exactly Mr Cook. If you fill your body with the equivalent of two star, it will run like shit." Snapped Neil.

"I suppose so boss. I get what you're saying." Tony's brain slowly digested what his boss was telling him.

"Good Tony I'm glad you understand. I'm not just getting at you. I know most of you are the same, but I've been doing a lot of research on this lately and I'm telling you, if you look after your body and make a few changes, you will reap the benefits and therefore as a team, we all will." Neil felt quite pleased with how he was able to get his point across using Tony.

"What you suggesting then boss?" Neil's faithful captain Carl Pilford enquired enthusiastically.

"I challenge you all to not drink alcohol from now until the end of the season. I also challenge you to eat as healthily as possible by eating only fish, chicken and vegetables, with the odd bit of rice and pasta now and then. You will be giving yourself, the team and the club, the best possible chance of promotion." Neil could see some of his team were concerned and could not believe what they were hearing from their boss. There were lots of murmurs coming from the players.

Carl Pilford spoke up.

"I'm sure I speak for all the lads by saying it's a bit far out and a bit of a tall order but I'm up for it and I'm willing to believe in you boss. I think fines should be in order if anyone is found to have had a drink.

"I'm well up for it. And I agree with the fines boss." Agreed Dave Jenkins.

"Yes, good idea. The fines, if there are any of course, can go to charity. I will weigh you all today and every week until the end of the season. I will fine you for not losing or gaining weight. If you take my advice the weight will fall off." Neil was enjoying the look on some of the players' faces who clearly did not agree with any of it.

"And what about those of us who do look after ourselves already boss?" Roy Cairns piped up in a militant fashion. Neil knew if anyone would moan about this it would be Roy Cairns. PFA steward and rabble rouser.

Neil composed himself.

"There is always room for improvement. I will have the final say if anyone gets fined or not. You know I'm a fair man Roy." Neil felt he squashed any potential uprising with this statement.

"Yes Boss." Roy knew his boss was a fair man. Not like his last manager at Islecarl, who bombed him out of the club for becoming a PFA steward. He couldn't prove it, but he knew it.

"There are some good books down the library on nutrition, so I suggest you all have a look. Right! Let's get on with training. Ah! Here comes a visitor!" Neil seemed a little surprised, but he should have known.

Billy Thorpe was on crutches. He was making his way over to his teammates. Neil had specifically told Billy not to come onto the training ground until he was off crutches, just in case he fell over on the uneven ground and in case his crutches damaged the already terrible training ground surface. The whole team started cheering and clapping.

"And we want to do our best for our injured team mate now don't we boys!" Shouted Neil above the cheering and clapping.

They all cheered even louder.

"Alright you lot that's enough of that bollocks. You better fucking get promoted cause if you don't, I'll ram these crutches right up your arses, one after the other!" Billy Thorpe gestured with one of his crutches.

"Calm down hop along Cassidy!" Laughed Tony.

Billy moved quickly on his crutches towards Tony.

"I'll give you hop along Cassidy you fat fucker!" Billy hit Tony across the stomach with his crutch.

"Look at the state of you"

All the players laughed. Neil Glover gave Tony a knowing look.

"Alright! I'm fucking giving this healthy lark a go!" Conceded Tony.

All the players cheered again. Billy gave Tony's stomach two soft taps with his crutch.

Tony jerked back expecting to be hit harder

"Billy is here to help out by coaching the full backs. So, from now on, I will coach the strikers, Dave will coach the midfielders and as I said, hop along Cassidy here, will coach the full backs."

Carl leaned in towards Bobby.

"Blimey things are changing Bobby boy. You listen to Billy mate."

"I will mate. I want to get promoted!" Bobby thought he had whispered his reply.

"Did you hear that lads? Young Bobby just said he wants to get promoted! That's the spirit lad! Right then let's crack on. Strikers over here with me, Dave you take the midfielders over there and Billy you can take your very first coaching session over there." Boomed Neil.

"Thanks boss I really appreciate this. Especially with not being able to play anymore." Billy said forlornly.

"No problem, Billy. I know you've been a good servant to this club. You can sit on the bench with us on matchdays too if you like?" Neil said with his eyebrows raised and his eyes wide with excitement which accentuated even more so, the deep furrows in his receding brow.

"You try and stop me Boss!" Billy enthused.

His eyes moistened slightly as he was slightly overcome with emotion.

"Thanks boss!" His voice cracked slightly.

"It's my pleasure Billy now go and coach those full backs to promotion!" Neil clapped his hands and pumped his fists, almost overcome with emotion himself.

Neil walked over to the strikers as Billy wiped a tear from his eye. He set his crutches and made his way over to the full backs.

"Right then you lot, let's get you sorted out!" A huge smile spread across his normally grumpy face.

MANCHESTER PICCADILLY STATION

The sun was shining through the glass of the Victorian roof. Bobby was looking up at the train timetable boards that rotated every so often until he saw what he was looking for:

KINGS CROSS - PLATFORM 10 - DEPARTS 1:47PM

Bobby pulled some change from his pocket and took a five pence piece from the pile which was a mixture of old and new coins. Some of the five and ten pence pieces were the old one- and two-shilling type that were still in circulation after decimalisation eleven years ago in nineteen seventy one. He put the rest of the change back into his pocket. He walked over to a red phone box. He opened the door and walked in. He smelt the familiar smell of urine as drunk men often used phone boxes to relive themselves in. He put his finger into the zero and pulled the dial around. Then he did the same with number one, then seven, then two, then nine, then five, then six, then three, then three again. He had become lighting quick at this since living away. He waited. The ring tone kicked in. Brrrp Brrrp, Brrrp Brrrp.

"Hello?" His mother's voice sprang from the receiver.

Bobby pushed the five pence into the slot. It clunked through.

"Hello Mum." Bobby said matter of factly.

"Hello Darling! You coming home?" Liz shouted demandingly.

"Yes mum. I'm getting the thirteen forty-seven so should be

home for dinner." Bobby could almost smell the kitchen as he spoke the words.

"Lovely! I've got all your favourite grub in" Liz said excitedly.

"Thanks mum. How's dad?"

"He's alright. He's looking forward to having you home. He's going to meet you at the station after work." Liz said excitedly

"Oh good... Tell him I'll meet him out the front with all the brasses!" Bobby said cheekily.

"You be careful babe." Liz either chose to ignore Bobby's remark or was oblivious to it. She was only concerned with seeing her boy again.

The pips started to make their ominous sound.

Doop doop doop.

"I will mum. The pips are going now so I'll see you later." Bobby was keen to get moving anyway.

"Ta ta love see you......"

The line went dead. Bobby put the phone down. He opened the door and headed towards platform ten.

OUTSIDE MARK'S HOUSE

The sunny day had brought out all the kids straight out after school. A group of local young kids between the ages of ten and thirteen years old were hanging around outside Mark's house.

MARK'S HALLWAY

"Come on then Porty mate, time for walkies." Mark attached the lead to the collar of his gigantic House Rabbit. He opened the front door and let the rabbit lead the way out.

OUTSIDE MARK'S HOUSE

"Oi you lot! Clear off will ya!" Mark shouted at the kids. He had already clocked them through his front room window a few minutes previously. He knew what was coming and was not in the mood for any of it.

"Here he is, here he is! I told you, look!" Said one of the older looking kids of the group.

The rest of the group of boys started laughing at what they saw.

"Why ain't you got a dog? Why you got that big silly rabbit on a lead?" Asked another member of the group.

The rest of the group laughed again.

"Go on piss off! The lot of ya!" Mark gestured his hand for them to go away as he walked down his pathway.

"Fucking weirdo!" Shouted another kid.

"Yeah! Who takes a rabbit for a walk?" Shouted the older kid.

"My old man says your probably a kiddie fiddler!" Shouted another of the group.

You can tell your old man to fuck off! I ain't no kiddie fiddler! If you lot come around here again, I'll brain the lot of ya." Martin was fuming at the accusation just hurled at him.

"And he's a Portham fan as well!" Said another one of their group.

"Scum!" The older kid followed up.

"Hockport! Hockport! Hockport!" They all started chanting.

One of the kids threw a stone which hit Mark on the right cheek, startling him and his rabbit Porty. The kids ran off laughing.

"I'll fucking get you lot. You fuckin little cunts!" Mark held his face. His chubby cheek had absorbed the force of the stone, so it hadn't caused too much pain.

He bent down and picked up his Porty and comforted him.

"There there Porty Portham... It's OK. It's OK they've gone now. I'll deal with those little shits don't you worry..."Mark looked in the direction of the kids who were still running. One of them turned back and gave him the bird which Mart duly responded to.

451 FELLOWSHIP COURT

Albert came through the front door followed by Bobby.

"Here Liz, look what the cat's dragged in!" Albert presented their son.

Liz entered the hallway from the kitchen holding a Tea towel. She threw it back into the kitchen and walked over to Bobby and gave him a kiss and a cuddle.

"Hello darling! Ooh I've missed you so much!" Liz squeezed the air out of her son's lungs.

"Hello mum! Missed you too!" Bobby just about got his words out.

"Mind him Liz! He don't wanna go back injured!" Albert chuckled.

Liz let her son go. Albert ruffled Bobby's hair. Bobby gently brushed Albert's hand away. They both smiled at each other.

MARK'S KITCHEN

Mark was making a sandwich for his dinner. He threw a lettuce leaf to the floor.

"There you go Porty, dinner time!"

The rabbit started eating the lettuce leaf. Mark picked up the sandwich and a bag of crisps. He placed a lettuce leaf and half a carrot on the plate along with the sandwich and walked out of the kitchen. The rabbit followed him, hopping through into the front room. Mark put the plate of food down on the coffee table and went over to the TV to turn it on. He sat down on the settee. The rabbit jumped up and snuggled up to Mark who started feeding Porty Portham the house rabbit, more lettuce.

"What more can a man want eh mate? A bit of food in his belly, a bit of peace and the telly on. Oh, hang on, I forgot the beers!" Mark remarked to Porty.

Mark got up and walked briskly out to the kitchen, leaving Porty munching on the lettuce leaf. He came back with two cans of beer and a small bowl. He opened one of the cans and took a big swig. He then poured some of beer into the bowl and put it on the floor. As soon as the bowl touched the floor, Porty jumped down from the settee and started lapping the beer up from the bowl.

"Silly me eh! How could I have forgot the most important thing. You must be thirsty."

The rabbit was eagerly drinking the rapidly depleting beer from the bowl as Mark poured some more in.

"Don't go too mad mate! Remember what happened last night when you fell asleep on the floor and pissed all over it you little fucker!" Martin chuckled to himself and sat down.

Suddenly, a brick came crashing through the front window. It landed on Porty's head then bounced off on to the floor. Mark hadn't noticed that the brick had killed his companion instantly as he ran out of the front door looking for who had thrown it.

Mark ran down his front pathway and turned left and then spun right but could not see anyone in the dusky evening.

"You fuckers!" Mark shouted at the top of his voice.

He looked around again, then went back up his pathway over towards the broken window. He inspected it. The net curtain, that was grey from hardly being washed in years, was flapping in the breeze.

"Fucking little bastards!" Mark thought that it wouldn't be too hard to repair as he had some board out in the garden. He noticed that Porty was motionless. He ran back into the front room, leaving the front door open behind him. He stopped in his tracks as he entered the front room. He saw that Porty. Blood was trickling from his left ear. He slowly picked up Porty Portham the house rabbit, his faithful companion of twelve years and cradled him in his arms. Mark broke down in tears and sobbed uncontrollably.

CHAPTER VI
TEENAGE KICKS

HAGGERSTON PLAYING FIELD LONDON

Bobby Gorman and Tommy Williams were having a kickabout on the field that they played so much football as they grew up together. They first met at the One o'clock club nursery that was based there as toddlers. They went to the same primary school at Randal Cremer, around the corner on Cremer Street. Named after the former Liberal Member of Parliament for Haggerston, Pacifist and Noble Peace Prize winner, Sir William Randal Cremer. The boys had both played for the same junior sides from five years of age until they both signed for the Artillery academy team. They were both released on the same day.

"What's it like up there then?" Tommy kicked the ball to Bobby.

"It's alright. It's a bit colder and more rain. But not too bad. What's Brentford Park Rangers like then? I've never been down that part of London." Bobby responded then flicked the ball up with his left foot and headed it back towards Tommy.

Tommy trapped the ball as it fell to his feet.

"Don't see much of it really... Apart from match days. The training ground's rubbish and not even in Brentford Park Rangers. I get the train to Hanwell then the training ground's a bit of a walk. It takes me two and a half hours door to door to get there every day." Tommy kicked the ball back to Bobby.

Bobby flicked the ball up with his right foot and started doing keepy uppy.

"It's better than having to be away from home up north though!" Bobby booted the ball towards the goal which was about 40 yards away. The ball sailed through the air and hit the cross bar.

"Oooohhh nearly mate! I wouldn't mind coming up there to see you and maybe go out up there." Tommy replied admiring his best friends shot and started to think of the laughs that they would have up north.

"Yeah come on, you're off next week." Bobby replied enthusiastically.

"Go and get it then!" Tommy gestured towards the static ball by the goal.

"I'll race ya!" Bobby dared his mate and started to run.

Suddenly the two of them ran as fast as they could towards the ball near the goal.

"That weren't fair! You got a head start!" Tommy was out of breath but jumped on Bobby as they got to the ball.

They both fell on the floor laughing.

"I'd love it if we play against each other one day." Bobby spun away from Tommy and laid on his back.

"You lot would have to get promoted first. And there ain't much chance of that with you playing for 'em." Tommy had also laid on his back next to Bobby.

Bobby swung fist down onto Tommy's bicep giving his old mate a dead arm.

"Aarrrgghh!" Tommy cried out in pain

"At least I'm in the first team!" Boasted Bobby.

Tommy sat up and swung his fist down onto Bobby's thigh

giving Bobby a dead leg.

"Aarrrgghh!" Cried Bobby.

They both started laughing.

"That would be blinding though!" Bobby said wishfully.

They both just laid there in their own thoughts for a while staring up at the sky.

"You coming to ours later then?" Asked Tommy.

"Yeah, it should be good watching them get drunk!" Bobby said with a smile on his face.

"I've got some beers stashed up for us though." Replied Tommy with a glint in his eye.

"Sweet as a nut! By time they're all pissed they won't notice anyway. I'll bring a bottle of Blue Smirnoff." Bobby replied enthusiastically.

"Blue Smirnoff? What's that?" Tommy spun onto his side to face Bobby.

"You know the vodka our mum's drink?" Bobby asked

"Yeah…" Tommy replied.

"Well, it's a stronger version of that." Bobby replied, all pleased with himself that his friend didn't know about this.

"I've never seen it." Tommy was sceptical of this new information.

"It blows your head off! I think they only sell it up north. I brought a bottle down specially." Bobby said proudly.

"I think my mum and dad's mates from work are coming. And I think they are bringing their daughters. I've seen them before, they're right sorts and a bit older than us. I'm sure one of them was giving me the eye down the club." Tommy convinced himself.

"It must have been her glass eye! What's the Lion like these days?" Bobby couldn't help but cane his old mate.

"Len's still there and big tit Lisa's behind the bar now." Tommy said with a glint in his eye, reminiscing on how him, Bobby and the rest of their gang had fantasised and likely wanked over, the thought of her bare breasts.

"Is she? I might have to get down there before I go back. I'm sure she was giving me the eye when I was last there." Bobby had dreamed of Lisa ever since he first laid eyes on her. Back when he was a young teenager, she was a pot girl, retrieving the glasses from the pub tables. His dad and his mates would perv over her, making her the enemy of all the wives down the pub.

"Yeah bollocks!" Tommy was having none of it.

Each one of their gang thought that one day, they would have her as their girlfriend and were always protective over anyone else making comments about her.

"She was!" Bobby was convinced.

Any member of their gang would at some point protest that it was they who thought Lisa was eyeing up, when in fact, Lisa eyed up any young male. She loved the attention and enjoyed playing all the young, testosterone filled, young bucks off against each other. She used to let the some of guys who were a few years older than Bobby and Tommy's gang have a snog and a grope now and again, in exchange for a few free drinks. Lisa was a player.

"Me and my old man see her jogging the other day. He shouted out the car window at her, mind you don't give yourself two black eyes! It was proper funny. She didn't look happy, but she looked fucking lovely in her jogging gear." They both started laughing.

TOMMY'S GARDEN

"You should have seen 'em! They were going wild mate!" Said Albert enthusiastically as he was whenever he regaled anyone with tales about his sons exploits for Portham FC.

"I'm pleased for him Alb. Perhaps we'll come up with you one time." John replied.

"That'll be lovely. Me and Jean could have a look round Manchester. Ooh there's some lovely shops up there Jean, considering its up north... You know what I mean?" Liz gave Jean a knowing look.

"Bleedin shopping! I'll take John to me Manc local." Sniffed Albert.

"Sounds good to me Alby!" Replied John enthusiastically, rubbing his hands together at the thought.

"Oh, you wanna see this place Jean, it's a right dive! It's like the Manchester version of The Alfred's Head!" Liz explained, shaking her head in the process.

The Alfred's Head public house was a wretched hive of scum and villainy. Albert would go there now and then as some of his old school friends drank in there. Liz refused to go there again after the last time she went there. The woman's toilets were closed, and a drunk woman stripped off her top and bra and started dancing around the place, swinging her breasts around.

"I can just imagine!" Jean replied, looking at the two smiling men, already scheming their first pint together up north. Jean had heard all the stories about The Alfred's Head. There wasn't a month that went by without a story going round of a punch up happening in there.

"They all love him up there though and they ain't too bad. Course, he tells anyone who listens in there about Bobby!" Liz was lightly scolding her husband but in a proud way.

"Right an all!" John responded, backing his mates' actions. He could imagine Albert proudly holding court with the northerners, who he knew would love Albert and his infectious character.

"So, how's Tommy getting on now then?" Enquired Liz.

"They say he's not ready yet for the first team, but he's training with them now and they let him sit on the bench for games so he can get a feel for it, so not bad I suppose." Jean knew that Tommy was not quite at Tommy's level.

"We still go down there on matchdays, and I've got a little Brentford Park Rangers local too Alb." Beamed John trying to change the subject.

"That ain't much better than The Alfred's either!" Said Jean shaking her head at Liz.

"I bet! What's a matter with 'em? They do love a shit boozer don't they, eh?" Liz looked at Jean with a perplexed look.

"We'll have to go down there with em eh Liz. Suggested Albert.

He was now intrigued about this boozer. He felt like he needed to go there, to conquer another pub and claim it like his prize. Discovering a new boozer was like conquering unknown land to his circle of friends especially if none of them had drank in it, or not even heard of it. Many a tale was told at work regarding the taste of the beer, the clientele, the bar staff, the décor and the toilets, after someone had been into a new drinking establishment.

"No! We'll go shopping and you two can go to the Brentford Park Rangers Alfred's." Liz took control of the situation swiftly.

"Bleeding shopping again!" Albert rolled his eyes firmly to the back of his head.

"That'll do us though eh Alb?" John backed his mate in this

rising tension.

"Sweet as a nut Johnny boy!" Albert felt victorious

"Where's them two anyway?" John sensed the victory but also felt the glare of both Jean and Liz. He cut while the going was good and changed the subject.

"Probably sneaking a beer in!" Albert welcomed the change of tac, employed by his trusty shipmate in this rough sea battle, with the two well-armed frigates bearing down on their two battleships.

"They bloody better not be!" Liz's attention was turned. The battle was over, for now.

"They're all right! The records will start in a minute!" John knowingly assured them all.

TOMMY'S BEDROOM

"Stick that dressing gown by the door. It'll stop it opening properly if anyone tries barging in." Tommy said with a slight pang of paranoia, realising the situation that was very quickly about to unfold.

"Good idea!" Enthused Bobby, thinking that he should have thought of this idea long ago as he pulled out a bottle of Blue Smirnoff vodka that he had hidden down his jeans.

Tommy pulled out some cans of Long Life beer from under his bed.

"Bloody hell Bob! How did you manage that!" Tommy could not believe he had not clocked it.

"It was a bit painful, but I made out I'm carrying a little knock." Bobby replied, all proud of himself.

Tommy burst out laughing

"Nice one mate!"

"Are they coming?" Bobby was like a little puppy begging for a treat.

"Supposed to be. I hear they're both right up for it after a few drinks!" Tommy was egging his desperate looking mate on.

"Right let's have a couple of shots of this. Then we can go downstairs, nick a beer and drink it in front of them so we've got the smell on us. We can wait for the birds to get here then after a while, we can get them up here to listen to records, get them pissed and have a little play, eh?" Bobby had it all worked out but was seeking approval for his master plan.

"Now that is a plan Bobby boy!" Tommy gave his full backing to his friends elaborate plan which all he heard of it was basically booze and girls in his room.

Tommy looked on eagerly as Bobby unscrewed the cap from the bottle of vodka. He carefully poured the vodka into the cap and passed it to Tommy.

"Get that down your Gregory!" Said Bobby, using a rhyming slang phrase his dad had used recently.

Tommy took the capful of mysterious liquid smuggled down from the North of England. He downed the vodka then pulled a face that made Bobby laugh hysterically.

"You got a face like the smell of gas!" Another classic Albert phrase which Bobby just used for the first time in a perfect situation, due to the face Tommy pulled as he winced at the ferocity of the alcoholic drink. Bobby pulled a face like Tommy. After Tommy had caught his breath, they both started laughing.

"Fuckin hell mate! That is Firewater! That must be what Jackie Chan was drinking in The Drunken Master!" Spluttered Tommy as Bobby started doing kung fu moves. He was trying to use the bottle of vodka in the same way that Jackie Chan had used the jug in the film. Tommy was laughing. He started doing karate moves too from the film that they both loved so much. They had seen it on their well-off mate John Hunter's Betamax home video recorder when they were all staying there for the night. John was showing them the video recorder and how it worked. The film was already in the machine as their friend's dad had rented it from the local video shop. They watched it and were all so fascinated by it as they had never seen a film like it before.

"Come on let's get down there with the old timers. I think I just heard the girls come in through the back gate."

Bobby looked out of the window.

"Yes, mate they're here! And their daughters are with them!" Bobby could not contain his excitement.

"Sweet!" Shouted Tommy, clapping his hands together.

TOMMY'S KITCHEN

Tommy opened the fridge and got two cans of Long Life beer out. He handed one to Bobby. They both cracked them open in unison and took long swigs and stopped at just about the same time.

"Let's get out there then!" Bobby demanded as he wiped his mouth clear of excess beer with the back of his hand.

They both walked through the kitchen's back door out into the garden.

TOMMY'S GARDEN

Tommy and Bobby walked out into the garden, proudly carrying their beers.

Tommy, his mum and dad, Jean and John lived on Fellowship

Court estate too. They had opted to take a maisonette on the ground floor of one of the Low-rise blocks, situated opposite the High-rise block where the Gormans lived. Being on the ground floor, they had the luxury of a small garden area. There was no grass as it was paved, but Jean had brought some nice colourful potted plants from the nearby Columbia Road Flower market, to make it look like a garden. Liz had wanted to take one of ground floor maisonettes in this block, but Albert had wanted to live in the High-rise block because of the view and because he had heard stories of the ground floor maisonettes being broken into on the estates.

"Oi you cheeky little fuckers! Have a look at these two will ya!" Shouted John.

"You mind you don't get pissed you two, that's strong old gear. You don't want to wet yourself again do you son!" Albert chuckled.

Everyone laughed. The two girls, Debbie and Linda, nudged each other.

"I never wet myself!" Bobby snapped, annoyed that his father was mugging him off so badly in front of the girls.

Bobby looked across at the girls.

"I never wet myself, honestly." Bobby tried reassuring them.

"You don't mind, do you? You lot won't drink them all anyway and there's still loads in the shed" Tommy remarked. He always knew how many beers there were in the shed as he would always steal one or two cans every time his dad stocked up as John would bulk buy them from the cash and carry.

"Well get out there and get some to put in the fridge will ya!" Retorted his father. Giving his son an evil stare. He knew that Tommy had been nicking his beers.

"Yes dad." Tommy replied forlornly.

John got up.

"You both know Dave and Marian, but I don't think you've met their two daughters, Debbie and Linda. They're a bit older than you two." Explained John.

"Alright. I remember you two from school. You were a couple of years above us." Tommy said a bit cockily as walked back out of the shed with the beers.

"Hello." Bobby said quietly.

"Hello boys!" Debbie said very confidently.

Linda just nodded and looked a bit sheepish. She just about looked up and smiled.

TOMMY'S BEDROOM

They were all sat around Tommy's bed. They had all had a few beers. Go Wild In The Country by Bow Wow Wow was playing in the background. Tommy and Linda stared kissing.

"Go on you two!" Bobby said loudly.

Bobby started singing along to the song that was currently battling it out for the number one spot with Frankie Goes To Hollywood's song, Relax. Relax had recently been banned from Radio One by Mike Read due to the lyrics of the song. Bow Wow Wow had also caused controversy two years earlier with their debut single C30 C60 C90 Go. The song was a homage to people taping songs from the radio and TV with small tape recorders, which had microphones built into them. The song was also the world's first cassette single.

"Go wild, go wild, go wild in the bedroom!" Bobby sang, altering the lyrics to Go Wild In The Country slightly.

"Linda! Bloody hell sis! A few cans and you're anyone's!" Exclaimed Debbie.

Linda and Tommy were snogging each other's faces off. Linda opened her eyes and gave Debbie the V sign with her fingers.

"For fucks sake!" Debbie sighed.

"They're alright!" Assured Bobby. He moved nearer to Debbie.

"So, come on then, what's it like being a footballer up North?" Debbie moved a bit closer to Bobby, keen to hear about his life.

"Not bad. It's quite a laugh really, I do miss home but I'm playing in the first team, which I probably wouldn't do here. Like Tommy, still being in the reserves!" Bobby kicked his mate's leg.

Tommy gave Bobby the Wanker sign with his hand while still kissing Linda.

Bobby pulled the bottle of Blue Smirnoff Vodka from under Tommy's bed.

"Here, do you want a drop of this?" Bobby asked Debbie.

"Blue Smirnoff? I didn't know they made this!" Debbie was intrigued, also not knowing that any other vodka existed other than Red Smirnoff.

"Yeah, they fookin loov it oop North!" Bobby said in his slightly more honed, although slightly exaggerated, hybrid accent of Mancunian and Lancastrian, which was spoken in the Portham area of Greater Manchester where he resided.

"Oh, go on then! Debbie laughed.

Bobby opened the bottle and poured the vodka into the bottle top. He handed it to Debbie who greedily downed it, barely wincing.

"Not bad! Do us another one then." Debbie asked wiggling the bottle top at Bobby.

"Good girl!" Bobby was excited by Debbie's behaviour.

Bobby poured another shot for Debbie. She downed it again. He poured himself one, downed it, then poured himself another one and downed that, which made him cough.

"Take it easy! Don't go wetting yourself will ya!" Debbie giggled.

"Bollocks! I didn't wet myself!" Bobby said sharply.

Linda and Tommy both burst out laughing breaking them off from their snog.

"Give us one of them then!" Demanded Tommy.

"And me!" Demanded Linda.

Bobby poured them both a drink which they both downed in one. They got straight back to kissing each other. Debbie grabbed two can of beers from the floor. She put one between her thighs and opened the other one and passed it to Bobby. She took the other can from between her thighs, opened it and took a swig of beer.

"So, you got a girlfriend then?" asked Debbie nonchalantly.

"Nah! I'm young free and single me!" Bobby said very confidently, sensing something could be happening.

Bobby poured another shot of Vodka and passed it to Debbie which she downed in one again. She then took a big swig of beer.

"Blimey you don't hang about!" Bobby was beaming.

Bobby poured himself a shot, downed it and then took a big swig of beer too. Debbie leaned over and gently squeezed Bobby's crotch.

"Well, if I'm going to get off with you, I need to blame it on the drink, don't I?" Debbie beamed back at Bobby.

Debbie leaned in and started kissing Bobby. He saw Tommy open his eyes. They made eye contact. Tommy gave the thumbs up to Bobby who winked back at Tommy. The door suddenly opened slightly. They all jumped and moved away from each other. The dressing gown on the floor by the door had done its job, stopping the door from opening fully.

"Now you boys better not be taking advantage of Dave's daughters in there!" Chuckled Albert.

Tommy jumped up and took the dressing gown away. Albert walked in as Bobby concealed the Vodka under the bed.

"You all having a good time listening to that rubbish?" Sneered Albert. He was slightly unsteady on his feet.

"Yes, thanks Albert." Tommy replied cheerily, in the hope that Albert would not notice anything and leave quickly.

Albert peered his head around the door.

"Dad!" An embarrassed Bobby shouted.

"You girls don't be letting these two little sods get their hands on ya!" Albert said with a glint in his eye.

"Don't worry, they wouldn't know what to do!" Debbie said very casually.

Albert burst out laughing.

"Good girl! And don't worry, I won't say nothing about the beers!" Chuckled Albert.

"Dad leave it out! You're pissed anyway!" Snapped Bobby.

"Have a good time kids. If you can't be good, be careful. I ain't ready to be a Grandad yet!" Albert chuckled and retreated from the bedroom.

Bobby got up and closed the door on Albert.

"Told you they'd all be pissed. Now who wants another shot?" Bobby asked the group excitedly, now that the embarrassment of his inebriated father had passed. He gave them all a beaming smile which was returned by them all, as they were all relieved too.

TWO YEARS LATER OUTSIDE MARK'S HOUSE

It was a bright sunny morning. Sammo was knocking on Mark's front door. He was dressed head to toe in Portham FC clothing. He waited for a few seconds then bent down and pushed the letterbox open.

"Mark!" Shouted Sammo.

"Alright! I'm coming!" Shouted Mark from behind the door as he approached to open it.

He unlocked the mortice lock and took off the chain. The door swung open revealing Mark, all dressed up in his Portham FC clothes, topped off with a Portham FC coloured wig. He was holding his new house rabbit. Mark had decided two weeks ago to bring a new companion into the house, he had been lonely without Porty for the last two years and couldn't bear the thought of replacing his old mate but felt that the time was right.

"Fuckin hell Mark... What the fuck is that?" Sammo could not believe what Mark had in his arms. He was not at all perturbed by Mart's attire.

"It's me new rabbit... Cornelius! Come in come in, we've overslept ain't we mate." Mark nuzzled up to his new companion Cornelius the house rabbit as they headed into the house.

Sammo walked in and closed the door behind him. They walked into the living room. Mark sat down and put Cornelius down next to him. The rabbit hopped off straight away towards Mark's previous house rabbit, Porty, which had been manipulated into the lying down position during the taxidermy process and was now situated beside the fireplace. Sammo was a observing the live and stuffed large rabbits, of the Flemish Giant breed, in front of him.

"So, what does Porty think of his new mate then, and where's that name from?" Asked Sammo.

"I'm sure he would have loved him like a brother and I've named after my old Grandad" Mark said proudly.

Cornelius mounted the stuffed Porty. Sammo laughed uncontrollably which was unusual for this stoic, calm man.

"I think the new one likes Porty in a bit of a different way mate and giving him more of a stuffing!" Sammo could hardly breathe with laughter.

Mark darted out of his seat toward the humping house rabbit.

"Cornelius!" Mark Shouted.

Mark picked up Cornelius and put him out in the hallway and slammed the door.

"You can stay out there and think about what you've done! He keeps doing that. I might have to move Porty somewhere else." Sighed Mark, not realising the hilarity and horror of the situation.

"That ain't right!" Chuckled Sammo.

Mark shook his head in acknowledgment.

"Anyway, hurry up and get ready... We got a game to get to!" Sammo said excitedly, diverting their thoughts away from the Leporidae, homosexual necrophilia they had just witnessed Cornelius the house rabbit commit.

"I know, I couldn't get to sleep last night, that's why I slept in." Said Mark.

"One game and we could be in the big time." Sammo said in hope.

"Go on Portham! I won't be long. Make yourself a cuppa." Mart nodded towards the kitchen.

"Sod that! I fancy a beer! You got any?" Sammo was slightly disgusted that his mate had offered him only a cup of tea on such an important morning.

"Oh, go on then! Get me one an all! I need something to steady me nerves after the last two seasons. If he don't get us up this time, then he's gotta go." Mart said looking directly into his old mate's eyes.

Sammo nodded in acknowledgement. He opened the door and walked out to the kitchen to get the beers.

"I think we'll do it this time. Third time lucky an all that." Sammo shouted back as he walked, tilting his head back slightly.

"I dunno." Mark raised his voice so that Sammo could hear him.

Cornelius darted into the front room just as Sammo walked back in with two cans of beer He had a large Portham FC coloured top hat on that Mark had left out there for him as a surprise. Sammo tripped over Cornelius and fell to the floor, the hat fell off, but he still had the cans gripped in his hands.

"Fuckin hell!" Groaned Sammo.

"Bloody hell!" Mark shouted in shock, but he soon started laughing at the site of Sammo on the floor.

"Poxy rabbit!" Shouted Sammo.

"Oi! it was an accident!" Mark went over to the corner of the room where the TV was. Cornelius was cowering behind the TV. Mark bent over and picked him up.

"You alright mate?" Mark nuzzled up to Cornelius.

"Never mind, bloody Cornelius!" Sammo rose to his feet, he was ok.

"Cornelius wants to know if you like your new hat that he brought you?" Chuckled Mark.

Sammo got up and started laughing hysterically which made Mark laugh even more. Sammo handed Mark a can of beer. They both cracked open the cans which sprayed out due to being shook up when Sammo fell over.

"Whay hey!" Shouted Mark.

Cornelius started licking the foamy beer that had sprayed onto Mark's hand.

Mark and Sammo touched their foamy dripping cans together.

"Cheers!" They both spoke in unison and chuckled and took nice long sips.

PORTHAM FC HOME CHANGING ROOMS

The Portham players were all finishing off putting their kits on and psyching each other up.

"Right lads sit down please and listen up!" Neil Glover shouted over all the chattering voices of the team.

Everyone quietened down and sat down on the benches.

"You all know the importance of this game. We have all failed in the last two years to get to where we need to be for lots of reasons but, here we are again. We have all become better for the experiences but, the Chairman does not have the money to keep funding the club as he has done so far. If we do not go up this time, he is going to have to cut his cloth accordingly. My contract is up tomorrow and so are a lot of yours. As you know, the Chairman has said he can only sit down with us once we know where we are playing next season. Not only that, our fans have become restless. Without them this club would be nothing. In just over ninety minutes time we could be in Division One for the first time in this club's history and nearly all the problems will go away. We won't talk about the other possibility anymore. You know the drills. You have played this lot enough times and know what they will do. Now get out there and get us promoted. You can do it! Let's go! "Neil Glover clapped his hands, encouraging his team.

The team and backroom staff all cheered then started to make their way out of the changing room.

PORTHAM FC COMMENTARY GANTRY

"So here we are on the last day of the season at Links Road, the home of Portham Football Club, for this all-important promotion clash against Brentford Park Rangers. So much rides on this game for both clubs. There are reports coming from Portham that this could be Manager Neil Glover's final game in charge if he doesn't get them promoted. Plus, lots of players contracts are up. Both sets of players are out on the pitch now and we see young Bobby Gorman of Portham and young Tommy Williams of Brentford Park Rangers, shaking hands and embracing. What a story for these two young men. Best friends from school who both served apprenticeships at Artillery. Both were released, joined their respective clubs and now find themselves about to play a game where one of them could be playing against Artillery next season." Sam Wellesley informed the radio audience.

"That is some story for these two young lads, especially for young Gorman, who had to leave his family home in central London to come and ply his trade up here. It is a credit to him, his parents and Portham Football Club that he finds himself here today." Replied Tony Court.

PORTHAM FC PITCH

Tommy and Bobby broke from their embrace.

"Can't believe it mate! Weren't that long ago we were playing over Haggerston for Wickside Youth!" Tommy said proudly.

"I know mate... This is unbelievable. Us Tin Soldiers marching into the big time eh! We're still going to do you though..." Bobby replied with a smile.

"Yeah! Good luck with that!" Tommy spat out his repost with a wry smile.

"We'll see about that!" Bobby ran off to take up his position ready for kick off.

PORTHAM FC NORTH BANK TERRACING

"That's good to see look. The two old mates playing against each other." Mark said very proudly of the two young men out on the pitch who were sharing an experience that he could only dream of.

Mark was the fat kid at school who was not good at football but loved the game. His dad George was a Portham fan and used to take Mark to Portham home matches from the age of seven, right up until George passed away suddenly from a heart attack, at the age of thirty-two. This tragic turn of events was not long after Mark's mother, who was the local bike and constantly cheated on George, ran off with a local waiter who she had met on a girl's holiday to Tunisia. This whole sorry episode had left a sixteen-year-old Mark to organise his dad's funeral and to fend for himself. Luckily George was sensible and had life insurance, which paid off the mortgage. George had changed all the relevant insurance and pension paperwork, to make Mark sole beneficiary, as soon as he had found the "Dear John" letter from his wife Lynne on the kitchen table one morning. George had a good job which came with good benefits. He had worked his way up to shop floor manager at the local toolmaking factory since starting their as an apprentice. Since living on his own, Mark had been in relationships on and off over the years but had trust issues. This left him always either finishing with the woman, or them leaving him.

"Don't like too much familiarity. They should be worrying about the game not themselves. They should leave all that till after." Sammo said with a sneer.

Sammo had been a good player and had played youth football for his school team and district. He had trials with Boldham and Hockport and played for Tolton Wanderers academy but got released at sixteen. He played semi-pro for Droylsden Football Club after being released but had sustained a cruciate ligament injury after landing badly, jumping for a fifty-fifty challenge for a header. He underwent surgery at the local hospital, but the operation was botched. After recovering, he had played again for the local team that he had played for in his youth, Chalkonians FC but he was never the same player. He played on until he was thirty-five for the Vets team at Chalkonians. Sammo officially retired by way of letting his teammates know in the club bar after a home game. He often visited Chalkonians, to watch games and to catch up with his old teammates and coaches.

A supporter a few feet to the left of Sammo, struck a match to light a cigarette. The thick plume of acrid smoke, created from the pink Swan Vesta match head as it was drawn against the rough side of the matchbox, causing the reaction which ignited the matchhead, got caught by the breeze and drifted in a perfect cloud towards the unsuspecting Mark. It would have floated past his face had he not inhaled sharply at that precise moment. The full plume of smoke disappeared into his mouth, down through his trachea, filling his lungs with chemically filled smoke. The human body's natural defence system forced Mark to cough violently.

"Who just light that match? That Phosphate went right down

my throat!" Mark struggled to get his words out. He coughed and retched.

Sammo cracked up laughing as he watched the coughing and spluttering Mark. The referee blew the whistle. The whole crowd started cheering. Mark was still coughing. His eyes were bulging.

PORTHAM FC COMMENTARY GANTRY

"Portham kicking from left to right." Sam Wellesley informed his listening radio audience.

"Looking at the way the teams seem to be set up, it looks for an entertaining game with both teams fielding what looks to be an attacking formation but no breakthrough from either team so far" Tony Court responded to his colleague.

"Ball over the top by Knight, straight into the path of Dawson... One nil Brentford Park Rangers!" roared the Sam.

"What a ball by Knight! He looked up and saw Dawson making the run. The Portham defence were all over the place there and Neil Glover and his assistant are livid down on the touchline!" Summarised Tony.

PORTHAM DUGOUT

"Carl for fuck's sake wake up! You're the bloody Captain for Christ's sake." Shouted Neil Glover.

"Carl! Pick Knight up! Pick him up... For fuck's sake! Jonesy... You're supposed to be on Dawson! Fucking wake up!" Shouted an incensed Dave Jenkins

"All of you, switch on, now!" Neil shouted between his hands that were cupped to his cheeks for amplification.

PORTHAM PITCH

Carl raised his hand in acknowledgment to his manager and coach. He knew that the goal that they had just conceded was his fault.

"Sorry lads! Come on we've got to keep alert! Heads up now!" Carl Pilford relaying his bosses' orders as a good club captain should.

Martin Jones was thumping the turf.

"For fuck's sake!" Shouted Martin. He also knew that he was at fault just as much as Carl.

PORTHAM FC COMMENTARY GANTRY

"Defender Martin Jones is furious and so is the Captain, Carl Pilford, who really should have done better." Sam said with an air of disappointment because of what he had just witnessed.

"You have to give credit to Knight for the awareness he showed in picking out Dawson. And what a finish by Dawson. He just touched the ball down with his right shoulder, on the run, and blasted the ball past the keeper, who had no chance!" Tony exclaimed.

"Almost half time now. Gorman dispossesses Dawson, makes space, takes the ball away, passes to Jones who passes back to Gorman with a lovely one two there. Gorman kicks the ball diagonally up into the Brentford Park Rangers half. The big striker Kenny Northolt chests down into the path of Pilfooooord... What a goal! An absolute rocket! Portham are level on the stroke of half time." Screamed Sam.

"Oh, my word! What an absolute screamer by the captain who makes up for his earlier mistake and drags his team level at half time! A delightful ball from Gorman from just outside his own box, big Kenny Northolt chests it beautifully down and chipped the ball into the path of Carl Pilford, who broke from midfield and caught it sweetly on the half volley from about twenty yards out! It literally almost tore the onion bag apart with the keeper rooted to the spot." Tony informed the radio audience.

"And there's a scuffle going on in the goalmouth as the Brentford Park Rangers keeper Jason Lane is slow to give the ball back as Northolt finally wrestles it from him. Portham are keen to get going again but there must only be seconds left." Sam explained.

"And you wouldn't fancy getting into a scuffle with big Kenny, I can tell you!" Tony said with a chuckle.

"Definitely not! As the referee blows for the kick off, the ball is put high up the field. The referee blows his whistle. Half time score, Portham one Brentford Park Rangers one. It's still all to play for in the second half." Sam laughed his reply, knowing Tony was spot on.

PORTHAM NORTH BANK TERRACING

The home crowd were going mad with excitement seeing their young player giving his all and fighting for the team.

Mark and Sammo were cheering their hearts out. Mark had now fully recovered from the match smoke inhalation.

PORTHAM FC HOME DRESSING ROOM

The players were coming back into the changing room. They were congratulating each other and shouting.

Dave Jenkins shouted above everyone in the changing room.

"Calm down you lot! We're lucky to be back in it but for fuck's sake... we were terrible out there! We won't get promoted playing like that!" Dave Jenkins shouted over everyone in the changing room. He was furious with what he had witnessed.

"Get sorted out you lot! Dave's right. We were terrible and that goal has masked it. Forty-five minutes more like that and it will be all over for us as a unit. I will probably be gone, and this club may not survive as it is. You all need to be as switched on as Bobby, Kenny and Carl were in that last minute for the next forty-five minutes. This club needs to get promoted and you players deserve to be promoted. Those fans out there were going wild when you scored! They are good fans that have stuck by us... Imagine the memories you will give them if we go up... Imagine the memories you will give them if we don't. We can do this lads, we can do this... You Full Backs push up at every opportunity. We have been sitting back too much and letting them play. It's time for us to play. We need to press them high up the pitch and suffocate them. We are going 3-5-2 for the second half, just as we have practiced. You all know your drills. Let's do this and make our fans happy! I've said enough... I will see you all back out there." Neil turned and walked out of the changing room. A few of the players looked shocked that he had walked out already.

"Focus lads, focus... A draw won't be enough. All we have to do for forty-five minutes is score more than them and we are up. Concentrate! Get some water down you and try and cool off. Give your legs a shake and have a stretch. Help each other out. Let me know if you need a hand." Encouraged Dave.

The players started stretching out. Some laid on the floor and pushed their legs up to encourage other players to push their legs back to stretch their hamstrings, in an effort to prevent cramping.

PORTHAM PITCH

The home crowd were roaring as the referee blew the whistle to start the second half.

"Come on lads let's get this done!" Carl Pilford was trying his best to motivate his team.

PORTHAM FC GANTRY

"And it's kick off for the second half of this promotion battle between Portham and Brentford Park Rangers for the chance to get into Division one... Brentford Park Rangers immediately take possession." Sam broke freely into his rhythm as the game started.

"It looks to me like Portham have gone three at the back in what looks like a three-five-two formation. This is a surprise as I don't recall them ever playing in this formation." Tony was trying hard to remember if this had ever happened before.

"I think you're right. It seems a bold move by the Portham manager Neil Glover. He looks to be really going for it in the second half. Maybe this is his last throw of the dice for promotion and in fact, if reports are to be believed, maybe keeping his job." Sam was divulging what he had heard from one of his trusted spies in the game.

"Well, it doesn't appear to be working out as Portham haven't had a sniff of the ball yet. "Tony pointed out.

"And Brentford Park Rangers are pouring forward now and... Oh, what a save from the Portham keeper and once again Neil Glover is furious with his team." Sam could see from his vantage point far away from the dugout that Neil Glover was red with rage.

"You can see what this means to him as he is normally quite reserved on the touchline compared to most managers. He sits down now and folds his arms as Dave Jenkins is having a word." Tony could see the body language was not good on the Portham bench, having experienced this kind of thing as a player.

PORTHAM DUGOUT

"Shall we change back formation boss?" Asked Dave.

"No way Dave! They're just getting used to it. Give them a chance." Neil said with a slight air of hopefulness.

PORTHAM PITCH

"Carl! This ain't working mate! We're getting over run!" Bobby was not happy and felt the need to challenge his Captain for the first time since he had joined the club.

"Stick with it! Just worry about your positioning. OK! The manager knows what he's doing!" Assured Carl. He also felt uneasy about the situation but had to back his manager and assure his young teammate.

Tommy was positioned between Carl and Bobby.

"It don't look like it!" Laughed Tommy.

"Fuck off!" Bobby was incensed that his mate who was his foe right now, was getting the better of him and his team.

PORTHAM DIRECTORS BOX

As Vicky was bringing a tray of drinks over to Albert, Liz, John, Jean, Dickie and Maggie. She noticed Dickie gently squeezing the left cheek of Maggie's gluteus maximus. Maggie nudged Dickie. Nobody else seemed to notice.

"Here you go." Vicky announced herself, a bit loader than usual, as she entered the fray.

"Oh, thanks Vicky love." Dickie quickly moved away from Maggie as he spoke.

Vicky looked Dickie in the eyes as she placed the tray of drinks down on the table. She walked off straight away due to the shock at what she had just witnessed.

"Young Vicky don't look so happy today, Dickie. You ain't give her a pay cut, have you?" Albert chuckled.

Dickie shook his head and pulled a face if to say that he didn't know what was wrong with her, oblivious that Vicky had seen him squeezing Maggie's arse.

"Looks like the boys have just had words. Looks like they are over Wickside again arguing like that..." Liz said knowingly.

"They were always like that whenever they played against each other at training or on the same team during a game, but they were always best mates again as soon as the game was over." Jean smiled uncomfortably.

"Ooh they used to hate losing against each other. Mind you to be fair, they both hate losing all together." John stated.

"Terrible losers. The pair of 'em." Liz was remembering how the two boys were as youngsters.

"I reckon I might have this one Albert. Fancy double or nothing?" John encouraged his old mate.

"Piss off! It ain't over yet Johnny Boy!" Albert said confidently.

"You can see where the boys must get it from then!" Chipped in Maggie

They all laughed, apart from Albert and John, who were both staring intently toward the pitch.

PORTHAM FC COMMENTARY GANTRY

"Just under ten minutes remaining with the score still deadlocked at one-one, with both teams attacking and defending equally well but as it stands, Brentford Park Rangers will be promoted." Sam stated the facts of the current situation.

"Portham are fighting for every ball, but Brentford Park Rangers are shading it for me. It looks like this change of formation has not worked out for Neil Glover." Responded

Tony.

"There seems to be some crowd trouble in the South stand as some of the away crowd seem to have gotten into the home section. The police are wading in with their truncheons." Sam was trying to communicate the goings on to his audience, without sounding too shocked at what he was witnessing.

"This kind of behaviour really has no place in the game and will ruin things before long! It's the honest folk who just come to watch the game with their children I feel sorry for." Tony was sick of this kind of behaviour. The disdain was loud and clear in his voice.

"Our attention has been diverted but Portham are on the break here and Carl Pilford has fed a lovely ball through to Kenny Northolt and as he... Oh, he's gone down awkwardly from a challenge by the Brentford Park Rangers Goalkeeper, which surely must be a penalty. The Portham players are incensed and both goalkeeper and striker are down as chaos reigns both on the pitch and off it, as a brawl has erupted on the pitch with fighting still going on in the stands behind the brawling players." Sam could not believe his eyes as he was relaying the massive brawl between the rival players on the pitch and the rival fans in the Portham home stand. The police were steaming into the crowd with truncheons, hitting anyone that moved.

PORTHAM FC HOME STAND

Mark and Sammo were apoplectic with rage and were both venting their spleens at the sights beholding them both further along the stand and on the pitch.

PORTHAM FC GANTRY

"The Brentford Park Rangers keeper is up. Northolt is back on his feet, remonstrating with the keeper. He is limping badly and signals to the bench. The Portham Physio, Gary Casey runs onto the pitch. The referee has just calmed things down and is now speaking to the linesman and... Yes, he has blown for a penalty and points to the spot." Tony could hardly contain himself with all the excitement.

DOWN ON THE PORTHAM PITCH

"I'm gonna stay on and see how I get on... We ain't got long now." Kenny Northolt said, wincing in pain.

"Well, there's nothing broken but you could have strained your ligament again." The long serving physio advised.

"Get some spray on there will ya... I'm staying on!" Demanded Kenny

Gary pulled some Deep Heat out of his bag and sprayed Kenny's ankle. Kenny pulled his sock up and slid his shin pad back in. Gary packed his things up and jogged off back towards the dugout, just as the Brentford Park Rangers Goalie walked over and offered to help Kenny up.

"Sorry mate. I didn't mean to take you out. I went for the ball... Honestly." The Brentford Park Rangers Goalie Was sincere in his apology.

Kenny looked up at his foe for a second. He then held out his hand. The Brentford Park Rangers Goalkeeper pulled him up.

"Don't worry. I'll get you next season. Mind you I probably won't get the chance now after we score this penalty! "Joked Kenny.

Kenny limped away as the crowd cheered him on. He applauded toward the home crowd. Everything had calmed down now both on the pitch and in the crowd.

"Carl, Bobby… Get over here." Summoned Kenny as he waved Carl and Bobby over toward him.

PORTHAM FC COMMENTARY GANTRY

"The referee and police now have everything under control both on and off the pitch as some supporters from both clubs are being ejected from the ground. The teams are back in their positions waiting for the penalty to be taken." Advised Sam.

"It looks as though Northolt is staying on, but he has called the Captain Carl Pilford and Bobby Gorman over. Northolt is the main penalty taker but both Pilford and Gorman have taken them in the past although Pilford took the last one and missed. Northolt looks as though he is struggling after that challenge." Tony remarked.

PORTHAM FC PITCH

"I can't take this. I'm staying on but I ain't gonna be able to take this penalty. Carl? "Kenny offered the ball to his captain.

"I've been struggling for a while. I've pulled my hamstring." Carl said, rubbing his hamstring.

"And I missed the…"

Bobby cut Carl off.

"I'll take it!" Bobby snatched the ball from Kenny and walked off towards the penalty spot and the waiting referee, who was starting to look agitated at the time it was all taking.

"Pick your spot, and don't change your mind!" Shouted Kenny.

"If he scores, get back and defend. If he don't, do what you can up front." Carl instructed Kenny.

PORTHAM FC GANTRY

It's the eighty ninth minute and unbelievably, young Bobby Gorman has started walking towards the spot. This was after a bit of deliberation between Northolt and Pilford, which must be due to Northolt looking injured... Gorman is going to take the penalty. He's striding very confidently towards the spot. He's now taken the ball from the referee.

PORTHAM DIRECTORS BOX

"I can't watch!" Liz held her hands to her eyes.

Come on son you can do it." Albert said through gritted teeth, holding his clenched fists at chest height.

PORTHAM DUGOUT

"Kenny's staying on but can't take the penalty." Gary Casey deduced.

"Carl's struggling and he did miss the last one he took. Bobby was staying behind this week doing shooting practice and taking penalties..." Dave was remembering Carl's miss as it was very painful. He was trying to be convincing in what he was saying as he was sure that Neil Glover was having a thousand thoughts about what was happening.

Neil Glover was standing right on the touchline, motionless. He was looking towards the away goal at the young left back who he had brought to the club and who he had showed so much faith in.

PORTHAM FC GANTRY

"Bobby Gorman places the ball on the spot, the Brentford Park Rangers fans are doing their best to put him off. But he seems unfazed as he takes a few steps back and... BURIES IT IN THE TOP LEFT CORNERRRRR! PORTHAM SURELY PROMOTED NOW! WHAT A GREAT PENALTY!! HE KNEW EXACTLY WHAT HE WANTED TO DO AND HAS SURELY FIRED THEM INTO DIVISION ONE FOR THE FIRST TIME IN THEIR HISTORY!"

Roared Sam Wellesley.

PORTHAM FC DUGOUT AND HOME STAND

Neil Glover started jumping for joy and turned and ran towards Dave and Gary. They all embraced and jumped up and down together. This was annoying the Brentford Park Rangers bench even further and one of their coaches kicked a water bottle into the air.

The home crowd were going crazy. The place was rocking. Mark and Sammo faces were red. Their eyes were bulging, and they were cheering at the tops of their voices. Sammo even hugged Mark.

PORTHAM DIRECTORS BOX

Albert and Liz were hugging each other tightly. Dickie hugged Maggie and then mouthed yes to the sky. Jean and John were smiling as even though their son was on the losing team, they knew how much this meant to their friends. Vicky was looking down towards Bobby and smiling.

PORTHAM PITCH

Bobby ran away from his teammates who were chasing him. He got near to the Portham director's box and blew a kiss upwards, hoping his family would see him. He then pumped his fist towards the fans before he got mobbed by his teammates and forced to the floor as they all jumped on him in jubilant celebration.

The Brentford Park Rangers players were all looking despondent. The Brentford Park Rangers manager was shouting and waving at his players to get back for the kick off and signalling to them to concentrate by pointing his finger to his head. The players eventually got back to the centre circle.

Brentford Park Rangers kicked off.

PORTHAM FC PITCH

"There can only be seconds remaining now as Portham kick it high up into the Brentford Park Rangers half... That's it! The whistles gone and it's all over! Portham go up to the First Division for the first time in their history as runners up and Brentford Park Rangers miss out on goal difference and finish third. QPR already confirmed as Division Two champions. The Portham fans are pouring onto the pitch now as it turns a sea of yellow and black stripes. The players are being mobbed." Laughed Sam.

"There will be one hell of a party in this part of Greater Manchester tonight! Congratulations to Portham Football Club and their fans, their chairman and of course, the Manager Neil Glover, who made a bold change in formation which paid off. What a great story! Young Bobby Gorman has scored the penalty that has taken them up and will surely go down as a legend of the club for evermore. Commiserations to Brentford Park Rangers as they did everything, they could but it just wasn't their day. Its third time lucky for

Portham now though. Young Bobby Gorman has been lifted up by the fans. He is waving towards the director's box where I'm sure his mum and dad are looking down on him very proudly. He has been picked up by two fans onto their shoulders. He is pumping his fists to the supporters and now blowing kisses to all the fans and up to the director's box again." Tony was sounding slightly emotional.

PORTHAM FC DIRECTORS BOX

Vicky was waving at Bobby. She blew him a kiss. Albert noticed and nudged Liz. Liz smiled as she saw what Vicky was doing then hugged Albert again.

PORTHAM FC DRESSING ROOM

Neil Glover was sitting on one of the benches with Dave Jenkins and Gary Casey either side of him. They had run straight down the tunnel to avoid the madness of the pitch invasion that they knew would happen if they were to win.

"We've done it then." Dave said in a mock, nonchalant way.

"Yeah, we have done it…" Gary responded in the same manner as Dave.

Neil Glover put his arms around Dave and Gary.

"Yes! We have done it! We have done it and I cannot thank you two enough for sticking with me. Now get them beers open. They'll all be in soon enough and there won't be any left! I told Godders to bring champagne down here if we did it!" Neil said enthusiastically.

They all referred to Dickie Godstone as Godders, when they were on their own.

Gary got up and went over to the crates of beer, which were stacked up underneath a wallpaper pasting table that had food on it. He pulled out three bottles of beer and opened them with one of the bottle openers that had been left on the pasting table. He walked back over to Neil and Dave and handed them both a bottle of beer.

"Cheers boys!" Neil said with the biggest smile on his face that Dave had ever seen.

They clinked their bottles together.

"I have no doubt that now we have reached the top division, we can go on and achieve greater things together… As long as you wish to stay together of course?" Asked Neil.

"Yes boss of course boss!" Said Gary very excitedly.

"As long as you'll have me, I'm here! You know that gaffer." Chuckled Dave.

"Thank you, gentlemen, that has made me a very happy man! Let's hope the chairman wants to keep me now! So, let's drink to our success and down these in one!" Neil was encouraging his trusted men.

They all clinked their bottles together again and downed their beers. Neil Glover got up as he had swallowed his beer the fastest.

"Let me get the next round." Chuckled Neil.

They all chuckled together as Neil Glover got them all another beer.

The door opened. Dickie Godstone came in accompanied by two stewards. The stewards were each carrying a case of Champagne. Dickie was carrying a box of champagne flutes as it was lighter than the wooden cases of champagne.

"I've had this cooling in the cellar boys!" Dickie couldn't hide his delight.

They all put their luggage down.

"Thanks lads. Now get yourselves back upstairs. Vicky has a beer waiting for you." Dickie didn't think it appropriate that the stewards stayed in the changing room.

Although the stewards didn't look too pleased, they both nodded in acknowledgement and walked out and closed the door behind them as Dickie ran across the dressing room towards Neil, Dave and Gary with open arms and tears in his eyes. They all stood up as the big bear of a chairman grabbed them all in a group hug. They all started jumping up and down. Dave and Gary broke away. Dickie didn't let Neil break away from his embrace.

"Thank you, Neil, Thank you so much! With the extra money the club will be alright so I can stay. Will you stay?" Dickie pleaded.

"As long as you want me Mr Chairman." Neil assured his pleading chairman whispering in his ear.

They pulled away from their embrace and were looking into each other's teary eyes.

"I will sort a new contract with you as soon as we stop celebrating but trust me, it will reflect what you have done." Dickie was nodding, trying to reassure his manager that he really meant what he was saying.

"And what about these boys? They're just as important as me." Neil Glover held his hands out furrowing his brow and nodding at Dickie turning his head in the direction of Dave and Gary, who were enjoying their beers and deep in conversation, but both turned toward their manager and chairman when they heard their names mentioned.

"Yes, lads I will be getting you new contracts as well don't you worry about that! Now let's crack open the champers! Get some glasses out please Dave." Asked Dickie.

Dave shot over to the box of champagne flutes while Dickie popped the cork of the champagne. It spurted out a little. He poured it into the four glasses that Dave has placed on the food table.

"Here's to a brighter future for the club and all of us... Cheers!" Dickie raised his glass to his management team.

They all clinked their glasses together and then each took a sip.

"Mr Chairman, this seems expensive considering we are struggling financially?" Dave pointed out.

"I like your thinking Dave, but don't you worry. I got it for the club bar on sale or return... Just in case like!" Dickie joked.

They all laughed.

Muffled cheering could be heard from outside then the door suddenly burst open. The players started pouring through the door. They were all cheering and shouting and singing the songs that the fans sang on the terraces.

"Yeeeesss!!" Shouted Dickie at his players

Dickie shook up the bottle of champagne he was holding and sprayed it at all of the players. They all laughed and cheered then they all made a grab for the chairman and started hugging him. They all picked him up. One of the players snatched the champagne bottle and poured the rest of the contents over him

"Drink up lads! There's beers, champagne and a bit of grub too!" Dickie chuckled as he lost his balance and fell but they managed to keep him up and settle him back onto his feet.

The players left the dishevelled, champagne soaked chairman, chuckling away as they all started grabbing bottles of beer and champagne and frantically opening them. They held their thumbs over the opened tops and started shaking the bottles up and down and then sprayed each other. They then started drinking the beer and champagne and pouring it over each other's heads.

"Well done lads. Well done indeed! I'm so proud of you all!" Shouted Neil Glover at the top of his voice.

Carl Pilford made his way through the mass of bodies and alcohol that was raining down on everyone. He eventually made it to Neil Glover.

"So, then Boss... You staying or what?" Enquired Carl slightly aggressively.

"Oh yes Mr Pilford, I'm most definitely staying! The Chairman has asked me to stay, and I have accepted. Now we have been promoted, and with the extra revenue that comes with it, the

Chairman is able to stay too." Neil replied enthusiastically.

"That's great boss!" Carl was genuinely pleased to hear this news.

"I'm pleased too Carl and thank you for all of your efforts." Neil grabbed Carl's hand and shook it.

"No problem boss." Replied Carl. He started shaking Neil's hand vigorously.

Carl cupped his other hand to his mouth and shouted to his team.

"Here lads, the boss and chairman are staying!"

Big cheers erupted. The players all steamed towards Neil and hoisted him up and started giving him the bumps. Neil was grinning like a child as he was thrown into the air. A local newspaper photographer had managed to get into the changing room. He took a picture at the exact moment as Neil was thrown into the air, capturing Neil mid-air. His eyes were closed. He had the biggest grin on his face. All of the players were looking up, smiling and laughing at their manager, who had pulled off the almost impossible task of getting his team promoted to the top-flight. A wonderful snapshot in time which would become a legendary photo for Portham Football Club.

CHAPTER VII
THE NIGHT BEGINS TO SHINE

C'EST BON NIGHTCLUB

"In you go lads. A few of your lot are already in there. Well done by the way. Go straight through. There's an area for you. I'm Man United so at least we'll be guaranteed six points off you lot!" Laughed the Bouncer.

The other Bouncers started laughing along with their colleague.

"Yeah! Yeah! Come on then you lot." Carl laughed with the bouncers as he gestured to his entourage to follow him in.

The group of players and staff started filing in as Carl guided them past himself and the Bouncers.

"Here mate, there are a few more coming down in taxis in a bit. Can you make sure they get in alright please?" Carl asked the big, hefty head bouncer, Benny Blackwell. Carl knew him well as this was the go-to club in town and Carl always sorted out the guest list with Benny and looked after him with a few quid for doing this and to make sure that the bouncers kept an eye on the players while they were at the club.

"I've got a list here. As long as there on it, they'll get in." Assured the thick set, bald man mountain.

"Cheers mate." Carl gave the thumbs up and followed the rest of the party.

C'EST BON NIGHTCLUB BAR

"Here come the players." Vicky said excitedly.

"Oh yeah! They're pissed already by the look of some of them." Laughed Tammy Wood.

"Probably. They had loads of booze and champagne in the dressing room." Vicky informed her colleague from the Portham Football Club hospitality team. They had hit it off instantly after starting work at Portham on the same day.

"I wish I could have got in there with them. I would have helped them celebrate!" Tammy did the motion of giving oral sex to a man. They both burst out laughing.

"You're disgusting!" Laughed Vicky.

"I don't think I could do anything with Glover or Godstone though!" Tammy said with a dismissing look on her face.

"Uuurrrgghh! The thought of it! Thanks for that image in my brain! Talking of Godstone, I think he's knocking off Maggie Braithwaite you know…" Vicky gave Tammy a knowing look.

"Who?" Tammy asked inquisitively.

"Maggie, you know, the one who looks after the apprentices who live too far away from home…" Vicky remarked as if to say that her colleague should have known who he was talking about.

"Oh yeah! I have heard some rumours in the past… How do you know?" Asked Tammy, eagerly.

"Have you? I saw him squeeze her bum in the lounge and it's just the way they are round each other sometimes…" Shrugged Vicky

"Probably is then. She's a widow so I suppose she has her needs!" Tammy shrugged too and held her hands out.

"I don't think I'd need it that much!" Vicky said with a grimace.

They both started laughing.

"Come on, let's go and get a drink off this lot." Tammy gestured towards the Portham FC team that were approaching the bar.

Some of the players headed toward the bar as the rest of them headed toward the roped off VIP area. Vicky noticed Bobby among them. He saw her and they both smiled and waved at each other.

"Oh yeah! Bobby Gorman, eh? I saw you eyeing him up back at the club." Tammy nudged her colleague as she noticed Bobby and Vicky gazing at each other.

"He's lovely... He doesn't seem interested, but we always have a good chat, and his mum and dad are really funny. Proper cockneys. There always like..."

Vicky adopted her best cockney accent.

"You're a such a lovely gel Vick fanks for the drinks darlin!" Vicky laughed at her own impression.

Vicky suddenly felt a bit bad for doing the impression though as she absolutely loved Albert and Liz to bits. She also loved Albert's tips which nicely augmented her wages from Portham FC and the Youth Training Scheme hairdressing course. Both of which did not amount to much.

"Bloody hell you'll be marrying him next! My old man hates cockneys! Come on..." Tammy dragged Vicky towards the players at the bar.

"Come on lads, get them in then!" Tammy said as she got in amongst the players.

"Hello girls! What can I get you?" Asked Carl.

"Well, you can get me a pint of snakebite and her a large vodka and lemonade for starters!" Tammy told Carl.

"Blimey you ain't shy! Yes, please mate." Carl gestured toward the barman who was already walking towards him

"You are something else!" Vicky sighed loudly as her face broke into a big smile.

"They've got plenty of money! They love getting the drinks in for the girls! Don't you Carl?" Tammy shouted.

"Er... Yeah course I do. But don't be getting too pissed! There'll be all sorts in here later, especially after what's happened today!" Carl said sternly.

"Go on Portham!" Shouted Tammy with her fists clenched.

Some tough looking men that were near the other end of the bar, glared over with menacing looks. Carl clocked them.

"Tammy, leave it out will you!" Carl glared at her.

"Yeah, calm down a bit Tam, we just got here!" Agreed Vicky.

"Alright you two. I'm just having a bit of fun..." Tammy acquiesced.

"Come on Portham" Tammy mouthed silently as she clenched her fists. She couldn't help herself.

"Shut it!" Vicky laughed as she put her hand over Tammy's mouth.

Bobby walked towards them. He looked a bit dishevelled.

"Bloody hell mate! What happened to you?" Carl was laughing at his young teammate who was definitely looking worse for wear.

"I got mobbed by a load of fans outside. They were alright though... I didn't mind." Bobby said calmly

"You sure you're ok Bobby?" Vicky asked in a concerned manner.

"I'm alright thanks Vick. You look nice. Alright Tammy?" Bobby tried to hide his admiration for the beautiful Vicky, who looked stunning in a tightly fitting black dress and high heels.

"Fine thanks Bobby. Don't I look nice then?" Tammy asked in a mock disappointed voice.

"Course you do!" Laughed Bobby.

How's your mum and dad?" Asked Vicky, vying for Bobby's attention.

"They're still up the club with Godstone and Maggie." Remarked Bobby.

DON'T YOU WANT ME BABY by THE HUMAN LEAGUE started to play.

" Oh, come on Vick. Let's go and have a dance! I love this song!" Tammy dragged Vicky off to towards the dance floor.

"See you later! Thanks for the drinks, Carl!" Vicky said as she was dragged away by her voracious work colleague. She gazed back at Bobby but had to turn her head quickly to avoid tripping over.

The two young women disappeared into the throng of people on the dance floor.

"I bet that Tammy loves it!" Bobby remarked as he watched the two Portham FC bar staff scurry off to the dance floor.

"She does love it mate, trust me!" Carl smirked.

"Oh yeah? You had a go then?" Bobby nudged Carl.

"Let's just say that bird could suck a golf ball through a hose pipe!" Carl enthused.

They both cracked up with laughter.

"I might have to get her round to my room!" Bobby said, very enthusiastically.

"I thought you and Vicky might get it on. I wouldn't mind a go..." Carl said wistfully.

"She's too young for you! I think she's up for it. You never know…" Bobby said with a cheeky smile on his face.

"You're in love with her! It's written all over your face you little Jessie!" Carl grabbed Bobby in a headlock and ruffled his hair.

"Fuck off!" Bobby wriggled out of his captain's grip.

"Come on get these down you." Carl pointed to the bar where two pints of lager and two large whiskey chasers were sitting. They both picked up the pints.

"Cheers Bobby you've done well this season. I'm proud of you mate, we all are." Carl said very seriously to the young cockney left back.

"Cheers Carl thanks for all your help." Bobby patted Carl on the shoulder.

Bobby looked across to the dance floor. Vicky and Tammy were dancing and really laughing at each other.

C'EST BON STAGE

The C'est Bon owner, Drew Edge, took to the microphone.

"Tonight, ladies and gentlemen, we have the radio commentary team from today's big match earlier today, which I'm sure a few of you were at, as our guest DJ and MC tonight. So, let's give Tony Court and Sam Wellesley a big C'est Bon welcome as they take to the record decks and microphone for you tonight.

Sam and Tony walked up the stairs to the left of the stage. They both shook Drew's hand. They both waved to the punters, then made their way to the DJ booth to the right of the stage.

"And may I take this opportunity to congratulate Portham Football club on promotion to Division One! Let's hear it for Portham!" Shouted Drew, who was an avid Portham supporter but also had a soft spot for Artillery, so he was a big Bobby

Gorman fan too.

Most of the crowd cheered but there were boos from some sections of the nightclub from rival supporters of other local clubs who were rivals to Portham FC. An empty pint glass flew past Drew's head and smashed on the red sequin covered wall at the back of stage.

"Right lads, find out who that was and have him out! Same kind of accuracy as the Hockport striker today, eh?" Laughed Drew as he pointed to his bouncers.

The whole crowd went wild. A Britvic bitter lemon bottle flew through the air which just clipped Drew on the head slightly. The blow was cushioned by his bouffant hair. This was followed by another pint glass, which wasn't empty this time. It smashed onto the stage, splashing its contents and bits of glass over Drew's neatly pressed trousers. Drew winced and shook his leg.

"Boys it came from over there." Drew pointed to the back of the dance floor, gesticulating to his Bouncers and the general direction of the thugs that had thrown the bottle and glass at him, for daring to support Portham FC.

"That was piss in that pint glass! The smell reminds me of Hockport's ground! Right, with no further ado I will hand you over to our DJ and MC for the evening." Drew winced, shook his leg, then ran off of the stage.

There was a bit of a melee on the dance floor as the bouncers waded in, grabbed some men and dragged them away to throw them out. They were protesting their innocence as they were pushed along. Vicky and Tammy were caught up in the middle of the whole thing.

"Hey! It wasn't them it was that lot! We see him pissing in the glass the dirty bastard!" Sneered Tammy.

"Well, these lot are going! Now out the way!" Shouted the

bouncer as he barged past the two women.

"Stay out of it Tammy! Come on let's get a drink." Urged Vicky.

Vicky tried to grab Tammy, but she carried on following the Bouncers and men who were getting thrown out.

Bootsy Callaghan, a well-known Hockport hooligan, approached Vicky.

"Yeah, you're right love! You should be keeping out of it. That's a good girl. No one likes a grass! Your mate should be careful who she blabs her mouth off at! Some of the bouncers are my mates you see. And now she's getting thrown out too... Look!" Sneered Bootsy.

Vicky looked across as she saw Tammy being pushed out of the fire exit doors along with the three other men she was trying to protect. Vicky went to go after her colleague, but Bootsy held her back.

"Let go of me!" Demanded Vicky.

"You don't want to get thrown out as well, do you? Come on, why don't you have a dance with Bootsy?" Bootsy pulled Vicky towards him.

"Get off of me!" Demanded Vicky as she tried to pull away from the leering fat psychopath.

Bobby suddenly appeared and pushed Bootsy away from Vicky.

"You alright Vick? "Asked a very concerned Bobby.

"Yeah. I'm going after Tammy." Vicky ran off. Bobby turned around to confront Bootsy.

"What the fuck are you playing at?" Bobby demanded.

Two of Bootsy's friends walked over and stood next to Bootsy.

"Oh, look who it is chaps. Bobby fookin Gorman. Why don't you fuck off you dirty cockney bastard!" Laughed Bootsy, trying to dismiss Bobby.

"What 'd you fuckin say?" Bobby squared up to Bootsy.

"I said you're a dirty cockney ba..." Booty's speech was violently interrupted.

Bobby threw a right hook that caught Bootsy square on his open jaw, breaking it instantly with a loud crack which floored him. His two friends piled into Bobby who tried fighting them off, but they all ended up on the floor. Two bouncers waded in and pulled them all apart. Bobby took a punch from one of the bouncers as he was trying to get back up.

"Stay there you!" The bouncer who just punched Bobby, pointed straight at him.

The bouncers threw Bootsy and his two friends out of the club. Vicky came running back over to Bobby who was slowly getting up. He was being helped by some Portham supporters.

"Listen mate we see everything. We'll back you up if anything comes of it. That was Bootsy Callaghan. He's top boy for the Hockport lot. I'll spread the word round our lot about what he did and what you did." Assured the Portham supporter

"Nice one mate. Don't get any bother over it though will ya." Bobby said, thinking about the kind of repercussions that would occur back home in Hoxton should anything like this ever happen.

"Mate don't you worry. You've just made a great day into an even better one. Here, your birds back now, I'll see you later." Laughed the big Portham FC supporter.

"Cheers boys. "Bobby patted the guy on the chest. They shook hands and hugged then the Portham boys walked off nudging each other and gesticulating with excitement.

"Bobby are you alright? Oh my god you've got a fat lip." Vicky was horrified.

"Yeah, from the bloody Bouncer! Anyway, you alright?" Bobby was more concerned for Vicky.

"I caught up with Tammy. She was copping off with one of the guys who got thrown out. She ended up getting in a cab with them all, so I came back in to see if you were ok, and all hell were breaking loose. The bouncers threw the wrong guys out for throwing them bottles and glasses at the stage. Tammy got involved and ended up getting thrown out and then that bloke started on me!" Vicky explained, still visibly shaken up by her ordeal.

"Alright calm down, calm down. I'm alright, you're alright and Tammy's probably getting a good seeing to, so she's alright an all." Bobby chuckled a bit in a bid to reassure the trembling Vicky.

Carl Pilford approached them.

"Fuck me! You alright lad." Carl was laughing a bit nervously as he saw his beat-up teammate.

"Yeah, I'm alright. One of Hockport's hooligans was giving it the big'un to our Vicky... So, I put him on his arse and his mates waded in then the bouncers steamed in and one of 'em give me a bit of a dig... I think he did it to calm me down and keep me safe to be honest." Bobby smirked.

"Come on. Let's get to the bar and get a drink and calm down." Carl said reassuringly.

"I think I'm going to go home to be honest." Vicky looked sad.

"I'll take you home in a cab. Here Carl, would you mind getting your mate behind the bar to order us a cab and ask him to get us out the back way, just in case." Bobby was concerned there could still be more trouble waiting for him,

Carl looked at the two youngsters and thought that it was a good idea. He could see this young love story going further.

"Ok mate." Carl said, assuring his dishevelled teammate.

They all walked towards the bar. A few of the clubbers were clapping and cheering as Bobby walked past them. As they got to the bar, Carl ushered over the bar manager and whispered in his ear. The bar manager pointed towards a door behind the bar.

"Right follow me." Ordered Carl.

The bar manager lifted the entrance flap at the end of the bar and let the three of them through and closed it behind them. Carl took them through the door which opened into a small office. Carl used the phone in there to call a cab.

"Hey its Carl Pilford... That's right. I need a cab please to pick up from the back door of C'est Bon nightclub down the alley. Tell the driver to knock and I will come out. Put it on my account please. Thanks." Carl put the phone down.

"I like your style, Carl!" Bobby was well impressed with his Captain.

"Being captain of the local club does have its perks. I've spoke to the bar manager, and he will sort out the bouncers. I've told him what happened. He knows what a prick that guy is. Oh, sorry Vicky..." Carl looked at Vicky slightly embarrassed.

"Thanks Carl. Don't be silly. Thanks for helping us out.

"I don't know what the fallout from this will be, but I suggest you keep your heads down for a while. It's not really good for the club." Carl knew that Dickie hated any bad publicity for his club.

"Bobby was only looking after me. God knows what that arsehole might have done if it wasn't for him." Vicky looked at her beaten up hero.

"Look don't worry, I'll deal with anything that comes of it." Carl knew he could get this all swept under the carpet. He had done this a few times over the years.

There was a knock at the door. Carl went and answered the door.

"Ok mate, just coming."

Bobby and Vicky walked out. Carl grabbed Bobby. Vicky carried on going out through the door into the alley and got into the cab.

"Don't do anything I wouldn't do!" Carl joked.

Bobby shook Carl's hand.

"Thanks for sorting things out mate."

"Now get going so I can get back in there and start enjoying meself!" Carl ruffled Bobby's hair and pushed him away towards door.

Bobby stumbled out through the door and got into the cab. Carl closed the door once he saw Booby safe in the cab.

IN THE MINICAB

"Fancy coming back to my gaff for a drink?" Asked Bobby. He was trying not to sound too enthusiastic.

"Yeah, why not. It's still early. What about Maggie?" Vicky asked. She too was trying to play it cool.

"She's staying out tonight she said. She stays at her mates now and again." Replied Bobby, very innocently.

"Yeah! More like a hotel with Dickie!" Vicky exclaimed.

Bobby kind of laughed then stared out of the window, remembering.

C'EST BON NIGHTCLUB DJ BOOTH

Sam Wellesley, who was the MC for the night, had a microphone in his hand and an earpiece in his ear. Tony Court, who was the DJ for the night, had a telephone receiver to his ear that he was using for mixing the records together. Tony had started DJing as a hobby at the end of his playing career.

He only liked playing records and once he teamed up with Sam doing commentary, they had really hit it off and as their popularity grew, they came up with the idea of doing guest spots in the local nightclubs in the towns and cities wherever they were commentating on matches during the day. Sam was more than happy to take on the MC duties.

"Well, that was KOOL AND THE GANG with THAT'S THE WAY I LIKE IT. Ah ha, ah ha! After all the excitement of earlier, I hope you have all COOLED down a bit. And keeping on the cool theme here is DADDY COOL from BONEY M!" Sam said smoothly.

The music kicked in and the pair of them looked at each other. Tony flicked a switch. He was talking through his telephone to Sam who was listening through his earpiece. This is how they communicated to each other due to the noise. Sam could flick a switch on his microphone and could talk to Tony so that they could talk about how the crowd was reacting to songs and so that Sam knew what songs were being cued up to play next. Tony had custom made this equipment. The crowd could not hear them.

"Well, we've almost reached halftime in this story, which ended with quite a bang in the end!" Chuckled Sam.

"It sure did, with lots and highs and lows throughout the first half but it's not quite over yet and may end up with an even bigger bang if young Bobby gets his way with young Vicky there!" Chuckled Tony.

"Only time will tell with that situation! But let's go through the talking points of the first half." Sam said, slipping seamlessly into giving the pundit his chance to break the action down as they did when they worked on live matches together.

"Well young Bobby's rise has been phenomenal and was of course aided inadvertently by Billy Thorpe's bad injury. Then of course we had Bobby having to deal with being away from

home and of course his bit of action with his landlady Maggie."
Tony gave his partner his chance to respond.

"Yes, his rise was phenomenal, especially when it came to
Maggie of course! But that situation never arose again, which I
suspect is down to her relationship with the chairman, Dickie
Godstone." Sam loved using double entendres to get his point
across.

"Yes, young Bobby has never seemed to really get that one out
of his system, but he will have to tonight, especially as he will
be playing at the same ground so to speak!" Tony was having a
field day challenging his colleague to better his remark.

"Well, it may even end up on the same part of the pitch if he
chooses to make the challenge in Maggie's six-yard box of a
bedroom, as he did before." Remarked a chuckling Sam.

"Well, if there's any goalmouth action later, then he may
choose to do it at the other end of the pitch in his own room or
take a shot in the living room." Surmised Tony with a grin.

"Well that remains to be seen. Let's move on now, to the
incident on the dancefloor here earlier and how Bootsy
Callaghan came to have his jaw broken in three places, if some
early reports are to be believed, by that vicious right hand shot
from Gorman." Sam said slightly more seriously.

"Well, I think the problem with that is, is the fact that
Callaghan was mid-way through saying the word bastard."
Advised Tony.

"Can you elaborate further on this please?" Enquired the
unsure Sam.

"Well, if you look down at the monitor...." The pundit pointed
to small monitor in amongst the DJ equipment, which was
connected to cameras around the dancefloor. It started to
rewind and then stopped on the point where Bobby hit Bootsy.

"Well, the thing is, with different accents, certain words are said differently. The way the jaw moves depends how you say things. When southern people say bastard, they pronounce it bastard which sounds like its spelt B A R S T A R D and hardly open their jaws when saying the word, but Northern people, especially around the Greater Manchester area where we are now, say bastard how it should be pronounced. They accentuate the first two letters which of course are B and A. By doing this they open their jaws wider. It was at this point, where his jaw was almost fully open, that Bobby's fist connected with it. Add to that the fact that Callaghan was probably drunk and shouting the word, Gorman's fist connected with Callaghan's jaw at its most open point. He probably did break it in three places, if not more. Gorman has probably shattered Callaghan's jaw as Gorman was an amateur boxer before giving that up to become a professional footballer. I think Callaghan will be eating his meals through a straw for the next few months now." Tony chuckled through a grimaced face, thinking of the pain and suffering

"I'm sure he will. What great analysis there. But surely there will be some fall out from this." Sam chuckled at first but got serious.

"I think between the club and the supporters, it will be sorted out in some way." Tony said knowingly.

"Well, we are running out of time as we need to get the next song on, but we haven't even spoken about Portham's promotion yet with all the other excitement going on." Noted Sam.

"Well, I hear that Dickie Godstone is going to stay and I'm sure there will be money to spend with the promotion. It will be a struggle for them but with Neil Glover sure to stay now too, I think all the building blocks are in place for a brighter future. I have also heard through the grapevine already, that some high-ranking members the Portham FC hooligan firm, The 5:56 Mob, have already made noises that Bobby Gorman is to be left alone and that if anything happens to him, there will be serious repercussions. I tell you Sam, you wouldn't want to be on the end of that early train coming at you!" Tony said sternly.

"Well on that note, its back to the story!" Sam said cheerily.

They both laughed then switched their equipment switches back to carry on their nights work.

BOBBY'S BEDROOM AT MAGGIE'S HOUSE

There was frantic movement in Bobby's bed. The sounds and the groans of sexual pleasure could be heard which reached a crescendo then the movement stopped. Bobby kissed Vicky and then they turned onto their sides and cuddled up to each other.

"I think I love you, Bobby. I have done for ages but not realised it." Vicky said breathlessly.

"I think I love you too... Well, I've always fancied you anyway." Bobby giggled.

Vicky dug Bobby in the ribs. They both started laughing. Bobby leaned over and kissed Vicky passionately he laid back and they got into the spoons position. Bobby hugged Vicky. They were both very contented and both started to drift off into a deep sleep.

SECOND HALF

CHAPTER VIII
BACK TO LIFE

JANUARY 4th 2004

Bobby and Vicky were lying in each other's arms. Twenty years had passed since the C'est Bon nightclub fight and subsequent sexual encounter between them, which resulted in them staying together ever since and marrying and having two children. Vicky was stirring. She turned and laid on her back. Her eyes were open, staring at the ceiling. The digital alarm radio lit up. ALL DAY AND ALL OF THE NIGHT by The Kinks burst into their eardrums. Bobby was lying on his side.

"That's a bit lively for this time of the morning ain't it?" Croaked Bobby.

"Well, it woke you up, which makes a change from you snoozing it loads." Vicky replied softly.

"I ain't really slept properly." Bobby said a bit louder this time.

"You could have fooled me. You've been snoring all night! I'm the one who's hardly slept more like!" Vicky said loudly.

"It's Sunday nights, I can never sleep properly Sunday nights." Remarked Bobby.

"Drinking beer don't help your bloody snoring!" Vicky wasn't happy.

"It numbs the pain! I can't keep doing this Vick, it's bloody killing me all this working for a living lark!" Bobby said sadly.

"Well, you ain't dead yet and we've got bills to pay, so up you get! Anabel needs stuff for Uni as well." Vicky informed her husband.

Vicky got up and opened the curtains. The sunlight filled the room in an instant. Her body was silhouetted against the sun for an instant. Bobby turned and looked at his beautiful wife. She left the room.

"Bloody hell!" Bobby pulled the covers over him.

OUTSIDE BOBBY AND VICKY'S HOUSE

A crew bus styled work van pulled up outside Bobby's house. Bobby was already waiting. He opened the back door and climbed in. The work van drove off.

INSIDE THE WORK VAN

Bobby walked through the middle of the van and sat down at the front where there was a space on one of the long benches that ran either side down the length of the van. There were five men in the back, now that Bobby had got in. Most of them were snoozing or trying to get comfortable on the wooden benches as best they could. Tony Ellingham was sitting in the front passenger seat. He turned to face Bobby.

"Morning! We didn't think you'd be back again!" Laughed Tony.

"That's a fiver you owe me Tony!" Johnny Holness rubbed his hands together.

"Well at least you had faith in me Johnny." Bobby nodded towards Johnny

"You let me down Gorman, like you let me down against Noke that day when you missed that sitter." Tony turned around and faced the front again.

"You let yourself down mate... Betting that we'd beat Noke that day!" Retorted Bobby.

One of the snoozing heads chuckled.

"Fucking useless in the end you lot were... Mick! Pull over at Bennet's will you, I need to get some fags." Ordered Tony

"For fucks sake Tony! Fucking buy them the night before in future! I'm not stopping again after this so anyone else who wants anything get it when I stop." Moaned Mick.

They pulled up outside Bennet's newsagents. Tony and Bobby got out and walked into the shop.

BENNETS NEWSAGENTS

The newsagent had all the day's newspapers laid out. The paperboys were loading their sacks. One paper boy was behind the counter. Bobby went to the cold drinks fridge and picked out a bottle of Original Lucozade. Tony went straight to the counter. The newsagent walked around behind the counter. Bobby turned and walked towards the counter and noticed one of the paperboys behind the counter, stealing a packet of Benson & Hedges. The newsagent brushed past him as he walked back around the front. The paperboy also stole a bar of chocolate too as he walked past the display at the front of the counter. Bobby smiled to himself.

"Forty Superqueen Black and fifteen Scratch cards please." Requested Tony, as if this was a normal request so early in the morning.

Bobby was now behind Tony at the counter.

"Bloody hell Tony you do love a gamble don't you!" Bobby was surprised at what he was seeing and hearing.

Tony paid the newsagent. The newsagent put the money in the till then handed Tony his change. Tony walked out of the shop already scratching the first card with one of the coins in his hand. Bobby and the Newsagent looked at each other in disbelief as Bobby paid for his Lucozade.

INSIDE THE WORKVAN

Tony had already settled into his seats and was furiously scratching at the long strip of Scratch cards. Bobby settled into his seat, opened the bottle of Lucozade and took a long swig of it, all the while watching Tony.

"Yes! Fifty quid!" Tony said quietly but excitedly and carried on scratching the remaining cards.

"Nice one!" Bobby said excitedly

"That won't last long!" Exclaimed Mick.

BUILDING SITE IN MANCHESTER PICCADILLY

Tony was up on a set of bandstands laying bricks on part of an internal wall while Bobby was pouring a bucket of mortar on to Tony's spot board, which was propped up on four bricks on edge.

"That'll do with the muck for now. That should do me to finish then I'll point up." Tony said confidently.

Tony turned around and threw his trowel into the fresh pile of mortar. Tony reached into his pocket, pulled out a Scratch card and passed it down to Bobby.

"Go and cash that in for me and get me ten more scratch cards and a quarter bottle of whiskey. Get yourself a can of beer for your trouble." Tony nodded with encouragement hoping Bobby would accept his kind offer for the trouble of going to the shop

"Fucking hell Tone! What about Mick? And the Arab?" Bobby was concerned. Mick Hattersley was their boss. The client that Mick was working for was a Saudi Arabian investor who was on site earlier to meet Mick.

"Don't worry Bob! Mick's gone over to the other job for the day and left Noel the keys to the van to drive us home. The Arab and his Berk of Works have gone to another meeting for the rest of the day so no one's about." Tony smiled at the knowledge he had unexpectedly gained from eaves dropping from outside of the old existing toilet that was next to the room that was acting as the site office, where the meeting was taking place.

"Alright then." Bobby said with an air of confidence knowing that he would not get caught by anyone and that he was not putting his job at risk which he could not afford to lose.

Bobby took the scratch card and walked off towards the stairwell.

"Don't let anyone see mind!" Tony said in a hushed tone.

IN THE SHOP LOCAL TO THE SITE

"Ten Scratch cards, a quarter bottle of Bells and these please." Bobby handed the shopkeeper two cans of Stella Artois and the winning scratch card.

ALLEY WAY BESIDE THE BUILDING SITE

Bobby was walking down the alleyway carrying a blue plastic carrier bag containing the booze. He stopped and pulled one of the cans of premium lager out of the bag. He opened it and downed half of it. He burped then drunk the rest of the contents of the can. He crushed it, threw it into the air then volleyed the can into a large skip that was in the alleyway. He took the other can of lager and bottle of whiskey out of the bag. He pulled his jumper off as the day had turned quite hot. He had a t-shirt on underneath, so he pulled that up and stuffed the booze down into the waist of his Jeans. He pulled his t-shirt back over his jeans and then tied his jumper around his waist.

He scrunched the carrier bag up and put it in his pocket. He turned and walked into the building site through a gap in the hoarding.

BUILDING SITE

Tony was pointing up the freshly laid brickwork as he noticed Bobby walking towards him.

"You've put on a bit of weight son!" Laughed Tony

"That's very insensitive of you Tony!" Chuckled Bobby.

Bobby lifted his jumper and t-shirt up and pulled the can of beer and the bottle of whiskey from his jean's waist. He placed them up onto the bandstand scaffold. He pulled the empty carrier bag out of his pocket and started to put the whiskey in it, but Tony snatched the whiskey, opened it and started to drink out of it pulling a funny face and crossing his eyeballs as he swigged the neat whiskey.

"Bloody hell Tone!" Laughed Bobby

"Where's them scratch cards?" Demanded Tony as he wiped his mouth with the back of his free hand.

"Oh yeah..." Bobby straightened himself then pulled the scratch cards from his back pocket. They were all folded into one. Bobby handed the thick wedge of scratch cards up to Tony. He took them and flicked them, causing the ten cards to fall and hang down in a long line. Tony was holding the line of cards from the top card in his left thumb and forefinger and started scratching it with his pointing rake.

"That's another tenner. We're going down the pub at lunchtime!" Smiled Tony.

Bobby was staring up at Tony in disbelief. Tony carried on, furiously scratching at the next card.

THE OLD BELL PUBLIC HOUSE NEXT TO THE SITE

"Right! I'll have two pints of Guinness and don't worry about letting them settle. I'll have them poured straight through and a large whiskey chaser please. And whatever this lot are having." Tony said with largesse as he held up his hand and pointed downwards with his right index finger, swirling his hand around, gesturing to the barman.

"Nice one Tone. I'll have a Guinness please, but I'll have it the right way thanks very much and I'll have a large whiskey chaser as well." Alan Pressman asked with a big greedy smile on his face.

"Bollocks! You can buy your own chasers! I ain't won that much." Tony sneered.

"Scrap the whiskey mate." Alan said softly.

The Irish barman was pouring the Guinness and nodded at Alan in acknowledgement.

"I'll have a pint of Carlsberg please Tony." Asked Tim Lynch politely.

"And I'll have a Stella please mate." Chipped in Bobby

"Ooh! Wifebeater eh?" Remarked Tim.

The barman had poured the first Guinness straight through and handed it to Tony. Tony held it in front of him, watching it swirling around in its unsettled state.

"Fuck all that settling bollocks! It'll settle soon enough in me guts." Roared Tony.

"Tony started gulping the unsettled Guinness and downed it in one. He slammed the glass down on the bar just as the barman was bringing the other pint of Guinness over. Tony held his hand out to receive it.

Thanks governor." Tony acknowledged the barman's work

which he was very impressed with.

"That's my kind of customer." Remarked the barman in his heavy, deadpan Cork accent. He would never have performed such sacrilege when pouring Guinness had he not been asked to, and neither would he argue with anyone spending their money like that at that time of the day.

"I'll have a shandy as I'm bloody driving. Of all days to be bloody driving the van. Micks stitched me right up!" Noel Grimwood said sadly, shaking his head.

All of them laughed. Tony started downing the next pint of Guinness but only drank half of it then put it down and wiped his mouth. The Barman was pouring the rest of the drinks.

"He's going for it today, even by his standards." Tim whispered into Bobby's ear.

"That ain't the half of it mate. He's had me up the offy already for more scratch cards and half a bottle of whisky, which he's nearly drunk already. I've had a couple of sneaky cans meself. Is it always like this on site?" Whispered Bobby back into Tim's ear

"Not really but sometimes we do have a couple at lunchtimes during the week, but mostly Fridays. Be careful though, because if Mick ever finds out, your gone!" Whispered Tim

"Ok." Bobby whispered his reply back.

The Barman had finished pouring the drinks and put them all on the bar. He handed Tony his whiskey chaser last. Tony pulled out some cash from his pocket and handed the Barman a twenty-pound note.

"Have one yourself mate." Nodded Tony.

"Thank you, sir. I'll have a small whiskey with you." The barman responded appreciatively

"Lovely sir!" Tony acknowledged the barman and turned to

face Bobby.

So, Mr Bobby Gorman, tell us what really happened at Portham then? Everyone's been dying to ask." Tony now had the Dutch courage to ask the question that everyone had been dying to ask as he was half cut.

The rest of the crew all looked a bit sheepish.

"Nothing much to tell really." Bobby replied, shrugging his shoulders.

"Oh, go on!" Johnny egged on Bobby.

"You probably all know the story anyway. But alright... I suppose you should hear it from the horse's mouth. Well as you all know, the Icelandic lot took over from Dickie when he had to sell up as he wasn't well. As soon as they took over, they started shouting the odds to us all. Neil was having none of it and told them to stick it. He retired as he said he couldn't face managing another club and was probably going to retire at the end of that season anyway. He put a word in for me to take over as manager as I had been made up to his assistant after Dave had passed away. I had just done all my coaching badges and really wanted to have a go at it, but the Icelandic lot said they would keep me on but had their own bloke they wanted to bring in as manager. So, I thought I would stay but me and the new bloke didn't see eye to eye. Now this is the bit you probably don't know about... The new bloke tried giving it the big'un in the changing room, right in front of all the players and his new coaches. He was trying to blame me for the losing run we were on, so I ended up losing it. I steamed into him, as it was all his fault what was going on, and the players knew it too. They all fucking cheered when I put him on his arse and kicked fuck out him, but his coaches waded in and started putting the boot into me. Some of the players joined in on my behalf so it was fucking bedlam. Some of the players broke it up because the new chairman just happened to walk in, right in the middle of it going off. Needless to say, I was sacked straight away and most of the players were sold on for siding with me. You know the rest. They ended up getting relegated and going down again the season after. All our hard work getting there and staying there all that time, against all the odds, all those good times, were suddenly all gone.

"Well fuck me... Mick better watch out then!" Laughed Tony.

The rest of the crew started laughing.

"I did hear there was some kind of fight, but nobody ever knew for sure." Tim remarked, shaking his head at the information he had received.

"The club put out a statement that I had been a disruptive influence. They blamed me and the players for it all, even though we were fine until the change of ownership. Most people knew it was bullshit. The tossers had me nicked an all." Bobby said, as he looked at the crew of builders, who were hanging on to his every word

Bobby took a sip of his beer.

"I've tried getting back in the game, but nobody seems to want to know, so here I am with you lot. My old landlady knew Mick and got me a start keeping you lot in bricks and muck." Bobby shrugged his shoulders with an air of defeat.

"I bet you never thought that would happen eh lad?" Alan said sarcastically

"You're fucking right there! But I've got bills to pay, kids and a mortgage... I don't know fuck all other than football, so until I can get back in, I'll be labouring for you lot!" Bobby said with a grim smile on his face.

Bobby finished his pint.

"Anyway, I'll get them in." Bobby put his glass on the bar and reached into his pocket.

Alan gestured with his hand to stop Bobby.

"No, you won't lad. You've given me enough good times and memories over the years... You don't need to get the drinks in." Alan assured their new labourer.

"That's right. Me and Al used to get over there all the time. You can tell us a few more stories along the way." Tim said with an air of reminiscence.

"Listen to you Portham tossers!" Sneered Noel.

"At least we ain't glory hunters like you lot. At least we support our hometown club." Retorted Tim smugly.

Bollocks! You ain't been for years!" Noel screwed his face up

"Noel here..." Alan pointed towards Noel.

"Is a Man united supporter. So, he probably won't be too forthcoming with buying you a beer." Alan said very sarcastically.

"I really enjoyed scoring that goal that knocked you lot out the cup that year!" Bobby said very sternly but couldn't help smiling.

Bobby stared off into the distance for a split second of reminiscence then stared at Noel with a big smile on his face.

"Fuckin tosser! But don't worry, I'll still stand my round... Begrudgingly! Even though I'm drinking fuckin shandy, cos I've got to drive you fuckin twats home!" Noel said with an air of disappointment.

Noel was staring back at Bobby giving him an evil stare but they both ended up smiling at each other.

"Don't worry Noel, I'll get them in. We'll let you off... As your driving!" Alan laughed.

The rest of the crew all joined in the laughter.

BACK ON THE BUILDING SITE AFTER THE LIQUID LUNCH

Bobby was walking into a room with a bucket of mortar on his shoulder. He was ready to pass it out through the window reveal out onto the scaffold for Alan. The sun was shining brightly through the opening and was dazzling Bobby's eyes, forcing him to squint.

"Here are Al.... Al..." Bobby was trying to get Alan's attention

Bobby put the bucket down on the floor. He looked out through the window opening onto the scaffold and saw Alan sat down asleep, snoring, resting back against the scaffold handrail.

"Leave it there Bobby. That fat lazy cunt's been asleep for the last quarter of an hour. That's what an hour an half down the pub does to you in this heat. Glad I was on the shandy." Noel said proudly.

Bobby passed the bucket of muck through to Noel then climbed out onto the scaffold through the window.

"He's just about covered his money today, so I'll finish these last few courses, so Mick won't clock on tomorrow if he checks up. Stick a bit on his board and come and put the rest on mine." Noel said softly.

Bobby picked up Alan's trowel and started knocking up the mortar on Alan's spot board then tipped some of the mortar from the bucket onto the mortar board. He then walked towards Noel then emptied the rest of the bucket's contents out onto Noel's spot board.

"You stink of booze son!" Chuckled Noel.

Bobby cupped his hand to his mouth and smelled his breath.

"Here... Fancy laying a few?" Noel asked inquisitively.

"Yeah, fuck it why not. You have to stink of booze to do this job don't you? I thought that was part of the training. You all stink of booze most of the time anyway." Bobby said confidently. Feeling reassured that he wasn't the only one in the world who liked a few beers.

"Aye, most people in this game are pissheads. You should think of doing something else other than this lark. But while you're here, you may as well learn something. Watch and learn. "Noel said with an air of smugness, due to his thirty plus years in the game.

"Now listen very carefully, I shall say this only once! "Noel said in a mock French accent.

Noel picked up his trowel and leant down to the mortar board and sliced some mortar away from the main pile. He scooped it up and dropped it down on to the board.

"Doing this, knocks it up again as best as possible." Noel informed his eager looking protégé

Noel spread the mortar onto the brickwork then laid some bricks. He then used his spirit level to level the bricks by tapping the handle of his trowel onto the spirit level then scraped the excess mortar off with his trowel in one quick movement.

"That's all there is to it really. Once you've laid a few, you make sure they're level. Go and grab his trowel and have a go. I'll keep an eye on you. Once you've done that, I'll show you how to point up." Noel was getting excited at being able to pass on his knowledge and that it would save him some work in covering for Alan.

"Cheers Noel. I've been dying to get on the trowel." Bobby was excited too.

Bobby walked over to the still snoozing Alan and picked up his trowel from the mortar board and started knocking some mortar up.

"I know you're awake you lazy fucker!" Whispered Bobby.

"Well keep the noise down and wake me up when you start wrapping up. At least you're getting an education!" Alan whispered back.

IN THE WORK VAN ON THE WAY HOME

Noel was driving and Alan was in the front passenger seat. Tim, Tony, Bobby and Johnny were in the back. Everybody apart from Noel had a can of beer in their hand.

"I'm fucking dying for a piss now!" Shouted Alan

"I fuckin told you lot I'm not stopping anymore. Piss in a can if you have to!" Noel turned his head slightly as he shouted back to his workmates.

"Here Bobby, pass us one of my marigolds from my bucket will you." Alan asked, as is if it was a normal thing do be asking.

"Oh, for fuck's sake!" Bobby spat as he knew it was down to him to grab the glove as he was the nearest and because he was the labourer for them all. Which he hated but knew he had to suffer this to bring home some much needed cash.

Bobby turned around and pulled one of the yellow marigold gloves from Alan's tool bucket. As he turned back around, Tony was standing up with his tracksuit trousers and pants around his ankles, with his scrotum fully stretched out in his clenched fist with his testicles bulging out of the other end of his fist.

"Fucking hell Tone!" Bobby was disgusted for a millisecond before he could not help but burst into laughter.

The rest of the men erupted with laughter.

"He's been waiting for a new victim for his party trick!" Laughed Johnny

"Put them fucking things away before they hurt someone!" Bobby laughed.

The whole van erupted with even louder laughter. Bobby pushed past the still standing Tony and passed the Marigold glove to Alan who was already undoing his jeans. The van had slowed down, but Noel put his foot down and accelerated quickly, catching Tony off balance making him fall backwards, still with his trousers around his ankles. His bare buttocks ended up pressed against the back-door window. Two women in a car behind them looked utterly shocked. The whole van was rocking with laughter as Tony fell over onto the floor.

"Oh, shit I forgot this window won't open! Someone get rid of this please. Quick!" Demanded Alan.

Alan was holding aloft the yellow marigold glove with his thumb and forefinger by the wrist part of the glove. The glove was full of urine and looked as if there was a hand actually in the glove. The index finger had a small pinhole at the fingertip. Urine was spurting out of it. Everyone was trying to avoid the jet of urine as it arced towards them all. Tim slid open the sliding window in the side door of the van.

"Fuckin give it here will ya!" Tim demanded, slightly panicking, trying to take control of the situation, as he did not want Tony's warm urine splashing over him or anywhere near his limited amount of seating space.

Tim grabbed the wrist of the marigold glove with his thumb and forefinger and threw it out onto the hard shoulder of the M6. Tony had managed to get to his seat but still had his trousers and pants around his ankles.

"I need a piss now after all that excitement!" Tony said as he tried to adjust himself. His penis and scrotum were hanging off of the bench.

"You should have seen them old dear's faces!" Johnny laughed.

"I thought the driver was going to have heart attack!" Bobby was hysterical.

Tony picked up an empty beer can and started to urinate into it. His aim was somewhat off, due to the amount booze he had a consumed throughout the day. The slit of his glans was fully open with the jet of urine flowing out of it. The tip of his glans touched the cans tab opener, causing a ricochet which resulted in the urine splashing off the tip of the can down onto Tonys pants and trousers around his ankle and onto the floor.

"I'm going to need a jab after this journey!" Remarked Bobby.

Tony had finished urinating. He put the can down and started pulling his pants and trousers up but accidentally kicked the can over. It started rolling down the middle of the floor between the rows of seats either side of the van. It was spilling urine out of it. Tim picked it up, opened the sliding window and threw it out.

"Uuurrrghh! I could feel the warmth of his piss through the can!" Tim said with a distorted, disgusted face.

A river of urine was now flowing toward the back of the van, where a crumpled bunch of flowers laid on the van floor.

"This is fucking disgusting!" Bobby sneered.

"I bet you didn't get any of this on the old team bus eh Bobby?" Noel remarked smugly.

"No! We fuckin never! Them flowers you bought for your missus are well and truly fucked now Tony." Bobby was not impressed all.

"They needed watering!" Tony shot back.

All of them were laughing except for Bobby, who took a big swig from his can of beer then looked out of the window.

BOBBY AND VICKY'S BEDROOM

Bobby staggered into the dark bedroom. He started to undress himself, banging into the bedside table as he went. Vicky was already in bed.

"Where have you been? You fuckin stink! You better have a shower before you get in here!" Vicky snapped.

"I can't fucking do this job much longer. They're fucking animals..." Slurred Bobby.

Bobby pulled the covers back and fell into bed.

"Bobby? Bobby? Get up and have a shower will you! Bobby?" Pleaded Vicky.

Bobby was snoring.

"Bloody hell!" Shouted Vicky.

Vicky got up, grabbed her pillows and stormed out of the bedroom.

TEN MONTHS LATER OUTSIDE OF BOBBY AND VICKY'S HOUSE

The work van pulled up outside of Bobby's house. Bobby jumped out.

"See you in the morning chaps." Shouted Bobby.

Bobby slammed the van door shut and walked towards his house. He pulled his keys out of his coat pocket as he was walking. He stopped at the front door of his house and put the key into the lock.

HALLWAY OF BOBBY AND VICKY'S HOUSE

"Hello dad. You alright?" Asked his daughter Annabel in her Manchester accent.

"No comment darling!" Bobby said as he walked into his house, his castle. He had managed to buy the house while still playing. They still had a few years left on the mortgage. Vicky's parents were from Denton and so were some of the players at Portham and it wasn't far from the ground or from Manchester, so it made sense to move there.

He kicked his trainers off and walked over and hugged Annabel. He kissed his daughter on the forehead.

"Is that you love? Vicky shouted from the kitchen.

"Yes love, it is the labourer extraordinaire!" Bobby said with mock enthusiasm.

Bobby walked through the hallway and into the kitchen where Vicky was chopping an onion. He kissed her on the cheek.

"Anyone rung?" Bobby asked hopefully.

"Nope!" Responded Vicky sharply.

"I really can't take this anymore. I really can't babe." Bobby said with open arms.

"Maybe it's time to start looking at doing something else." Vicky said as she turned from the chopping board to face Bobby, looking him squarely in the eyes

"Like what?" Asked Bobby in a defeated manner.

Annabel walked in.

"Dad, I'll leave uni if it's going to help you..." Annabel said reassuringly.

"Darling, I've told you before. You ain't leaving uni. But I really appreciate your offer darling I really do. I'm so proud of you!" Bobby grabbed his daughter and gave her a kiss on her forehead and cuddled her tightly.

THE BRITISH LION PUBLIC HOUSE

Albert was sitting on a stool at the bar, reading his paper and drinking a light and bitter. Dave Peters, the landlord, was pointing a remote control toward the TV on the wall out in the bar area. The door opened and Jimmy Archer, a short, well-dressed man, walked in. He stopped for a minute to look around, then walked over towards the bar.

"Albert Gorman!" Boomed Jimmy.

Albert looked up towards Jimmy.

"Bloody hell Jim! Where you been hiding?" Albert smiled.

Albert got up and walked towards Jimmy. They hugged each other hard and slapped each other on their backs. They broke off from their embrace and shook hands warmly. They held each other's other arms. They looked into each other's eyes for a moment then broke away from each other.

"Dave! Get him a large whiskey please mate and I'll have one an all." Albert ordered loudly.

"No, I'll get these in! How are you, Jimmy?" Asked Dave warmly.

Dave held his hand out over the bar towards Jimmy's already outstretched hand.

"Not too bad Dave, not too bad!" Jimmy said as they shook hands.

They broke off their handshake. Dave then reached under the bar and pulled out three small glasses. He slammed them down on the bar with one hand and then reached back under and pulled out his most expensive bottle of whiskey. An 18-year-old Glenvalley.

"For special occasions." Dave pursed his lips and nodded his head towards his old pals.

"A fine choice David! So, come on Jim, what's been happening? You look well..." remarked Albert

"Well to answer your original question, I had been hiding out in Spain, but I got grassed up and ended up getting extradited back home. Ended up doing five years down in Dover nick in the end!" Jimmy informed his old mates.

"You don't look like you been in nick though?" Albert said with prying eyes.

"Well, I have been out for a few months. I had to nip back out to Spain. To tie up a few loose ends shall we say, but now I'm back." Jimmy announced.

"What about your gaff in Spain? Asked Albert.

"Still got it. Cindy always owned it so they couldn't take it off me." Jimmy remarked with a mock air of smugness.

"Nice one!" Albert nudged his old mate.

"I lost a few quid but I'm not on the breadline just yet!" Jimmy assured them all.

Dave lined the drinks up.

"No, I bet you ain't! I still wouldn't mind being a pound behind ya!" Dave laughed, feeling slightly bitter at some of the chances he never took when Jimmy had offered from time to time in the past. He always turned them down as could never face the prospect of going to jail.

They all picked their drinks up and raised their glasses to each other. They all proceeded to down their whiskies in one. They all winced in their own way as they put their glasses down.

"So... What brings you back then Jim?" he asked inquisitively.

"Well, I always had a little share in Wickside didn't I... The other blokes wanted to sell up. They were pretty desperate, as I think they were in a bit of trouble, so they got hold of me and I ended up getting the whole club for a song!" Chuckled Jimmy as he still could not quite believe it himself.

"It's not been good over there for a while now." Said Dave.

"I know mate but there's a lot of potential there. You still get over there Alb?" Jimmy asked in a probing way, to try and gauge if his investment had been worth it.

"I don't really take much notice now Jim." Smirked Albert.

"I've got Stevie Cootes coming down. He should be here soon."

Jimmy informed his friends.

"Yeah, he was in the other day. He mentioned there were going to be some changes, but he didn't say what was happening." Dave said.

"Fuck me he's been there some years now! Part of the double winning side eh Jim?" Albert said.

"One of the greatest sides ever Alb, if not THE greatest!" Exclaimed Jimmy.

"We still beat you twice that year!" Dave piped up.

"Well, you never won fuck all that year though!" Albert jumped in.

"Yeah, and you only ended up playing for them because you couldn't get a game with us." Jimmy retorted

"It was a tough decision. He needed to get some games, so we reluctantly let him go." Albert said in a mock football managers voice.

They all laughed except Dave.

"Bollocks! Old Jonesy said it was the worst decision he ever made letting me go. He did try getting me back, but I wanted to stay loyal." Remarked Dave, in his own recollective way.

"Now that's fuckin bollocks!" Albert said confidently.

As Albert was speaking, the door opened. Stevie Cootes, who was a large man, wearing a tracksuit and glasses, walked in.

"Bloody hell! Now let me guess... Are we discussing our double winning triumph in sixty-four and how Dave had to be let go?" Boomed Stevie.

Stevie looked over to a faded part of the wall.

"Where's the picture?" Stevie was not impressed.

"I had to take it down... It was scaring all the customers!" Joked Dave.

"Fuckin liberty!" Remarked Albert.

"Your jealousy finally got the better of you Dave?" Sniffed Stevie.

"Calm down girls! Rose knocked it down when she was cleaning. As much as it cheered me up seeing it all smashed on the floor, I'm getting it repaired. Gary the glazier's putting a new bit of glass in." Said Dave.

"Alright, nice one Dave, but tell him to hurry up please, it's part of our heritage!" Sniffed Steve.

"I see your photo's still up! Rose didn't knock that one down did she! There's something missing in that picture... I can't quite put me finger on it..." Albert said in a mock questioning style.

"Yeah, I can't either Alb. What can it be Jim?" Stevie agreed.

Jimmy walked towards the picture.

"Looks like there's a trophy or two missing chaps!" Jimmy chuckled.

"Oh, change the bloody record will ya!" Dave snorted.

They all laughed. Dave walked over to serve another customer.

"I'm glad you're here Albert. Shall we all take a seat? We've all got a bit of catching up to do." Said Steve.

Jimmy got a fifty pound note out and held it in his thumb and forefinger, holding it to catch Dave's eye.

"Stick that behind the ramp Dave. Same again and keep them coming mate, drinks are on me tonight lads! Have one yourself as well Dave." Jimmy offered.

"Lovely jubbly!" Dave responded acceptingly.

The three of them took a seat as Dave started pouring the drinks. He opened up a door behind the bar which had a stairway leading down to the cellar and another stairway which led upstairs to where Dave lived.

"Sue! You better get down here! It's getting busy now!" shouted Dave

Alright! Be down in a minute!" Sue shouted back.

"I take it Jimmy's filled you in?" Steve said as if everyone knew what he meant.

"Yeah. Well sort of anyway. So, I take it you already knew?" Albert stumbled with his words.

"Yeah, but it's all come about a bit quick. The brothers have gone skint! Their building firm got knocked for a load of money, so they sold their stake in the club to Jimmy to keep themselves going." Said Stevie.

"Yeah, I'd been speaking to Stevie, and he told me what was happening, so I stepped in. Otherwise, the club would've been fucked and probably would've gone under an all. Trouble is, I played football, but I know fuck all about actually running a club." Jimmy said without any airs or graces to try and communicate that he did not have a clue what he was doing.

"That's where you come in Alb…" Stevie said with a kind of knowing look on his face which he tried to impress upon to Albert.

"Go on…" Cajoled Albert.

"When we got up, we wanted to be challenging for the promotion straight away, but the brothers didn't put any more money in, so I knew things weren't good with them. We've struggled ever since. The managers lost the dressing room now and he's going to have to go. I've put the feelers out, but no one wants to know because of all the grief.

"And if I'm honest, I can't be involved for too long as the whole things just a money pit. I ain't as flush as I used to be, so I'm talking to a few contacts who might be able to take it off me hands and make a good fist of it. The only thing is, they won't really touch it until things have settled down." Said Jimmy.

"So, like I said, that's where you come in." Assured Stevie.

"So, you said..." Albert said pensively.

"We've got to get the club back on an even keel or its fucked." Stevie informed them.

"What... Proper fucked?" Albert asked with a perplexed expression.

"Proper fucked." Nodded Stevie in a matter-of-fact way

"For good probably." Chipped in Jimmy.

"Go on..." Albert remarked inquisitively.

"Well, I'm going to have to sack Clive. He knows it's coming but he's holding out for a pay off." Stevie shook his head in dismay.

"A fuckin pay off?" Albert spat in disbelief.

"I'll have to... when we went up, we turned pro to keep the lads on and to try and get us to the next level. All the clubs are paying now in this division." Conceded Stevie.

"Well fuck me! I'll have a go if you get paid for it!" Chuckled Albert in disbelief.

"It weren't you we had in mind Alb..." Jimmy remarked with a frowning smile.

CHAPTER IX
ONCE MORE UNTO THE BREACH

BOBBY AND VICKY'S BEDROOM

Bobby and Vicky were in bed making love. Their movement stopped. Vicky fell breathlessly towards Bobby.

"I'll have to get a new job offer more often! That was fuckin lovely!" Said a breathless, post coital Bobby.

Vicky slowly manoeuvred herself off of Bobby.

"Yeah, it was fuckin lovely weren't it!" Mimicked Vicky in a very good cockney accent.

They both laughed.

"I'm not really sure about it... I didn't really understand it all. You were a bit too excited, and your dad sounded pissed out of his head on the phone!" Vicky chuckled.

"Right! What it is, it's our old local football club. Wickside FC. Me dad and his mates all played for them and me and all my mates played for them. It's a proper old club by Hackney Wick. It was one of the first clubs to join the Football league. It was formed by the blokes from the toy factory that made the little toy tin soldiers that all the young boys had before they started making them in plastic. So, the team were nicknamed The Tin Soldiers and because it was right next to Hackney Wick, they called themselves Wickside Football Club and..." Vicky interrupted her husband who was in full nostalgic flow.

"Alright that's really boring! How much you going to get paid?" enquired Vicky, laughing as she spoke.

Bobby laughed.

"Alright! This is an important bit of family history I'm talking about here. They did well, but fell out of the leagues and went right down, but in the last few years they got themselves into the league below the Conference but..."

"How much?" Vicky more sternly.

"I'm getting to that bit now. They've offered me a grand a week to be the manager... And to help them get the club running right, with a view to some new investors taking it on. There's a lot of potential, but investors or any decent managers won't go near it at the moment and what with nobody wanting to go near me, it all makes sense. It gets me back in the game and it will show bigger clubs that I'm prepared to do things the hard way to get back in." Bobby assured his wife.

"The money's brilliant but it means you being down there though. You mentioned a flat?" Probed Vicky.

"Well Jimmy, who's me dad's old mate and the one who owns the club now, has got a few flats that he rents out and one of them is his old council flat near mum and dad. It's coming free soon, and he says I can live there rent free. I'll just have to pay the gas and electric." Bobby enthused.

"So, you're gonna be at your mum and dads for a while then?" Vicky asked knowing the answer.

"Yeah. But I can come back up a couple of days a week and if you want to come down, I can afford to sort an hotel out until I'm in the flat. It's too good to turn down Vick!" Bobby was looking at the ceiling.

"I'm worried though! What it'll do to us..." Vicky turned towards her husband.

Vicky turned on her side and cuddled up to Bobby, who was

still on his back, looking at the ceiling.

"We'll be fine darling seriously. It's what I've always wanted. It's just ended up being at a club out the league. If I can get them stable and maybe get promoted, it can all change. If it doesn't work out, I can always come back to carting bricks and muck about for Mick and his crew." Bobby assured Vicky.

"Are you fuckin joking? You fucking hate it and its turned you into a right pisshead!" Sneered Vicky.

"I know, but it kept us going. Your right though, if this goes tits up, I'll get a nice office job or something." Bobby said.

"You in an office? I don't think so. You'll end up beating someone up!" Laughed Vicky, punching Bobby gently.

"Well, that's why I've got to give this a go love. But if you don't want me to, then I won't..." Bobby was serious as he loved his wife more than anything.

Bobby pulled himself onto his side and faced Vicky.

"If you really don't want me to then I..."

"It's fine! Let's give it a go!" Interrupted Vicky

Bobby leant across and kissed Vicky on the lips.

"Thanks darling."

Vicky turned over onto her other side and Bobby cuddled up to her back. The hallway light was shining on her face. She had tears in her eyes.

"It's alright Vick. It's gonna be alright." Bobby was trying to reassure his wife.

"I know. I'm alright. Ring them tomorrow and tell them you'll take it." Snivelled Vicky.

"Only if you're hundred percent?" Bobby was willing to turn this down if Vicky didn't want him to go.

"Yes, Bob take it. It's what you know. We'll get by." Vicky said softly, wiping her eyes.

"Sweet as Vick. I fuckin love you!" Bobby was excited.

"I love you too. We'll talk to Anabel and Liam about it tomorrow." Vicky closed her eyes.

BOBBY AND VICKY'S LIVING ROOM THE NEXT MORNING

Bobby was sitting down on the sofa wearing a dressing gown and gorilla slippers, which were a bit of a joke Christmas present from Vicky, but he loved them as they kept his feet warm as he had bad circulation which was a hangover from his playing days He was speaking on the phone.

"Is that you Jimmy? "Bobby asked enthusiastically knowing it was Jimmy.

"Yeah... who's this?" Jimmy answered groggily

"It's Bobby Gorman." Smiled Bobby as he imagined Jimmy in bed probably hungover after a skinful in the pub.

"Bobby... Fuck me boy do you know what time it is?" Jimmy chuckled. His voice slightly hoarse probably from a few cigars that Bobby knew that Jimmy would have smoked whilst having a drink.

"Yeah, sorry mate I know it's a bit early, but this is when I get up for work." Bobby joked.

"Sorry son... I'm feeling a bit delicate. I was out with the old man and Stevie weren't I... I take it that's why you're ringing. I don't normally get up for another couple of hours."

"Yeah. I'm in!" Bobby could hardly contain his excitement.

"Good boy! Nice one! When can you start?" Asked Jimmy, sounding very pleased that his plan had come to fruition.

"As soon as bloody possible!" Bobby exclaimed.

"Alright, lovely Bob. I'll get things moving from my end and sort things out with Stevie. Replied Jimmy, chuckling.

"When will you know? I need to know when I can pack this poxy job in." Pleaded Bobby.

"Tell 'em today mate." Jimmy replied very casually.

"Yeah, that's alright, but when will I start getting paid by you?" Bobby asked nervously.

"Shall we say from Monday then? I'll have to pay you cash until we get the other manager sorted." Jimmy said quickly.

"What, sack him you mean?" Laughed Bobby nervously.

"I prefer the term, part company with. That's what they say ain't it?" Jimmy laughed.

"Something like that... It all feels a bit moody to me." Bobby felt a pang of guilt wash over him.

"Listen son, he has to go. It hasn't worked out. It's not your problem. He's getting a payoff. You're a proper football bloke. We think he's out of his depth really, which is a shame, but you can come in and really sort this place out. They'll respect you for what you have done in the game and because of your ties to this club." Jimmy reassured Bobby. He did not want Bobby having any second thoughts.

"Maybe, but it just don't sit right with me really but I suppose that's how it goes. Look what happened to me!" Bobby felt a bit better about the situation.

"Exactly! So, don't worry. Now you go and jack your job in then I can get a couple a more hours kip!" Jimmy instructed his new manager.

"Alright Jim, thanks for all this, I really appreciate it." Bobby replied very gratefully.

"That's alright mate, thanks for giving it a go. I'll give Stevie a ring and get him to get a contract sorted then I'll get him to give you a bell." Jimmy sounded a bit more upbeat but wanted to get his head back down and sleep off some more of the whiskey.

"Cheers Jimmy. See you later."

"Ta da mate. Ta da." Bobby put the phone down. He slumped back into the chair, staring into space, deep in thought.

Vicky walked in. She was in her dressing gown, brushing her hair.

"Morning love." She bent down and gave him a kiss. She rose back up.

"Well?" Enquired Vicky.

"I just spoke to Jimmy and he's going to start paying me from Monday." Bobby was staring into space, trying to comprehend everything that had transpired in the last twelve hours or so.

"Oh Brilliant! What are you going to do? Are you going to work?" Vicky was genuinely pleased for her husband.

"I'd love to ring Mick now and tell him I'm not going back but I want to give him some notice. You never know, I might need him if it all goes tits up with this thing." Bobby looked at Vicky.

"Just have a chat with him today. We'll have a few things to sort out." Vicky was already a few steps ahead of Bobby with regard to what would have to be sorted out to facilitate the change that was coming to their lives.

"Yeah, I'll have a word with him today." Bobby stared into space again. A thousand thoughts flowing through his mind.

CAFE UP THE ROAD FROM THE BUILDING SITE

"So, what do you want? You either want a pay rise or your leaving!" Mick got straight to the point.

"How do you know?" Bobby was taken aback.

"Blokes don't normally want to take me for a cup of tea unless they want a pay rise! So, come on, spit it out!" Mick Smiled.

"There's no flies on you eh Mick!" Bobby smiled back at his very soon to be former boss.

"Nope!" Mick smiled even more at his insight that had been gained from over forty years in the building game.

"Look Mick, I've had a job offer, a manager's job back in London. Mine and me dad's old team." Bobby felt uncomfortable as he had grown to like Mick's no-nonsense attitude and because he was the only person who was willing to give him a job at the time.

"Well, it's better than the other option!" Mick said very seriously.

"Eh?" Bobby was confused.

"Well at least I don't have to give you a pay rise!" Smiled Mick.

They both laughed.

"Listen pal. It's what you do. I always knew you'd be off as soon as something in football come up. I just didn't think it would take this long!" Mick chuckled.

"That's why I've gotta take it Mick. The offers ain't exactly been flying in." Bobby said forlornly.

"It's alright. I'll be gutted to see you go. You're a grafter. I think the boys will be sad to see you go too. But listen, if you ever need a start, you just give me a bell. You know... If it don't work out... Or you end up chinning some cunt!"

They both laughed out loud.

"Thanks Mick it means a lot. As much as I've hated it. I've loved it as well. When the boys get in here I'm gonna buy 'em all breakfast. Even Tony!" Bobby smiled.

"When you finishing?" Asked Mick.

"Well straight away really Mick, today if possible, as they want me to start Monday and I'll have a lot to get sorted but I don't want to leave you in the lurch like..." Bobby said a bit sagely.

"It will but fuck it! Go and follow your dream son. We'll manage. I suppose I'll have to knock the fucking muck up now won't I!" Mick looked to the sky. This is what happened whenever a labourer jacked in or got sacked. Mick always did the labouring until he got a replacement.

They both chuckled. They looked each other in the eyes. Bobby offered his hand and Mick responded. They shook hands across the table.

"Nice one Mick." Said a relieved Bobby.

"If it does go tits up then you give me a ring and I'll sort you out." Mick said sternly. He had grown to like Bobby too. He wasn't sure about him at first, but he knew he must have had something about him to take a job labouring to support his family.

"That means the world mate." Bobby was feeling a bit emotional.

"No problem. You better get the breakfasts in. Here come the troops!" Mick nodded towards the entrance door.

Bobby looked around. Tony, Alan and Johnny were walking towards their table.

"I'll leave you to it. I've got to get to the other job for a meeting." Mick pushed his chair back.

They shook hands again and embraced and patted each other's backs. They broke away from each other and Mick walked off, acknowledging the others as he passed them.

"What's all this about?" Tony was shocked at what he saw.

"Could our lad be leaving us?" Alan could tell.

"I'll let him tell you" Mick said as he hurried out. He did not want to be pestered by his workers with small talk and banter as he had to get away.

"What's all this cuddling the gaffer bollocks then?" Tony asked loudly for effect.

They all sat down at the same table.

"I'm off lads! Got a manager's job down in London. I'm going home to manage the club I played for as a boy, before I went to Artillery." Bobby beamed.

The weight had been lifted from his shoulders and now he could relax. He was ready for the grilling he was about to receive from the stalwarts of Mick's firm.

"I knew it! I knew you were leaving as soon as I walked in." Alan was happy with his own quick deduction of the situation.

"What's the club called? As I suppose I'll have to look out for the results now then!" Tony said begrudgingly.

"Wickside. They're in the Isthmian south, one down from the Conference." Bobby said trying to sell it as best as he could.

"Fuck me, we'll have to go on Ceefax to find them results!" Laughed Johnny.

"I doubt their results will even be on there!" Chuckled Tony.

They all laughed.

"Yeah, funny as ever Tone! At least I won't have to look at your stretched-out bollocks anymore!" Bobby started giggling.

"You'll miss em! No, good luck to you kid. It's about time you got another chance." Tony said very seriously. He liked Bobby but didn't like to let it on too often.

"How much you getting for that then?" Asked Johnny, thinking that it would be a lot.

"Put it this way, a little bit more than I'm getting now!" Bobby replied and smiled and winked at Johnny.

"It's probably not as much as you think though Johnny. There's no money down them leagues. I think the equivalent up here is the Evo-stick league, you know, Hyde, Hinkley..." Alan informed his colleague.

"Oh right! Not too glamorous then." Johnny sounded a bit disappointed.

"Nope. It's gonna be hard work. The clubs not been run very well and I'm going to have to sort it from top to bottom. They're not too far off being able to push for promotion. Anyway, go and order your grub... My shout." Bobby pointed to the counter encouragingly.

"Lovely!" Alan got straight up.

"Look at him, fat bastard! Straight up there!" Tony sneered.

Johnny got up, then Tony got up and followed. Bobby sat for a moment, staring at them with a smile on his face. He got up and walked towards them all at the counter, happy and hoping that this would be the last time he would be coming in here at this time of the morning.

PORTCULLIS STREET OUTSIDE WICKSIDE FC GROUND

Jimmy, Steve, Albert and Bobby were standing outside of the Wickside FC football ground which had turnstiles either side of the main entrance, which led to the boardroom and changing rooms. They were all looking up at the club crest which consisted of two Grenadier Guards wearing red jackets, black trousers and bearskin hats, holding rifles at their sides, standing guard either side of an old fort. Underneath the image were the words "The Fort" all of which was encapsulated in a vesica piscis shape to form a shield.

"What happened to the old one?" Asked a very puzzled Jimmy.

"It went years ago! Good job an all. It wasn't very PC was it!" Sneered Albert.

"Well, it weren't really. It was derived from the top of one of the old tin boxes that the little tin soldiers were sold in by the old toy factory, which depicted Rourke's drift. It showed dead or wounded soldiers with spears hanging out of 'em and Zulu's being shot and bayoneted. The actual club crest wasn't as detailed, but everyone knew what its roots were. There were complaints so it had to go... And rightly so." Stevie remarked casually.

"It was pretty naughty. I'm glad it's gone too. I think this ones much better... The Fort! Who'd have thought it eh dad? Me, managing our club." Bobby said proudly.

"It's a proud day son!" Albert beamed.

"We're all proud." Said Jimmy.

Stevie was standing between Bobby and Jimmy. He put his arms around them.

Yes Bobby. Tin soldiers together, eh? Thanks for doing this lads." Stevie was so happy with this situation, having gone through heaven and hell with the club in recent years trying with all his heart to keep it in existence.

"No worries. It's my pleasure." Bobby put his arm around Stevie's waist and squeezed in acknowledgement.

"I couldn't stand by and see our old club in trouble." Remarked Jimmy.

"Do they still play Tin Soldier when the players come out?" Bobby asked excitedly.

"Nah! The brothers stopped it years ago when they tried to modernise the club. Same time as they changed the crest. The fans still sing their version though." Smiled Stevie.

"We're definitely playing it from now on! Anyway, how did my predecessor take the news?" Bobby asked.

"He said if I was a bit younger, he would've give me a dig so I told him to give it a try but he never did… All mouth!" Smirked Stevie.

"He did get a bit lemon, but I advised him it wasn't a good idea and he soon shut up. I waited while he cleared his desk and the rest of his gear. Anyway, he's paid off and gone now." Jimmy said proudly.

"Shame really, as Clive was a nice bloke. It started off well, but it just didn't work out in the end. He's got it in his mind that he's been stitched up, but he had to go for the good of the club. I'm sure he'll get another job." Stevie assured Bobby, who he could see still felt uneasy, about how everything that had transpired.

Bobby stared intently at the club crest.

LIVING ROOM OF MATT AND DORIS HOOPER'S THIRTEENTH FLOOR HIGH RISE FLAT

Matt Hooper, a shabbily dressed, overweight man, with long greasy hair was slumped on the sofa. He had a table on wheels in front of him which had open Chinese take away foil dishes on it and a plate with some of the food on it. There was a half full, two litre bottle of coke which was squashed in the middle, next to the plate. There was also a pair of glasses, a notepad and a pen on the table. The television was on very loud. The light of the television filled the room as there weren't any lights on. The national lottery update came on to the television screen. He sat up and dug his spoon into the food on the plate and then stuffed the spoonful of food into his mouth. He put the spoon back onto the plate. He picked up the pair of black rimmed glasses that contained thick glass bottle type lenses. He put them on then picked up the note pad and pen. He poised himself to write.

"Tonight's draw used set of balls number nine and the machine

used was Guinevere. Our independent adjudicator was John Phillips. Tonight's winning numbers in ascending order are three, seven, fifteen, sixteen, nineteen and twenty-seven. The bonus ball is number forty." The BBC continuity presenter said with an air of cheeriness.

Matt was writing the numbers down and suddenly stopped.

"Mum!" Shouted Matt.

"And once again, those winning numbers are, three, seven, fifteen, sixteen, nineteen, twenty-seven and the bonus ball is number forty. Tonight's jackpot is a whopping twelve point two million pounds. Results indicate that there is one lucky jackpot winner. And now, it's time for Match of the day."

The Match of the day theme tune started playing. Matt was looking at his ticket in disbelief and then stared at the television.

"Mum!" Matt shouted louder this time.

Matt's mother, Doris Hooper walked into the living room. She was wearing a dressing gown, headscarf and slippers. She was wearing thick lensed glasses, similar to her son's. She was half asleep.

"What's the matter? What's all the shouting about?" Asked his mother, who had not long drifted off into a nice deep sleep.

Matt was taking a big swig from the bottle, making a crunching noise as the plastic crushed together in his hand as he sucked the coke out in big gulps. He slammed the coke bottle down. It fell over before he could put the top back on. Brown liquid spilled out of the misshaped bottle onto the table and flowed over the edge of the table down onto the carpet.

"What have I told you about drinking out the bottle. I'll get a cloth." Doris scolded her son as she went to go out to get a cloth to clear up her son's mess.

"Mum?"

"What!" Doris shouted back from the kitchen.

"I've won the lottery! I've won the bloody lottery!" Matt could not believe the words coming out of his mouth.

"Eh?" Nor could his mum believe what she was hearing.

She came shuffling back in with a cloth in her hand.

"What do you mean you've won the bleedin lottery?" Doris thought that her son was on a wind up again as he always liked winding up his mother.

"I need to check the numbers... I need to ring them up!" Matt was going into a panic.

"Calm down. You drunk all that coke? You shouldn't drink that much it's no good for you, you know!"

Matt was fumbling with the remote control. The Match of the day theme was coming to an end. Les Dynam's face appeared, and he started introducing the programme. His face and the rest of the picture on the screen was replaced with the Ceefax title page. Les Dynam's voice was still audible. Matt was pushing the buttons on the remote control with his chubby greasy fingers, trying to get the lottery page up, but was struggling to see. The horse racing page appeared.

"Bollocks!" Matt was getting agitated.

"Here let me put the lamp on." Doris shuffled over to the table lamp.

Light filled the room. Matt pushed the buttons on the remote control again. The lottery page appeared. Matt was looking up and down in a nodding motion as he checked his numbers.

"All six numbers! The bloke on the telly said one winner. I've won..." Matt shouted.

"Oh, my gawd!" Doris laughed nervously.

"Yes!" Matt pumped the air with his fist.

He cuddled his mother and started jumping for joy.

CAMELOT NATIONAL LOTTERY OFFICES

Matt and Doris were sitting down at the Camelot Executive Manager Joseph Cavendish's desk.

"We just need you to sign there and there Mr Hooper. This is to activate your new bank account with Coutts and for us to transfer the money to them. It also states that you are not taking us up on the offer to manage your money for you." Joseph said sternly.

"I just want it in an account where I can get to it at any time. I don't want it tied up in anything. Cash all the way please." Matt did not trust anyone at this place and nor would he until he saw the money in his new account.

"He's good with money. And I'll be helping him look after it." Doris reassured the Joseph.

"Mum's better than any financial advisor." Matt smiled at his mum. His teeth yellow from all the coke that he drank and from not brushing them regularly.

Doris smiled back an almost toothless grin.

"As you both wish. But if you decide to change your mind, you have my details. Sign here please." Joseph pushed a piece of paper towards Matt who was sitting opposite him in the plush opulent offices in London's west end.

Matt took the document and signed it in the three places that were marked with crosses. He handed it back.

Joseph took the piece of paper and looked at it.

"That's it then! All signed. Your advance has already been paid into your current account and the remaining balance will be in your new account within the next few minutes..." Joseph smiled through gritted teeth at the sight before him. Feelings of jealousy clouded his mind.

"I want to see it in the new account." Demanded Matt.

"Yes Mr Hooper. A car will pick you both up shortly and take you to Coutts where your account manager will be only to pleased to help you and issue you with your card.

"Yeah, I bet he will. I bet he can't wait to get his hands on my dough!" Sneered Matt.

"Matthew! Don't be so rude! I'm sorry about him, it's all been a bit much." Doris looked at the Joseph.

Joseph laughed.

"It's fine! You have nothing to worry about. After all, you now have an account where the Queen does her banking." He smiled.

"Here are look Matthew, the same bank as the queen. Who'd have thought it eh?" Doris said excitedly.

"Can we go now?" Matt wanted to get out of there. He started to get up from his seat.

"Yes, Mr and Mrs Hooper you..."

"She's my mum not my wife!" Snapped Matt.

"Yes Mr Hooper." Joseph said uncomfortably. He thought that it could be a possibility.

"I'm sure he didn't mean it how it sounded." Doris tried to reassure her son who she could see was very agitated.

Matt was glaring at Joseph who was now out of his seat and was walking towards the door. He got there and opened it.

"Whatever! I'm rich and he don't like it!" Matt smirked.

The manager was standing holding the door open. Doris walked out followed by Matt.

"I can assure you that is not the case."

He closed the door behind them and exhaled loudly. He started loosening his tie as he walked back to his desk. He sat down and pressed on an intercom device.

"Becky, Mr and Mrs Gorman are on their way out. Can you show those ghastly people to the car please?" Joseph was very distressed as he always was after giving people millions of pounds that he could never have the chance to get, as being an employee of the company, meant that he could not ever participate in the lottery.

"It's not here yet. Becky's voice crackled through the intercom.

"Just get them out of this building!" He demanded.

A SOUTH LONDON BROTHEL

Matt had decided to treat himself. A prostitute was performing fellatio on Matt. She stood up then climbed on top of Matt and started having sex with him. He grabbed at her breasts

"Oh, that's it love... Oh yeah... I love them fuckin tits of yours oh fuck... Oh fuck... Aaaarrrghh!"

Matt convulsed in orgasm, unable to hold out any longer. The prostitute slowed her movement down and came to a halt.

"All done?" Asked the prostitute.

"Yeah, all fuckin done! Shame I couldn't last a bit longer for ya eh?" said Matt with a grin.

The prostitute climbed off.

"Here love, any chance of taking that off for us?" He pointed towards his penis.

"No." she responded sharply.

She took some wet wipes from a pack on another table. She wiped herself and threw them in the bin which was almost full to the brim with soiled condoms and more wet wipes. She threw the pack of wet wipes at Matt. He tried to catch them but missed. They hit the wall and bounced back onto his stomach.

"Use those." She sniffed.

"Charming! I was going to give you a tip as well but sod ya now!" Matt retorted.

"Sod you too!" The prostitute walked out of the room slamming the door behind her. Matt was just looking at the door, shocked.

"Slag!" shouted Matt at the door.

COURTENAY AND SONS TAILORS SAVILLE ROW LONDON

"And how would you be paying sir?" Asked the shop manager, Gilles Dufresne, looking Matt up and down as he spoke.

Gilles' lineage could be traced back to a Huguenot tailor, Pierre Dufresne, who had been one of Louis XVI's tailors. Being a known royal employee and sympathiser, Pierre had fled for his life to London to escape the French Revolution. With his few belongings, tools of his trade and with the help of some his contacts, Pierre had managed to get a job as a tailor and eventually set up his own tailor shop. Pierre's offspring and descendants had kept the shop going but it eventually closed after being bombed during the blitz. Giles father, Bertrand had to take a job working in the shop where Gilles worked now. Gilles was his father's apprentice. The Dufresne men always took French first names and had French as a second language. Gilles had the notion that he should be considered royalty because of the Dufresne family history both in France and in London. Nobody else thought this, especially customers such has Matt Hooper who Gilles hated with a passion.

"How's he paying? We've only just walked in here!" snapped Doris.

"I've only said I want a suit! I ain't even looked at anything yet!"

Matt was getting angry.

"Sir. When one states that one would like a suit, we do not just offer suits off a peg. We are not Burtons sir." Sniffed Gilles, putting his nose in the air.

"I know you ain't! That's why I'm here!" Growled Matt.

Matt pulled his wallet from his back pocket. He pulled out a black bank card which had the Coutts logo on it.

"Sod him! Let's go to that other one we see down the road." Doris started to walk away.

"No hang on mum."

Matt handed the card to the Gilles.

"Will this be alright as payment... Sir!" Matt said with a scowl.

Gilles smiled broadly.

"Oh yes of course sir. Please accept my apologies. We offer a very bespoke service here and we have lots of time wasters whom we spend a lot of time and effort on only for them to tell us that they cannot afford our prices." Gilles had completely changed his tune after seeing the Coutts card.

"Hmm." Matt gave him a side look.

"But you sir, most obviously are our type of customer. We shall be only too willing to offer you our best possible services."

Gilles gestured towards a door at the back of the shop.

"Now sir, madam, would you care to follow me into our exclusive fitting area please. We shall offer you an extensive measuring service and any refreshments that you would like." Gilles could almost smell the money that he would be making from Matt.

"Oooohh!" Doris was excited.

FITTING ROOM

Matt was standing on a fitting stool in a suit jacket worn over his vest. The shops master tailor, Eugene Raine, was measuring Matt's inside left leg.

"Easy mate!" Matt said with a chuckle

"Yes sir. Sorry sir." Eugene replied. He was not happy that he had been assigned to Matt.

"Ooohh! Was he trying to cop a feel!" Laughed Doris.

"Anyway, where's our grub and drink?" demanded Matt.

"Yeah! I thought you were going to look after us. Me stomach feels like me throat's been cut!" Doris chipped in.

"Yeah, come on mate! My mums starving and I'm spitting feathers here! I'm going to be spending a lot of dough in here today judging by your prices!" Matt knew he could afford it but still had the mind of poor man so didn't like the thought of spending an obscene amount of money without him and his beloved mother being looked after.

"I do apologise sir but what you have requested will take slightly longer than usual as we have had to send out our apprentice out to procure the items, which are very specific items and..." Gilles, who was presiding over operations, was interrupted.

The fitting room door opened suddenly. James Garvey, the apprentice tailor, walked in. He was carrying a large tray that had on it a box of Kentucky fried chicken, two Marks and Spencer ham sandwiches in their boxes, a bottle of Stella Artois and two empty plates stacked on top of each other.

"Ah! Here we are! Put it over there please James!" Gilles clapped his hands to hurry James up.

"Oh, hello James!" Doris was eyeing up young James

Doris looked at Gilles.

"He looks a lovely boy! Will you get me a nice cup of tea James? Milk and two sugars please love." Doris smiled.

"Yes of course Mrs Hooper. Coming right up Mrs Hooper." James was getting a bit panicky.

Matt got down from the fitting stool and took the bottle of lager and started to down it. He drank half then put it down and belched loudly, to the dismay of Eugene and Gilles who looked at each other very briefly to convey their disgust to each other.

"Keep 'em coming Jamie!" Demanded Matt

"No problem, Mr Hooper. I got you a case of them, just like you asked." James was pleased with himself.

"Nice one James my boy!" Bellowed Matt.

Matt picked up his trousers and pulled out his wallet. He opened it and pulled out a ten pound note. He handed it to James.

"And, if I ain't drunk them all before I go, you can take the rest home with you!" Smiled Matt at his own largesse. He was so happy to help someone who, like himself up until his win, did not earn a lot of money. After trying lots of different jobs, Matt had ended up as a Logistics operative on various building sites in the City of London over the years. Or glorified labourer as some of his mates used to call him and wind him up about.

Matt pressed the note into James' hand.

"Thank you very much Mr Hooper!" James was so happy with this tip.

"Now go and get me mum her cup of tea please mate." Asked Matt in a soft tone.

James nodded and went to leave the room. Gilles gave James a dirty look, jealous of the good treatment Matt had given the young apprentice. Matt pushed past the Gilles and Eugene towards the tray. Matt opened one of the sandwiches, put it on a plate then handed it to his mother.

"Thanks babe." Doris smiled at her son with a loving look.

Matt then opened the Kentucky fried chicken box which was filled with two chicken thighs and two chicken legs. He picked up one of the chicken legs and the bottle of Stella Artois. He climbed back onto the fitting stool with the chicken leg in one hand and the bottle of Stella Artois in the other. He took a bite of the chicken leg Henry VIII style and swigged from the bottle of Belgian lager.

"Crack on then mate!" Matt ordered what he now considered to be his minions. He was standing over them regally on the fitting stool.

Eugene and Gilles were staring in disbelief at what they were seeing in their exclusive fitting room. Doris was tucking into her ham sandwich and Matt was eating the chicken leg. Bits of the crispy coating from the chicken leg were falling onto the floor.

"Yes sir. Of course, sir..." Sighed Eugene.

HAMMONDS OPTHALMIC OPTICIANS

Matt and the Optician, Nathaniel Hammond, were standing next to a display cabinet

"Yes, Mr Hooper you must take them out each night. But may I suggest that when you are at home in the evening, you wear glasses, thus avoiding the possibility of leaving your lenses in overnight. It's up to you of course. Could I perhaps interest you in a new pair of glasses?" Nathaniel was being more helpful than usual.

"I know your game mate... But I could do with some new ones, some of them really thin ones rather than these bloody coke bottles that me and me mum have to wear!" Matt knew how bad their glasses looked and had he been teased mercifully at school being called names like coke bottle boy, Mr McGoo and x-ray specs and worst of all, kiddie fiddler.

Matt pointed towards his glasses and then to Doris who was sitting down but looking around at all of the nice frames.

"Yes Mr Hooper. We can sort that out for you. I can see it's been a while since you and your mother have had new glasses. There have been some wonderful innovations in how lenses are made these days." Assured the Nathaniel.

Matt was looking at the selection of frames in the glass counter.

"I must advise you Mr Hooper that they are our more... Expensive range." Nathaniel looked at Matt.

"That's alright... I think I can afford it. I'll have two pairs of them." Matt pointed towards some Giorgio Armani frames.

"He can afford it don't your worry Mr Hammond." Piped up Doris.

"And two pairs of them for me mum." Matt pointed towards some outrageous Juicy Couture frames.

"You like them, Mum? I see you had your eyes on them." Smiled Matt.

"Ooh they are nice...You sure love?" Doris knew how expensive they were. She still couldn't easily forget not having much money and would not have dreamed of spending such vast amounts on glasses. Hence her and Matt having the same types of glasses for so long.

"Course mum!" Matt smiled down at Doris in the chair.

"Thanks, my little soldier!" Doris beamed back at her son.

"The same lenses we always have but the best money can buy. Nice and thin like, no more coke bottles." Matt pointed at the

Nathaniel.

"Yes of course Mr Hooper. Right away sir! We have all your records. We should be able to have them ready by the end of the week, along with your contact lenses." Nathaniel said with a smile.

Nathaniel handed Matt a pair of the frames that he had chosen. He took off his glasses and tried on the new pair of frames. Nathaniel handed Matt a mirror. Matt took it and looked into it.

"Sweet!" Matt couldn't see that well, but he knew anything was better than what he had. This money was going a long way to getting him looking better.

SPORTSWEAR SHOP

"Two pairs of them in size nine, one in black one in white. One pair of them in size nine and one pair of the same in size six for me mum and I'll take them seven tracksuits." Matt felt like he was buying the whole shop.

Matt pointed to a pile of tracksuits laid across a clothes rail.

"No problem sir, my colleague will come and get the tracksuits and I'll go and get the trainers." The shop assistant took the display trainers that Matt has picked out and walked off.

"I'll take the tracksuits to the counter in case anyone else takes them." Matt did not want anyone to ruin this moment for him.

The shop assistant stopped and turned around.

"Oh. Ok. I won't be long. I'll see you at the counter."

GEORGES BARBERS

Matt was sitting in the barber's chair with the gown around him. The Barber, George Papa Charalambous, was standing behind Matt, lifting up his ponytail. They were both looking into the mirror.

"Blimey Matthew, it's been a long time since you been in!" remarked George in his heavy Greek accent.

"I know. Not since dad died." Matt looked down.

"God bless him. He was a good man your dad. I remember when he first bought you in here. He was so proud." George said with a smile.

Matts eyes were welling up. George noticed.

"You sure you want this off?" George said cheerily, holding the ponytail aloft to change the subject.

"Yep!" Matt pointed to one of the posters.

"I want it like that geezer! He looks a cool dude don't he!" Matt chuckled.

"I'm a barber Matt, not a magician!" George laughed.

They both laughed.

"You sure now?" Checked George.

George had Matt's ponytail between his thumb and forefinger in one hand and a pair of scissors in the other, poised ready to cut.

"Get rid of it please George. Me dad wouldn't have liked it anyway and me mum hates it." Matt conceded.

"Okey dokey!" George said cheerily, a look of glee on his face as he started cutting into the thick bunch of greasy hair.

MARKS AND SPENCER'S CHILLED FOOD AISLE

Doris was walking down the chilled food aisle. She was pulling her shopping trolley with one hand and holding a shopping basket in her other hand. She was pale and breathless. Her legs gave way and she fell towards the ground.

GEORGE'S BARBER SHOP

George cut one final time and Matt's ponytail came away from his head. George let it fall towards the ground.

Matt's ponytail hit the floor.

MARKS AND SPENCER SHOP CHILLED FOOD AISLE

Doris fell. Her head bounced off of the chiller, down onto the floor. The side of her head hit the floor with a dull thud.

GEORGE'S BARBER SHOP

"Feel a bit lighter?" enquired George to Matt's reflection in the mirror

Matt smirked. George carried on cutting.

MARKS AND SPENCER CHILLED FOOD AISLE

There shop manager and an assistant were helping Doris, who was sitting with her back against the chiller unit. The right side of her face was bruised and swollen.

"Are you ok love? Can you hear me?" The shop assistant asked Doris.

"I've fell over but I'm alright…" Doris responded softly.

"We've called an ambulance just in case. Where do you feel pain?" The shop manger informed Doris.

"I've banged me head and the side of me face hurts but everything else seems alright…" Doris tried to get up but fell back again.

"Please don't try to get up for now. What's your name?" The shop manager asked, trying to hold Doris up.

"My name's Doris love. A bang on the head won't do me any harm. I could do with a cup of tea though..." Doris smiled painfully.

GEORGE'S BARBER SHOP

Matt was looking in the main mirror, turning his head from left to right. George was holding up a smaller mirror at the back of Matt's head.

"Yep, yep... Lovely George. Lovely. Cheers mate." Matt was happy with the transformation.

George put the mirror away. Matt's hair was now short and slicked back with gel now rather than natural hair grease.

"No problem my friend. You look better without the ponytail. Mum will be happy now, no?" George laughed.

Matt was still looking in the mirror moving his head around from left to right coming to terms with his new hairdo.

"She will mate, she will." Matt smiled, imagining his mum's reaction when she sees her little soldier.

DORIS' BEDROOM - LATER

Everything was blurry. Everything then became clear as Matt finished putting in his new contact lenses. Matt was standing in front of the full-length mirror on the back of the wardrobe door. He was wearing one of his new tracksuits and a new pair of trainers. The transformation was complete. He was almost unrecognisable with his new clothes, trainers, haircut and because he was wearing contact lenses now instead of wearing glasses. Both he and Doris had had their teeth cleaned up at the Dentist and Doris had had new dentures made. Matt pulled his lips apart and gritted his teeth together. His teeth were almost white now. The phone on Doris' bedside table started to ring. Matt walked over and picked up the phone.

"Hello? Yeah, who is it? Oh? Yeah, I'll be right there! Is she conscious? Alright, I'm on my way. Tell her I'm on my way will ya!" Matt slammed the phone down and rushed out of the bedroom.

CHAPTER X
THE DON OF ALL DONS

ST THOMAS'S HOSPITAL CASUALTY WARD

Doris was in a curtained off bay laying on a bed fully clothed. She was connected to an intravenous drip. The curtain moved and Matt rushed in. He stopped, just staring at his mother. He burst out crying.

"Don?" Doris asked very confused.

"No mum it's me!" Matt burst into tears.

He walked round and leant over and gave his mother a kiss and a cuddle.

"Ya silly sod stop crying, I'm alright!" Doris chuckled softly.

Matt pulled away and stood up.

"I see now! You've had your hair cut!" Doris' expression lightened into a smile.

"And I've got me new lenses in and me new tracksuit and trainers on. Oh mum! When they phoned and said you were in hospital, I was so worried..." Matt said wiping the snot and tears away with the back of his hand.

Matt sat down on the seat next to the bed and held his mother's hand.

"I'm alright ya silly sausage! You look so much like daddy!" Doris said proudly.

Tears were streaming down Matt's face as he tried to hold it together.

"I'm so pleased you chopped that bleedin silly pony tail off. And you've had a proper shave I see. Keep letting that stubble grow... Hiding that handsome face!" She rubbed his cheek.

"What happened?" Matt smiled through the tears.

"Well, I was in Marks' and I had a funny turn. I come over all funny and fainted. Hit the freezer then hit me head on the floor." Doris rubbed her head and face.

"Why? What they said?" Matt held his mother's hand.

"Dehydrated they reckon. That's why I'm hooked up to this bleedin thing." Doris pointed to the bag of saline solution that was hanging on the small wheel trolley which was connected to a tube into her hand via a canula.

"I said all I need is a nice cup of tea but the girls in Marks' said they weren't allowed to. The nurse has just gone to get me one now. I say nurse but he's a bloke. I think he's a poof but he's a lovely fella." Doris chuckled.

The curtain moved to the side and the male nurse, Craig Michaels, walked in.

"That's right Mrs Gorman. I am a poof. Thank you for noticing and I'm over the moon you think I'm a lovely fella, but you must keep yourself hydrated from now on, ok?" Craig berated her with a false smile.

Craig looked at Matt.

"Ooh! Who's this lovely handsome young man?" Craig really camped it up, looking Matt up and down.

Matt looked agitated.

"You leave my son alone you dirty sod!" Doris laughed.

"Ooh he's gorgeous!" roared the Craig.

Matt didn't know where to look.

"A lovely looking bloke like you Craig... I'd have turned you back in my heyday I can tell ya!" Laughed Doris.

"Mum!" Matt wasn't happy.

"I'm very flattered Mrs Gorman but this worms not for turning! Anyway, you can go home now." Craig screwed his face into a reassuring smile.

Craig turned to Matt.

"You must make sure she keeps hydrated. And don't be letting her do anything strenuous now ok..." Craig pointed at Matt.

"Alright..." Matt replied uncomfortably.

"And don't look so worried. I was only pulling your leg earlier." Chuckled Craig.

Matt looked relieved.

"You're not my type anyway!" Cackled Craig.

They all laughed. Craig walked out through the curtain.

"He's a cheeky so and so! I love him though, he really looked after me..." Doris chuckled.

Matt was staring at the bruising on Doris' face.

"Come on mum, let's get you home, eh?" Matt was happy and relieved that his mum could come home.

THE TIN SOLDIERS CAFE PORTCULLIS STREET

Bobby and Jimmy were sitting at their usual table in the busy Tin Soldier Cafe. It had been there for over one hundred years and was a favourite with the Wickside fans and the various local businesses and residents that were located around Hackney Wick. It was first opened to serve the nearby Bryant and May match factory in Bow and more importantly, the Tobacco Box toy factory which made tin soldier toys and many other toys, which is where Wickside Football club had originated. The team were originally named The Bacca, which was short for and a cockney slang word for, Tobacco. This was due to the tobacco tin size boxes that some of the toys were sold in by the factory. They were nominated into the original Football League in eighteen eighty-eight, due to their success as part of the original Association of Football, which was formed in eighteen sixty-three, and their subsequent success against Barnes FC in winning the inaugural Association of Football Challenge Cup in eighteen seventy-two. There were old and new pictures of Wickside FC teams and individual players adorning the walls. There was also a sprinkling of various Artillery, Haringey Hotboots and East Ham United pictures, due to the proximity of these clubs and the residents of the area and local business owners. There were a few scrap yards and car breaker businesses that had taken root nearby, mainly after World War Two, whose workers also frequented the Tin Soldier Cafe. Irish travellers or Tinkers, as they were commonly known in Ireland, the name being derived from the sound their tools made hitting metal when many Travellers worked as Tinsmiths, also frequented the Tin Soldier Cafe. The Travellers were also commonly, and wrongly known in London, as Gypsies. The Travellers had set up sites for their caravans on a lot of the abandoned land around the river Lea, which ran through Hackney Wick and Bow, much to the chagrin of the local residents and businesses.

"Well Bobby boy we're doing well son, we are doing well!" Jimmy smiled and rubbed his hands together.

"It ain't over yet!" Bobby said forlornly.

"The players love you, the fans love you... I fuckin love ya... We're in the play-off places with three games to go..." Jimmy was confident and excited.

"Jimmy... Don't get carried away please mate... It ain't over till it's over. Believe me!" Bobby knew this from the many painful experiences the had lived through during his football career.

"I know, I know... But take the credit where it's due mate. We're getting full houses every game for the first time in years, which is really helping with the finances, and I'm getting some interest from potential investors who I know. They weren't interested at first but now your here and were doing well, they're saying if we go up, they're in!" Jimmy was still being too enthusiastic for Bobby's liking.

"And if we don't go up, they ain't in... Let's talk about it at the end of the season. I can't be having me, or the team distracted by any of this. Alright!" Bobby looked Jimmy square in the eyes to let him know in no uncertain terms that this conversation was to end there and then.

"Blimey you are serious ain't you son... Which is exactly why we got you in! But no, you're right. I'll keep it all schtum for now." Jimmy said, a bit taken aback.

Jimmy wasn't used to having the law laid down to him. It was usually the other way round, unless of course he was being interviewed by the local constabulary.

Bobby downed the rest his coffee.

"I'd better get to training..." Bobby said as he got up, glad that he had put an end to Jimmy's aspirations, for now.

"You crack on son. I'm going to hang on here for a bit as I'm meeting with a potential investor." Jimmy raised his eyebrows and winked at the retreating Bobby.

Jimmy looked towards the door and waved to Iranian Ali, an Iranian immigrant who had fled to London to escape the Islamic Revolution back in nineteen seventy-eight. Before the revolution, Ali already had ties with London. He was a bald-headed man, smartly dressed in a tailored, black three-piece suit accompanied with a white shirt, black tie and black Ray

Bans.

"Here he comes now." Jimmy nodded towards the approaching, potential investor.

"See you later Jimmy..." Bobby replied sarcastically.

Bobby got up and walked off towards the door. Iranian Ali looked at Bobby as he recognised him. They both acknowledged each other. Bobby carried on walking on and out of the door. Iranian Ali walked over to Jimmy. They shook hands, hugged each other and slapped each other's backs. They eventually broke off from their embrace.

"Iranian Ali! Well, I never! How are you son?" Jimmy asked enthusiastically.

"Jim Jim! Good to see you, my brother. You look well. They must feed you well in English jail, no? Unlike jail in my country where you must eat rats to survive!" Ali gave Jimmy a knowing look as he had experienced the hell of an Iranian jail during the Islamic revolution as very young man. Ali was a throwback to how a vast number of Iranians, prior to the Grand Ayatollah Ruhollah Khomeini replacing the Pahlavi dynasty under the Shah Mohammed Reza Pahlavi. Ali was Westernised, as opposed to Islamic. Wearing a suit as opposed to traditional Islamic male attire. He had never got over his treatment in jail and the death of most of his family, during the revolution.

"There must be no more rats left in the jail you were in then... You fat bastard! look at the bloody size of ya!" Jimmy retorted merrily.

They both sat down. The waitress came over to the table.

"No no Jim Jim. I have very bad thyroid problem. Full English please darling." Ali asked, oblivious to what he had just said in one sentence.

The waitress wrote down the order.

"Fucking thyroid problem my arse! Yeah I'll have the same

please love." Jimmy looked at Ali then the waitress.

"Any drinks?" Asked the waitress, looking completely uninterested

"Tea please love." Jimmy replied

"Two cans of coke please." Ali looked up to the waitress and then down to the table again.

The Waitress wrote down the rest of the order.

"Thank you." The Waitress walked away towards the counter.

"So, my brother, tell me all about this investment opportunity." Ali asked intensively.

SEAFORD WAY FOOTBALL CLUB CHAIRMAN'S OFFICE

Matt was dressed in one of his new suits. He was sitting down at a desk, opposite the Seaford Way Football Club chairman and owner, Wally Rainham.

"So that's my story. You can see I'm telling the truth..." Matt pointed towards his Coutts bank statement that was on Wally's side of the desk.

"Like I say... I want to buy the club."

"You see Mr Hooper... Owning and running a football club is not as easy as you think. There is so much to think about, and you have said yourself, that you have no experience at all. We must think of the long-term future of Seaford Way, for we are only custodians of the club. It is the fans that truly own it." Wally Rainham was trying his best to convince this potential buyer, that it was a bad idea to purchase the club that he had owned, to his chagrin, for over twenty years. Wally had let his heart as a supporter, rule his head when purchasing his beloved club himself. Seaford Way FC had become a labour of love over the past few years and as his children kept reminding him of, had eaten into their inheritance.

"Look, I know all that. I'm a fan of this club and so was my old man god bless his soul... I know what you and your family have done for this club, and I want to help take it to the next level." Matt enthused, feeling pleased with himself for saying a phrase that he had heard on a programme he had watched recently.

"Yes Mr Hooper, I understand, but who will run it for you? Who will do the accounts?" Wally was starting to feel that he was fighting a losing battle.

"Well, my offer is to clear the club of its debts and pay you back what you have invested over the years. For that, I get full control of the club, but I pay you to keep running it day to day. Simple, eh?" Matt shrugged his shoulders.

"Are you serious Mr Hooper?" Wally asked in disbelief.

"I've never been more serious about anything in my life... Ever!" Matt replied with conviction.

"Well, with the way things are, I am struggling to pay the debts off, but the club is pretty solvent. I'm not getting any younger and none of my family are interested... They all have their own thing going on...." Conceded Wally, comfortable now that he had secured the best deal of his whole life.

Matt was getting excited.

"Well?" Matt asked, pleadingly serious.

"Well Mr Hooper, there will be a lot to do with paperwork, but we can let the solicitors deal with that so... I'm prepared to shake on it for now Mr Hooper and..." Wally was interrupted by Matt as he walked around the desk.

Wally got up from his chair. Matt's hand was already outstretched.

"I'm willing to do the deal Mr Hooper!" Wally smiled in a very controlled way as he could not believe that the buffoon in front of him was about to make his dream of at least the last ten years, come true for him, as he had been struggling, against his families wishes, in keeping Seaford Way FC afloat.

They shook hands.

"Please, call me Matt." Matt requested, as he felt uncomfortable being called Mr Hooper, as had his father.

Ok then, Matt! You've got yourself a deal!" shouted Wally.

They broke off from the handshake.

"Yes! Yes! Yes!" Matt clenched both of his fists and raised them to near his face.

Wally sat back down. He pulled open the top draw of his desk. He reached down and pulled out a bottle of Glenfiddich whiskey and slammed it down onto the desk. He reached down again and rummaged around for a few seconds then pulled out two tumbler glasses. He opened the bottle and poured out two large measures of whiskey and then handed one of the glasses to Matt. They clinked the glasses together and then raised them.

"Cheers Matt!" Smiled Wally.

"Cheers Wally!" Smiled Matt.

Matt downed his whiskey in one, while Wally only drank half of his measure.

"Another?" Wally moved his glass up and shook it in a provocative way, smiling as he did the motion.

"Yes please!" Matt greedily replied.

Wally poured another large measure for Matt and topped his own glass up. They both took a sip then sat back down.

"What do we do now then?" Matt asked innocently.

The owner took another sip confidently, as if he were a python, restricting its prey of air.

"Well, if you leave me your details, I shall ask my lawyers to proceed with things." Wally was closing this deal as quickly as possible, knowing that Matt was now putty in his small, sweaty hands.

Wally grabbed a note pad and pen and slid it over his desk towards Matt. Matt grabbed it straight away and started writing.

THE LADYWELL ARMS PUBLIC HOUSE

The Ladywell Arms was packed, due to a televised League Cup football, match between local teams Carlton Football Club and Brickwall Football Club. Matt was standing at the bar. Lucy Benson, the barmaid, approached Matt to serve him.

"Yes love?" Lucy asked.

"The usual please Luce." Matt asked.

"Sorry... Do I know you?" Lucy asked in a very confused manner.

"It's me Luce, Matt. Matt Hooper." Matt said encouragingly.

"Matt? Matt! Oh my god... You look so different... What's happened? I didn't recognise you!" Lucy laughed nervously.

"I don't look that different, do I?" Matt was a bit concerned.

"You look that different I half fancy you!" Lucy laughed in shock at the complete transformation of Greasy Haired Matt, as he was known in some circles of the local clientele due to another, tidier Matt, who frequented the establishment.

"Well, you better get yourself one then!" Laughed a nervous Matt, at the sudden interest shown in him by one of the many barmaids that he had lusted after in this pub, since as long as he could remember.

Lucy was staring at Matt.

"I can't believe how different you look..." Lucy walked off to get

Matt's drink.

"I'm just off to the khazi." Matt walked through the packed pub towards the toilets. He looked back towards the bar and winked at a smiling Lucy as he walked.

WICKSIDE FC MANAGERS OFFICE

Bobby was sitting at his desk writing. The door opened. Jimmy and Stevie walled in. Bobby looked up.

"Jimmy, Stevie. What you doing here?" Bobby asked in a happy way.

"We knew you'd be here!" Jimmy remarked.

"Don't you ever go home?" asked Stevie, knowing how dedicated Bobby was.

"Someone's got to do the graft round here... Anyway, what do you want?" Bobby wasn't in the mood for their usual joviality.

Jimmy sat on the side of the desk. Stevie pulled up a chair and sat down opposite Bobby.

"It's looking good on the investment front. My old mate Ali is well up for it." Jimmy said a bit tentatively, as he could feel Bobby's mood easier these days, now that he had got to know him a bit better.

Bobby looked up at Jimmy who was perched on the edge of his desk looking down at him.

"Oh yeah?" Bobby responded flippantly.

"But he wants us up before he commits..." Interjected Stevie, who was also a bit more reserved about these things since Bobby blew up at him last week.

"He's got the dough but like Stevie says, he wants us to go up first." Jimmy said softly.

"Chaps. I want us to go up that's why I'm here till all hours, but

I'm not having ultimatums put on me like this, I've told you before!" Bobby knew this was coming.

Jimmy got up and walked around and put an arm around Bobby.

"It's not like that!" Jimmy tried to reassure him as he ruffled Bobby's hair.

Bobby pulled his head away slightly.

"No, it's not Bobby." Stevie reassured Bobby.

"We just want to keep you up to date with matters. This is the most serious offer we've had and like I said, I ain't got enough dough to keep this club going..." Jimmy said forlornly, looking Bobby straight in the eyes.

THE GENTS TOILETS IN THE LADYWELL ARMS

Matt was at the urinal doing his trousers up. There were whispered voices and sniffing sounds coming from one of the toilet cubicles. The lock clicked and the cubicle door opened. Matt turned and zipped up his fly as Jackdaw and Deckchair both emerged from the cubicle, one after the other, respectively.

"You doing that shit again?" Matt asked the pair of lowlifes.

"What the fuck's it got to do with you?" Jackdaw replied aggressively, taking a step towards Matt.

"Hold on..." Deckchair interrupted his best mate and held him back.

"You old bill or something?" Jackdaw was charged from the fat line of cocaine that he had just snorted, added to what he had already previously inhaled that evening.

"If he was old bill, we'd all be in trouble..." Deckchair held out his hand to Matt then pulled it back.

", wash your hands first eh!" Laughed Deckchair.

Matt laughed then walked over towards the basin and turned the taps on.

"How's it going you old dog?" Matt arched his head around as he washed his hands.

Jackdaw was looking between them both, looking confused.

"It's alright mate. Its Matt Hooper. You remember, ponytail and coke bottle glasses?" Deckchair put his hands to his eyes and made circles with his thumb and forefingers, to imitate wearing glasses.

Matt turned the tap off then turned around, shaking the water from his hands as moved.

"Oh yeah!" Jackdaw finally clocked on.

"I definitely ain't old bill!" Matt assured the gawping Jackdaw.

"What's all this about then? That whistle looks a bit dear." Deckchair remarked.

"I'm celebrating! And I think it's time I tried a bit of gear." Matt said very seriously.

"Eh?" Deckchair looked shocked.

"Fuck it! I wanna get right on it tonight... And I know you got some, coz I heard you both in there..." Matt smiled and pointed towards the cubicle.

"Unless you were sniffing each other's arseholes?" Chuckled Matt.

 They all laughed.

"You sure?" Deckchair asked.

"Yep! I wanna see what all the fuss is about!" Insisted Matt.

"Come on then!" Deckchair gestured towards the cubicle.

"I'll see you out there." Jackdaw walked out of the toilets as

Matt and Deckchair walked into the cubicle.

"Lucky I weren't old bill then!" Matt shut and locked the cubicle door behind them.

"Old bill don't come in here mate." Deckchair assured Matt.

Deckchair pulled out a clear plastic bank coin bag, containing small, white paper packages. He pulled one of the packages out and unfolded it, revealing white lumpy powder.

"Looks like speed." Matt casually remarked.

There was an old, green British Telecom phone box card, lying on the toilet cistern. The card, which was now almost obsolete as telephone boxes became rarer and rarer due to the increase in people owning mobile phones, was attached to a piece of string which was wrapped around a screw in the wall next to the toilet cistern. Deckchair used the card to scoop out some of the cocaine onto the cistern and started cutting up the powder into lines.

"I can't believe that card's still there!" Matt shook his head.

Deckchair showed Matt the phonecard up close. It had some black permanent marker writing on it.

"In case of emergencies!" they said in unison then both cracked up laughing

"If they didn't let people do gear in here the place would lose all its customers!" Smirked Deckchair, as though that he was doing the pub a favour by selling and sniffing Cocaine Hydrochloride in the establishment.

"True!" Matt acquiesced.

"You got a note?" Demanded Deckchair, as he surveyed the two thick lines of cocaine he had carefully racked up.

"Yeah." Matt said sarcastically, as he pulled out his wallet which was stuffed full of fifty-pound notes.

"Fuck me! You finally had a win on the horses?" The cash had piqued Deckchair's predatory instincts.

Matt pulled out one of the fifty-pound notes, rolled it up into a tube and handed it to Deckchair. Matt was by no means a stranger to drugs. He had been heavily into speed before his dad died but had since stopped and had become a recluse. He used to bomb speed in drinks mostly but snorted it sometimes, which is why he knew how to roll a banknote with skill, precision and accuracy.

"A fucking fifty an all! Look at him!" Deckchair's mind was working overtime on how to relieve Matt of some of the enticing wad of cash in Matt's wallet. It would be in the form of wraps of cocaine and drinks from the bar. He was thinking of maybe borrowing some, but he thought he would wait for a while before pouncing, at least until Matt had had a few more lines and beers.

Deckchair took the note and bent down to inhale a line of cocaine through his right nostril. He leant back up and passed the note to Matt, who then bent over and inhaled the other line of cocaine through his right nostril.

"Nice!" Matt said as he swung back up from the cistern.

"Seeing that you're so flush, you can buy some. You ain't sniffing mine all night!" Deckchair sniffed hard to get the cocaine into his brain.

"Fuck it! Go on then!" Matt sniffed hard too.

"Well, you give me that nifty fifty..." Deckchair snatched the rolled up fifty pound note out of Matt's hand.

"And I'll give you one of these." Deckchair pulled one of the wraps of cocaine from the coin bag and handed it to Matt, who greedily snatched it.

"Fifty fuckin quid?" Matt wasn't happy.

"It's good stuff mate!" Deckchair said confidently.

Deckchair was proud of his product as he kept the cocaine content quite high, rather than cut the hell out of it, which most of his contemporaries did. Although to do this, he kept his measures slightly light. What should be one gram, usually weighed in at point seven of a gram and what should have been half a gram, would usually weigh in at just under point four of a gram or, the arse end of point three, as he and Jackdaw used to say and always laugh at. He often referred to his rival's gear as having been trampled on by a herd of wildebeests. Deckchair put the clear bank coin bag into his pocket and unrolled the fifty-pound note. He pulled out a wad of money from his other pocket and added the fifty-pound note to it. He then put the wad of cash back into his pocket. Matt unlocked the door.

"It fuckin better be." Matt said.

They both walked out of the cubicle.

"Don't go mad on it though... You don't need to keep doing it like some of the other shit that's going about." Advised Deckchair.

"Yeah yeah!" Matt said dismissively.

"Hang on... Have I got any round me hooter?" Deckchair tipped his head back.

Matt peered into Deckchairs outstretched nasal cavities.

"Nah." Responded Matt as he tipped his head back.

"What about me?" Matt asked nervously as he did not want anyone knowing he had been sniffing cocaine and he certainly did not want Lucy the barmaid to see any shit around his nose.

"Yeah. Have a sniff and a wipe on the right nostril." Deckchair pointed to his own right nostril.

Matt sniffed and wiped his nose with the back of his hand, then tilted his head back a bit.

"Sorted?" asked Matt.

"You're all clear kid! Now let's blow this thing and go to the bar!" Deckchair responded in an American accent, mimicking Han Solo from a Star Wars when he saves Luke to enable him to blow up the Death Star. He knew Matt was a Star Wars fan, as he was. They used to sit up all night watching the films and reciting the dialogue whilst on Speed.

They both laughed and walked out of the toilets back into the bar.

DORIS' BEDROOM

Mr Blue Sky by ELO was playing on the digital alarm radio on the bedside table. Doris was sitting on the end of her bed pulling on one of her new trainers. She already had one on. She bent forwards to tie one of the laces up. She sat back up. She was breathless and pale. She bent down to tie the other shoelace but didn't stop, falling headfirst to the floor. She came to a motionless halt, contorted in a heap.

THE LADYWELL ARMS

Matt, Deckchair and Jackdaw were sitting down at a table, watching the match.

"That thing ain't doing anything..." Matt looked unhappy.

"Fuck me it was only five minutes ago, give it a chance!" Jackdaw's jaw was clearly reacting to the cocaine that he had been snorting.

"Chillax bruvver! Don't you chicken curry about that thing my pedigree chum! Go and get the beers in..." Deckchair ordered Matt, waving his hand towards the bar.

"I will! Then I'll do another boot of that thing and if nothing happens soon, I'll be taking my fifty back." Matt got up, scowling at Deckchair.

"There ain't no refunds round here bruv. Sold as seen! Sold as seen!" Laughed Deckchair.

Sold as seen was in reference to the statement that they wrote on all the logbooks of the old banger cars that they sold on, as a cash enterprise to cover for their cocaine dealing. If anyone did dare come back and complain about a car, they would always quote what was written on the logbook. Deckchair and Jackdaw would take cars from people who couldn't pay their off their tick bills and would go to car auctions to acquire stock. If they thought that the punters buying their cars were sweet, they would sell them cocaine too. They operated on the corner opposite the pub, which was a busy place and left alone by the police. They would handwrite the For Sale signs in the pub, then stick them to the windows of the cars. They would both walk around near the cars and pounce on anyone who showed an interest in the cars. They would also be in and out of the pub drinking, selling and snorting cocaine. Jackdaw started laughing at his partner in crimes recital of their trusted statement.

Matt walked off towards the bar, wiping the sweat from his top lip as he walked. He got to the bar and pulled his wallet out from his back pocket and opened it. He saw the wrap of cocaine. He pulled a fifty-pound note from the wallet. He caught Lucy's attention with the green and slightly orange banknote that he was holding aloft in his thumb and forefinger.

"Yes, please Luce!" Shouted Matt.

"What can I get you handsome?" Lucy smiled. She was still impressed at Matt's transformation and now even more impressed at the fifty pound not he was waving around.

"Three pints of Stella, three sambucas and whatever you're having… Stick this in a glass behind the bar for me, Deckchair and Jackdaw over there please." Matt instructed confidently.

Lucy looked shocked and then impressed. Lucy snatched the fifty-pound note.

"Hey big spender! Will do." Lucy sang in the style of the song Hey Big Spender, sung by Shirley Bassey.

"I'm off to the bog, I'll get 'em on me way back."

"Lovely!" Matts vulgarity at first put her off but soon amused Lucy. She smiled at Matt as she schemed to somehow get hold of his cock and entice him into her bewitching spell of easy sexual relations.

Matt walked off. Lucy started to pour the drinks.

Matt walked into the toilets. He went straight into the same cubicle as he had used on his previous visit. He locked the cubicle door behind him. He undid his trousers and started to urinate.

"Oh, that's better." Matt whispered to himself.

He finished urinating then did his trousers up. He pulled his wallet out and opened it. He pulled out the wrap of cocaine and opened it. He pinched some cocaine from the warp and snorted it up both nostrils. A noticed that few lumps had fell out from his nostrils, so he inhaled harder to stop anymore of this valuable drug from hitting the urine-soaked cubicle floor. This caused him to violently gag and retch. He held himself rigid, clenching his teeth for a few moments. He let out a big breath. He put the cocaine back into his wallet and put it away. He spat into the toilet then turned around. He unlocked the door and walked out to the mirror. He looked at himself in the mirror. He was smirking and feeling good, but his face was covered in sweat. He washed his hands and splashed his face with water. He looked back into the mirror and grinned broadly, thinking of how his life had completely changed as much as his appearance.

"Fuck me he's been a while!" Deckchair noticed.

"Probably having a coke pony!" Jackdaw responded.

They both laughed.

"There he is!" Deckchair saw Matt approaching the bar.

Matt approached the bar. His drinks were already on a tray. Lucy was serving somebody but looked across to Matt.

"Feeling better now?" Lucy asked with a big grin on her face

"Don't worry, I weren't having a pony... You cheeky mare!" Matt looked a bit embarrassed.

"You feeling alright? You don't look too good!" Lucy remarked with a concerned grin on her face.

Matt picked up the tray of drinks.

"Never felt better love!" Matt winked at Lucy. She winked back. Matt turned and headed of towards the waiting vermin that was Jackdaw and Deckchair. Matt had the biggest grin on his face.

"Here he is! I see that things kicked in then." Jackdaw pulled a gurning face towards Matt as he put the tray of drinks down.

"Yeah, it ain't so bad after all!" Conceded Matt whose face was showing the effect of cocaine.

The whole pub erupted in cheers as Brickwall scored a goal. Jackdaw and Deckchair both stood and clenched their fists.

"Yes! Fuckin get in!" Shouted Deckchair.

"Sweet!" Jackdaw shouted, but not as loud as Deckchair.

"I fuckin missed it!" Moaned Matt.

"I shall go and celebrate with a nice big fat line!" Jackdaw was worse for wear and unbalanced.

As Jackdaw moved around the table, he tripped up on one of the table legs. Matt and Deckchair laughed out loud, as did some of the people round them. Jackdaw straightened himself up and the laughter subsided. He started to walk away from the table and one of the crowd who was standing watching the game on the television held his leg out and tripped Jackdaw, making him fall over. The laughter erupted again. Everybody was cracking up at the fallen Jackdaw. Jackdaw got up and stomped off towards the toilets.

"What a plank!" Matt guffawed at the sorry site in front of him.

Lucy was pushing her way through the crowd towards them.

"Is he alright?" Lucy asked chuckling away.

"He'll be sweet. Don't worry love" Deckchair tried palming her off.

"He fuckin better be!" Lucy's mood changed as she knew what these two could be like, especially Jackdaw, who was either on the verge of beating someone up or more often than not, getting chinned for being abusive.

Lucy got to the table and started collecting the empty glasses from the table. She bent across the table between Matt and Deckchair. Matt squeezed the left cheek of Lucy's derriere. This made her jump almost dropping the glasses. Deckchair squeezed the right cheek of her buttocks. She shrieked in laughter, loving the attention, whilst Matt and Deckchair giggled their heads off like two naughty boys. She put the glasses down and smacked the pair of them round the head. She picked the glasses back up.

"Pair of bastards! You can fuckin cut that right out!" Lucy laughed but she was annoyed with Deckchair rather than Matt.

"You feel like you're carrying a bit of timber there girl!" Deckchair was trying to breathe through the giggling.

Deckchair and Matt both laughed even harder.

"You can fuckin talk!" Retorted Lucy.

She turned back around.

"Fuckin cheek!" Lucy was really annoyed with Matt now as he was laughing along.

"Cheek being the operative word eh, Matthew my son!"

They high fived each other. Jackdaw walked back towards them, steadier than before.

"I suppose you thought that was funny!" Jackdaw remarked glumly as he sat back down.

"Yeah, it was fuckin hilarious actually!" Deckchair laughed.

"I'll get the drinks as it'll be closing time before we know it. Plus, you two seem a bit allergic to wood tonight!" Matt clocked that none of them were rushing to get the drinks in, but he was on one now. The cocaine had taken hold and he had to keep drinking.

"Well as you're so flush..." Jackdaw gurnily grinned.

Matt glared at Jackdaw and Deckchair as he got up to walk to the bar. He pushed his way through the crowd.

"He's through on his own and... He scores! Brickwall surely have this game wrapped up now with only seconds to go." The TV commentator's voice could just about be heard as the whole crowd erupted. Matt turned to the television and cheered along with all the rest of the pub. He managed to push his way to the bar. Lucy saw Matt. She was pouring a pint but called over to Matt without taking her eyes of the lager flowing into the glass.

"Same again love?" Lucy was trying to keep Matt interested in her as best as she could. She knew men loved a bit of special attention from a barmaid.

Matt nodded. Lucy picked out more glasses from under the bar while she was pouring a pint. She finished pouring the pint, handed it to the customer, took his money and put it into the till. She walked over towards Matt. She started pouring the first pint.

"Do you fancy having a drink with me after everyone's gone?" Matt had Dutch courage enough now that the cocaine and stella were coursing through his system, fuelling him with a confidence that he hadn't quite felt before.

"You asking me out on a date?" Lucy replied cheekily. Knowing that she was going to take him up on his offer.

They both laughed.

"Yeah, why not. Just hang around until everyone's cleared off. Only you mind. You'll have to ditch them two!" Lucy pointed to Jackdaw and Deckchair who were singing Brickwall terrace songs.

"No problem!" Matt was buzzing even more now.

They both smiled at each other. Lucy handed the tray of drinks to Matt. He took it back over to the table. Jackdaw was pinching cocaine from a wrap and snorting it.

"Fuck me!" Matt was shocked at the blatancy.

"Fuck it!" sneered Jackdaw.

Matt put the drinks down. They all took their drinks from the tray. Matt sat down and pulled his wallet out then opened it and pulled his wrap of cocaine out. He pinched some cocaine between his fingers and inhaled it through his nose.

"When in Rome..." Matt replied.

"He's bang on it!" Laughed Deckchair

The crowd cheered as the game ended after extra time.

"Rotherham in the semi then! We should piss that and then have a nice day out at Wemberleeee!" Jackdaw clapped his hands and rubbed them together

The bell for last orders rang.

"Here, you fancy going round The Monarch? I've heard they were going to do a lock in if we got through to the semi-final..."

Deckchair enthused.

"I'll have some of that!" Jackdaw was happy at this news as he always loved a lock in as it was an opportunity to sell more gear.

"Nah. I'm gonna hang about here thanks. I've just got these in"

Deckchair and Jackdaw downed their remaining drinks then grabbed a pint each.

"Well sod you then! If we don't in there before closing, they won't let you in once the doors are locked. Tossers! Let's down these together like the Three Musthavebeers!" Deckchair was slurring his words.

Matt grabbed his pint. They all proceeded to down their pints. Jackdaw was struggling with his and slammed it down about halfway through, causing some of the lager to spill over the edge of the glass onto the table. He grabbed a sambuca off the tray and downed it. Deckchair broke off from downing his pint about three quarters through. He slammed his glass down and grabbed a sambuca and downed it straight away. Matt carried on draining his glass until it was empty.

"Fannies!" Spat Matt, as he picked up the last remaining sambuca and downed it.

Matt got up. They all shook hands and hugged each other. Jackdaw did not look good.

"You still got my number ain't ya?" Deckchair gestured as if he had a phone to his ear.

"Yeah mate. I'll give you a bell." Matt did the same phone gesture.

"See you later Matt. Cheers for the drinks!" Jackdaw was puffing his cheeks out, suffering from downing the drinks.

"No problem. See you lads." Matt could not wait to get rid of them now. His focus was solely on getting back to Lucy and having a drink with her on their own.

Deckchair and Jackdaw walked off and out of the pub. Jackdaw inhaled deeply as he opened the door out onto the street. The fresh air hit him. He retched. His cheeks suddenly looked like a squirrel's face full of nuts for the winter. His facial skin already stretched beyond its limit, couldn't take anymore. He spewed his guts up onto the pavement. The combined liquid of alcohol and gastric acid sprayed out of his mouth hitting the pavement, sounding like hard pouring rain. It ricocheted off the concrete back over onto his trainers. Some of the puke hit Deckchair's new blue suede Patrick Cox loafers as he tried in vain to avoid the splatter. Jackdaw kept walking as he puked. He stopped for a split second before another bilious attack occurred but this time not as long. He stopped and steadied himself.

"For fuck's sake you cunt! These are brand new!" Deckchair shouted.

Jackdaw spat the remaining puke and spittle from his mouth and carried on walking.

"That's better! Don't worry about them shoes... I'm sure your mum will clean 'em up for ya!" Jackdaw walked on.

Deckchair followed trying to avoid the puddles of puke.

"Shut up you cunt!" Deckchair ran up behind Jackdaw and rubbed his shoe down his leg, trying to wipe off the puke. Jackdaw didn't notice as he was only focused on getting to The Monarch to get another pint to wash away the puke from his mouth.

Back inside The Ladywell Arms, Matt had just got to the bar, which was very busy, due to last orders being called. Matt waited and eventually caught the eye of Lucy, who smiled and walked over to him.

"I see you got rid them two nutters then!" Lucy was pleased.

"Yeah, they've gone round The Monarch for a lock in." Matt assured Lucy with a glint in his eyes.

"Good! Same again?" Lucy was just about to grab a pint glass.

"Nah. I'll have a large whiskey please Luce, with a little drop of water in it please." Matt could not stomach any more beer or sambuca.

"That's a bit old school ain't it? Anyway, why do they call him Deckchair?" asked Lucy.

Lucy grabbed a glass and turned around to the optics. She poured Matt a treble without him noticing. She knew Matt was admiring her bum.

"I'll tell you later... Whiskey and waters nice. You should try it sometime." Matt smiled. His eyes were firmly transfixed on Lucy's well-rounded rump of an arse.

Lucy poured some water from a small Toby jug into the whiskey glass. She turned around and presented it to him.

"Nah! White wine all the way for me! I've had a couple already! Is that enough water?" Lucy wasn't sure due to the treble measure she had dispensed into the glass.

"Looks lovely!" Matt admired the drink and its pourer.

Lucy turned around towards the bell next to the optics and rang it for drinking up time.

"Time gentlemen please!" Shouted Lucy.

The pub started to clear quickly as word had spread about the lock in at The Monarch. The other bar staff were clearing up.

"Don't worry peeps. You can go now, I'll finish up." Lucy ordered the other bar staff. Her quickly formulated plan that had started earlier when Matt came to the pub, was slowly coming to fruition. Her net was closing around Matt.

They all hurried off and said their goodbyes. They too had

heard about the lock in round The Monarch and were happy to be let off early for the night. Lucy locked the door behind them. She then proceeded to draw all the curtains at the windows. She drew the last set.

"Right! Time for a well-earned drink!" Lucy was excited.

Lucy strode over towards the bar. She walked behind the bar and opened a bottle of cheap Pinot Grigio and poured herself a large glass of it. Almost to the brim of the glass.

"Sounds good to me!" Matt was almost in heaven at this point.

Matt wiggled his glass in the air. Lucy was downing her wine as she walked over to take his glass. She put her empty glass down. She pulled the whisky bottle down from the optic wall. She pulled the optic out and poured Matt a very large whisky then topped it up with water from the Toby jug. She then poured herself another large glass of wine. They clinked their glasses together and each took a sip of their drinks. Lucy switched off most of the lights in the bar using the grid switch behind the bar. They were left in dim yellowish light.

"Come on then, get your gear out!" demanded Lucy, with an almost demonic smile on her face.

"What you on about?" Matt tried to brush it off.

"I've seen you all in and out of the toilets all night... And cuffing at the table!" Lucy looked at Matt with a knowing smile.

"Alright, you got me! What about your mum and dad?" Matt seemed suddenly concerned, remembering that they lived upstairs and what they were like when it came to their only daughter.

"They're away for the week!" Lucy squealed. Her eyes widened.

"By the way Matt, I'm sorry to hear about your mum's fall the other day."

"Matt steadied himself as he always immediately got upset

when he thought of his mum hurt and in the hospital.

"Thanks. Matt was fighting back the tears and wanted to change the subject.

Matt pulled his wallet out.

"Oh, that's nice. Understand if you don't want to talk about it but I'm here if you need a chat." Lucy was being sincere but she also had one eye on Matt's wallet.

"Thanks Luce really appreciate it but I'm going to live my life the best I can now and you only live once so I'll rack 'em up!" smiled Matt.

Lucy walked from behind the bar and pulled up a stool. Matt was busy chopping up two lines of cocaine on the bar. He finished cutting the lines then rolled up a fifty-pound note then offered it to Lucy. She took it and bent over towards the cocaine that was awaiting her nostrils. He knew this was going to be a good night.

"And no pinching my arse this time!" She said, just before she snorted a line. She came back up then bent down again and snorted the other line. She came back up and gave the note to Matt.

"You greedy cow!"

They both burst out laughing. Lucy then took a huge swig of wine.

"I better do some more then!" Matt said with mock enthusiasm.

"Excellent behaviour!" Lucy clapped her hands together.

Lucy reached over the bar and grabbed her cigarettes, lighter and an ashtray. Matt had chopped up the rest of his cocaine into four big lines. Lucy light her cigarette and inhaled deeply. Matt snorted one of the lines.

"I know I keep saying it, but I can't believe how different you look. You're a bit of a sort all of a sudden. Jo couldn't believe it either." Lucy had spoken to her friend Jo who was in earlier. Lucy informed Jo her of her plan to corner the now handsome and wealthy Matt and shag him as soon as possible.

Matt took a big swig of his drink. Lucy put her cigarette in the ashtray.

"Whose Jo?" asked Matt, interested that two women had been talking about him.

"Never you mind." Lucy leant in and kissed Matt full on the lips.

She then grabbed the rolled fifty-pound note and sniffed two of the lines. She came back up, swigged more wine and took a deep drag on her cigarette. As she was doing this, Matt snorted the last line then downed the rest of his whiskey. They both looked at each other for a moment. Matt leaned in to kiss Lucy. Their lips locked together. They kissed passionately. They started to undress each other. They were almost naked when they moved to a table. Lucy sat on the table and spread her legs. Matt moved towards her and inserted his penis into her sopping wet vagina. They started having furious sex for a few seconds

"Fuck me from behind!" Demanded Lucy

They changed positions and continued having sex. Lucy was now moaning in ecstasy as Matt started moaning too. Matt couldn't hold on any longer and climaxed

"Aaahhh fuckin hell!" Matt shouted as he unloaded deep into Lucy's vulva.

"Mmmmmmm!" Lucy was climaxing as she could feel Matts penis pulsating his hot semen into her.

They held their position for a while then broke away.

"You never did tell me why they call him Deckchair..." Lucy said breathlessly.

"Fuckin hell! Talk about kill the moment!" Matt was standing and swaying as the blood had rushed away from his head. Matt was feeling the effects of his massive orgasm coupled with the amount of booze and cocaine he had ingested.

"Oh! Tell me!" Lucy giggled.

"Alright!" Matt wasn't happy with this conversation so soon after this special occasion. After all, Matt had not had sex with anyone other than prostitutes for as long as he could remember.

"When he was a kid, him and his family always went on holiday down to Clacton every year. They were on the beach one day and he sat down on a deckchair. It collapsed and cut half his little finger off."

"Oh, that's why his little fingers missing! That's awful... what about Jackdaw then? How did he get that name?" Lucy asked very inquisitively

"For fuck's sake! I don't know... I'll find out and tell you next time, eh? "Matt was seriously pissed off that after this encounter, all Lucy could talk about was the pair of vermin. Matt was feeling unsteady and slurred his words.

"Who says there's going to be a next time? I really need a wee..." Lucy walked off towards the toilets holding her vagina.

Matt was left standing there, looking towards Lucy, trying to comprehend everything that had happened to him tonight. He looked at the table that they just had sex on. It was the same table that he was sitting at earlier with Deckchair and Jackdaw. He didn't feel well and couldn't comprehend if he was awake or dreaming, as the effects of the long day that he had experienced all began to grip Matt at once. The rush of blood from the sexual intercourse, coupled with the mix of strong lager, sambuca, almost half a bottle of whiskey and cocaine, had now taken full effect and control of Matt's mind. An apparition of Deckchair suddenly appeared in exactly the same position that he was sitting at earlier.

"I bet you didn't expect to see me again tonight, eh?" said the apparition of Deckchair, which was looking towards Matt's penis and waggling the stump that was left of his little finger. An apparition of Jackdaw suddenly appeared in the exact same position that he was sitting at earlier.

"Or me! Great performance! Not that it lasted too long, eh?" Said the apparition of Jackdaw smarmily.

"Yeah! The force was strong with you tonight eh mate..." Said the apparition of Deckchair with a chuckle.

Both apparitions disappeared. Matt was staring at the empty seats. He rubbed his eyes and shook his head. He was unsteady on his feet.

"Fuckin hell..." Matt whispered to himself.

MATT AND DORIS' FLAT

The front door opened. Matt staggered into the hallway. He quietly closed the door behind him and staggered upstairs to bed.

CHAPTER XI
GOODBYE HELLO

Matt was lying in bed. The curtains were closed. He stirred and woke slowly then jolted. He was awake now. He stretched out. He looked up at the clock by his bed. It read twelve fifteen PM. He sat upright. He got out of bed. He staggered a bit as he walked out and downstairs to the kitchen.

Matt shuffled into the kitchen. He grabbed the kettle. He pulled the lid off and saw it was almost dry. He shuffled around to the kitchen sink. He turned on the tap and started filling the kettle from the tap. He lifted the kettle and drunk some water from the spout as the water from tap gushed into the sink. He moved the kettle back under the tap and continued filling it. He turned the tap off. He put the kettle on to its holder, put the lid back on and switched it on. He turned round and peered into the microwave. He pushed the open button causing the door to swing open. He pulled out a dinner plate that was covered with another dinner plate. He pulled the heavy plates containing last night's dinner. Matt grinned with glee wondering what it might be. He put it down on the kitchen table and pulled the top plate off. It was four sausages, mash, peas and onions covered in a thick skin of gravy. Matt ate one of the sausages whilst looking out of the kitchen window. He put the plate back into the microwave and turned the dial to three minutes and pushed the start button. It was a hot sunny day, so Matt walked out of the kitchen, through the passage and into the living room. He opened the balcony door and walked out onto the balcony which overlooked South London across to the city. He stood there for a while, taking in the view. The kettle's whistle broke him from his trance. He walked back into the living room and noticed his mother's handbag on the table with wheels that he was eating his Chinese off the night he won the lottery. He also noticed a pair of her glasses on the arm of the armchair.

"Mum?" Shouted Matt.

He walked out of the living room into the passageway and straight up the stairs. He got to his mother's room, but the door was shut. He knocked on the door.

"Mum?" He knocked again.

"Mum?" He opened the door and saw his mother in a contorted heap on the floor, motionless. Doris had fell forward her head was turned towards the door. He could see his beloved mothers face. Her skin was pale. Her eyes were open, but she was dead. Matt stood there motionless for a split second. Matt could smell death.

The microwave downstairs started bleeping and made him jump.

"Oh Mum..." Matt's voice croaked with emotion.

PORTCULLIS STREET OUTSIDE WICKSIDE FC GROUND – ONE MONTH LATER.

The entrances to the turnstiles of Wickside FC all had queues formed at them.

WICKSIDE FC PRESS AREA

Two local newspaper journalists were seated just behind the dugout, busy making notes. A lone radio commentator wearing headphones and holding a microphone, was sat beside them. Behind him was a crude set up of an array of yellow and white power extension leads and black audio leads to the microphone and headphones and a yellow 240 volt to 110 volt step down transformer which all fed into and out of, a beaten up old green and black Long Wave broadcast unit, that had been donated to the local Homerton Hospital radio station by The Royal Electrical and Mechanical Engineers or REME for short, to allow commentary from Wickside FC's ground to be broadcast to the hospital.

"Today is the day! It's do or die for Wickside! The Tin Soldiers must win this game against Highbridge Swifts, who are chasing promotion themselves, to secure automatic promotion to the conference or face the lottery of the play offs. By twist of fate, any team that they may face in the play offs, have already beaten them this season. By all accounts, no pun intended, Wickside could be in serious financial trouble if they do not get promoted this season as potential backers to this ailing, but once great club are only interested if they are a Conference side and current owner Jimmy Archer cannot afford to keep the club afloat past this season." Local man Ian Pearson, spoke into the black foam windscreen of his handheld microphone.

Ian was an ex REME serviceman. He was responsible for getting the equipment donated by his regiment. Ian looked after and serviced the equipment as well as doing the broadcasting. He had aspirations of getting into mainstream radio since leaving the army after joining at sixteen and serving his twenty-two years with distinction and receiving a full pension. He also helped at the hospital doing odd jobs after his radio shifts. Ian was a lifelong Wickside supporter.

WICKSIDE FC DRESSING ROOM

All the players were sitting down. Bobby was standing and

addressing them all.

"This is it boys, the time has come. We all know what we have to do, you all know your drills. To not win this game will invite catastrophe to this club. To win this game will invite a whole new era to this club that we can all play a part in. I know you can do it, you know you can do it. Now get out there and do yourselves proud."

Bobby clapped his hands together twice.

"Let's get out there and win this game!" Shouted Bobby as he pumped his fists.

All the players rose as one, fully pumped up for the game, hitting each other and shouting and pumping their fists in the air. As they started walking out of the dressing room door, Bobby was slapping each player on the back to encourage them.

WICKSIDE FC PITCH

The Highbridge Swifts players were already out on the pitch as the Wickside team came running out. Tin Soldier by The Small Faces was playing on the pitch side speaker system. The players took their positions on the pitch. Bobby was last out. He shook hands with the opposing manager Don Fryer. Both managers sat down on their respective benches. The Wickside FC fans were singing their version of the Tin Soldier song with their own lyrics.

"WE ARE THE WICKSIDE TIN SOLDIERS

WE ARE THE BOYS FROM THE FORT FORT FORT

WE KISS THE BADGE ON OUR SHIRTS

WHEN THE BALL HITS THE BACK OF THE NET NET NET

THEN WE'LL GIVE YOU A KICK

'CAUSE WE ARE THE BOYS FROM THE WICK WICK WICK

WICKSIDE GIVE US A GOAL

WICKSIDE

WICKSIDE WIN THE GAME

WICKSIDE

WICKSIDE WE CHEER FOR YOU

'CAUSE WE LOVE YOU

WICKSIDE

THE FORT

The Wickside fans sang their hearts out.

"Come on boys this is it!" Shouted Bobby towards the pitch from the ramshackle bench area.

The music stopped as the fans stopped singing. The referee flipped a fifty pence coin with his thumb and fore finger. The silver hexagonal coin shone in the sunlight as it flipped over and upwards through the air as it ascended for a split second then stopped spinning and descended to the turf, landing heads up.

"It's heads. Highbridge, it's your kick off." The referee said sternly.

The two captains shook hands then stepped back to take their positions. The referee blew his whistle. The Highbridge players passed the ball between each other. The partisan crowd were shouting from all sides of the pitch.

Over here!" shouted the Highbridge number eight.

"Highbridge pass the ball out towards the wing. Wickside 's Terry Cross slides in to intercept but the Highbridge number eight jumps out of the way and picks up the ball. He takes a few strides and crosses the ball into the area the ball into the area and it's met with a header by Highbridge striker Tommy

May and the ball hits the back of the net. One nil Highbridge Swifts." Ian reported solemnly.

"For fuck's sake!" Bobby threw his water bottle down in disgust.

The fifty or so Highbridge Swift supporters behind the goal went crazy in celebration.

"Poor defending by Wickside! Highbridge were all over them. Wickside all over the place! They won't go up playing like this! Wickside nil Highbridge one after only nineteen seconds. I think that's a record for this season!" Ian said in disbelief.

Bobby cupped his hands to his mouth.

"Wake the fuck up you lot. Johnny, Pete you're defenders so fucking defend! Terry! Don't go to ground so fuckin easily! He sees that tackle coming before you even thought about it!" Bobby was furiously shouting and admonishing his defenders for their poor display.

"Lovely goal lads. Lovely. Keep it up. Now let's go straight for the jugular!" Shouted Don Fryer, standing near enough to Bobby to allow him to hear his snide remark.

"I'll go for his fuckin jugular in a minute!" Whispered Bobby under his breath.

"The Wickside manager Bobby Gorman is fuming down there. Berating his defenders. Being a defender in his day, it's got to hurt seeing defending like that! Meanwhile the Highbridge manager Don Fryer is as cool as a cucumber looking very relaxed." Remarked Ian.

WICKSIDE FC PITCH – LATER IN THE GAME

"Get me the ball please! I cannot score if the ball is not with me!" Louis Ngunde, or The Student, as he was known affectionately, was holding his hands out pleading for the ball

"Try getting back just a bit and you might be able pick it up for fuck's sake!" Terry Cross angrily replied.

"We are almost at the halfway mark. The Wickside players are arguing out there which is never a good sign. And there goes the whistle its half time Wickside nil Highbridge Swifts one." Summarised Ian.

WICKSIDE FC DRESSING ROOM

The players were filing back into the dressing room. Bobby and Billy Thorpe, his assistant, are the last in. Billy had said yes to Bobby straight away when he got the call to come down to London to help his old protégé. Bobby slammed the door behind him, almost rattling it off its rusty hinges.

"Right sit down you lot!" Bobby ordered loudly.

The last few players sat down.

"Anyone need any attention." Bobby asked, checking if anyone had any cuts or knocks.

The players all shook their heads.

"No? Of course, none of you need any attention. That's because you haven't been pushing yourselves... You haven't been putting your bodies on the line." Spat Bobby in disgust.

A few players were looking down at the floor. Some were looking at Bobby.

"If you lot don't buck your ideas up that's it, finito, end of fucking story! What the fuck are you lot playing at eh? Their lot are fucking laughing at us. They can't fucking believe how easy it is!" Bobby's face was red with anger. His head was tingling.

"The gaffer's right. You lot have been piss poor. And on a day like today for fuck's sake!" Chipped in Billy aggressively.

"Yeah, a day like today that could put us on the road to

greatness or send us down the rubbish chute. If it stays like this, you won't see me again so if you want to say your goodbyes now then let's shake hands right now and save some time after the game. If you want the chance to play in the conference and start getting noticed, then buck your fucking ideas up right now. What do you lot want?" Bobby asked with his arms held out to them all.

"We want promotion boss!" Answered Terry Cross straight away.

"Good answer son! What do you all want?" Bobby acknowledged Terry who he had respect for but was disappointed with so far today. He held his arms out again to his team

They all mumbled.

"What? I can't fuckin hear any of ya!" Bobby shouted at the top of his voice.

The players all jumped.

"Promotion." They all responded.

"I can't fucking hear you!" Bobby shouted even louder.

"PROMOTION! PROMOTION!" everyone in the room was shouting at the tops of their voices

"FUCKING LOUDER! LOUDER!" Screamed Bobby. His eyes were bulging, and spittle was flying from his mouth.

"PROMOTION! PROMOTION! PROMOTION!" The players and coaches responded even louder now. The players were now up on their feet pumping fists, kicking chairs and banging walls.

AWAY DRESSING ROOM

Muffled shouting, crashing and banging could be heard coming from the home dressing room.

"Ignore all that bollocks boys!" Don Fryer said with a wry smile on his face.

Some of the players were laughing but most of them were looking at each other sheepishly.

WICKSIDE FC CHANGING ROOM

The players were still going mad.

"I think it's time to get the medicine out. I think this lot have finally found their bollocks at last!" chuckled Billy.

"Do it!" Spat Bobby

Billy reached down to an old kit bag and pulled out a large bottle of Brandy and a stack of white disposable plastic cups. He lined the cups up on the treatment table, opened the bottle and started pouring.

"Gentleman's measures William!" Bobby said in a mock posh voice.

"Yes of course Robert! Nothing less would suffice in our current predicament." Replied Billy in an even more posh, Mancunian accent.

"Not in an old brown bottle like the old days?" Chuckled Bobby.

"Nah. Had one years ago when I was managing Scunthorpe. It was in a kit bag and the old fucker that I had as kit man, threw the bag down as we got into the away dressing room. It were Halifax I think... Local derby so I had a full bottle like, and it smashed! All the boys kit soaked in the finest Courvoisier! I think the fumes had the desired effect as we beat them three nil!" Billy replied proudly.

"Sweet!" Bobby replied. He had calmed down a bit now,

The players noticed what was going on

"Right gentlemen! You may wonder why our Billy is pouring

the Brandy or, in our day, as our old physio used to call it, medicine. This will sort you all out." Bobby said with a scowl on his face.

Billy handed out the cups of brandy to all the players. They were all staring at the cups and at Billy and Bobby, who now had a cup each.

"Now get this down you boys it will give you a good jolt. Greyhound racers squeeze their dogs' bollocks to get em fired up for the race. This is the equivalent. Although some of you would probably prefer having your balls squeezed by me, eh?" Billy said with a wink and a smile

The whole dressing room erupted with laughter.

"Especially you eh Godber?" Billy smiled at Godber.

They all roared with laughter.

"I reckon you'd enjoy it more!" Said Godber in a camper than camp accent. Although he had never came out and told the players or coaches, it was an open secret that Godber was gay. Everyone was happy with the status quo and Godber was one of the hardest players at the club anyway, so nobody would dare mess with him, gay or straight.

"Right then boys I propose a toast... To what can be..." Bobby raised his cup and downed his drink in one followed by Billy. All the players followed suit. A few of them grimaced at the strength of the brandy. The Student Louis Ngunde was the only one who hadn't drunk his. The rest of the players were more fired up and start chanting again.

"PROMOTION! PROMOTION!"

Bobby approached Louis.

"What's up mate?" Bobby asked nicely.

"But I do not drink alcohol boss." Louis replied proudly.

"I thought that might be the case and I admire you for it, but today is a different day. A day you may never experience again. You're part of a team and we do things together!" Bobby patted Louis on the back and looked his player in the eyes.

The Student looked Bobby in the eyes then looked at the cup in his hand. He looked back at Bobby then downed the drink in one, grimaced, coughed then crushed the cup and threw it to the ground.

"PROMOTION! PROMOTION! PROMOTION!" Louis was shouting at the top of his voice. His eyes were bulging and welling with emotion.

His teammates all suddenly took notice, laughed and started patting him on the back and hugging him. Billy approached him and slapped him on the back three times.

"Now go out there and fucking terrorise them my son!" Shouted Billy, in respect to what Louis had just done.

Louis Ngunde was more fired up than he had ever been during a match. He didn't drink because his earliest memories were of the warlords that terrorised the people of his home village back in Liberia. They all used to drink to excess, even though the rest of the villagers had nothing and could barely eat. This afternoon was somewhat cathartic and had helped Louis immensely. It was like a weight had been lifted and he wanted to win this game for his family and all the villagers that had been raped, beaten, tortured and killed by the oppressive regime which had forced his family to flee to the UK for asylum.

Bobby poured two more brandies for him and Billy. He handed Billy the drink. They touched their cups together in silence and downed their drinks. Bobby grimaced and has an aggressive look on his face as his players started making their way out. He slapped Billy on the back.

"Let's get out there Bill."

"Aye."

WICKSIDE FC PITCH

Both sets of players are out on the pitch. The Wickside players seem fired up. Bobby Gorman must have given them a right rollicking during the break." Chuckled Ian.

"Let's do this!" Shouted Louis.

"Right boys this is it! I don't know about you lot, but I don't want to be playing this lot next season in this poxy league!" Shouted Terry, turning to his teammates on the pitch and shouting so that the other team could hear him.

"You won't be playing us that's for sure! We'll be up and you'll still be playing in this, poxy league." Laughed the Highbridge Swifts captain, sarcastically.

The referee blew his whistle and the game kicked off.

"And here we go for the second half of what is such an important game for both teams and... Oh, a beautiful ball over the top from the Wickside captain and Ngunde is clear through. GOAL! Ngunde has smashed it into the top left corner. The Highbridge goalie had no chance with that rocket. The Highbridge players are appealing for offside, but the referee has given it. A wonder goal from Ngunde and what a story! They call him The Student as all he has ever done since his family fled war torn Liberia to start a new life in England, is go to school, college and university and is qualified in things ranging from Sports Science to Law but ended up choosing football as his profession after being scouted playing for his local Sunday league team. His watching parents must be so proud!" Ian screamed proudly.

The Student ran towards the bench and hugged Billy and Bobby with tears streaming down his face. They were all shouting and cheering. He looked over to see his parents hugging each other and blew them several kisses. He was then mobbed by his teammates. The whistle blew and they all ran back to their positions for the kick off, eager to capitalise on their sudden equaliser.

"Now go for their fucking jugular!" shouted Bobby.

Bobby looked towards Don Fryer, who had a dejected look about him but couldn't help giving a wry smile to Bobby, who smiled back.

"Once again Wickside have taken control of the game and are pouring forward leaving themselves very exposed but the back. The ball is moved into the path of Ngunde who is certain to score but... Oh! A crunching tackle has just come in from the Highbridge number six completely taking Ngunde out! Surely, it's a penalty and yes, the referee has pointed to the spot! Oh, Ngunde looks hurt, he seems in real pain. And the referee has red carded the Highbridge defender who can't have any complaints about that." Said a worried Ian.

The Highbridge centre back was walking towards the bench. A furious Billy Thorpe was gesticulating towards the player.

"What the fuck were you thinking lad eh? You fucking better not have fucking hurt the boy." Screamed Billy.

The defender walked towards Billy.

"Fuck off you old cunt!" shouted the Highbridge centre back.

"Old cunt Eh? I'll fucking show you!" Billy went to grab the player, but Bobby grabbed Billy and pulled him back.

"There seems to be a bit of an altercation going on down by the dugout. Billy Thorpe looks furious and is being held back by his manager as the Highbridge manager pulls his player away from the trouble and shoves him towards the dressing room entrance." Ian was fired up. The fan in him could not help but get excited and angry at what he was witnessing.

"You ok mate?" asked a concerned Terry

"Yes, I think so. I will take the penalty. Let me show them my strength!" Insisted a wincing Louis.

"Are you ok? Do you need treatment?" asked the referee who was breathless with all the running and shouting he had just done.

Louis got to his feet slowly and walked his injury off a bit.

"Give to me the ball please ref. I am ready!" Demanded Louis, who had a good grasp of the English language but did slip up now and again.

"You sure mate. I'll take it if you want?" Terry knew this was a futile gesture.

Louis grabbed the ball from the referee and slammed the ball down onto the penalty spot. The Wickside crowd went wild. Louis gesticulated to the crowd to shout louder. He walked slowly backwards then rubbed his injured leg. He said a quick prayer and crossed his chest.

"Ngunde and his family were devout Christians, and his father is the pastor of the local church hence his silent prayer. It doesn't seem a good idea for him to take the penalty as he does seem quite badly injured but... Oh his prayers have been answered! He smashes the ball straight down the middle and scores again! The Wickside players go to mob Ngunde, but he signals for them to be careful of his injury. The Highbridge manager looks dejected as his team are losing and down to ten men with only minutes left to go now." Ian could hardly keep his composure having been a Wickside FC for fan his whole life and he was currently working his dream job albeit he would be back to his boring office job as a Postmaster for Swiss a bank in the city which could be seen from the ground, due to its very close proximity to the City of London. The Radio shifts, odd Jobs and commentary for the hospital were welcome respite from the boredom of the job he had taken via an old mate from REME who also worked at the bank. While his Army pension was decent, he still needed to work and keep himself busy. The postmaster job was boring but the social side of it after work down at the Flying Horse pub was always good fun.

Bobby and Billy were hugging each other on the touchline.

"The Wickside management team of Bobby Gorman and Billy Thorpe are ecstatic. Another great story with these two as Billy Thorpe was Bobby Gorman's mentor when Gorman moved from the Artillery youth team up to Portham Football club in the North-West of England in the early eighties. Gorman took Thorpe's place when his career was cut short by injury. Thorpe went on to be a manager but retired a few years ago but came out of retirement to help his old teammate and protege. You can see the love and respect they have for each other right there in that embrace!" Ian was very emotional and had a lump in his throat.

"Right let's concentrate now and finish this. Let's make them two old fuckers on the touchline proud of us and give those fans something to brag about!" Terry clapped his hands to encourage his teammates.

"Right lads let's calm this down and get kicked off." Said the referee trying to calm himself down as well as the twenty-one players that were still on the pitch. He was hoping he would not have to send anyone else off.

"There's not much time left now as the referee blows for the re-start. The ball is pumped high into the Wickside half but is cleared straight away by Wickside centre half Gary Branch with a powerful kick straight back into the Highbridge area. Wickside 's Captain Terry Cross takes the ball and smashes a spectacular volley which cannons off the bar straight into the path of the on running Ngunde who lashes it through the legs of the Highbridge keeper for his hat trick! Wickside surely promoted now with only seconds left of the game!" Ian's voice was croaky.

"We've done it Bill! We've fucking done it!" Bobby hugged his mentor hard.

Bobby pointed towards the seats where all his family, Jimmy and Stevie were all celebrating wildly.

"Well done my son! Well done!" Albert shouted towards his son. His eyes were moistening

Jimmy and Stevie are hugging each other.

"Yes!" shouted Jimmy.

WICKSIDE AWAY STAND

Matt Hooper and the former Wickside FC manager Clive Atwell were sitting amongst the Highbridge Swifts fans. Both were wearing Highbridge Swifts scarves, dark glasses and baseball caps, in a vain attempt to disguise themselves. Clive leaned into Matt.

"Right if you're serious about this Mr Chairman, then we buy the Captain Terry Cross, Ngunde, the Centre Half Gary Branch and the Goalie Glenn Peters. They'll compliment what we have already and what with the others that are coming in, we'll have a good enough squad to get us promoted out of the Conference..." Clive whispered into Matt's ear.

"And weaken them for next season." Matt wasn't whispering. He pointed towards the Wickside bench who were all celebrating wildly.

"I was about to say that." Clive whispered.

"And give you a bit of revenge." Laughed Matt.

"I'm telling you, if they had given me more time, I would have got them promoted. That's nearly all my team out there anyway." Whispered Clive a bit louder this time, due to still hurting from being sacked.

"Well, you're promoted now anyway, now you're manager of Seaford Way. And you get to fuck them up now too!" said Matt with an evil grin.

"Yeah, well it is what it is now. Anyway, are you serious about this or what?" Clive wasn't whispering anymore and was looking at the pitch.

"Yes, I'm fuckin serious about this. I went for higher calibre managers and players but none of them wanted to know, even players near retirement in higher leagues. I was offering top dollar as well but they either weren't interested or were taking the piss in what they wanted in wages, so I changed tack and went for managers and players from around this level. That's where you came in. So yes, I am fuckin serious about taking Seaford as far as I can fuckin get them. My old man was a fan and so am I. I want to make him proud so he can look down on me taking this club up." Matt said proudly.

"Fair enough. I get the message. Nice to know I weren't first choice though! But fuck it! Let's do this! You get the ball rolling by talking to that cunt of a chairman Jimmy Archer. In the meantime, I'll tap them up. I've still got all their numbers, and most were sad to see me go. We'll sort it. As long as you offer them a lot more than they're on now, I'm sure they'll come." Clive said confidently.

"Don't worry. I'll make them all offers they won't be able to refuse." Matt said with conviction, knowing his windfall was enough to give them all massive pay rises to achieve his goal.

WICKSIDE PITCH

"And that's it! The referee has blown his whistle. Wickside are back in the Conference for the first time in twenty years. Wickside three, Highbridge Swifts one. The crowd are now on the pitch and are lifting some of the players up and carrying them. They are ecstatic. This could signal a new chapter for this club who have been through the mill this last twenty years and were rumoured to be going out of business if they didn't achieve promotion. It looks like the Wickside chairman Jimmy Archer is making his way down onto the pitch now. He has a bottle of champagne and is spraying it all over Bobby Gorman and Billy Thorpe, who are jubilant. They all embrace each other. What wonderful scenes here at The Fort in Portcullis Road!" Ian Pearson had tears in his eyes.

FINAL THIRD

CHAPTER XII
SALE OF THE CENTURY

ONE WEEK LATER SEAFORD WAY FC MANAGERS OFFICE

"Hello Terry... It's Clive... Congratulations on promotion... I just wanted to run something by you... "

PLAYA BLANCA LANZAROTE
AROUND THE SWIMMING POOL OF THE FRUIT DE LA MERE RESORT

Bobby was lying on a sun lounger with earphones on that were connected to Walkman tape player. Vicky was on a sun lounger next to him reading a book. His mobile phone rang.

"For crying out loud!" Vicky said disappointedly as Bobby's phone had not stopped ringing.

Bobby picked the phone up from under the sun lounger and answered the call.

"Hello?" Bobby was not happy.

"Bobby... It's Jimmy."

"Yeah, I know."

"Oh yeah it comes up on the phone don't it. I'll never get used to

that! Anyway, Ngunde's going as well now..."

"What do you mean Ngunde 's going an all?" Bobby's voice raised in anger.

"That fat Wanker has poached him as well!"

"That's half the team... The best bloody half!" Bobby was devasted.

"That's why he's poached them. Weaken us and strengthen them. "

"There's rules against it but there ain't a lot we can do I suppose, with the kind of money he's offering... It's out of hand now though Jim!"

"I know. Ali's well fucked off! But there are other ways..."

"What do you mean?"

"I'm gonna pay that fat fucker a visit and hopefully bump into that snake Clive while I'm there."

"Jim don't be doing anything stupid now will you?"

"Don't worry son. I'll just let him know he needs to back off a bit that's all."

"No Jim I don't want..."

JIMMY'S LIVING ROOM

"Sorry mate What's that? What? The lines going funny I'll call you later!" Jimmy smiled as hung up on Bobby.

AROUND THE SWIMMING POOL OF THE
FRUIT DE LA MERE RESORT

"Tosser!" Bobby said through gritted teeth. He could not be bothered to call him back to remonstrate with him as he just wanted to enjoy his holiday.

Vicky sat up from her sun lounger. She gave Bobby a dirty look then tossed her head back onto the sun lounger.

SEAFORD WAY FOOTBALL CLUB CHAIRMAN'S OFFICE

Matt Hooper and Clive Atwell were sat opposite each other at Matt's Desk.

"So how we doing then Clive?" Matt asked eagerly.

"I'm almost there with Ngunde and that's it then. The plan will be complete." Clive said proudly, clapping his hands and rubbing them together gleefully.

The phone on Matt's desk rang. Matt picked it up straight away.

"Matt Hooper." Matt had started answering the phone in this manner as he had remembered somebody important in one of the soap operas, he and his mum watched, doing it which impressed him. He thought that it made him sound important to whoever was calling him as he was now receiving phone calls from all sorts of people since he had become involved in Seaford Way.

"Hi Matt, it's Katie. I have Jimmy Archer at reception to see you, but he's not booked in." Katie the receptionist said nervously.

"Oh really? Hold on..." Matt held his hand over the phone receiver.

"It's only Jimmy Archer downstairs!" Matt said slightly nervously but seemed pleased.

"Fuck! Don't let him up for fuck's sake!" Pleaded Clive.

Matt took his hand off the receiver.

"Show him in please Katie. Thanks." Matt put the phone down. Clive looked at Matt with a very worried expression. The colour had drained from his face.

"What the fuck are you doing? He's a fucking nutcase. And well connected... If you know what I mean?" Clive was trying to talk

Matt out of letting Jimmy Archer into their world.

"Fuck him the old cunt! I've heard he's well past his sell by date these days... I've done me homework. He's still on license. And I've got cameras all over the place." Matt said very cockily and pointed to the cameras in the two corners of the room which gave a full view of the office.

"He'd be mad to do anything here. Plus, it will be good to see you squirm!" Matt said vindictively.

"That's nice of you! This is a bad move if you ask me." Clive was scared.

"Well, I ain't asking you. I own this club and I'm the chairman... So, I can do what I fucking like." Matt shouted.

There was a knock at the door.

"Come in." Shouted Matt.

The door opened into the office. Katie showed Jimmy Archer in. Matt stood and walked towards Jimmy. Clive got up more slowly and turned around. Matt held his hand out to shake hands with Jimmy, but Jimmy walked past Matt straight toward Clive. Matt nodded at Katie. She walked out closing the door behind her.

"You fucking piece of shit. We looked after you!" shouted Jimmy.

Clive was nervous and uneasy and looked to the floor. Matt walked towards Jimmy and Clive.

"Oi! You don't just walk in here shouting the odds." Matt shouted confidently, knowing that everything was being caught on camera.

"Fuck off! I'll deal with you in a minute! What the fuck do you think you're doing tapping up our players?" Jimmy demanded.

"You didn't look after me... You fucked me over!" Clive shouted back.

"Gents! Let's sort this out nicely please." Matt interjected.

Jimmy poked Clive in the chest.

"You don't contact any more of our players... Do you hear me?" Jimmy made Clive jump. Clive looked to the floor.

"I own this club and my manager can do what he likes..." Matt was trying to protect Clive and felt bad now.

Jimmy turned to Matt.

"And you... You fat prick! You can go and fuck yourself! Throwing your money round like some fucking bigshot! You're a fucking clown and I warn you now, stop fucking with our club!" Spat Jimmy

"Right, you old cunt! I've tried to be civil with you but that's it! You can fuck off out my office or I'll call security!" Matt was getting nervous now, cameras or no cameras. He knew he had made a mistake.

"I'm leaving. But I warn you now, I'll be back here the minute I hear anymore of you fucking about with our players. Next time I won't be so fucking nice!" shouted Jimmy.

"You know the way out!" sneered Matt.

Jimmy walked out and slammed the door behind him. Matt ran over to his desk, picked the phone up and punched in three numbers.

"Katie... Its Matt. Make sure that crusty old arsehole leaves... Oh ok." Matt put the phone down.

"She's good that girl."

"What?"

"She called security to make sure he goes."

The phone rang. Matt picked it up.

"Yeah? Lovely. Cheers Katie." Matt put the phone down.

"He's gone." Sighed Matt.

"I told you he was a fucking loon! Don't fuck with him." Clive shook his head as he spoke.

Matt was deep in thought.

"Matt?" Clive hissed, trying to get Matt's attention.

"I won't fuck with him... But I know some people who will!" Matt pulled his mobile phone from his inside suit pocket, searched for a number then dialled it on the office phone.

"Why don't you just use your mobile?" Clive asked, slightly confused.

"It's cheaper to use the landline! Look after the pennies and the pounds... Deckchair... It's Matt Hooper... Yeah... I've got something I want you and Jackdaw to do for me." Smiled Matt.

Clive sat down and slumped in the chair holding his head in his hands, knowing that Matt was about to fuck with Jimmy.

OUTSIDE JIMMY ARCHER'S HOUSE – LATER THAT NIGHT

Jimmy was fumbling with his door keys trying to get the key into the lock. He finally opened the door. Two masked men with baseball bats ran through the darkness behind Jimmy. As Jimmy walked in, he went to close the door behind him. The door hadn't quite closed before it burst open. The door hit Jimmy and made him stumble through the hallway which was in complete darkness. The door closed and all that could be heard was heavy breathing. Jimmy moved toward the kitchen door, opened it and went in. He felt around and pulled a bottle of wine from the wine rack and kicked the kitchen door shut. There was total silence. He stood dead still, taking deep breaths. He heard some fumbling around.

"You go in first and I'll follow." Whispered Deckchair

"Fuck off you cunt! You go first!" Jackdaw hissed back.

"You fucking go, or you don't get paid!" Deckchair hissed back.

Deckchair found the hallway light switch and turned it on. He looked at the masked face of Jackdaw and pointed his baseball bat in his face.

"Fuck sake!" whispered Jackdaw.

Jimmy saw the light from under the kitchen door. The door burst open and a masked figure holding a baseball bat strode in. Jimmy swung the bottle of wine which connected fully to the side of Jackdaw's masked head causing him to fall to the side. Deckchair followed through the door and swung the baseball bat down onto the top of Jimmy's forehead. A trickle of blood started to roll down Jimmy's head. He was dazed but stumbled across to a knife block and pulled a large knife out of it. Jimmy was very dazed as Jackdaw swung his baseball bat wildly at Jimmy but missed. The bat crashed into the cooker, smashing the glass in the door. Jimmy lunged towards Jackdaw and managed to stab him in the left buttock causing Jackdaw to howl in pain. Deckchair found the light switch and turned it on then his baseball bat at Jimmy, who held his hands up. The bat connected with his right arm, breaking it and causing Jimmy to fall to the ground and drop the knife. Deckchair hit Jimmy on the back of the head. Jimmy stopped moving.

"You alright?" Deckchair whispered, looking down at the motionless Jimmy.

"The cunt stabbed me in the arse man! I've got to get it sorted I'm bleeding!" Jackdaw whispered breathlessly, holding up a bloody hand.

Deckchair saw a tea towel on the sink draining board. He grabbed it and threw it to Jackdaw.

"Hold that on it. Don't let any blood get on the floor. DNA and all that. Get outside and keep an eye out. I'm gonna see if this old cunt has got any cash lying about." Whispered Deckchair

274

"Nah man, let's just fuckin chip now!" Pleaded Jackdaw.

"Go and get in the caaaarrrrgghh!" Deckchair screamed out in pain.

Jimmy was in immense pain and had come around from the blow to the head and had grabbed the knife and stabbed wildly at Deckchair and caught him in the leg twice. Deckchair dropped his baseball bat. Jimmy got up and stabbed Deckchair twice in the stomach. He picked up Deckchair's baseball bat. Jackdaw was running away towards the front door but before he could open it, Jimmy smashed Jackdaw on the head knocking him out. Jimmy walked back into the kitchen holding the knife in his right hand which was limp from it being broken earlier. The baseball was in his left hand. Deckchair was slumped on the floor holding his leg and stomach Jimmy walked past him and opened the back door to the garden.

"Get the fuck outside! I don't want you bleeding all over the place." Jimmy said nonchalantly.

Jimmy pulled him towards the door and started kicking Deckchair, forcing him outside. Jimmy walked back to Jackdaw and picked his legs up and dragged him face down towards the garden through the kitchen. Jackdaw's head thudded face down as he was dragged out of the back door. Deckchair was up and trying to climb the fence. Jimmy ran towards the fence and swung the baseball bat into Deckchair's back, causing him to howl and fall.

"Everything alright Jim?" shouted Jimmy's next-door neighbour from over the fence. He could be heard but not seen due to the height of the fence

Jimmy walked over to his shed, opened the door and walked in.

"Yeah! Just the grandkids fucking about!" Jimmy shouted back with a chuckle.

Jimmy walked out of the shed with a roll of duct tape and some rope in his hand.

"Little buggers! I had mine round the other night. Run me ragged they did!" chuckled his neighbour from the other side of the fence.

Jimmy held the knife to Deckchair's neck and started taping his mouth up.

"Shut your mouth and it will all be easier." Whispered Jimmy to Deckchair.

"Yeah, these two have given me a right going over but I'll survive." Jimmy shouted over to his neighbour.

"I'm gonna get back to me beer. Goodnight mate." Shouted the neighbour.

"Goodnight!" Jimmy shouted back as he tied Deckchairs legs and wrists.

He then did the same to Jackdaw, who was still out cold.

"I'm gonna clear up the mess then get you two sorted out." Hissed Jimmy.

Deckchair eyes looked horrified. Jimmy walked into the kitchen and pulled out his mobile phone and dialled a number.

"It's me. I've got a couple of boxes that need picking up and storing. They're in a bit of a mess so you need to be careful. I'll need to be dropped off at the special A and E so ring and tell them I've hurt my arm and it might be broke. Get to my gaff. You'll need some help as the boxes are heavy and fragile." Jimmy said as he looked at them both.

"And not in good shape." Jimmy informed the man he was speaking to as Deckchair was rolling around groaning.

LA ROTE RESTAURANT IN LANZAROTE

It was a lovely balmy evening in Lanzarote. Vicky and Bobby were sitting opposite each other eating dinner in their favourite restaurant on the island.

"I'm gutted it's our last night." Bemoaned Vicky.

Bobby leant across the table and kissed her.

"I thought I had forgotten something..." Bobby smiled and winked at his beautiful wife.

"Everywhere we go!" Blushed Vicky as she noticed a couple of the other diners looking and smiling at the loving gesture, her husband performed at every restaurant they went to, wherever they were in the world.

"Don't worry love. We'll get away again in the winter. See how the season goes." Bobby assured Vicky.

"I know. Maybe even come back here? The weather's good all year round." Enthused Vicky.

Bobby was looking into the distance.

"Yeah... maybe..."

"What's up love?"

"It's not looking good for us. I'm gonna have to work like mad to get some more players in now and don't have a lot of time before the season starts."

"I'm sure you'll sort it out. Our Maria's Darren has moved down. You always said he was a good little player. And Liam would much rather play full time than do what he's doing at the moment."

"Those two are already on my radar."

"They'll love that. It would be like old times over the rec. Cousins playing in the same team."

"Yeah, if they're both up for it they'll go straight into the first team. But don't tell them that!"

"I'll let Maria know you want to talk to him. I'll have to get his number off her."

Bobby was looking into the distance again.

"What else is wrong Bob?

Bobby looked Vicky in the eyes.

"I'm worried Jimmy's going to do something stupid..."

A WAREHOUSE IN EAST LONDON

It was morning now. The sun was beaming through the skylight in the warehouse roof. Jackdaw and Deckchair were tied up and blindfolded. They were both sitting on chairs with their legs stretched out with their feet resting on two other chairs. Their feet tied to the other chairs. Two large, masked men were standing behind them. They were both wearing white examination gloves that were smeared with blood. Another slightly smaller masked man was walking towards them. He had an air of authority as he walked over and took charge.

"Right, you pair of maggots! You're gonna tell me who sent you round to Jimmy's. Take the tape off them mushes please." The lead masked man ordered.

The two large, masked men each started pulling at the tape across the mouths of Deckchair and Jackdaw, who looked pale and very scared. They had both been beaten around the face and both pairs of their jeans were stained with the blood from their stab wounds. They hardly moved as the tape was ripped off.

"Aarrrgh!" Deckchair moaned.

"Owww!" Jackdaw moaned.

The lead masked man stood between the two sorry looking cardboard gangsters. He bent down to their head level.

"Talk to me!" He said softly.

"It was just a job mate! We was only supposed to scare him..." Jackdaw started to cry.

The masked man turned his head towards Jackdaw.

"And fucking rob him!" The masked man hissed.

"That was his idea!" Jackdaw sobbed and tilted his head toward the direction of Deckchair.

"You cunt! What happened to honour amongst thieves you grassing little piece of shit!" Moaned Deckchair.

The masked man turned around towards Deckchair.

"Oh, that's right..." The masked man stood up and made quotation marks with his fingers. One arm was slightly lower than the other

"Let's see if the old cunts got any money lying about..." Remarked the masked man and pointed to Jackdaw.

"Well, you didn't scare him..." The masked man pointed towards Deckchair.

"And you didn't get any of the old cunt's money! So, tell me who sent you and I might let you go home. And by the way, I know where home is for both of you two little rat cunts! I took the liberty of going through your wallets... Raymond and Andrew!" Chuckled the masked man as he looked at Jackdaw.

"Your mum's a bit of alright for her age. Bit of a MILF as they say! I definitely would..." The masked man laughed dirtily

"Fuck!" Jackdaw could not believe what he was hearing. Everyone wanted a go on his mum, so he knew the masked man was serious. He was starting to think that his voice sounded familiar but couldn't quite put his nicotine and hashish-stained finger on it.

"Tell him fuck all!" Deckchair laughed as he knew a few of the older generation had been with Jackdaws mum.

Deckchair reminisced in his mind. He even tried himself once but as pissed as Jackdaw's mum was that night, he still couldn't persuade her, due to his lifetime friendship with her son Jackdaw, as she said it would be like shagging her son. Jackdaw never found out, so he had respect for his mate's mum. He always thought that when the time was right, he would have another crack.

The main masked man nodded to one of the other two masked men. The masked henchman walked silently up next to Deckchair. He jumped up and landed one of his feet right down onto Deckchairs left knee, separating the knee bone from the tendons and splitting both the Tibia and Fibula in two, bending the leg the wrong way into a slight crescent shape between the two chairs, curving his foot that had been resting on the opposite chair, upwards.

"Aaaaaarrrrrggghhh" Deckchair's reminiscence about his best mate's mother was broken as suddenly as his leg had just been.

"Sorry? What was that?" The main masked man cupped his hand to his ear.

"It was Matt Hooper, he got us to do it!" Shouted Jackdaw.

"Thank you, Raymond! See Andrew, you could have saved yourself a broken leg there son."

The masked man nodded to the third masked man. He walked up next to Jackdaw and jumped up and brought one of his feet down on Jackdaw's right knee, breaking his leg in the same way too.

"AAAAARRRRRGGGGHHHH! What the fuck was that for? AAAARRGGGHHHH!" Jackdaw screamed in agony.

The lead masked man leant right into Jackdaw's ear.

"That was for singing like a bird you little cunt! No one likes a grass Raymondo... Untie their hands." Commanded the masked man doing all the talking.

The two other masked men untied Deckchair and Jackdaw. They immediately both held their damaged legs and the stab wounds in turn. The main masked man walked behind them and picked up a baseball bat from the floor. He climbed over Deckchair's legs and stood over him.

"You also clobbered him over the head with this fucking thing." The masked man examined the baseball bat in his hand for a second. He brought the bat up next to his head and swung it down toward the top of Deckchairs head, but he managed to cover the top of his head just in time with his now freed up hands. The bat smashed onto his fingers, crushing and breaking them all. This action protected his head somewhat, but pain seared through his head as well as his hands and fingers.

"Aaaaarrrgghhh!" Deckchair screamed as he held his hands in front of his face, looking on in horror at his broken buckled fingers. The main masked man swung the bat down again. This bat fully connected with Deckchairs cranium with a dull thud this time, fracturing his skull instantly and knocking him unconscious. Jimmy swung the bat round to the left which smashed into the side of Jackdaw's face with a load smack, shattering his cheek and jaw bones, knocking him unconscious too.

"Get this place cleaned up and get them dropped off outside that place. Call reception and say there's a delivery for that bloke I told you about. You know the drill."

The two other masked men both nodded then started to untie the two injured men's legs. The main masked man walked off. When he was out of sight, he pulled off his mask. It was Jimmy Archer. He took off his jacket to reveal that his right arm was in plaster. He pulled a sling out of his jacket pocket and put it over his head and set his broken arm into it.

OUTSIDE SEAFORD WAY FC GROUND – LATER

Katie was outside on an office mobile phone, looking around.

"They said it was a delivery for you, but I can't seem to... Oh my god!" Katie held her hand to her mouth.

She saw Jackdaw and Deckchair lying in a crumpled heap together. Jackdaw was barely conscious. Tears were rolling down his face. Deckchair was not moving.

"Call a fucking ambulance... Call a fucking ambulance..." Jackdaw hissed through gritted teeth, due to his broken jaw. He passed out

Matt Hooper came running towards them both.

"What happened to that delivery... Fucking hell!" Matt saw the two sorry looking men on the floor.

"I was looking out for it then found these two guys! They look like they've been mugged... Or something..." Katie was shaking and scared. She started to sob.

"Ok darling. You get inside and call an ambulance and I'll wait with these two and see if I can find that delivery." Matt ushered her away looking at his two compatriots

"Yes Mr Hooper!" Katie scurried away snivelling as she went.

Katie started dialling on the phone as she walked back in. Matt saw that she had gone in and bent down to them both. He nudged Deckchair but got no response. He checked his breathing. He pushed Jackdaw who jolted awake.

"Matt?" Jackdaw whispered through clenched teeth.

"What the fuck happened?" Matt was shocked.

"That geezer, he's a fuckin nutcase. It all went wrong mate! It all went wrong!" Jackdaw wheezed through clenched teeth, red spittle flecked Matt's shirt.

"Listen this can't get back to me right. If the police get involved tell em, it was rival supporters or something." Matt looked at the red flecks of the spit and blood mixture on his tailor-made white shirt.

"Yeah mate I ain't grassing that geezer up, he knows where we both live. What about Deckchair?" Jackdaw was speaking as best as he could through the immense pain of the broken bones, stab and impact wounds around the various parts of his body. He was concerned for his best mate.

"He's breathing. There's an ambulance on its way." Matt reassured Jackdaw.

"Sweet mate." Jackdaw started to sob.

"The geezer stabbed us both then we got took to a warehouse where they broke our legs and beat us with baseball bats. They broke my fucking jaw and smashed him over the head and he ain't woke up since." Tears streamed down Jackdaws blood-soaked swollen face. His left eye had started to swell and close where it had been punched so hard.

"It's alright mate. Don't worry I'll look after you." Matt was trying his best to placate Jackdaw.

"Don't fuck with this geezer anymore, he'll go after our families." Jackdaw sobbed even more and winced in pain.

"Don't worry I fuckin won't!" Matt looked around hoping nobody was watching him.

WICKSIDE FC MANAGERS OFFICE – ONE WEEK BEFORE THE NEW SEASON STARTS

Bobby was on the phone. Jimmy walked in. Bobby nodded to him.

"Alright then mate, you can stop at my flat for a while and we'll see how we go. Vicky will give you the details. Me you and Liam living together! We'll have right old giggle! See you next week then. Bye mate." Bobby put the phone down. Jimmy sat down opposite Bobby at his desk.

"What you done to your arm?" Bobby asked curiously.

Jimmy pointed to his broken arm in the sling.

"Oh this... I was doing a bit of gardening and tripped over in the shed and broke it." Jimmy shrugged his shoulders.

"You. Gardening..." Bobby was sceptical.

"Yeah, it needed doing but the sheds in a bit of a mess. That's how I ended tripping over! Anyway, at least I'm left-handed so it ain't too bad." Jimmy shrugged again.

"Oh right... Well, let me know if you need any help with anything." Bobby said cheerily.

"Oi! I ain't an invalid just yet!" Jimmy chuckled.

"I know, I know!" Bobby chuckled along with Jimmy.

"How was your holiday?" Jimmy was glad to be able to change the subject.

"Not bad, but all the fucking phone calls didn't help! And half the teams fucking off! Other than that, it was lovely thanks! Mind you, it's all gone quiet on Ngunde..." Bobby remarked.

"Has it?" Jimmy said with as much conviction as could, knowing why this had happened and feeling pleased with himself.

"Yeah. I've spoken to him... He hasn't heard anymore. He said like the others, he didn't want to go but..."

"Couldn't turn the money down?" Jimmy asked rhetorically.

"Yeah yeah, but he wants money for good things like sending to Africa and helping his dad's church." Bobby said sternly.

"Well let's make him an offer somewhere near what they were

offering and see what happens. If we don't hear anything he'll have to take it and it'll send out a message to the others that we are trying. I'll have a word with Ali about the money." Jimmy reassured his manager.

"Yeah, good shout. I was just on the phone to her nephew as you come in. That's all sorted now. My boy's already up for it and if Ngunde stays, then we should only need two more. We could go with a couple of the youths to get the season started plus I've got a couple of trialists to look at. We're a lot weaker but I'll do my best. Let Ali know that please." Bobby enthused.

"Don't worry about Ali, he's sweet with you."

"Is he gonna come to the games?" Bobby asked enthusiastically.

"You try and stop him. I hope he brings some of his mates with him as we need investment more than ever now. That Seaford cunt has fucked our plans right up!" Jimmy spat in disgust.

"Well, it's the first game next week so let's put on a good show on and off the pitch for him." Bobby smiled.

"You sort it on the pitch, and I'll sort it off the pitch!" Jimmy reminded Bobby of the way he wanted things.

Bobby gave Jimmy a sarcastic smile.

"Talking of things off the pitch, did you ever go and see Hooper and Atwell?" Bobby asked inquisitively.

"Yes, I did… Let's just say we had a little chat and that's all you need to know son." Jimmy said with a mock smile. Jimmy's face straightened into a scowl. He stared directly into Bobby's eyes.

"Comprende!" Jimmy snarled.

"Yes Jimmy! Comprende. Fuckin bonne de douche! I don't wanna fuckin know, merci becoup!" Bobby gave Jimmy a stare.

CHAPTER XIII

THE BARE BONES

WICKSIDE FC GROUND - MORNING

The team was standing in a semi-circle with Bobby, Kenny Northolt, Billy Thorpe and Graham Reid standing in front of them.

"Today is the start of a new era. As you know, there have been a few changes... More than we anticipated, but we could never have accounted for what happened with some of our first team players leaving like that. We've moved quickly to replace those that have left. I would like to say thank you to our very own Louis Ngunde who has decided to stay with us despite initial interest from others. And I would like to congratulate him on becoming the new captain of the team." Bobby smiled and started clapping his hands.

Louis looked shocked. But soon started grinning from ear to ear. The rest of the team started clapping. A few looked surprised.

"Thank you boss I will be a good captain for you. It is an honour." Louis thumped his chest.

Bobby walked over and shook his hand. Louis shook hands with the rest of the coaches and the players started to clap even harder. A few whistled as he walked back to them. They were all patting him on the back and shaking his hand. Some hugged him.

"Alright alright calm down you big jessies! Well done, Louis!" Billy shook Louis' hand.

"One of the new players is my son Liam, who's a winger and another one is my nephew Darren, who's a goalie. They're here because they are family. That's how I knew about them. I know their ability and if they don't cut the mustard they won't play. The other reason they're here is because I get a family discount... So, they were bloody cheap!" Bobby laughed a little bit nervously as he was worried about accusations of nepotism.

The team and coaches all laughed.

"But seriously they won't be getting any preferential treatment I can assure you and I don't want you to treat them any different. I don't want to hear any bollocks from anyone about it, or any backbiting. I've also promoted young Luke from our Saturday under eighteen team. He's our youngest player at sixteen and he has been playing up for the under eighteens since being plucked from the under sixteens not so long ago, so please bare this in mind. He's good enough, so he's old enough as far as I'm concerned." Bobby looked around at his coaches and players.

Luke nodded, slightly nervous and embarrassed.

"I don't mind a bit of a laugh but if any of you have any problems you come to me or Billy. The door is always open. We are a team. So, we win together, and we lose together... Billy..." Bobby turned to his trusted lieutenant.

"Right, we're gonna change a few things around with the training this season. Let me introduce you to Big Kenny Northolt. He played with me and Bobby back in the day and he was a top striker." Billy pointed towards Kenneth Northolt.

Kenny was bristling with pride at the chance he had been

given, having also been out of the game for a few years. He had been coaching at several lower league and non-league clubs previously.

This is our Goalie coach Graham Reid for the new lads who don't know. I'll coach the defensive midfielders, Kenny will coach the forwards and attacking midfielders and Bobby will coach the defenders. Paul is still physio, but he is off getting geared up with supplies." Billy had finished his address.

"I'm here to help in anyway and I'm sure I won't be speaking out of turn when I say we'll be going for promotion." Chipped in Kenny.

"Spot on Ken! That's exactly what we're going for and we'll go as far as we can in any competition, we're in." Assured Billy.

"Yep. We're all in agreement on that. As well as coaching the goalies, I'll be doing a lot of the fitness work with you all and I'll work on that lot's fitness too!" Graham Reid pointed to Bobby, Billy and Kenny.

Everybody chuckled.

"As well as what Billy said about how we will all coach you, I'll mix it up a bit now and again, so Graham will coach the strikers to give a goalie's perspective on what a striker should do, and I'll coach the strikers from a defender's perspective and so on and so on... You'll be getting coached from all angles... You lot won't know what's hitting you!" Bobby said with a wry smile.

Bobby clapped his hands and rubbed them together.

"Right, we'll head back in and sample the delights of our new chef and then we'll hear our new guys sing a song for us!" Bobby smiled at the new youngbloods.

"What's all that about?" Liam whispered to Luke.

"I don't know!" Luke whispered back.

The coaches were laughing. Bobby's lanky goalie nephew Darren was looking around very bemused.

"And that includes the new coach!" Shouted Bobby with a sinister cackle.

Billy started laughing at Kenny who suddenly stopped laughing. Bobby looked at Kenny and Billy, remembering his song that he sang when he first joined Portham FC all those years ago. They must have all shared the same memory at once as they all looked at each other and started laughing again.

"Boss?" Louis interrupted the cacophony.

"Yes Captain Louis?" responded Bobby.

Louis looked slightly moved and smiled at the thought that he was now captaining Wickside Football Club.

"I do not believe that Mr Thorpe sang a song when he joined us Boss?" Louis said with a cheeky but slightly nervous smile.

Billy threw Louis a dirty look then looked at Bobby.

"Have you heard his singing?" Laughed Kenny about his old teammate.

"I think you're right Captain!" Chuckled Bobby.

"I'll sing you all a song!" Billy replied confidently although not entirely happy with being stitched up by Louis.

"Boss?" Louis was looking slightly more nervous now.

"Yes Captain Louis?" Bobby responded sarcastically as he knew what was coming

"I do not recall you singing us a song when you joined either?" Louis was smiling again.

"Louis... I think you're taking this Captain lark a bit too far now!" Bobby responded sternly.

Everybody fell silent.

"Fuck it. We'll all sing a song. You're right! All the coaches, the new players and me, will all sing a song every lunchtime until we have all done it. In fact, we'll all sing a song! From now on every one of us, one person a day, will sing a song to make it fair and for the craic!" Bobby clapped and surveyed his version of the team and coaching staff stood before him., seeing that this now had his stamp on it.

He was satisfied that this was the best he could have possibly done in the circumstances that had befell him and the team.

JACKDAW'S HOUSE

Jackdaw was sitting on the armchair in the living room. His leg was in plaster and his jaw was wired up. There were a set of crutches lent against the sofa. Jackdaw's mum Bernice was sitting on the settee watching TV. The doorbell rang.

"I'll get it." Bernice said cheerily.

"Well, I can't fucking get it can I!" Hissed Jackdaw through his wired jaw.

"Shut up you miserable so an so! At least you ain't in a coma like poor Raymond. His poor mum is worried sick she is..." Bernice said sadly as she walked out of the living room.

Jackdaw huffed as he heard the front door opening.

"Hello Matt... Come in."

The front door closed. Matt and Bernice walked into the living room.

"Cup of tea boys?" Asked Bernice.

"Yes please" Replied Matt in an especially nice voice.

"Don't make it so hot this time. It fucking almost melted the fucking straw last time!" Hissed Jackdaw, some spittle flew from his clenched together yellow and brown teeth.

Bernice picked up an empty mug with a straw in it.

"He ain't stopped fucking moaning... Considering he's lucky to be alive!" Bernice stomped out in a huff.

Matt leaned over towards the debilitated Jackdaw.

"What did you tell the old bill?" Matt's voice was back to normal and a touch sinister.

Jackdaw huffed through the wiring in his jaw. The spittle crackled through and some of it sprayed into the air.

"Oh! Not fucking how are you or anything!" Jackdaw leaned forward as if to give Matt a close up of his sorry state and bogged at Matt for a few seconds.

Matt was nonplussed. He sat down on the settee at the end nearest Jackdaw and just stared back at the sorry state of a man who still lived with his mother.

"Don't worry, they believed we got beat up alright but no, I didn't say by who. And fucking Deckchair certainly ain't said anything! Anyway, fuck all that, where's our fucking money? We need more on top coz of all this!" Jackdaw hissed out his demand then slumped back into his chair.

"Did any of you tell the blokes it was me that sent you to Archer?" Matt leaned in even further his hushed tones demanding an answer.

Jackdaw leaned forward again a bit quicker this time. It caused him to wince as the pain from the stab would that had been stitched up, stung through his body.

"Course we never!" Jackdaw's cheeks puffed out as he tried hard to whisper and sound hard at the same time.

"Thank fuck for that!" Matt's tone lightened as he slumped back into the armchair, thankful in the thought that the two idiots had not grassed him up.

"Where's our fucking money?" Demanded Jackdaw who was

not in any state to be demanding anything, but he was trying to be as menacing as his involuntary clenched jaw, crushed body and mental state would allow him to be.

Matt pulled out a thick brown envelope. He went to give it to Jackdaw. Jackdaw reached out to take it, but Matt pulled it back just out of Jackdaw's reach.

"You sure you didn't say anything?" Matt's brow burrowed above his designer glasses.

"No mate." Jackdaw's tone softened as he wanted the cash that was concealed in the brown envelope more than anything.

Jackdaw noticed that Matt's demeanour had suddenly softened, believing that he had not grassed him up. He saw his chance and snatched the envelope just like Jackdaws knew exactly when to steal eggs from other bird's nests, the split second that the mothers left the nest to gather food for their young.

Andrew "Jackdaw" Watson was an opportunist thief and the nickname just fitted perfectly the time that someone thought of it and blurted out that Andrew was like a Jackdaw, during a heavy Ganja smoke session one night. The name was so apt that the whole stoned room full of young men and women instantly pissed themselves laughing and instantly all agreed that the moniker fitted Andrew perfectly. And just like that, Jackdaw was his nickname forever more. Jackdaw stuffed envelope down the side of the armchair.

"Like I said we need a bit extra... You're fuckin rolling in it and me and Deckchair are fucked! Two hundred and fifty K each and the Old Bill never find out." Jackdaw hissed screwing his face up in anger and then even more from the instant pain that thumped through his jaw and head.

Matt was aghast and completely taken aback.

"You fucking little cunt! I ain't gotta pay you fuck all! You didn't even do the job properly!" Matt's voice was getting louder.

"You said he was some old cunt! You didn't say he was some fucking gangster... You must have known... Anyway, it ain't up for debate." Jackdaw looked away from Matt.

Bernice popped her head around the door.

"Do you want a sandwich boys?"

"No thanks. Don't worry about Matt's tea. He's just leaving... Ain't ya Matt!" Jackdaw glared at his mum and then at Matt.

"Alright..." Bernice looked a bit bemused. Her head popped back around the door frame as she went back to the kitchen.

"Half a mill into this account... I don't think I'm taking the piss considering your new found wealth Matthew..." Jackdaw hissed and crackled his demand through his painfully shattered jaw. His cheeks were bulging.

Jackdaw handed Matt a slip of paper. Matt snatched it.

"Why? How do I know if you'll even give it to Deckchair? He might not even wake up!" Matt was acquiescing slightly, knowing that he did not have much choice and that Jackdaw could ask for more and there wouldn't be much that he could do about it. He suddenly thought that this might be a good deal to buy their silence at this price as he had much more cash in the bank from his lottery win.

No matter how many times people had asked him, he had never let on exactly how much he had won and always stuck to the story that he had always told people, that he had won enough to not have to work for now and be comfortable, but he might have to start working again in a few years.

"If he don't wake up then his mum gets the cash... Anyway, I'm sure he will and when he does, we get free entry to all home games and free drinks forever... And we get to serve up at the games with no grief from any mug Stewards..." Jackdaw knew old Coke bottle Matt had no choice.

Jackdaw kind of smiled, revealing his brown ganja stained and yellow teeth and the hooks and bands that the surgeons had installed to repair the badly broken jaw.

The Doctor in charge of the operation to reset Jackdaw's jaw, had remarked about the sorry looking state of the teeth during surgery. The Doctor had jokingly remarked that he may as well pull out all of the teeth and start again. The Operating Department Practitioner had responded that the jaw would probably fall apart. One of the Nurses chipped in that they would never have the time to do it anyway as this was their last operation before ending a gruelling fifteen-hour shift and that they had arranged to go for a well-earned drink after. This made them all laugh as Jackdaw was lying unconscious and prostrate under anaesthetic, with a tube down his throat which was connected via a clear flexible tube, to breathing apparatus at the side of the operating table

"And you'll both keep schtum? The pair of ya?" Demanded Matt.

"As long as that money is in that account by tomorrow morning the latest..." Jackdaw pointed to the piece of paper in Matt's hand.

"It will be like nothing happened. Apart from the fact that me and poor Deckchair got the fuck kicked and stabbed out of us!" Jackdaw was starting to feel and look upset.

Matt got up to leave.

"I'll sort it." He looked Jackdaw in the eyes and turned to walk out but bumped into Bernice.

"See you later." Bernice said cheerily.

"Bye love." Matt walked awkwardly past Jackdaw's mother.

Matt quickly strode toward the front door. He fiddled with the door handle for a few seconds and then manged to escape the hell that he had just endured.

BOBBY'S FLAT

Bobby's mobile flip phone rang. He pulled it from his pocket and answered it.

"Hello?"

"It's me..."

"Jim is that you? You got a new phone?"

"Yeah, store the number in mate. I got my niece to do it for me, but I suppose you know how to do all this mobile phone stuff..."

"Yeah, I'm getting a bit of an expert at it in me old age but the boys do have to help now and again. Ok thanks for letting me know. First game next Saturday mate..." Bobby said excitedly.

"Can't wait mate." Jimmy sounded excited too.

"How's your arm?" Bobby asked.

JIMMY'S FRONT ROOM

Jimmy rubbed his plaster cast.

"Not bad. Not bad at all. Anyway, got to go. I'm cooking sausages. Ta da." Jimmy put the phone down.

GRAYS MECHANICS FOOTBALL CLUB GROUND

It was a mild sunny afternoon. The Grays Mechanics FC players were running out onto the pitch, followed by the Wickside FC players. Bobby was already standing in the away dug out, hands cupped to his mouth.

"Come on lads! Let's get this done. You know the drill!"

"Come on lads! A nice home win for the fans please! The Grays FC manager shouted to his team in response to Bobby's war cry.

"Yeah, all fifty of them!" Billy shouted sarcastically as the home end had what looked like fifty fans in it, but the away end had what looked like over one hundred and fifty Wickside FC fans in it. They were rocking at the sight of their team running out.

"I'm bloody pleased with our turnout today!" Bobby smiled as he pumped his fists towards the away end. They started to sing.

"THERE'S ONLY ONE BOBBY GORMAN! ONE BOBBY GORMAN! WALKING ALONG, SINGING OUR SONG, WALKING IN A GORMAN WONDERLAND!"

Bobby gave the fans the thumbs up. The fans cheered even louder.

"Cheers lads!" Shouted Bobby with his fists raised high above his head.

He turned to Billy.

"I wonder if old Pat made the trip?"

"I bet he has! It's not a long trip... It's only up the A thirteen." Smiled Billy proudly.

Since moving down South to London to become Bobby's right hand man at Wickside FC, he had a lot of spare time on his hands. Billy had been married three times and had two grown up kids from his first marriage who he barely saw. He was currently single and jumped at the chance to join his old protégé. He had rented a room in the same block of flats, downstairs from Bobby. Billy had taken a walk on a Sunday down through Colombia Road Flower Market right through to the top of Bethnal Green Road where it met Shoreditch High Street leading into The City. There was a Flea Market on the corner of the two old roads which stretched back centuries into London's history. He had bought a battered old A-Z off an old gentleman who was selling his surplus possessions that were laid out on the pavement. This was how people sold their wares at the old Flea Market. Some people even sold one shoe. Billy had gained a good knowledge of the London Streets and Roads as he was so fascinated by the road map book that he read it at night. Billy liked to know as much as could about just about anything.

Pat Bryce, an elderly gentleman with hair that was almost grey but still had the tinge of ginger that kept the two shades of colour fighting against each other and just about kept Pat classed as ginger. Pat was sitting at the front of the away stand. He was wearing a very old and frayed red and black Wickside FC scarf. He was cheering along with the rest of the away fans.

"Let's have it lads." Shouted Louis as the referee blew his whistle to start the game.

Louis passed it backwards and made a darting run forward, closely followed by a Grays player.

"Get it up to him!" shouted Billy.

The Wickside attacking midfielder Jack Ralford, made a darting run and passed it out wide to the Wickside left winger Dean Harris, who took one touch and crossed the ball into the box, where it was met by Louis' head, diverting it straight into the opposition net.

"Yeeeeesssss!" Cried the Wickside fans in unison.

The Wickside crowd went wild. Old Pat Bryce was almost knocked off his feet but was cheering and laughing.

"You alright dad?" Chuckled Pat's son, Little Pat Bryce as he was known, as he helped his dad.

"I'm bloody loving it!" Chuckled Old Pat Bryce as he steadied himself.

A young seven-year-old boy with bright ginger hair, emerged from the crowd.

"You ok Grandad?" Asked a concerned Pat Bryce Junior, as he was known.

Old Pat Bryce bent down and hugged his beloved grandson.

"You alright? Don't worry about your old grandad!" Old Pat Bryce squeezed his Grandson.

"I love it grandad! They all picked me up!" An excited, but still slightly out of breath, youngest Bryce kid of the clan replied.

Pat cuddled his grandson and then his son.

The Bryce family were a well-known family on the Fellowship Court estate in Shoreditch which was situated just off the Hackney Road. All the sons were named Patrick and they were always born with Ginger hair. It did get confusing at times. Therefore, every generation of the male Bryce's were unofficially christened with their own moniker. Names of which were borne, depending on their age, trade or what they drank in the pub. The current Old Pat Bryce's father was known as Whisky Pat Bryce in the pubs around the area for obvious reasons. He was banned from drinking from the top shelf in every pub that he played up in after drinking too much Guinness and then going on to whiskey when he couldn't stomach any more stout. His wife regularly went into the local pubs and told them in no uncertain terms that Whiskey Pat Bryce was not allowed to drink whiskey.

The Bryce family were an old Shoreditch & Hoxton family that stretched back generations to the time when Irish Immigrants travelled to London during the potato famine from eighteen forty-five to eighteen fifty-two.

GRAYS MECHANICS FC AWAY CHANGING ROOM

Wickside FC had won the game by one goal to nil. Bobby was standing, addressing his players and staff, who were all sitting on the ramshackle benches. Billy Thorpe was standing next to

Bobby.

"I have to say we were bloody lucky to scrape the win in the end but a wins a win. We can't just switch off at certain times like we did today. We defend as a team from front to back for the whole game. If we don't, we won't win against the better teams in this division." Bobby was relieved that they had won their first game but was not happy with the performance and knew that this was going to be a long season.

"Aye the gaffers right I think it's a case of a few too many bevvies in the summer eh boys?" Billy admonished the players.

"Yeah, most of you were blowing out your arseholes at seventy-five minutes so I'll be monitoring your weight closely from now on and you must keep to the diet plans." Bobby furrowed his brow as some of the players had clearly not been sticking to the strict regime that he had set for them over the summer.

"Yes, boss I will make sure this happens." Louis stood up and saluted Bobby.

"I can assure you sir!" Louis sat back down.

"Thanks Louis but you needn't go that far I know you're captain now but blimey, it ain't the bloody Third Reich here you know!" Bobby chuckled.

The whole room erupted with laughter. The laughter died down as some of the players near the wall, adjacent to the home changing rooms, gestured to each other that they could hear something. Muffled shouting could be heard. Billy Thorpe walked over and listened.

"Shush you lot!" Billy put his ear to the wall for a few seconds. He stepped back as the wall was thumped from the other side.

"It sounds like the bloody third Reich in there! He's giving them a right bollocking for losing to us!" Billy smiled at Bobby.

"He was giving it the right biggun on the bench as well!"

Bobby cupped his hands to his mouth.

"WHO ARE YA? WHO ARE YA?" Shouted Bobby at the top of his voice.

The rest of the team and staff joined in.

WHO ARE YA? WHO ARE YA? WHO ARE YA? Shouted the Wickside team in unison.

SEAFORD WAY FOOTBALL CLUB AWAY CHANGING ROOMS TWO MONTHS LATER

The Wickside players were changed and ready to take to the field. Bobby and Billy were addressing the players.

"Now we need to do these fuckers, or we will slip further away from them!" Billy snarled at the team.

"Yeah boys. They're romping it, but it's only October, and being nine points off them ain't bad but twelve points might be too much. Make no mistake we are going for the league... End of!" Bobby shouted.

SEAFORD WAY FC CHAIRMAN'S OFFICE

Matt was sitting at his desk. Deckchair and Jackdaw were sat opposite him. Deckchair was sat in a wheelchair and Jackdaw was sat in an office chair.

"I'm sure he knows... I'm sure he fuckin knows! I've been getting phone calls in the middle of the night and when I answer, they just hang up." Matt was manic and dishevelled.

Matt very paranoid. The paranoia was being heightened due to the amount of cocaine that he was snorting up his nostrils at every opportunity. The thought of Jimmy Archer coming after him and doing worse to him than he had done to the two sorry characters sitting in front of him in two very different chairs, was horrifying him. He had realised that he had got himself into an almost impossible situation despite his wealth which he believed that everyone was trying to take off him.

"He don't know... How do you know its him anyway?" Deckchair asked.

"It's probably some fan of another club." Jackdaw said assuredly.

"Probably a fan of this lot today, seeing that you took their best players, and we're top of the league now." Deckchair said smugly.

"You got anything for me then?" Matt asked enthusiastically.

"Course we have Matteus! Do the honours Deckus Chairus! Our Cocainus dealer has it hidden in his chariot!" Jackdaw chuckled.

Deckchair pulled open the compartment under the wheelchair. The compartment was there to house the small toolkit and puncture repair kit that were there for maintaining the wheelchair. On the day that Deckchair was finally discharged from hospital, Deckchair and his mother were receiving the wheelchair at the hospital. The Orderly in charge of the Wheelchairs had been explaining all the workings of the wheelchair to them. The Orderly had quite proudly remarked that he that had installed these boxes underneath every wheelchair because the toolkits came in a small bag which had to be signed for and issued along with the wheelchair. The Orderly moaned that the tool bags almost always got lost by the wheelchair users and never ended up getting returned despite all the well-meaning assurances from the healed patients. Deckchairs mother was listening intently but while the Orderly was waffling on, Deckchair had immediately thought that the box could be repurposed to carry cocaine. He thought that no coppers would dare try and search a man in a wheelchair. As soon as they had arrived home, Deckchair threw the toolkit in the bin.

"We should call you Wheelchair now instead of Deckchair!" Laughed Matt.

Deckchair stopped and looked at Matt.

"You're funny! I ain't heard that already, have I? About a thousand fucking times down the boozer!" Deckchair was not happy. He pulled out a plastic bag containing wraps of cocaine.

"How many?" Demanded Deckchair, who was not looking at Matt but only at his goods that he knew Matt would buy.

"Trois sil vous plait!" Matt replied eagerly.

"Deckchair pulled out three wraps and handed them to Matt. Matt went to take them, but Deckchair snatched his hand back.

"Money first!" Deckchair was now looking Matt square in the eyes.

"I'll give it to you later." Matt tried to dismiss the crippled Deckchair.

"Like fuck will you! You still owe for the last two, so I'll have what you owe and the money for these or, you get fuck all..." Deckchair remarked with an air of authority.

"Yeah, pay up you cunt or Deckus Chairus will run you over with his chariot!" Jackdaw got up and wheeled Deckchair around to where Matt was sitting and nudged Deckchair into Matt's chair.

"Alright... For fucks sake!" Matt reached into the inside pocket of his jacket and pulled out his wallet. He gave them both a dirty look. He opened the wallet and pulled out the wad of note that were in there and then preceded to count it all out onto the desk.

"That should cover it." Matt said begrudgingly.

"Another fifty'll cover it... You tight cunt!" Deckchair sneered.

Matt pulled open his drawer and took out a money clip full of notes and carefully eased out a fifty-pound note from it. He placed it on top of the pile of cash that he had just counted out.

"There you go... Don't get your wheels in a twist!" Matt said with huff.

Deckchair threw the wraps on to the table. Matt greedily picked them up one by one and then started to open one of them. He took a pinch from the wrap and snorted the cocaine up into his right nostril then took another pinch and snorted it up into his right nostril again. He offered some to Deckchair and Jackdaw.

"No thanks. I don't do that anymore. I just sell it." Deckchair said sarcastically,

"Me neither. We've both seen the light mate. Don't get high on your own supply!" Grinned Jackdaw smugly, looking at their cash cow who was well hooked on the bashed-up pub grub that they were constantly punting out to him.

"Fuck the pair of you then." Matt took two more pinches of cocaine.

SEAFORD WAY FC PITCH

Louis was running through on goal but was taken out by former teammate Craig Connor.

"Have that Ngunde! I never liked you anyway." Craig Connor was hoping that he had hurt Louis.

They had a training ground bust up a few months ago and Louis had got the better of him. He was going to retaliate but had been dragged away by his teammates and had never forgiven any of them for stopping him retaliating. He had been only too glad to take the money and join Seaford Way.

"REF! HE FUCKIN TOOK HIM RIGHT OUT!" An irate Wickside fan shouted from the crowd.

"WHAT A GREAT TACKLE! HE'S GONNA FIT RIGHT IN

WITH US! THERE'S ONLY ONE CRAIG CONNOR, ONE CRAIG CONNOR, WALKING ALONG, SINGING OUR SONG, WALKING IN A CONNOR WONDERLAND!" Sang a Seaford fan.

"Is that how you've been teaching him to defend? You dirty cunts!" Shouted Bobby, looking towards the Seaford bench.

"What did you fuckin say?" Clive shouted back from the Seaford bench.

"You fucking heard me!" Spat Bobby, staring straight at Clive.

Clive strode over towards the away bench. Bobby leapt to his feet and the two managers faced off. Billy Thorpe rushed in and dragged Clive away and pushed him back towards the Seaford bench, causing a melee to erupt between the two sets of opposing coaching staff. The referee blew his whistle to stop the game and ran over towards the melee.

"You lot cut it out! You stop it now or I'll send the fucking lot of you off!" Shouted the referee.

Some stewards and players managed to pull them all away from each other.

"You're a fucking disgrace to the game Seaford! Every man jack of you... From the top to the bottom!" Billy was apoplectic with rage.

What had happened since Matt Hooper had taken control of Seaford Way, systematically trying to ruin Wickside and other clubs, had boiled over in Billy's brain.

"Fuck off!" shouted Clive.

"Right that's it! You two are off!" Shouted the referee as he waved his red card to both the Seaford manager and the Wickside assistant manager. Both sets of fans were boiling mad. Clive and Billy exchanged filthy looks and walked off down the tunnel knowing they had both let their respective clubs down

"OFF OFF OFF OFF!" shouted the Wickside fans.

"OFF OFF OFF OFF! Responded the Seaford Fans.

"For fuck's sake ref! They bloody started it coming over to our bench!" Remonstrated Bobby.

"Shut it Gorman or you'll be next. Control yourselves and your staff!"

"You too while your managers off!" The referee pointed to the Seaford assistant coach.

Both benches settled down and the referee restarted the match.

"Attack them now lads! 4-3-3 to win the game! You know the drill. Louis? Louis?" Bobby was shouting at the top if his voice towards Louis Ngunde.

Louis turned to his manager. Bobby signalled four-three-three with his hands and fingers.

"Yes boss." Louis shouted back to his manager.

Louis barked the managers orders to the rest of the team.

SEAFORD WAY CLUBHOUSE TOILETS

Matt was in the disabled toilet cubicle snorting cocaine. He finished and walked out and started to wash his hands at the wash hand basin. As he finished and shook the water off his hands, he checked himself in the mirror.

Jimmy Archer walked in.

"Ah!" smiled Jimmy.

Matt froze and stared at Jimmy's reflection in the mirror.

"What?" Matt asked nervously.

"I had a bit of an accident at home a while back, just after I paid you a visit. I think you had something to do with it..." Jimmy rubbed his chin

Matt was petrified but the cocaine started to kicking in.

"What makes you think that then? You know fuck all old man now f..."

Jimmy rushed towards Matt and punched him square on the cheek, knocking Matt back into the disabled cubicle. Matt hit his head hard on the back wall. He was dazed and fell, ending up sitting awkwardly on the toilet pan. Jimmy pulled out a knuckle duster from his trouser pocket and punched Matt hard in the face. Matt was now unconscious. Jimmy started searching Matt and pulled out his wallet from his inside jacket pocket. It was full of fifty-pound notes. Jimmy took all the cash. He noticed Matt's cocaine in the bottom of the wallet and took that too. He carried on searching Matt and found a money clip full of cash in the other inside pocket of Matt's tailored suit jacket. He took that too.

"Like a bit of sniff too, eh? You fucking fat. Flash. Cunt!" Jimmy said with a sneer as he stood victoriously over Matt.

Jimmy opened the wrap, took a pinch in his thumb and fore finger and snorted it up into his right nostril. He then undid his flies. He pulled his boxer shorts down, held his penis and directed it at Matt and started to urinate.

"No hard feelings mate. Have a drink on me why don't ya?" Smirked Jimmy.

The urine splashed all over Matt's face, causing his lips to quiver under the pressure from the urine jet emanating from Jimmy's urethra. The urine started to fill Matt's mouth. The urine jet subsided. Spurting arcs of urine were reaching lower and lower, jetting spurts over Matt's chest and groin area. Jimmy's bladder was approaching emptiness. He shook his penis, which threw drops of urine all over Matt. Jimmy threw the rest of the cocaine all over Matt's face and rubbed the almost empty wrap around Matt's nose. Jimmy rolled the wrap into a tube and pushed it up into Matt's right nostril.

"I take it you're right nostrilled..." Chuckled Jimmy.

Jimmy then took out a small digital camera from his trouser pocket and took a picture of Matt. There was a bright flash. Jimmy inspected the camera display screen. There was a screenshot picture of Matt. The flash had made Matt's eyes open wide

"Even better!" Chuckled Jimmy.

Jimmy took another picture of Matt with his eyes wide open. The urine gave Matt a sweaty appearance in the picture and the rolled-up wrap was still wedged into his right nostril. Jimmy spat at Matt. A white foamy globule landed on Matt's forehead. It stayed still for a second then started running down Matt's forehead.

"A little chaser for ya! Any word of this to anyone and I'll bury ya. Understand?" Jimmy screwed his face up as he spoke.

Matt barely nodded as tears rolled down his cheeks. Urine dripped from his mouth. His own urine started flowing out of his penis, taking the shortest route down through and out of the bottom of his right trouser leg.

"I guessed you were right nostrilled. It turns out you're right legged as well!" Jimmy laughed at his own joke then punched Matt with a right hook sending Matt sprawling off the toilet and wedging him between the wall and toilet in a mangled heap.

"T T F N!" Jimmy did a mock wave at Matt whose eyes were open, but nobody was home.

Jimmy walked out of the cubicle and closed the door behind him. He reached into his pocket and pulled out a one pence coin. He used it to lock the cubicle door from the outside. He walked out of the toilets.

Deckchair and Jackdaw were at the bar. Jimmy walked out of

the toilets and towards the bar. Deckchair nudged Jackdaw. Jimmy noticed them and walked over and stood next to them.

"Your mates had a nasty fall in there. I think he might have had a bit too much..." Whispered Jimmy, tapping his right nostril with his index finger.

"I think you better go and see if he's ok. You two better keep schtum about our little deal or I'll come after you an all." Jimmy growled at them both.

"You didn't tell him that we told you then?" Deckchair asked nervously.

"Course not you thick cunt. I told him I worked it out myself, I mean, I go and visit him and the next thing I've got two masked men in my house trying to beat me up! It don't take too much working out does it? You're all as thick as each other you South London scumbags!" Jimmy said with an air of authority.

A big cheer erupted from outside. They all looked towards the window facing the pitch.

"And it looks like we've scored. This day just gets better and better!" Jimmy punched the air.

"Go on Wickside! Large scotch please love!" Jimmy called to the barmaid.

Jackdaw wheeled Deckchair off towards the toilets. The barmaid handed Jimmy his drink and he downed it in one.

SEAFORD WAY PITCH

The away crowd were going wild after their team had scored. Billy was in the stands. Old Pat Bryce was hugging him.

"We done it Pat! We fucking done it!" shouted Billy

"They might have took a few players but they ain't took our heart!" Smiled Old Pat Bryce

Little Pat Bryce was holding his son and kissing him on the cheek.

"Is it finished now daddy?" Asked an inquisitive Pat Bryce Junior.

"Hopefully in a few seconds son..." Responded his proud father.

The referee blew his whistle to signal full time.

"YES!" shouted the Wickside fans in unison.

Some of the Wickside fans ran onto the pitch.

"No! Don't do it! Don't run on the pitch!" Shouted Billy Thorpe.

Some of the Seaford fans had also ran onto the pitch. Fighting ensued with their rivals Wickside. The players were running off the pitch.

"Fucking silly cunts! Come on boys let's have it on our Bromley-by-Bows!" Shouted Old Pat Bryce.

"What's cunts daddy?" Asked Pat Bryce Junior.

"Dad! You mustn't say that word! Basically, son it's that lot fighting on the pitch!" Little Pat Bryce stared at his dad who was moving to get away.

"Thanks for coming boys but I'll have to get going." Said Billy, shaking Pat's hand.

"Thanks for sitting with us." Smiled Old Pat Bryce.

"It was my pleasure mate and thanks for all your support."

"Been watching this lot all my life. I know Bobby's old man you know. Ain't seen him for years since I moved out." Old Pat Bryce remarked.

"Yeah, he's told me. He'll be at the next home game." Billy assured Pat.

"I'll look out for him." Smiled Pat.

"No doubt he'll be in the bar! I'll see you later." Billy jogged off.

"Ta Ta son. Hang on! That's Bobby!" Remarked Old Pat Bryce.

Bobby ran over to the Wickside fans and took a scarf from one of them and tied it around his neck. He then grabbed a Wickside flag from another fan and ran back onto the pitch towards the centre circle. He stabbed the flag into the centre circle. The Seaford fans were incensed with rage as Bobby ran off towards the changing rooms.

WICKSIDE TEAM BUS

Most of the team had cans of beer in their hands.

"Two each and that's it! We've got the Vase game next week." Shouted Bobby.

"Are we going to give the boys a go in that game?" Billy asked Bobby.

"We've got to mate. And besides, we were playing at that age. If we don't play them now, they won't get the experience. If we pick up injuries, they're all we have as back up anyway." Bobby said concerned as he looked towards Liam and Luke who were chatting away together. They had become good friends.

"Your mad by the way, with the that flag and scarf stunt!" Giggled Billy.

"If their fans weren't so fat and ugly, they might have been able to catch me! I've still got the required turn of pace you know, Mr Thorpe!" Chuckled Bobby.

"Lucky nobody clocked it was you or we'd have the FA on us by now!"

"It was the scarf disguise that done it. In Cognito! And by the way, we might have a bit of investment coming our way…"

"Nice one gaffer!" Billy gave Bobby a thumbs up.

CHAPTER XIV
BLUE, YELLOW & GINGER

WICKSIDE FC VS BROMLEY FC

Old Pat Bryce was at the bar. Albert was approaching him from behind. He tapped Pat on the right shoulder then moved quickly to the bar to Pat's left. Pat looked to his right then to his left.

"Hello Pat! How you doing? Long-time no see!" Smiled Albert.

They shook hands.

"Bloody hell Albie! How you doing son?" Pat touched Albert's ear.

"What's that bloody thing in your ear... An hearing aid?" Asked a confused Old Pat Bryce.

"It's me Bluetooth for me phone. Saves me getting me phone out!" Albert said proudly of the device that he had come to love.

"Bleedin Bluetooth? More like yellow tooth! You sure it ain't an hearing aid?" Chuckled Old Pat Bryce.

"Bleedin cheek! The reason it's called Bluetooth is because some Viking bloke who used to eat loads of blueberries, was good at bringing the warring Viking tribes back together. He was good at connecting. That's what this thing does. It connects. They called him Bluetooth see, coz all the blueberries he ate turned his teeth blue. That's why these things are called Bluetooth devices." Albert said smugly at the information he had learned from the young mobile phone salesman who had talked him into the device that came as five pounds extra per month. Albert was so convinced that he needed it, he couldn't do without it now.

"Oh really! I don't bother with all that! Anyway, How's the Mrs?" Asked Old Pat.

Albert seemed a bit put out that Pat was not interested in his story.

"Not too bad. She's alright. Here y 'are! You can ask her yourself..." Albert pointed towards Liz as she walked over towards them.

"Pat! How you doing?" gasped Liz.

Pat held out his arms and they cuddled each other.

"Lovely to see you love! I can't believe you let him out the house with that thing on!" Chuckled Old Pat.

"I know! No one ever rings him... Apart from me anyway!" Laughed Liz.

They broke off from their embrace.

"He's a Wally ain't he! I'm just getting them in... What can I get you both?" Asked Pat.

"Lovely Pat. I'll have a light and bitter and Liz'll have a G and T please mate." Albert replied.

"I got that. How's it going?" Asked George the barman.

"Lovely thanks George." Replied Old Pat.

"How's Little Pat?" Asked Liz

"He's over here with his Little Pat." Old Pat pointed to his son and grandson.

"Oh, I didn't know he'd had a boy. Oh, that's lovely. Little Pat and Little Little Pat!" Gushed Liz.

"And he's got lovely ginger hair too!" Smiled Old Pat

"Oh, I can't wait to see him! Bless!" Smiled Liz.

"You hanging about for the draw?" Asked Albert

"Yeah! Oh look, here they come now Liz." Old Pat informed Liz.

Little Pat Bryce was walking over with his son, Pat Junior or PJ as everyone called him.

"Here Pat? You remember Liz and Albert from upstairs, don't you?" Old Pat asked his son.

"Yeah, how you doing? You were on the second floor, weren't you?" Remembered Little Pat.

"That's right! You and Bobby used to knock about together sometimes. Lead him astray a bit an all if I remember!" Chuckled Liz.

"I'm not saying we didn't nick the milk float once and set traps in the dust chutes now and again!" Smiled Little Pat.

"Yeah, you little fuckers! I had that quality street tin come down on me head once, when I walked into the rubbish chute room! Gertcha!" Growled Old Pat with a smile.

Old Pat pretended to swing for his son.

"Did you really do those things daddy?" asked PJ.

"Here he is. Little Little Pat! Come and give us a cuddle you sweet little thing." She squeezed him hard and whispered in his ear.

"Us gingers have got to stick together!" Whispered Liz.

"That's what my grandad says." PJ whispered back into Liz's ear.

Liz let PJ go. Albert ruffled his hair.

"You look just like your old man." Albert remarked.

Albert shook Little Pat Bryce's hand.

"I remember when you nicked that milk float and drove it round the estate with my Bobby on the back. The milky went mad didn't he! How you doing son? "Asked Albert

"Good thanks Albert. He did have the hump didn't he! I'm so pleased Bobby's here. Let's hope we get a good result today and get a decent team in the draw, eh?" Little Pat was excited.

Vicky and Rosie walked over.

"And here's my beautiful granddaughter Anabel and this is Vicky, Bobby's wife." Liz said proudly.

"Hello Liz." Vicky kissed Liz on the cheek.

Hello my beautiful darling. How's university? Albert gave his granddaughter Anabel a big hug.

'Yeah, it's really good thanks Grandad." Replied Anabel.

You don't' be letting them boys got near you now will ya!" Albert broke off his embrace and looked at his granddaughter in the eyes.

"No, I won't grandad!" Anabel rolled her eyes and smiled.

"Hello. You must be Pat?" Vicky said to Old Pat.

"Hello love. Nice to finally meet you." Old Pat said.

"It looks like the boys are going to be playing today." Vicky said excitedly.

"Magic! "Albert rubbed his hands together.

WICKSIDE FC CHANGING ROOM

Bobby was addressing his squad.

"Right chaps... Because of our situation, we are a bit thin on the ground. I'm concerned if we do pick up injuries, the boys who would come in are not experienced enough. That's the reason behind my decision to rest some of you today. This being an

FA vase match and us in this afternoon's draw for the FA cup proper." Bobby said sternly.

"Boss we are fully behind you! We will help the boys in any way we can to win this game. We wish to win every game!" Louis said proudly.

"Thank you, Louis, and thank you all for understanding. Liam, Luke and Darren are coming in. Now you three. We've done all the drills in training so just think of this as another level of training. Go out there and enjoy yourselves. The rest of you help them along. Understand?" Bobby looked around at his players.

The whole team nodded in acknowledgement.

"We've all been there, you all know what it's like. Let's go out there and have it!" Bobby voice reached crescendo.

The team cheered and were in good spirits, cajoling and ruffling the hair of the three young players

WICKSIDE FC PITCH

"Let's do this boys" Louis clapped his hands and waved his arms to rile the players. The referee put his whistle to his lips and blew to start the game. Louis passed the ball to Liam who passed it back to Louis.

"Now make a run straight for goal!" Louis commanded Liam.

Louis then kicked the ball over the top of the opposing midfield into the path of attacking midfielder Jack Ramsay. Liam ran pass Jack who passed it into the path of Liam who took a touch then lashed the ball past the opposing keeper. The crowd went wild with emotion.

"Yes! Fuckin yes!" Bobby eyes were moist with emotion. Billy Thorpe ran over and hugged Bobby. Liam ran over to his proud father. Bobby had his arms open, and they embraced. Bobby lifted Liam up into the air.

"I'm so bloody proud of you son!" Bobby's voice was croaking with emotion.

"Thanks for giving me a start dad!" Liam was emotional too.

Bobby put his son down. Liam was immediately bundled over by rest of the Wickside team.

"Come on you lot! Get on with the game now. Let's go, let's go!" Billy Thorpe ordered the team up. After a few seconds the players all get up and took their positions for the re-start.

WICKSIDE FC HOME END

Vicky, Anabel, Albert and Liz were all hugging each other and cheering and crying. Old Pat, Little Pat and PJ were all cheering and pumping their fists.

The Wickside fans started singing their version of Tin soldier.

WE ARE THE WICKSIDE TIN SOLDIERS

WE ARE THE BOYS FROM THE FORT FORT FORT

WE KISS THE BADGE ON OUR SHIRTS

WHEN THE BALL HITS THE BACK OF THE NET NET NET

THEN WE'LL GIVE YOU A KICK

'CAUSE WE ARE THE BOYS FROM THE WICK WICK WICK

WICKSIDE GIVE US A GOAL.

WICKSIDE

WICKSIDE WIN THE GAME.

WICKSIDE

WICKSIDE WE CHEER FOR YOU

'CAUSE WE LOVE YOU

WICKSIDE

THE FORT

WICKSIDE FC PITCH

Wickside had got off to a poor start. Bromley were on the attack. Their striker lashed the ball towards the top corner, but Darren got his fingertips to it and pushed it out for a corner.

"What a fucking save Bobby!" Remarked Billy.

"Fucking beauty!" Responded Bobby.

Bobby cupped his hands to his face.

"Stay alert! Stay alert! Remember your marking!" Screamed Bobby.

Bromley took the corner. The ball floated into the goal area, but Darren rose above them all and punched the ball back towards the opposing goal.

"Fucking magic kid! Did you see that jump Billy?" Bobby was shocked with amazement.

"Fucking excellent!" Billy was in awe at what he had just witnessed from the young goalkeeper.

The crowd were going wild.

The ball was stopped by the opposing centre half and kicked back into the goalmouth. There was a scramble and Louis Ngunde scored an own goal as he had anticipated what might happen and got back trying to defend. He had attempted to clear the ball but had sliced it into his own net.

"No No No!" Shouted Louis, distraught at what had just happened.

"Bollocks! Fucking Bollocks!" Shouted Bobby in tremendous disappointment.

"Fuck it! There's only a minute left!" Billy said disappointedly.

Both sets of players were running for the re-start, eager to score a goal in the closing seconds to win the game. The game re-started. Louis kicked the ball to Luke, but the ball was intercepted by the Bromley midfielder and kicked into the Wickside area. The Bromley striker ran onto the ball. The striker was one on one with the Darren who rushed out from goal and touched the ball away from the striker's feet, causing the striker to fall over. The referee immediately blew for a penalty. Darren ran straight towards the ref.

"I got the ball first ref!" Darren was pleading with the referee.

"It looked like a penalty from where I was standing." The referee said sternly.

Corey Stonewood the Wickside centre half ran over.

"He got the ball first ref. No fuckin doubt about it. Never a penalty." Corey shouted at the referee.

It's a penalty. Now Fuck off before I send you off!" The referee was having none of it.

"No fucking way ref! I got the fucking ball!" Darren was losing it.

The Bromley captain walked over.

"Ref, he got the ball." The Bromley captain said.

"Too late. Penalty!" The referee ran off towards the penalty spot.

"Good save young un!" The Bromley captain congratulated Darren.

"Cheers mate! I can't believe it!" Darren was really upset.

The referee pointed to the spot. The Bromley striker placed the ball down on to the spot. He took a couple of steps back as Darren walked to the goal and turned and faced the Bromley striker.

"I can't watch!" Albert said as he covered his eyes.

"I can't watch!" Bobby said as he covered his eyes.

Darren lifted his arms up in the air. The Bromley striker ran and kicked the ball. The ball flew through the air dipping and curling slightly to the right as it went. Darren dived and got a hand to it which directed the ball onto the right post. The ball bounced off the post and back out onto the pitch. The Bromley striker was alert and smashed the ball into the net for the goal. Darren dropped to his knees and slumped onto the floor. The referee blew for full time. Bobby rushed onto the pitch to confront the referee. Some Wickside players were running towards the referee, and some were on their way over to console Darren.

"What the fucking hell are you playing at?" Bobby was apoplectic with rage.

"You need to calm down Gorman!" The referee was walking off the pitch.

The Bromley captain ran over.

"I told him that he got the ball first, but he was having none of it!" The Bromley captain was clearly shocked at what had transpired.

"You fucking what?" Bobby couldn't not believe what he was hearing. He got nearer to the referee, but Billy Thorpe jogged over and pulled Bobby away.

"Leave it mate. We've got bigger fish to fry." Said Billy has he grabbed Bobby by the arm and steered him away from the referee.

"Something's not right with that ref. Their captain even told him he got the ball." Bobby turned and shouted his words towards them referee

"Let's go and get them all in. Our boy's in pieces over there." Billy pointed to Darren who was distraught.

"Oh, fuck yeah! Let's get them in." Bobby came to his senses and ran over to Darren. The Wickside crowd were angry.

WICKSIDE FC STANDS

"That's a fucking disgrace. That ref should be fucked off out of it!" Raged Albert through gritted teeth,

"Calm down Alb! You know what the doctor said..." Liz grabbed Albert by the arm and squeezed him slightly to calm him down.

"I know I know!" Albert's rage subsided as the doctor's words rang through his head about keeping calm and changing his diet and drinking habits.

WICKSIDE FC DRESSING ROOM

The players were angry and distraught, especially Darren. Bobby had his arm around his shoulder.

"You played out of your skin today mate. You were robbed, we were robbed. But this kind of thing happens." Bobby tried to reassure his young keeper.

Billy walked over.

"It's ok son. That was an unbelievable performance!" Billy enthused.

"Yeah, but it was my fault for the penalty." Darren said dejectedly.

"No son you got the ball. It was the team's fault. Ok!" Billy held Darren by the shoulders.

"Yeah, we shouldn't have let that happen. It was my fuck up if anything." Chipped in Richard.

"We win as a team..." Billy said, waiting for the inevitable answer.

"And we lose as a team. Got it!" Bobby replied as he ruffled Darren's hair.

"Right you lot! Let's get changed and get up to the bar and watch this draw. Forget about today's result. We move on. Right now!" Bobby shouted.

WICKSIDE FC BAR

After the game, the bar was packed with Wickside FC fans, staff and their families. The smell of stale beer and cigarette smoke filled the air. There were some small children running around oblivious of why everybody had gathered. People were already focusing on the wall mounted projector screen that was slightly swaying in the breeze from the open windows. Bobby led the team into the bar area. A few people started cheering as they noticed their team walking in and then the whole place erupted with cheers and whistling. Bobby, his team and staff were getting their hands shaken and being patted on the back. People were shaking their heads in disappointment and discussing the result, some gesturing that the goalie got the ball. Bobby saw his family and walked over to them.

"Hello mum." Bobby gave Liz a big hug. Liz squeezed him tight.

"Ooh. Hello love!" she said warmly.

They broke away from each other.

"Alright dad? Bobby hugged his dad. His dad was never quite sure how to hug another man. They broke off.

"Alright son. That was a bit fucking harsh, weren't it?" Albert said disgustedly.

"Fucking Wanker that ref!" Responded Bobby

Old Pat Bryce emerged from the crowd.

"Oi! You watch your language in front of your mother!" Shouted Old Pat.

Bobby jolted a little bit in amazement.

"Hello Pat!" Bobby said with a big smile.

"He got the fucking ball you know!" Old Pat said with a grimace. His wrinkled face contorting.

"Well, I've started having the games filmed by some local film students so hopefully they've got it. If he did, then I'll appeal it. Anyway, talking about students, where's my Anabel? And Vicky? What's everyone having?" Bobby said trying to change the subject away from the horrible situation that had just occurred. He was looking around for his wife and daughter.

"No, I'll get them! You look like you need it!" Albert said with a knowing smile.

"Dad, you do this every time! Put your money away. I've got a tab ain't I!" Bobby chuckled.

"Oh, go on then!" smiled Albert, proud that his son was managing their team and that he had managed to get a bar tab paid for by the club.

Anabel and Vicky walked over.

"There you are he's been worried about you." Albert chuckled.

Bobby turned around and saw his beloved wife and daughter he hugged them both and kissed them both on the cheeks.

"We've been to the little girl's room dad! We've been crying happy and sad tears all game so had to do our make up again."

"I was so proud of our Liam when he scored… and our Darren in goal… Poor Luke at the end losing the ball and the penalty… Oh my god!" Vicky was very emotional.

A cheer went up around the place which made the Gorman family jump. Everyone focused on the screen. TV commentator Ross Williamson started to announce that the draw for the AF cup first round proper was about to start.

"And here we are for the draw for the AF cup first round proper. Our guests who will be making the draw are world cup winners Martin Chivers and Sir Bobby Charlton." Ross said smoothly. His voice sounded as silky as it did at six am every morning for the breakfast radio show that he presented on Virgil radio. He also loved sport and had been lucky to get this gig in his ongoing pursuit of presenting a regular sport show on tv and move away from radio if he could.

"Thanks Ross and good luck to everybody involved." Martin Chivers put his hand into the clear plastic bowl containing the red numbered balls and rummaged around. He pulled a ball out and held it towards the camera.

"Number twelve." He said confidently.

"Number twelve is Forest Green Rovers. Forest Green went out in this round last season but made it to the third round in nineteen eighty-five." Informed Ross. His encyclopaedic knowledge of the football game could only be bettered by the likes of John Tomson and Les Dynam.

Sir Bobby Charlton plunged his hand into the bowl and pulled out another ball and held it towards the camera.

"Number seven." Sir Bobby Charlton said slightly nervously as he did not like being in front of the cameras.

"And number seven is Fleetwood town. Fleetwood having made it to the fourth round only two seasons ago. So, the first game pulled out is Meadow Green versus Streetwood Town." Ross informed the audience of millions, so elegantly.

The Wickside FC Bar was tense with anticipation as Martin Chivers pulled out another ball from the bowl.

"Number forty-three." Martin placed the ball into the tray.

"Number forty-three is Wickside Football Club. The Tin Soldiers. Wickside having won the cup way back in nineteen thirty-seven." Ross said with a grin.

The whole bar erupted with cheers.

"You were at that final weren't you, Pat?" Albert shouted towards Old Pat.

Old Pat's eyes moistened slightly.

"Yes, I was Alb. Only a nipper. My old man and Uncle took me." Old Pat Bryce's eyes drifted off in deep thought. He was barely five years old when his father, Whiskey Pat Bryce and his Uncle Joey Bryce were swinging him by the hands between them walking up Wembley way. Pat could hardly see the game and his dad had put him up on his shoulders just as Wickside scored the winner. The memory was so vivid despite Old Pat struggling to remember what day it was these days. Old Pat was quickly snapped out of his beautiful daydream by Ross's voice calling out.

"And Wickside will be away to number sixteen... Harrow FC."

"Well at least we won't have far to travel!" Bobby shouted out to the whole bar who cheered in response

SEAFORD WAY CHAIRMAN'S OFFICE

At the same time as Wickside FC were watching the draw in their bar, Matt Hooper was sitting on his chair at his desk. He was watching the draw on a TV which was mounted on the wall.

"Harrow FC going as far as the fifth-round last season on that memorable run beating Middlesbrough and Luton before eventually losing to Portsmouth." Ross said smoothly.

Martin Chivers picked out another ball.

"Number twenty-seven..."

"Number twenty-seven is Seaford Way. Seaford Way looking to build on recent league success and new ownership, have always gone out at the first time of asking but could their fortunes change?" Ross knew what was happening in non-league just as he did with the League.

"Number fifty." Sir Bobby Charlton said more confidently now as he had got into his stride and used to all the cameras and lights.

"Number fifty is Northampton Town. The Cobblers. So, Seaford at home to Northampton Town, The Cobblers, who are one league above Seaford in the fourth division." Ross smiled.

Matt picked up the TV remote from his desk and pointed it towards the TV and pressed the power button. The TV screen went blank. He put the remote back onto the desk and picked up a glass tumbler containing a large measure of whiskey. He looked at it then greedily downed it in one. He turned on his computer tower and waited for it to boot up. He inserted a disk into the slot at front of the computer tower and sat back and waited. CCTV footage flickered onto the monitor on the desk next to the computer tower. The footage was of two people at the Seaford FC bar. Another man walked up to the bar and stood next to the other two. There was no mistaking who the three people were. One of them was in a wheelchair.

"Cunts!" Matt shouted at the monitor then hurled his Whiskey glass across the room. It hit the door and smashed on impact. Matt slammed his fists down hard onto the desk. His face was red with rage. He had tears in his eyes.

WICKSIDE FC PITCH – TRAINING DAY

It was a bright sunny day as the Wickside players were going through their paces. Half of them were at one end of the pitch. The rest of the players were at the other end of the pitch. Bobby was walking towards the centre circle. When he got there, he stopped and blew his whistle. He took the whistle from his lips.

"Right, you lot… Gather round." Shouted Bobby.

The players, coaches and physio all stopped what they were doing and jogged towards Bobby. They formed a line in front of Bobby.

"I need to address a problem that has cropped up in the analysis of your stats." Bobby said confidently as he had employed student statisticians to monitor everything from players weight, eating and sleeping habits.

"What does that mean boss?" Richard Jones asked, he was a bit confused.

"It means that most of you are too unfit and overweight!" Bobby looked around at the group.

"Really boss?" Asked midfielder David Cotton in surprise.

"Yes really! Even you!" Bobby said sharply as even he was surprised at the stats that showed David as being slightly overweight.

"Bloody hell! What does that mean then boss? Sweat suits with black bags on and loads of running like in your day?" David was horrified at the thought that they might have to do old school fitness stuff.

"Sweat suits yes. Black bags no. A bit more running… Yes. But most importantly, I'm putting you all on a stricter diet and the Paul the physio will monitor you all a lot more.

"But boss we are already on your diet." Protested Louis.

"I have to say that not all of you are sticking to it and the most important part of the diet is that it does not allow for any alcohol of any kind. Apart from certain times where I may allow it… If it's earned and deserved." Bobby smiled.

"But boss I do not drink and there is not one ounce of fat on me! "Louis lifted his training top up to reveal an impressive, chiselled set of abdominal muscles.

"As much as I love looking at your six pack Louis, the stats don't lie and I'm sorry to say that even your BMI is higher than it should be." Chuckled Bobby.

Louis dropped his training top down in disgust. The other players laughed.

"I've devised a diet with Paul. So, Paul, it's over to you." Bobby held his right hand out, palm upwards.

"I've got print outs of your diets. I've done my best to tailor them to your individual needs. If you need help with any of it, please give me a shout." Paul the physio said seriously, as he had spent many a sleepless night on this project.

"But I'm no good with cooking special stuff." Moaned Richard.

"I'll help you with it and I've spoken to the girls at the cafe down the road and they'll prepare you meals to suit your specific dietary needs, which you can take home." Paul said proudly, knowing that he had covered all the bases of what he knew the players would protest about.

"It'll probably cost an arm and a leg." Richard moaned again.

"Listen lads, you cannot put a price on success! If you lead the lifestyle, you'll reap the rewards and it'll prolong your careers." Billy said with a smile.

"You can eat and drink as much as you want when you retire. If you stick to this, you'll be much fitter and you won't be blowing out of your arses at the seventy-minute mark. Which is still what is happening. It affects concentration if you're gasping for air." Bobby had studied sports fitness and nutrition, via books from the library when he had retired from playing and got into coaching. He had got into it more after his sacking from Portham.

"Aye! You lot collapsed at the end of the last game. I'll be all over you on this. If you're not up for it, then you know where the door is. I'm even going for it." Billy said with an air of shock as he could not quite believe that he had got involved in the diet and volunteered to be monitored too.

"We all are. If at the end of the season we can all look each other in the eye and say we did everything possible to be the best we could be, then that's all we can do." Bobby glared at his players.

"The boys are right. I'm already on it but it's not all doom and gloom. There are days you can let your hair down a bit, but only when we all agree." Paul pointed his finger at the group of unhappy players.

"It sounds like a dictatorship to me!" Richard said, looking around at his teammates.

Billy walked over to him.

"And that comment sounds like it comes from somebody who's not up to the challenge..." Billy stood right in front of Richard.

"All your starting places are on the line. All of you! Our youth team has thrown up some interesting options so it's up to you. After our recent results and studying the stats, I will be re-assessing my squad over the next three games." Bobby shouted and looked around at all his players.

"Is everybody clear on this?" Billy looked at Richard and then stepped back and glared at all the players.

"Yes boss..." The Wickside players and staff responded in unison.

"My door is always open. So please feel free to come and talk to me. Anytime!" Bobby was almost challenging his group to challenge him on his methods.

"Me too lads, I'm here to help." Paul assured the group.

"We all are. But if you're not willing to help yourselves, then there won't be much that we can do to help." Growled Billy.

"Right let's start wrapping up." Bobby clapped his hands.

HARROW FC vs WICKSIDE FC FA CUP FIRST ROUND

The players were all out on the Harrow FC pitch on a slightly overcast afternoon as the referee put the whistle to his lips and blew for kick off.

"You made your mind up yet?" Billy asked his manager without looking at him.

"Not quite. I want to see how we perform today then get Paul to give me some stats on them all. Then I'll make my final decision." Bobby replied sternly without looking at his assistant Billy.

"I'll be honest, they've all been pretty good on the diet front, but some just don't have the right attitude." Billy said as he surveyed the pitch full of players.

"That's where I'm making most of my decisions." Bobby replied. He too was surveying the pitch.

"We'll see. Let's do a comparison. You do yours and I'll do mine without the stats, based on my intuition!" Billy said. They both turned and looked at each other with a smile.

They shook hands.

"You're on!" Bobby said confidently.

"Ref!" Shouted Billy as he had noticed a bad challenge out of the corner of his eye.

Bobby turned to the direction that Billy was looking in.

"Bloody hell!" Bobby saw Louis Ngunde writing in agony on the pitch after a nasty tackle from the Harrow FC central midfielder.

HARROW FC AWAY DRESSING ROOM

Louis Ngunde was lying on the treatment table. Paul was treating Louis's swollen knee.

"How does that feel mate?" Paul asked Louis softly

Louis winced in pain.

"That hurts!" Louis grimaced

"You aren't going back on for the second half unfortunately Lou." Paul said forlornly.

The rest of the team came in for half time. Bobby and Billy were straight over to Louis and Paul.

"What's the prognosis doc?" Bobby asked cheerily trying to lighten the mood.

"How you doing Lou?" asked Billy

"Not good Bill." Louis responded forlornly, still wincing in pain.

"Well, he needs to have a scan. I would say he's definitely stretched his ligaments, possibility a bit of tearing." Paul advised them all.

"How long will I be out Paul?" Louis looked Paul in the eyes.

"Don't worry about that for now mate." Bobby patted Louis on the foot.

"Don't worry Lou. I'll get you an ice pack and you can get back out there and watch the rest of the game." Smiled Paul.

"We'll get you a scan local, rather than round this way." Billy sort of jarred his head around in disgust.

"Yep. I've got a mate at Whipps cross. We'll get you scanned there." Paul said positively.

A tear formed in Louis's right eye.

"Come here you silly sod. You'll be right as rain in no time." Bobby hugged him.

The other players come over and started patting him and wishing him well.

"Now as you can all see, Louis is injured and won't come out for the second half. Liam will replace him." Bobby looked towards Liam.

"Get warming up now lad. Have a stretch!" Shouted Billy with a smile on his face.

"Now keep your shape out there. I don't need to say much more other than go out there and win this for our captain." Bobby clenched his fist.

"And let them know you ain't gonna take anymore shit from them. Hit them hard and take the fucker out who did this!" Billy shouted.

"Do it sensibly! I don't want anyone getting themselves hurt or sent off. What are we going to do?" Shouted Bobby.

"Win!" The Wickside players and staff responded in unison.

"What?" Bobby cupped his hand to his ear.

"Win!" The Wickside players and staff responded louder this time.

"Tell me what you're gonna do out there? Fuckin tell me!" Demanded Bobby.

"Win! Win!" The Wickside players and staff responded even louder this time.

Even Louis and the Physio were joining in.

"Win! Win! Win!" The whole dressing room was pumped up and shouting in unison.

HARROW FC HOME DRESSING ROOM

The Wickside players could be heard through the walls. Some of the Harrow players were laughing. Some looked shocked.

"Ignore all that!" Sneered the Harrow & Wealdstone manager Dennis Beale

The noise from next door was getting louder. The Wickside players were banging on the wall. The Harrow players were struggling to hear their manager.

"I said ignore all that! Get into them out there and don't let them fucking win. We want to be in the next round, not them." Sneered the Dennis, louder this time, but he was struggling to be heard.

The noise was almost deafening from next door. Dennis threw his mug of tea at the dividing wall. It smashed and sent hot tea and bits of ceramic all over the players who were sitting on the benches.

"Shut up you cunts!" Shouted the Dennis at the top of his voice.

The chanting stopped and then laughter could be heard.

HARROW FC AWAY CHANGING ROOM

"Right! Now let's get out there, win this fucking game and get into the next round!" shouted Billy with gusto.

"Four three three attack formation! ATTACK! ATTACK! ATTACK!" Shouted Bobby, his eyes were bulging, and veins were popping at the side of his forehead.

"ATTACK! ATTACK! ATTACK!" responded the whole Wickside team.

The players and staff were pumped up even further.

"LET'S GET OUT THERE!" Cried Bobby like a leader taking his troops to war.

The players and staff were all shouting as they started to go back out. As they passed the home dressing room, the whole team banged on the door as they passed.

"ATTACK! ATTACK! ATTACK!" They all shouted, ensuring that their opponents could hear them.

HARROW FC HOME DRESSING ROOM

The Harrow players were all looking towards the door that was getting banged on. Dennis strode towards the door and opened it. As he opened it, Tony Chaplin was poised to bang on the door but as the door opened the Tony's fist almost connected with the Harrow manager's face but stopped himself just in time. Tony laughed and walked off last in line behind the rest of the Wickside team. Dennis tried to kick the player but slipped over and fell backwards. His own players started laughing but his captain walked over and helped him up. Tony looked back and gave the Wanker sign.

"That's called karma mate... You always were a shit player." Laughed Tony as he walked away. He knew Dennis as an older player from years ago.

"You alright gaffer?" Asked the Harrow captain.

"Yes, I'm fuckin alright!" replied the irate Dennis as he got up.

"Right, you lot! Get up and get out there... And do the fucking lot of them!" Dennis was incensed and very embarrassed, his face was crimson red.

The home team made their way out onto the pitch.

HARROW FC PITCH

The game was nearly over. "Come on lads go for it! Push up. Push up! About a minute to go!" Dennis was waving his players forward.

"He's pushing them up. We need to be ready to catch them."

Noticed Billy.

Billy cupped his hands to his mouth.

"Tony, Richard! Stay up! Stay up!"

The Wickside players were pushed back into their own area. Tony and Richard were hanging as far up as they could as instructed. A Harrow player blasted the ball towards the Wickside goal, but Darren punched it clear. The ball sailed over the rest of the players. Rory trapped it and turned and ran with it. Harrow players were desperately running back. One almost caught Rory Maloney, but he passed the ball onto Tony who was brought down by a Harrow defender, but the referee waved play on. Richard managed to pick the ball up on the run. He was one on one with the Harrow FC keeper. He took a sidestep and passed it with power into the Harrow FC goal.

"Yes! Good shout Billy boy!" Bobby ran over to his assistant. They embraced.

Dennis Beale was apoplectic with rage.

"Ref that was offside! It was fucking offside!"

The Harrow FC players were surrounding the referee.

"Ref! It was offside! You can't give that!" Shouted their captain.

"I played the advantage when your player took theirs out. It was not offside. Your lot played him on as they were rushing back. So, goal. End of." The referee put his arms straight out in front of him.

The Harrow players were all moaning. Everyone retook their positions for the re-start and as the ball was kicked, the referee blew his whistle for full time. The Wickside players, coaches and fans were ecstatic.

Albert, Liz, Vicky and Anabel had made the trip with the Bryce family. Iranian Ali and Jimmy Archer had also made the trip. They had all been allowed into the clubhouse to watch the game. They were all celebrating wildly and were getting some nasty looks. A couple of Harrow & Wealdstone club members came over to calm them down.

"Do you lot mind?"

"Is there a problem here?" Jimmy had noticed them.

"Well yeah, you need to show a bit of respect..."

"Get out of it!" Shouted Albert who had had a few drinks."

"No problem gentleman we'll be on our way...Now we have got to the next round!" Jimmy laughed.

"Come on everyone...Let's get back home now before we cause any more trouble." Shrieked Liz who had also had a few drinks.

Vicky and Anabel were looking very embarrassed and started ushering Liz and Albert out. The whole clubhouse were giving the Wickside contingent dirty looks. Jimmy and Iranian Ali reciprocated as they both ushered the Bryce family out. Bobby had jokingly christened his and the Bryce Family the Wickside Ultras a few weeks back. They were certainly living up to their name today.

WICKSIDE FC TEAM BUS

"Right, you lot listen up! Seeing as we had to get out of there sharpish, I'll talk to you now. Well done. We won. I'm sure you'll all agree, you had a bit more in the tank towards the end, did you not?" Bobby said with an air of assuredness.

All the players nodded and murmured in agreement.

"Yes boss. The diet and no drinking is paying off." Tony conceded.

"Surely we deserve a beer now though boss?" Pleaded Richard.

"Actually, I agree! You do deserve a beer!" Bobby smiled.

Some of the players looked pleased and were smiling and

nudging each other.

"But you still ain't having one! We maintain the momentum! We ain't stopping at the offie, we ain't stopping at the pub. We ain't even going back to the club! Tell em Billy!" Bobby said smugly.

Billy got up from his seat and turned to the rest of the bus.

"We are going to pull up at a Tesco's or Sainsburys somewhere, grab a bit of healthy grub and have a picnic in the car park while we listen to the draw together." Billy smiled, knowing this would not go down well.

The driver half turned his head towards the back of the bus.

"There's one at Seven Sisters where we can stop off. Can be there pretty soon. Boots are away and Artillery play tomorrow. The traffic shouldn't be too bad." The driver said confidently.

"We'll stop there, listen to the draw, then get Paul and Louis to Whipps Cross. Then we'll get the rest home. We can cut through Stamford Hill and Dalston from here." Bobby had taken this route more times than he could remember.

"Aye. That way we know you've all got home safely and not slipped off to the pub." Billy said seriously.

Louis' leg was strapped up and he winced as he turned to face everyone.

"So that is why you insisted on picking us all up from home today!" Louis smiled slightly.

"When you said we would be going straight out I thought you meant out out boss!" Richard sighed.

"We are going out lad. That is alright with you and Paul isn't it, Louis?" Chuckled Billy.

"As long as Louis doesn't mind? Is this ok Louis?" Paul checked with his patient

"I wish to stay with my team for now. It's not too bad. I'm used to the pain now." Louis winced ever so slightly.

"Good Louis. Proper Captain! We're going for a picnic!" Bobby shouted.

"In a fucking Tesco car park... Cheers boss!" Richard said dejectedly.

"No problem son!" Bobby chuckled.

TESCOS CAR PARK SEVEN SISTERS ROAD

The team bus was parked in a parking bay. All the doors were open. Some of the players were outside the bus talking and eating while some were inside doing the same. The bus radio was on with the volume turned up as loud.

"We now cross live to the AF headquarters where the draw for the third round of the Association of Football Challenge Cup is about to take place." The voice of radio commentator Andy Crawford crackled through the medium wave radio frequency via the circular speakers in the sides of each of the front doors of the van.

The right speaker was slightly blown. It vibrated slightly and crackled more than its counterpart on the left-hand side door, due to it being on the driver side and bearing the brunt of the constant slamming of the door where the driver got in an out for football games and airport runs. These were the bread-and-butter jobs for the twenty-five-seater bus owner driver, taking pissed up young men and women to the airport or to various venues around the country in birthday, stag and hen dos.

"Here we go lads!" shouted the bus driver who was native to the areas of Shoreditch and Hoxton. He supported Artillery but had, as most young boys from those areas, been taken to Wickside FC for their first game of live football.

"Mike. What's the atmosphere like there?" Asked Andy Crawford

excitedly and inquisitively.

"Well Andy it's buzzing here! It's pleasing to hear that we still have one non-league team left today in Wickside Football Club, The Tin Soldiers..." Responded Mike Dawes, full of enthusiasm at the delight of the tie that Wickside had just won, which kept them in the magical draw for the AF cup. Mike Dawes was the roving reporter based at the AF headquarters that day.

The whole bus erupted with cheers, inside and out.

"Wickside beat Harrow & Wealdstone earlier on today with a controversial late goal in the final seconds of the game." Continued Mike Dawes with an air in his voice which assured the listening millions that Wickside had been fortunate to get to get through to the next round.

"We were a bit lucky there!" The bus driver agreed with a wry smile. He always watched the games.

"That's as maybe, but we fuckin deserved it!" Billy Thorpe responded proudly and loudly.

"Franny Flintlock is about to start drawing the balls out. Franny of course part of the nineteen seventy-one double winning Artillery team." Mike Dawes said with a chuckle as most of his listeners knew that he was an Artillery fan and was at times, guilty of some emotional outbursts in his commentary of the Artillery games, when things did not go their way.

"Lovely bloke Franny is!" Bobby said with a big smile, having met Franny, the double winning captain of Artillery, many times, stretching back to when he was a youth player.

"Aye a true gent! Loves a drop of whiskey that man, I can tell you!" Enthused Billy who had drunk with Franny on a few occasions when he had played against Artillery.

"Number forty-three." Said Franny in his Scottish Brogue.

"Number forty-three is Brentford Park Rangers Football club. The Bees. Who have never got past the fourth round in their entire

history." Remarked Mike Dawes matter of factly.

"That's Tommy's team..." Bobby went into a dream like state, thinking random thoughts about him and his best mate.

"*Number sixty-four.*" Franny announced.

"*Number sixty-four is Wickside football club. The Tin Soldiers who I just mentioned.*" Mike informed the listeners with a little bit of joy in his voice, that most would not have noticed.

The whole of the team and stuff erupted in cheers again, this time a lot louder.

"Fuck me... We're gonna be playing Tommy's team!" Bobby could not quite comprehend what had just transpired in his ears.

"*Wickside are one of the founder members of the football league and former AF cup winners back in nineteen thirty-seven. This once great club has been in the doldrums for decades but is seemingly on the rise. Wickside's opponents are managed by Tommy Eden, who is the Wickside managers former youth teammate at Artillery. Both went on to have steady careers, mostly in the lower leagues and then went into coaching after retiring from playing.*" Mike Dawes informed the listening millions.

Most of whom would probably not grasp the importance of this tie, which was about to bring the two best friends together against each other in a game of football, for the first time as managers.

"And you know who they're playing next in the league don't you son?" Billy asked in a rhetorical manner.

"Of course, I do William!" responded Bobby, who knew only too well who his old mate Tommy was playing next in the league.

Both Bobby and Billy knew this wonderful piece of information due to their thirst for all knowledge of football and because both Bobby and Tommy always kept an eagle eye on each other's fixtures, hoping that this day would one day come.

CHAPTER XV
JUST GOOD (OLD) FRIENDS

PORTHAM FC GROUND – NIGHT

A man and a woman were hugging outside the entrance of Portham Football Club. As they broke away it was clear that it was Bobby and an older looking Maggie.

"It's lovely to see you again Bobby." Maggie said warmly.

Her face was wrinkled slightly but she was still stunning.

"It's lovely to see you too Maggie. It's been a while! How's things?" Bobby asked enthusiastically as old memories rushed through his mind like an old black and white film, but in colour and very vivid.

"Not bad. Still a lady of leisure!" Maggie said with a cheeky side smile.

"Blimey! He must have really looked after you in his will!" Bobby said with a bit of shock, but he knew how rich Dickie was as he had been extremely pissed one night with him during the good times when Dickie had told Bobby that he had a nice few quid stashed away on the Cayman and Virgin Islands as well as the property that he owned around the Greater Manchester area.

"He did love. He did..." Maggie's eyes moistened.

"Sorry Maggie…" Bobby said forlornly.

He looked to the ground and then at Maggie, staring straight into her eyes

"It's ok love. Anyway, who'd have thought it eh? You coming up here, to watch a team, that you'll be managing against in the AF cup!" Maggie gushed.

"I can't believe it either! Do you ever come over here anymore?" Bobby asked, probably knowing the answer.

"No love. Never. I get asked all the time, but I just can't, not with everything that went on…" Maggie was clearly upset at the memories that this fixture had dredged up of her late husband and Dickie.

"You sure you're up for it?" Bobby squeezed Maggie's arm.

"On this occasion, I wouldn't miss it for the world! And as I'm a guest of yours, it just feels right." Maggie squeezed Bobby's arm back and smiled at him.

"Thanks Maggie." Bobby gave her a kiss on the cheek.

"Steady on! I've not had a voddy yet!" They both giggled like school children and walked towards the entrance. This was the first time that any mention of their one-night stand had been even slightly mentioned since it had happened all those years ago when they swore to each other never to mention it again.

They exchanged an ever so quick glance to acknowledge their night of passion. Maggie very quickly changed the subject.

"It's good we got here early. They still adore you up here you know. I don't think you would've been able to get in otherwise." Maggie smiled at the Portham legend that she had nurtured in more ways than one, as a young apprentice.

"I am trying to keep a low profile." Bobby responded with a little duck of his head as if he was incognito.

"Good luck with that! Everybody knows you'll be coming. I've heard folk talking about it in town all week!" Maggie giggled, feeling proud whenever she heard anyone referring to the game.

"Really?" Bobby responded with surprise.

"Aye, I think you might be in for quite a night chuck!" Maggie informed Bobby in her thick, Lancastrian accent.

"Eee by gum!" Bobby responded in a mock Lancastrian accent which was more than passable as he had honed it over the years, having lived in Portham, Greater Manchester, for so long.

Maggie playfully smacked his bum.

"You cheeky beggar!" Chuckled Maggie.

PORTHAM FC DIRECTORS LOUNGE

Bobby was talking to Maggie as they looked out onto the pitch. They were approached by an elderly looking man who was collecting the glasses.

"Bobby Gorman? Well, I never!" Said the elderly man with amazement.

Bobby looked at the elderly looking man for a split second as he was holding out his hand. Bobby stared in amazement for a few more seconds then shook the outstretched, thin and veiny hand.

"How you doing Sammo the superfan?" Bobby said warmly in recognition.

"Pleased to see you, Bobby. I knew you'd be here." Sammo responded proudly.

So, you working here now then?" Bobby asked merrily.

"Yes lad. It's a much better place now. The new chairman is a lovely bloke. He respects the tradition of the club. Not like that other lot. We were glad to see the back of them. Not you though!" Sammo smiled like a man relieved at the sight of his hero returning at last.

"How's Mark?" Asked Maggie knowingly.

"He's not well..." Sammo was holding back tears.

"I was with him earlier. He's on his last legs. Not long now..."

Maggie hugged Sammo tightly.

"What's happened?" Bobby was shocked at what he was seeing and hearing.

"He's got terminal cancer. Asbestosis. He was a pipefitter. He reckons asbestos was everywhere when he was an apprentice. It was very sudden. He got took ill here and been in hospital and then the hospice ever since." Sammo was holding himself together.

"Bloody hell! Where is he? St Augustine's?" Bobby asked.

"Yes, they've been lovely. And the club have too. They had a collection round the ground and the chairman made a nice donation. Some of the boys went and painted his room in our colours and put posters up." Sammo said with a proud smile.

"That's nice. I bet he loves it!" Bobby was feeling emotional now.

"Yeah, the hospice were more than happy for them to do it. You're even in there on a couple of the old posters! I'm back up there in the morning, first thing. Just hope he makes it through the night..." Sammo broke down.

"Come here mate..." Bobby hugged Sammo hard.

"I'm staying up the night. I'll come with you."

Sammo broke away. He was fighting back more tears.

"Really? He'd love that!" Snivelled Sammo.

"I'll come too." Maggie chipped in. She was also overwhelmed at the sudden turn of events.

"Oh, that's lovely. He always had a soft spot for you Maggie!" Smiled Sammo through the tears.

"I bet he did the dirty old sod!" Chuckled Bobby.

They all started laughing.

"Thank you both so much! I'm going to ring the hospice and tell him. That'll cheer him up no end and hopefully he'll wait for us one more night, eh?" Sammo scuttled off.

"Thank you!" Sammo shouted behind him.

PORTHAM FC DIRECTORS SEATS

Bobby was seated between Maggie and the Portham chairman, Ashley Michaels.

"Bobby! It's great to finally meet you. And to be actually sitting next to you watching a game! You're still a ledge up here you know!" Ashley gushed in his Oxbridge accent

"I don't know about that! Thanks for the hospitality by the way. Very generous!" Chuckled Bobby.

"It's the least I could do. There has been a bit of a buzz around the place. Most fans have guessed that at least someone from the club would be up. Either you or Billy." Ashley looked at Bobby in the slim hope that he might have two legends at his new plaything, so that he could boast to all of his rich friends.

"To be fair, I insisted that Billy came but he was having none of it. He's taking the training instead." Bobby informed Ashley, proud of Billy's commitment to the cause and that it had saved the club the train fare.

An old lady was walking towards her seat. Bobby and Ashley got up to let her pass. She stopped as she noticed Bobby.

"Bobby Gorman? It is you int it love? My eyes aren't what they used to be. I've left me specs indoors." Agnes Lyons informed them all.

"Blimey! Agnes my darling..." Bobby cuddled her.

"It's so good to see you chuck!" Agnes kissed him on the cheek.

"Hello Agnes!" Boomed Ashley.

"Hello Ashley!" smiled Agnes. Ashley had clued himself up on who he should keep happy when he bought the club so that he could enamour himself to the die-hard fans and existing staff, of which Agnes Lyons the long serving tea lady was one of them.

They exchanged kisses on the cheek.

"I've known Bobby since he was a fresh-faced young'un when he first come up here. Still as handsome as ever!" Agnes pinched Bobby's right cheek playfully.

"This lady looked after me! I love her to bits! It's so nice to see you again Agnes. I'll get you a gin at half time. She loves a drop of gin this girl!" Laughed Bobby.

"Ooh I'll look forward to that! I've had one or two already!" Giggled Agnes.

Maggie got up.

"Come on Agnes love. Let me help you to your seat." Maggie got up and linked arms with Agnes who she had known for what seemed like forever.

"You sort her out, I'm gonna nip to the loo quick." Bobby said with the look of someone who was breaking their neck for a piss.

PORTHAM FC TOILETS

Bobby was at the urinal reliving himself.

"Well, I'll be! I'm having a piss next to the legend that is Bobby Gorman!" Said the Portham fan proudly, as he was still urinating holding his spare hand out over the modesty panel.

"You certainly are! I've got me hands full at the moment! Let me shake this before I shake your hand!" Bobby said with a slight smile as he felt embarrassed and shocked as he was quite OCD about cleanliness.

"Of course, bud! Classic!" Laughed the Portham fan.

They both finished and then both went over to the basins to wash their hands. When they were done, they both went to use the electric hand dryer. The fan offered it to Bobby first

"No, you first. I insist mate." Bobby moved aside as he spoke.

"Cheers mate." The Portham fan slammed the worn-out chrome button on the hand dryer with a thud which kicked the dryer into motion with a loud whir. He placed his hands under the dryer's air outlet nozzle and started rubbing them together.

"I came to your last game as a player. My old man's been going all his life. Always says you were one of our best players. And he was in that club that night you done the Hockport knobhead." Shouted the fan over the noise of the hand dryer.

"Lovely!" Bobby said uncomfortably.

"What is that they sing... You dirty cockney tosser!" The fan said loudly.

"It's Bastard actually. But you lot pronounce it bit different up hear. as you lot say it!" Chuckled Bobby nervously.

"Oh, what a fuckwit plonker I am! I meet a club legend and fuck up his chant!"

"Don't worry mate! I've been called a lot worse! Anyway, I've got a bit of scouting to do so better get going." Bobby was sensing that things might start getting busy if he did not get away from such a public area.

"Yeah, course mate. Don't let me stop you."

They shook hands.

"Can't wait to tell the lads about this!" The Fan was so made up at what had just happened.

PORTHAM FC DIRECTORS SEATS

The game was in full flow. Bobby and Ashley were on their feet.

"Come on! Push up! Push up!" shouted Bobby.

"Go Portham! Go for it!" Shouted Ashley.

Some fans were looking back towards Bobby.

"I told you! See that's him oop there in t' director's seats." Pointed one of the Portham fans.

It bloody well is man... It bloody well is! Eh Bobby... Bobby Gorman! Give us a wave!" shouted the other Portham fan.

Fans around them heard what was just shouted. Bobby heard and duly gave a wave down to the two fans.

"He bloody well waved! The Portham fan two gave a thumbs up to Bobby, who responded with a thumbs up of his own. By now more and more fans were noticing Bobby.

"BOBBY BOBBY GIVE US A WAVE. BOBBY. GIVE US A WAVE. BOBBY BOBBY GIVE US WAVE. BOBBY. GIVE US A WAVE!" Shouted another fan up towards Bobby.

Other fans were nudging each other and joining in the song.

"BOBBY BOBBY GIVE US A WAVE. BOBBY. GIVE US A WAVE. BOBBY BOBBY GIVE US WAVE. BOBBY. GIVE US A WAVE!" Around thirty Portham fans were now singing the old song that they used to sing to him, years ago, when he was in his pomp.

Bobby stood up and waved with both arms down to the fans

and gave them the thumbs up.

"I told you Bobby, I told you!" Ashley Michael could not hide his glee at the admiration of a cult hero of the club. He was also thinking of the extra pints that would probably be drunk by these joyous fans who would be hanging around to try and catch a glimpse of or try and have a chat with Bobby.

Bobby sat back down. Maggie nudged Bobby as he seated himself.

"You are legend." Maggie whispered in his ear and kissed him on the cheek. And focused back on the game.

Then Bobby leant across and whispered in Maggie's ear.

"I couldn't have done it without you Mags. I owe you so much."

Portham scored a goal. The whole of the home crowd including all those in the director's seats went wild. Ashley Michael hugged Bobby.

"You are the lucky charm tonight!"

Bobby talked into Ashley's ear as they hugged.

"I aim to please Ashley!"

Ashley cracked up laughing. Then the fans started chanting a song that was very familiar to Bobby, Maggie and Agnes. It started to erupt and work its way around the ground.

"YOU DIRTY COCKNEY BASTARD! YOU DIRTY COCKNEY BASTARD! YOU DIRTY COCKNEY BASTARD! YOU DIRTY COCKNEY BASTARD!" Shouted the Portham fans.

The chant harking back to that infamous night in C'est Bon nightclub. Most fans of a certain age claimed to be there on that night, in the same way lot of people of a certain age from the East End, claimed to be in the Blind Beggar when Reggie Kray shot Jack "The Hat" McVitie

As the chant reached its crescendo, Bobby rose to his feet

very slowly and drank in the adulation. He had his arms outstretched, turning from right to left, acknowledging the whole of the Portham FC ground. He then bowed towards them all and pumped his fist, gave them all a thumbs up, then started urging the team forwards. He directed the whole crowd to do the same. As he did so, the whole crowd descended into another chant.

"COME ON PORTHAM! COME ON PORTHAM! COME ON PORTHAM! COME ON PORTHAM!" Bellowed the Portham Fans.

Ashley Michael looked at Bobby. And started chanting at him.

"You dirty cockney bastard! You dirty cockney bastard! You dirty cockney bastard! You dirty cockney bastard!" Ashley Michael's posh, Eton educated, Recital Pronunciation was not doing the chant any justice at all.

They both fell about laughing as they sat back down. Maggie leaned into Bobby's ear as he sat down.

"I know for a fact that you're dirty cockney bastard!" She leaned away with a wry smile on her face and focused on the game. Bobby then leaned into her ear.

"And I know for a fact that you're a dirty northern monkey when you want to be!" Bobby looked back towards the game with a wry smile on his face.

"There might be a replay at this rate!" Chuckled Maggie, who was still staring towards the pitch.

Bobby was looking dead ahead at the game.

"You should be so lucky!" They were both looking dead ahead, giggling.

They had after all these years suddenly felt a weight lifted from both their shoulders having spoken for the first time about it. After their night of passion. Maggie had become like a second mother to Bobby.

Bobby suddenly jumped out of his seat.

"Go on son take it all the way... Keep running... Shoot! Shoot!"

The Portham player had only one Brentford Park Rangers player to beat but decided to smash the ball from thirty yards. The ball flew into the top right corner of the Brentford Park Rangers goal.

"YES!" The Portham Fans celebrated extatically.

"There's only about a minute left! We've won. We've won!" Screamed Ashley.

"It ain't over yet!"

The referee blew immediately. Bobby stood and went wild and hugged Ashley.

"Yes!" Screamed Bobby.

PORTHAM FC INTERVIEW AREA

Tommy Eden was waiting to be interviewed.

"So, Tommy, a late goal has put a dent in the teams climb for promotion." Alan Bexhill the Cloud TV Interviewer asked an irate looking Tommy Eden.

"Yes Alan. The players are distraught in there. So am I to be fair... Our lack of concentration cost us at the end where we could have come away from here with a draw." Tommy said with an air of disappointment.

"On the balance of things, a draw probably would have been a fair result, but Portham really came at you in the end as the home crowd really got behind their team." Enthused Alan.

"The crowd really were the twelfth man at the end." Sighed Tommy.

"I heard there was a certain club legend in the stands tonight." Alan said with a twinkle in his eye knowing the connection.

"I believe there was Alan." Tommy knew where this was heading and wasn't entirely happy with the situation.

"A certain Bobby Gorman. Your old youth teammate from Artillery." Alan explained for the cameras.

"I tell you what Alan, that dirty cockney... so and so, has got a lot to answer for tonight! He's supposed to be my mate. He should have sent someone else to scout. He was the reason we lost tonight. You wait till I see him!"

They both laughed.

"But no, to be fair to Portham, they played very well at the end. They deserved the win. We let ourselves down by not keeping our focus. I feel sorry for the fans that have made the long trip up here, but I can assure them, I will get those lads to work on what went wrong tonight and bounce back for what is an important derby game against Leytonstone Cathay FC on Saturday." Tommy said, trying to focus away from the result that evening.

"That is an important game for both teams chasing promotion. We do have to return to the studio now but very briefly, do you have a message for Bobby Gorman tonight?" Alan asked, loving the friendly rivalry and knowing what it was all about, having been a former player himself during the same time that both Tommy and Bobby were playing, albeit a lot older.

"I've got a message for him alright! But I'll be giving that to him in person. I don't think I can say it on camera!" Tommy said reservedly and with a slight smile.

They both laughed.

"I would probably agree with you there! Thank you for talking to us tonight, Tommy."

"No problem, Al."

"Now let's return to the studio."

PORTHAM FC DIRECTORS LOUNGE

Bobby was at the bar with Ashley, Maggie and Agnes. Tommy saw Bobby as he entered the bar and strode quickly over towards him.

"You could have fucking kept a low profile couldn't ya?" Tommy said in a raised voice.

Bobby span around and faced his old friend.

"Blimey Tom! Hello, how are you? Would have been nice!"

They stared each other out for a few seconds, but their friendship took over and they both embraced in unison, hugging hard at each other, patting each other hard on their backs. Both sets of eyes met, as thoughts of their younger days engulfed both of their minds. They broke off from their embrace.

"You know it's your fucking fault we lost!"

"Bad management I say!"

"Fucking tosser!"

"You always were a bad loser! Your defence switched off and you know it."

"So, the crowd creaming their Y-fronts over you being here didn't have an effect then eh?"

"Shut it you tart! What do you want anyway?

"I'll have to invite you more often Bobby!" Ashley giggled.

"You can shut it as well!" Tommy said sharply.

Ashley suddenly stopped giggling.

"No. The commiseration drinks are on me..." Ashley offered an olive branch.

They all started laughing.

ST AUGUSTINES HOSPICE

It was a cold grey morning. Bobby and Maggie met and greeted Sammo by the front of the hospice, then walked towards the entrance door. All of them were looking solemn.

"I spoke to them first thing. He's deteriorated. They say he ain't got much longer..." Sammo's eyes were red from all the crying he had done since hearing the news.

MARK'S ROOM

A nurse was tending to Mark. She finished and nodded at the three visitors then left the room. Maggie, Bobby and Sammo were standing around the bed looking at Mark. He was pale and looked in pain. Death was in his face. The walls of the room were painted in the Portham FC colours. Posters of past and present Portham players adorned the wall, including one of Bobby Gorman. Scarves were pinned to the wall and tied to the bed. There was a picture on the bedside cabinet of Sammo and Mark in their younger days, outside the Portham FC ground. Both of them striking a fist pump pose, dressed in replica football shirts, hats and scarves. The room was a shrine to Mark and Portham Football club. There were also pictures of his pets, Cornelius and Porty. The closest things he had to children. Marty had so reluctantly given Porty to an animal sanctuary when he had become too ill. Sammo had taken him that day Mark was so upset that it had even made Sammo cry with him.

"Mark... Mark..." You've got some visitor's mate. Sammo whispered quietly, his voice choked with emotion at the sight of his old mate. He ever so gently shook Mark's arm.

Mark's eyelids moved and opened slowly.

"Look who it is look..." Sammo said softly.

Mark's eyes opened fully. They then rolled into the back of his head but returned slowly. He slowly moved his head and looked at them all.

"Am I dead?" Mark asked in a croaky voice.

Maggie started to well up and put her hand to her mouth.

"No mate. It's good to see you again." Whispered Bobby.

Mark was struggling for breath and was looking confused.

"It's Bobby Gorman... And Maggie." Sammo informed his old mate softly.

Mark looked at them both. He realised who they were. A broad smile engulfed his face. Sammo's hand was resting on Mark's arm. Mark grabbed Sammo's hand and squeezed it slightly.

"Thanks mate." Mark voice was very croaky. He was struggling for breath.

"We beat 'em last night. You should have heard them singing Bobby's name... And his song!" Sammo's excitement shone through, trying to make his dying mate happy.

Mark smiled slowly and broadly again, briefly removing the look of death from his face.

"Dirty cockney bastard." Marks eyes closed but he smiled as he struggled to speak.

They all laughed.

"Thanks for coming. I've missed you both. You look beautiful Maggie..." Mark was waning.

Maggie was fighting back the tears. She walked over and kissed Mark on the forehead. She sat at the seat to Mark's right and started stroking his hair. Mark was still holding onto Sammo's hand. Mark held up his left arm slightly. Maggie nodded to Bobby who acknowledged and walked over and took Mark's other hand. Mark opened his eyes and looked at them all. A kind of holy trinity in his life.

"I'm going now..." Mark's voiced trailed off.

His monitors started to beep. A nurse entered almost immediately. Mark's breathing became even more shallower then stopped. He gurgled slightly then slipped away. They all stayed still for a few moments.

"May I have some room please?" the nurse asked quietly.

They all gently moved away. Sammo and Bobby gently laid Mark's hands down beside him. The Nurse moved in then checked his pulse. She turned to them all. Her lips pursed.

"He's gone now."

Sammo and Maggie broke down. There were tears filling Bobby's eyes. His mind flashbacked to when they were all in the restaurant the time when Sammo and Mark asked Bobby for the first autograph that he had ever signed.

CHAPTER XVI
THERE WERE HEROES AND VILLAINS ON BOTH SIDES

RUMOURS & LIES NIGHTCLUB HACKNEY ROAD

The nightclub was packed and decked out with Christmas decorations. The team were all dressed as superheroes. They were all very merry, apart from Louis Ngunde. He was dressed as Superman.

"Take it easy lads. We have not even had food yet." Louis was already concerned at the amount his teammates had already drank.

Louis called the barman over.

"When can we sit down for our food?"

"Won't be long mate. Keep your cape on! There's another party just finishing. It should be ready for you in about fifteen minutes. Most of East London seem to be having their Christmas do's in here tonight!" The barman said, slightly stressed out.

"Ok. Can I have a diet coke please?" Louis asked politely.

"Yes of course. It's good to see Superman not having a booze! Ah! Here they all come now." The Barman pointed towards the restaurant area. A party of men plus two women, were leaving the restaurant and heading over towards the bar. They were all dressed as nineteen thirties gangsters. A few of them were swaying with drunkenness. The two women dressed as gangster's molls, were clearly very drunk. They headed straight towards the team of superheroes.

"Hello Superman. Can I be your Lois Lane?" Said one of the Gangster's molls.

"No that's OK thank you!" replied Louis who was feeling very uncomfortable.

She rubbed the S on Louis' Superman outfit.

"Very nice. What's your name? I take it it's not Clark Kent!" screeched the pissed up, gangsters moll.

"No! my name is Louis. Please stop touching me." Louis pushed her hand away. Some of the gangster party saw what was happening.

"Calm down Lois. I mean Louis!" The gangster's moll was laughing and swaying.

Some of the team saw Louis.

"Looks like Louis has pulled!" Liam laughed.

"Blimey he don't hang about!" Darren said with astonishment at what he thought he was seeing.

Two of the gangster party walked over to Louis and the gangster's moll.

"Is he bothering you?" Asked a man aggressively. He was dressed as Al Capone.

"No, she is bothering me. Can you take her away please?" Louis pleaded with the Al Capone look alike.

"I see you push her!" Another gangster shouted as he waded into the situation.

"It's ok!" Snapped the Gangster woman. She was swaying badly.

The Al Capone alike moved his Moll out of the way and confronted Louis and was in his face. The other woman from the gangster party arrived on the scene and dragged her friend away.

"I know who you are. You think just coz you're a footballer you can take the piss with birds!" The drunken gangster said angrily, spittle flying from his mouth.

"That is not how it is. She came to me and started touching me." Louis was trying his best to reason with him.

Liam and Darren saw what was happening. Darren was dressed as Batman and Liam was dressed as Robin. They made their way over.

"I just pushed her hand off me. That is all." Louis was getting agitated.

More of the gangster party moved in closer. One of them stood next to Louis.

"Don't give it all that! Anyway, Superman ain't a coon is he!" Shouted the gangster.

"Very clever you racist!" Louis pushed him out of his way to try and get away from the situation.

The gangster fell backwards. The Al Capone alike punched Louis. The rest of the gangsters started laying into him. Louis went down. Liam and David, aka Batman and Robin, arrived at the scene and started wading in. They were followed by Richard dressed as The Incredible Hulk, Luke dressed as Thor and Dean dressed as Captain America. More of the gangster party came over and a mass brawl of Superheroes versus nineteen thirties gangsters ensued.

BETHNAL GREEN POLICE STATION

There was a mix of bloody and bruised gangsters and

superheroes in the detention cage. Their costumes ripped and torn. Their masks and hats were gone. They had all sobered up.

This is so embarrassing!" Louis held his head in his hands.

"My old man's gonna kill me." Liam looked shell shocked.

"I can't believe this. I'm probably gonna get sacked for this!" The Al Capone alike said quietly.

"All because of those two silly birds. I told you we shouldn't have let them come!" Said the Gangster who Louis had pushed over, forlornly.

"No choice... It's a work do... Everyone had to be invited..." Al Capone alike shook his head.

"Perhaps you should not drink so much..." Louis was staring at the cold concrete floor.

"Shut it Superman! You're supposed to be the good guy." Snapped the gangster.

There was an awkward silence. Then they all started laughing.

"I'm sorry about all this... I shouldn't have gone that far... I was well pissed! The Al Capone alike said with an air of regret.

"I'm sorry too chaps... Too much booze..." Gangster man said meaningfully.

"That was a proper brawl though!" Liam said with an air of proudness.

"It's not good though! We will probably end up in court. This will embarrass the club." Louis was carrying the extra burden of responsibility as he was club captain.

"I used to go over the Wick with my Grandad sometimes. Go to the scrapyard and then go to a game. Good times!" Gangster man reminisced with a smile.

There was a tap on the cage. The Duty Sergeant was standing there.

"I'm glad to see you've kissed and made up. If you lot don't press charges against each other, it'll save a lot of grief for us all." The duty sergeant clearly could not be bothered with all the paperwork.

"We ain't going to." Gangster man looked around at the bruised and battered lot of drunk partygoers.

"That's right! Real gangsters don't grass do they!" Sneered the duty sergeant.

He looked at Louis and Liam. They both shook their heads.

"Well, there wasn't any damage to the premises, bar, excuse the pun, a few broken bottles and smashed glasses. You scared a few people though. It was one of those people you scared that called us. The premises confirmed the fracas, but they can't be bothered to press charges either. Other than that, you lot are barred for life from there and their other establishments. The rest are barred as well. The bouncers only seemed interested in you four as you were the only ones they could catch. The gangsters went into hiding, no one would talk and the rest of the superheroes must have used their special powers to escape!" The duty sergeant smiled sarcastically.

"Very amusing officer. But what happens now?" Louis asked curtly.

"Calm down! I would say keep your cape on but that seems to have flown off without you!" Chuckled the portly duty sergeant.

They all laughed. Louis felt the back of his neck. His superman shirt was ripped where the cape should have been.

"Looks like we'll both be losing our deposit. My cape and mask have gone... And I lost a glove and a shoe!" Liam said looking at what was left of the Robin suit.

"We both lost our hats..." Al Capone alike chipped in disappointedly.

"My heart bleeds! As nobody is pressing charges, and as its Christmas, you'll be let go with a warning. This could have been a lot more serious so think about your actions chaps, especially you Wickside lads." The duty sergeant raised his eyebrows.

"Your dad is going to fucking kill us..." Louis hissed.

"You must be worried! I don't think I've ever heard you swear..." remarked a shocked Liam.

BOBBY'S FLAT – THE NEXT MORNING

Liam came through the front door looking bedraggled. Bobby walked out of the kitchen and saw him.

"What the fuck happened? You alright?" Bobby hugged his son in a relieved way and then let go sharply.

"You won't be happy dad. We got into a bit of a fight down Rumours & Lies." Liam said nervously.

They walked through into the kitchen. Bobby pointed to the newspaper on the kitchen table. It was open. There was a picture of Liam, Louis and the two gangsters being dragged out of the club by bouncers and police.

"I know!" Bobby was disgusted.

"Bloody hell! How did it get in the papers so quick?" Liam was shocked at the sight of the picture.

"Someone's obviously took a picture and sent it in to make a few quid. It must have been bit of a slow news day, so they run the story. Its fucking embarrassing. My names even mentioned!" Bobby was furious and his face was crimson red.

"I'm sorry dad..."

"You fucking will be! The fucking phone ain't stopped ringing.

Jimmy and Ali have got the right fucking hump with me over it!"

"Oh, for fuck's sake!"

"Turns out the blokes you had the tear up with worked for some top bank in the city! You better tell me exactly what happened!"

WICKSIDE MANAGERS OFFICE

Jimmy, Ali, Liam and Louis were standing. Bobby was seated at his desk.

"Right then! What the fuck happened you two?" Jimmy asked menacingly. He was furious.

"Let's sit down first. Grab some chairs you two." Bobby was trying to calm the situation.

Liam and Louis grabbed chairs and arranged them round the desk. Two chairs next to Bobby and another two chairs the opposite side of the desk.

"Mr Chairman. A drunk woman started to touch me, so I moved her hand away." Louis said very quickly.

Jimmy looked astonished.

"And?" Responded Jimmy in a confused manner.

"It was inappropriate..." Louis said forthrightly.

"Inappropriate! You need to lighten up a bit!" Ali shrieked, not quite believing what he was hearing.

"Look he didn't want to know. Louis doesn't drink. He didn't want to know this bird, but these friends of hers come over. They were well pissed then all hell broke loose." Liam defended his captain, looking at the three older men in front of him.

"It really wasn't his fault. We just went to help him out as he was getting a kicking. Any one of you would have done the same..."

"No charges are being brought and we were let off with a warning. We are barred from that place and any other of their establishment's chain of bars." Louis informed them all.

"Fair enough boys but the bottom line is this! I said go out for a few drinks and a bite to eat... Not a full-blown piss up in fucking fancy dress!" Shouted Bobby.

"What you've done is bring unnecessary attention to yourselves and this club." Said Jimmy slightly calmer now.

"How will they be punished? Friends of ours own that place. They are not very happy." Iranian Ali was animated.

"The whole team will be fined... Amount to be decided. Louis you'll be fined double whatever we decide for allowing this to happen. You went against my strict instructions. You'll be stripped of the captaincy for now... Until I decide otherwise." Bobby looked Louis in the eyes

"Shouldn't they be dropped?" Jimmy asked.

"I would drop them both, but we simply can't afford to do that at the moment." Bobby said with a slight annoyance at what he thought was an intrusion into his territory.

"We're going to fine you too Bobby. You should have been with them. Or at least made a better job of making sure it didn't happen." Jimmy said looking at Bobby.

Bobby stared at both Jimmy and Ali for a few seconds, trying not to lose his temper and not lose his job.

"Right! I'll have to take that. But that's it now then. We draw a line and move on." Bobby said, starting at both Jimmy and Ali trying to hide how he was seething on the inside.

"Let this be a lesson to you all." Iranian Ali said calmly.

Louis and Liam were sitting ashen faced. Louis started to look furious.

"You can both leave now." Bobby waved them away.

The two teammates got up. Louis pushed his chair away hard. They both turned and walked out of the door.

"I just hope it doesn't have too much of an effect on things." Bobby said with an air of disappointment at the whole situation, worried what it might do to team morale.

"Well, you better make sure it doesn't. The league form has been piss poor. Lucky we're on this cup run." Jimmy was not pulling any punches.

"Listen Jim, with all due respect, the league form has suffered because of the cup run. Don't tell me you're not happy with the cash its bringing in..." Bobby tilted his head slightly, furrowed his brow and smiled slightly, again, trying to hide what he was really feeling inside. His head was tingling, and he wanted to lay both Jimmy and Ali out.

"Alright! I get that... But we need to be in this league to keep moving forward." Jimmy acquiesced.

"The remit was to keep us up this season. By hook or by crook I'll keep us up. But I'm going for it in the cup. We've got to, for all sorts of reasons." Bobby was getting passionate.

"Such as?" Ali chipped in.

"Well first of all, the money. Then exposure for the club. Our players will learn and become better players by playing against better players in the higher divisions and, if they get better, then they'll have a better re-sale value, should we ever need to sell. Or, if we get an offer we can't refuse..." Bobby was on a roll and knew exactly what this club required and how to do it.

"OK. That sounds fantastic. I'm glad you are thinking along those lines... The more exposure we get, the more chance of investment we get." Ali was warming to Bobby's thinking.

"Exactly Ali!" Bobby clapped his hands and rubbed them together.

"Alright then. So how do we improve in the league. Can we do anything to help you?" Jimmy asked in a genuine way, eager for some of what Bobby had explained.

"Just let me get on with it if you don't mind. I'll have a think on how we can improve things and perhaps next week we can talk about that further." Bobby knew that they would both get carried away if things got talked about anymore now.

"Ok mate we're here to help. We've got every faith in you... Haven't we Ali?"

"Yes, we do Bobby, but you must work to keep us up and we will do all we can to help. You must understand we have put a lot of money on the line."

Bobby looked them both in the eyes.

"I understand..."

SUTTON UNION AWAY DRESSING ROOM

The players were sitting down deflated. Bobby was addressing them.

"It's another loss in the league... We can't let this keep happening boys, we just can't. I've got the chairman and the main investor breathing down my neck and that ain't nice, trust me!"

"Boss, I'm at a loss." Richard said dejectedly.

"This is no time for fucking poetry! You're the captain at the moment! I need your help here!" Bobby shouted back to Richard, who had reluctantly accepted the captain's armband after the nightclub incident.

"We've had some terrible luck, especially today." Richard said defensively.

"We have had some bad luck, but we've also been very poor as a unit. No more league losses do you lot here me? We have to stay up, end of. We don't want to be known as one season wonders do we?" Bobby looked around at his team

A few of the players shook their heads.

"Do we?" Bobby was not impressed with his dejected team's response.

"No boss!" The players responded loudly this time.

"I want four points minimum from the next two league games... No messing up! I don't care how we get the points, we just get them. I want you lot to think long and hard about how far we've come as a group and how we don't want all that effort wasted. If we don't get the points, I'll have to look at changing things. Do you hear what I'm saying?" Bobby said in a threatening manner.

"Yes boss." The players responded better his time, worried at what might happen.

"Ok. Now let's get changed and all get home and get some rest. We'll train like trojans next week. We've got a nice little distraction from the league called Wickside v Brentford Park Rangers at home in the AF cup... With the cameras there! This is a big deal for us all but especially for me, for many reasons. So, if we let ourselves down, there'll be hell to fucking pay!" Shouted Bobby.

WICKSIDE FC DIRECTORS LOUNGE

Albert, Liz, Jimmy, his partner Connie, Ali and his partner Rhouska, were all standing near the Wickside FC club lounge bar.

"They're all over the gaff, runners, producers, cameramen. They've taken over!" Smiled Jimmy at the situation that he could hardly believe was happening.

"They've been nice about it though. They laid on a car to

SCOTT SAMAIN

pick us all up as well." Said Connie who was dressed very glamorously.

"Ooh look at you getting chauffeured about!" Liz said with a chuckle

The three women giggled.

"You could have come and got us!" Albert moaned.

"It wasn't a stretch limo mate!" Ali said with a smile.

The men all laughed.

"Here, ain't that that an old footballer who played for Orient and City? What's his name?" Jimmy was having trouble trying to remember.

"Where?" Ali looked around excitedly as he had been a Leytonstone Cathay FC fan almost as long as he had been in England. His first real friend's dad had taken them both to a match. He had been hooked ever since.

"Over by the bar." Jimmy pointed.

They all looked over to the bar.

"Don't make it obvious for Christ's sake!" Jimmy whispered and turned in the complete opposite direction.

"Alan Bexhill. Good player but had to retire early. Done his knee. Was never the same..." Albert recognised the Scottish ex pro who had been a classy centre forward.

"Time for a bit of networking!" Jimmy couldn't contain his excitement.

Jimmy walked over to the bar where Alan Bexhill was standing. Albert and Ali followed.

"I've met him before, he's a top bloke" Ali said to Albert as they walked over.

"Can I get you a drink." Asked Jimmy.

"No that's OK thanks." Alan politely refused.

"I insist mate!" Jimmy held out his hand.

"I'm James Archer the chairman of the club."

They shook hands.

"I'm Alan."

"Yeah, we know..."

Ali walked over.

"And I'm Ali. We have met before, a couple of times at Orient, years ago." Ali was hoping that he remembered him.

Alan looked at Ali for a few seconds.

"Ali!"

They embraced and patted each other hard on their backs.

"How you doing mate?" Alan asked with a chuckle.

They broke off and shook hands.

"Very well Alan. Very well. I am CEO of this club. We have big plans!" Ali said proudly.

"I bet you do!" Alan said with a smile.

"What can I get you?" Jimmy asked again.

"Believe it or not Ali... I'll have a coffee!" Alan knew that Ali would find it hard to believe.

"A coffee?" Ali could not believe what he was hearing.

"I'm commentating on the game today." Alan informed Ali and Jimmy.

Albert walked over.

"Really? Well I never!" Albert had heard stories of Alan's drinking exploits as a player.

"Well, we shall have a drink after then?" Ali asked excitedly.

"Win or lose on the booze!" Alan laughed.

"Make sure you say a few good words, Al!" Jimmy nudged Alan.

"And go easy on my boy and his team won't you! My boy's the manager of this club." Albert said proudly.

"Your boy's Bobby Gorman?" Alan asked enthusiastically.

Alan and Albert shook hands.

"It's an honour. He was a great player. I played against him when he hadn't long been in the Portham first team. A cup game if I remember?" Alan looked at Albert for help remembering.

"It was mate. Nineteen eighty-three up at Maine Road when you were at City. You lot won it with a late goal.

"Aye that was a tough game! I'm sure I remember your Bobby giving me a rough time!" Chuckled Alan.

"He did!" Chuckled Albert in reply.

A mobile phone rang. Albert pressed the button on the Bluetooth device in his ear.

"Hello… Hello… Blimey! Alright!" Albert was not happy.

Albert turned around. Rhouska, Connie and Liz, who had her mobile phone to her ear, were all laughing. Albert pressed the button on his Bluetooth device and turned back around to Alan, Jimmy and Ali who were also laughing.

"Important call, was it?" Alan smiled.

"Yeah! Hurry up and get the drinks in she said!" Albert was annoyed at the interruption at such a great point in his life, reminiscing with an ex-pro about his boy.

They all laughed even more.

"Right you are then!" Jimmy waved the barman over.

"Yes, please Geoff!"

Across from the men at the bar, Tommy's mum Jean walked in and saw Liz, who waved her over to come and join them.

"Hello darling!" Liz said as they cuddled

"This is Connie, Jimmy's partner. And this is Rhouska, Ali's wife." Liz said with a smile as showed off her important friends.

"Hello nice to meet you." Smiled Jean.

"They're just getting the drinks in. You want your usual?" Asked Liz, knowing what the answer would be.

"Ooh yes please love." Jean gushed.

Liz still had her mobile phone in her hand. She dialled in and put the phone to her ear and paused for a second.

"Me again! Jean's just got here... Can you get Jean a G and T please?"

"Stop bloody ringing me! It costs a fortune!" Moaned Albert through the phone.

"Alright!" Liz said laughing.

The woman all started laughing.

"Honestly you two and them phones!" Jean laughed.

"So, this is Bobby's best mate Tommy's mum, Jean. Tommy's the manager of Brentford Park Rangers." Liz proudly showed off her friend.

"Jimmy told me all about it. How lovely that they're still such close friends." Connie said with a warm smile.

"I hear they are not so good friends in situations like today though. No?" Rhouska said in her thick Iranian accent.

"You right there Rhouska!" Exclaimed Liz.

Vicky and Anabel walked through the doors and immediately saw Liz and the girls.

"Hello my darlings!" Liz hugged her granddaughter Anabel and then her daughter in law Vicky.

"Do you want a drink? You look like you need one the both of you! What happened?"

"The bloody trains were up the spout! Got stuck just outside of Wilmslow and then it crawled nearly all the way into St Pancras! We had to get a black cab as the tubes had all engineering works going on and we got stuck in traffic. Cost a bloody fortune! At least were here now though. I was worried we wouldn't make it for kick off... I'll have a large vodka and orange please" Frowned Vicky.

"Yeah, mum was well stressing! I'll have a large vodka and lemonade please." Giggled Anabel.

"Single for hr please Liz! And make sure it goes on our Bob's tab please... Don't you or Albert pay for it..."

"Don't you worry my darling. I'll get Albert to sort this..." Liz dialled Albert's number again on her mobile phone.

"Don't be like that your granddaughter and Daughter and law are here and need a drink... See you miserable old sod... Strict instructions from Vicky... Make sure it goes on our Bobby's tab...!" Liz smiled at Vicky. She had never liked it that Vicky always referred to Bobby as Bob sometimes.

CLOUD TV STUDIOS

"And we now cross live to Portcullis Street. To The Fort stadium, the home of the Tin Soldiers. What fantastic names! It's Wickside vs Brentford Park Rangers in the AF cup, live on Cloud sport. Alan, how is it there?" Asked Mike Dawes the main Cloud TV Anchor.

Mike Dawes was a veteran of TV broadcasting who had been a professional footballer for a short while, but never really made the grade. He had started out in broadcasting on his local radio station. He progressed to local news reporting on the Anglia TV network, then progressed to sport reporting. He got a slot on the inaugural British commercial television network's early morning breakfast TV show. After a few years, he eventually landed his dream job of TV sports presenting, on the fledgling British satellite TV company, Cloud TV's sport channel.

The TV screen was split to show Mike Dawes in the studio and Alan Bexhill at the Wickside FC ground.

"Oh, its lovely Mike. This is a real old-fashioned, old-school ground. So much history all around the place. The two teams playing today, Wickside and Brentford Park Rangers, have so many connections. Both teams were founder members of the football league, both winners of the cup back in the late 1800's and early 1900's and both managed by former Artillery youth teammates Bobby Gorman and Tommy Eden. Both local lads who played for this club as young boys and who both had solid careers in the lower leagues. They both have their families here and I was just speaking to the Wickside directors, one of whom I know by the way, and Bobby's father about that time that myself and Bobby Gorman played against each other in a cup game. A young Bobby Gorman gave me a hard time that day let me tell you." Chuckled Alan in his broad Glaswegian accent.

Alan Bexhill had an illustrious but short career that saw him play for his native Scottish national team at the European Championships, his hometown club Glasgow Foresters as a youth team player, winning the Scottish AF youth cup, which earned him a move down south to Manchester FC. Whilst at Manchester he won the AF Cup and EUFA Cup. He also played for Leytonstone Cathay FC and played in the North American Soccer league in the early eighties during the English close season, which lot of the more well-known players from around the world did, to boost their earnings in between the English league finishing and restarting for preseason.

Mike Dawes laughed.

"What's the feel around the ground? How do you think this will pan out Alan?"

"Well Mike, Brentford Park Rangers are the favourites being one league above Wickside, who have promotion hopes but are struggling in the league. But this is the cup and The Tin Soldiers have been on a fantastic cup run and are well up for it. I've been assured that Wickside are going for it today. On paper, it should be Brentford Park Rangers' game but, I think Wickside have a really good chance if they can keep up their rich vein of cup form going today."

"Thanks Alan."

"Thanks Mike."

The television screen reverted to a single shot of Mike Dawes in the studio.

"Alan Bexhill there, covering Wickside vs Brentford Park Rangers in the AF cup. We'll be right back, after the break."

WICKSIDE AWAY DRESSING ROOM

Tommy and his players were jogging lightly on the spot.

"Ok boys let's sit down." Tommy directed his players with his arms.

They all stopped jogging. Some of the players limbered up then slowly sat down.

"Ok. It's not quite what we as a group are used to, playing at a ground like this, but individually, some of us are. This is a special club. Their players have something about them so don't take it lightly out there. Look past it all and realise right now that this is a cup game. This is another stepping stone to move us forward as a group to bigger and better things. We must win this in normal time. End of. We cannot afford extra time, penalties or a replay. We need to put this to bed early and then shut up shop. Emotions will be running high today. They have a full house, and the cameras are here... So, let's put on a good display and show the world what we're all about. What Brentford Park Rangers football club is all about. Go and make those fans of ours happy!" Tommy rubbed his hands together softly.

WICKSIDE FC HOME DRESSING ROOM

The Wickside players were all seated. The manager and staff were standing.

"Right, you lot... Up you get! The gaffers got something to say!" shouted Billy.

The players all stood up. Bobby walked towards the players to address them.

"Alright boys. Now this is the biggest game this club has played in for God knows how long. As far as I know, It's also the biggest game ever for you lot. The cameras are here, your families are here and it's a chance to get into the next round where we will probably play one of the big boys. With all that in mind, all I'm going to say to you is, do your jobs, enjoy the occasion and win the fucking game!" Bobby clasped his hands then rubbed them together hard and briskly.

WICKSIDE FC HOME STAND

All the Gorman family were there along with Jimmy, Ali, Connie and Rhouska. Tommy's dad Dave was also there. Jean had gone to the toilet. The drinks and nervousness of her son Tommy playing against Bobby had got ton her bladder. They were all cheering, but Wickside were losing. Liam Gorman almost scored from long range. Albert jumped up out of his seat.

"Lovely boy! Come on Wickside! Aaahhh..." Albert's face contorted with pain. He was clutching at his chest. He fell against the seats in front of him.

"Oh my god! Albert!" Screamed Liz as she grabbed onto her husband.

"Alb? You alright?" Jimmy looked very concerned. He too grabbed hold of Albert.

Ali moved along from his seat to help. During the commotion, Albert's Bluetooth earpiece had fallen out. As they all helped him to sit down, Alberts beloved Bluetooth earpiece had got trodden on. It was crushed and broken into pieces, which then got kicked and scattered by all the feet moving around.

"Alb! Darling it's your heart. It's his heart!" Liz was sobbing.

Albert was pale and sweaty and foaming at the mouth. He was groaning and growling in pain.

"Oh my god!" Connie held her hand to her mouth.

"Go and ring an ambulance babe... Use the phone behind the bar... Quick!" Jimmy shouted.

"Yes Jim! Oh Liz!" Connie rushed off.

Alberts body went limp.

"Bloody hell Alb! Stay with us! Ali give me an hand. Let's get him down by the gate so we can get him straight in the ambulance." Ali and Jimmy picked Albert up.

"I'm going. I'm going..." murmured Albert.

"No, you bloody ain't!" Liz rubbed his cheek.

"I used to be a Nurse. Let's get him downstairs. Does he have heart problems?" Rhouska asked calmly.

"Yes!" Liz snapped as if everyone should know.

There was roar from the crowd. Jean was just returning from the toilets as they all rushed past her.

"Oh my god..." Jean grabbed Liz.

"It's his heart. We're getting him down. Connie's called an ambulance." Liz said with tears streaming down her face. Her perfectly applied mascara was running down her cheeks.

Connie came rushing over.

"They're on their way. Liz, you go down and me and Jean will get all our coats."

"Did they score?" Albert asked, his eyes closed.

"Yes, mate we scored. Don't worry about that now mate. The ambulance will be here soon." Jimmy was trying his best to reassure his old mate.

They carried Albert in the sitting position. Jimmy and Ali were either side of Albert, carrying a leg and a shoulder each.

"Don't tell the boys about this... They need to finish the game... Don't tell them boys out there Jim. Please don't tell them till after the game..." Albert pleaded.

CHAPTER XVII
A GOOD HEART WILL ALWAYS WIN

ST BARTHOLOMEW'S HOSPITAL

Liz was sitting next to Albert's bed. Albert was sleeping. He was hooked up to a heart monitor. The curtain opened and Bobby walked in. He saw his dad. Tears filled his eyes immediately. Liz stood up and rushed over to cuddle her son.

"It's his heart again..." Liz said hugging her son tightly.

"I know, Connie told me. They're all out there... Tommy followed me up as well." Bobby sat next to Albert's bed and held his dad's hand.

"I'm here dad. We won. We did it. Can he hear me?" Bobby asked hopefully, wiping away the tears that were rolling down his cheeks. He gently held his father's hand

"He's sedated now but the Nurse said he may come around."

The heart monitor bleeped slightly faster.

"Well... Done... Son..." Albert responded slowly his voice just about an audible croak

Albert squeezed Bobby's hand ever so softly. The monitor bleeps slightly slower again.

"I bet Tommy wasn't happy!" Liz's voice kind of laughed through the tears.

"He had the right hump. We had a proper row on the touchline. God knows what it looked like on camera!" Bobby smiled through the tears.

"What have I told you two about arguing... Only seems like five minutes ago I was holding you in my arms when you were born up here" Albert croaked with a weak smile. His eyes still closed.

Liz and Bobby both smiled through their tears.

"Dad, you got to fight this... I need you... I need your help. I need you to do some scouting for me... Like you used to on the teams I used to play against when I was little..." Bobby broke down.

Liz got up and walked round to comfort Bobby. Liz started crying too. Albert stayed silent. The machine was beeping slightly slower now.

"What did the doctors say. What do they think?" Bobby whispered.

"They think he had a heart attack due to another blocked artery. They need him to rest for a while. They had to bring him back at one point..."

"Yeah? What... he died?"

"He was gone for a little while. They've put a pacemaker on him for now but when they were adjusting it, he had another heart attack and they had to shock him. It was awful." Liz cried.

"Why didn't no one tell me? I should have been here!" Bobby was getting angry.

"You know what you father's like! When it happened, he give strict instructions not to tell you or Tommy. He didn't want to spoil the game for you both!"

"I hate the thought of you being on your own... Dealing with all this..."

Liz gave Bobby a cuddle again.

"It's alright love. It's not the first time either is it. Once he gets through this we're really going to have to look after him. He won't be able to drink or go football or do anything that excites him.

"He won't like that!"

"Well, we are going to have to give him tough love!' Liz looked her son in the eye then looked at Albert.

LAGRANGE HOTEL SUITE CENTRAL LONDON

Matt Hooper and three of his players were drunk and high on cocaine.

"I told you I'd look after you! Shame the other lightweights can't last the distance! The birds will be here soon... Here. Get this up your hooters!" Matt enthused as he showed off the fat lines of cocaine, he had just racked up for the cling ons that had only stayed with him for free booze and coke.

"Bloody hell Mr Chairman... With these lines you are spoiling us! And I have to say on behalf of the rest of the lads, thanks for the cash bonus! Everyone's well happy!" Smiled the Seaford Way captain Marlon Ryan as he bent down to snort one of the fat lines of cocaine on the glass table.

"Well, you all better keep schtum about that! You just keep winning games to win us the league and there'll be plenty more where that came from." Matt said with a coke gurn.

The other two players sniffed the lines that were on the glass table.

"And there'll be plenty more where that came from an all!" Matt assured the hangers on who were his only people who were even close to being classed as friends right now.

"Here Mr Chairman, don't your missus mind you being out all

the time?" Asked one of the players.

"She's too tired too even notice. What with looking after the baby. But never mind eh! Anyway, she's had a right result. She was only a barmaid before we got together. Only banged her once and she got up the duff. Now she lives a life of luxury. She always wanted a baby anyway." Matt informed the motley crew of ponces around him.

There was a knock at the door.

"Here we go!" Matt said enthusiastically as he got up and strode over to the door to open it. Four tarty woman barged in.

THREE MONTHS LATER

WICKSIDE FC DIRECTORS OFFICE

Jimmy, Ali and Bobby were all sitting around Jimmy's desk.

"So, is the old fucker on the mend then?" Jimmy's asked, but he had already been informed of Alberts condition.

"Yeah, he's doing really well now Jim. Thanks." Replied Bobby confidently.

"We have some good news, Bobby." Enthused Ali.

"I think I know what this is all about. I got a letter..." Bobby smirked.

"It seems our friend at Seaford has been a very naughty boy indeed!" Chuckled Ali.

"The AF and taxman have found out about his bonus schemes..." Chipped in Jimmy smugly.

Their club have been found guilty of financial irregularities and breaching AF rules on bonus payments. The Taxman is going to hammer them for it too!" Ali said proudly.

"We've just heard they'll be getting docked fifteen points!"

Jimmy said with a big smile on his face.

"Fuck me! That keeps us up then!" Bobby said excitedly.

"Yes, Bobby boy! We are guaranteed to stay up now and they will almost certainly go down! Ali assured Bobby.

"All the clubs in the league have been given the heads up." Jimmy assured Bobby.

"Well until I see it confirmed in writing, it hasn't happened yet! The letter didn't state that..." Bobby said in his usual cautionary manner to slow the two of them down as he usually had to do in moments of excitement t such as to his.

"I admire your caution, Bobby." Ali said gladly.

"Fair enough mate but it is happening. I'll tell you what else is happening... That stupid fat fucker has got himself into some other trouble as well..."

"Eh?" Bobby's head swivelled around to Jimmy.

"Well, he gets right on it. Bang on the gear see..." Jimmy imitates sniffing a line of coke by holding his finger to his right nostril and inhaling through it.

"Him and some of his players went out clubbing. They've ended back at some hotel room with a few birds and him and one of the players got hold of one of the birds while she was pissed up and out of her nut on gear for the first time. She's woke up the next morning with them two in bed with her and she's freaked out. Her fella found out and went down the ground and beat the fuck out the pair of them. He's blackmailing that silly cunt out of a nice few quid, so the story goes. He's fucked and the club are fucked an all!" Jimmy reported gleefully.

"Bloody hell!" Exclaimed Bobby at this most fortunate turn of events for his club, at the expense of their most hated rivals' club.

"With that in mind and with us now safe in the league, we want you to throw the kitchen sink at getting to the final. Getting us to the semi with everything that has gone on has been nothing short of a miracle Bobby and we are forever in your debt. The money it has brought in has been amazing and it has attracted the investors we needed." Grinned Ali.

"I would have done that anyway but thanks for the gratitude. I'm confident we would have stayed up anyway with our run in and we're due some luck in the league. I'm not giving up on it. We still have four games left but I'll rotate the players if we win the semi. I still can't believe it... Wickside versus Sheffield Thursday at Aston Park in the AF cup!" Bobby could not hide his excitement.

Jimmy walked over to Bobby.

"It's all down to you son!" Jimmy smiled broadly as he patted Bobby on the cheek.

ASTON PARK

The game was in full swing, but time was running out.

"Thursday on the attack again but Wickside are fighting this one out to the death. You can see how tired both sets of players are with only seconds remaining with the score level at one one after extra time. And there goes the whistle with this one heading for penalties..." Alan Bexhill informed the millions of viewers who had tuned into Cloud Sports to watch the fascinating encounter in the oldest cup competition in the world. The air in his voice was disappointment. He and millions of others had been rooting for little Wickside FC.

ASTON PARK PITCH

Bobby signalled to the players to form a circle around him and Billy Thorpe. They all ran over and surrounded Bobby and Billy.

"We know the list of takers. Any objections?" Bobby asked looking around his team, judging their emotions.

They all shook their heads.

"Good lads! But if any of you are unsure, then speak now or forever hold your piece!" Smiled Bobby, doing his best tom calm the most important moment in theirs and the club's history.

They all shook their heads again.

"We're well and truly up for this gaffer!"

Louis said on behalf of his team. He had been reinstated as Captain again.

"Now when you take them kicks, you be sure where you're putting them! Do not change your mind and do not fucking hesitate!" Shouted Bobby.

"Aye lads. You walk to that spot full of confidence and put the ball away... Simple as that!" Billy said, backing up their manager.

"Last step of the way lads and Wembley awaits us!" Bobby said, his eyes wild with excitement, trying to motivate his team to the best of his powers.

The referee blew his whistle to signal the start of the penalty shoot lout. The shrill of the pea in the whistle distracted them all.

"Right lads that's the whistle." Louis started to take charge.

The whole team embraced each other and moved off towards the centre circle. Billy and Bobby were patting all the players on the back for encouragement as they moved off away to the centre circle. Billy and Bobby embraced each other. They broke off. Bobby walked over to the Sheffield Thursday manager Teddy Frankham. They shook hands and embraced each other.

"Good luck Bobby."

"Cheers Teddy. Good luck to you too mate."

They both started to walk back towards the dugout.

"Who would have thought it eh?" Said Teddy.

"Yeah, Sheffield Thursday reaching an AF cup semi-final eh!" Bobby said dead pan.

Teddy Frankham burst out laughing.

This scene was captured by a photographer and immortalised in the national newspapers the next day and became synonymous with this day forever more.

"Yeah! You're right there!" Laughter Teddy, acknowledging the quick wit of his counterpart who he knew from their playing days around the same lower leagues where they had plied their trade.

"It's great to see the camaraderie going on there between the two managers. Fantastic! Their nerves must be shredded. This would mean so much to both clubs and their fans. Especially to Wickside." Alan said with an air of romanticism.

"Heads or tails Wickside?" The referee asked the Wickside captain.

"Heads please ref." Responded Louis.

The Referee flipped a fifty pence coin into the air. It landed almost perfectly in the centre circle.

"I couldn't do that again if I tried!" Chuckled the referee.

The referee bent down to pick up the coin.

"No. Its tails. Sheffield Thursday, would you like to go first or second."

"We'll go first." Said the Sheffield Thursday Captain.

The two captains shook hands.

"You'll both be shooting towards the Holte end to our right.

All players to stand well back but no further than the halfway line. Good luck gentleman." The referee picked the ball up and handed it to the Sheffield Thursday Captain. He took the ball straight to the penalty spot and placed the ball down hard.

"And its Thursday taking the first penalty at the Holte end in front of a sea of blue and white stripes having the advantage of taking their penalties in front of their own fans. He strides over confidently putting the ball on the spot. He takes a few steps back and... he scores straight down the middle sending the young Wickside keeper the wrong way." Alan shouted with an air of excitedness and relief as it was clearer who he wanted to win.

"Bollocks!" Shouted Bobby.

The Sheffield Thursday bench were celebrating.

"Next up it's the Wickside captain Louis Ngunde. Both captains leading the way. Leading their teams into battle! He doesn't look confident... oh he's skied it. He's missed. Advantage Thursday." Alan Bexhill said softly at the end, feeling sorry for Wickside.

"Fucking hell!" Shouted Billy.

Louis was distraught as he walked back to his teammates. They all comforted him.

"And he doesn't look confident either the Thursday midfielder. Walking very slowly to the spot but no, He's blasted it straight into the top left corner. Keeper no chance. Two nil to Thursday! Wickside have to score." Shouted Alan.

"I'm sorry I missed but you boys just do your thing. Just take deep breaths and pick your spot."

"We can do this lads come on we can do this!" Louis clapped his hands.

Dean Bowens walked towards the penalty spot.

"The Wickside captain urging his players on. As the next taker is up. The Wickside left back Bowens, who put some lovely crosses in

during the game. And he scores! The Wickside team are ecstatic!" Alan could not contain his delight.

Billy and Bobby hugged each other. The team in the centre circle were all cheering and pumping their fists. The next Thursday player walked to the spot and grabbed the ball and put it down onto the spot with force. He adjusted it again then blasted the ball wide.

"Oh, he's missed it. Took it past the right upright!" Alan said, feeling sorry for the player.

The Thursday player fell to his knees and curled up but quickly got to his feet and ran off towards his teammates as the next Wickside player Corey Stonewood, was running to take the penalty. He grabbed the ball from the referee and slammed it down on the spot. The Referee blew his whistle, and the player blasted the ball.

"Oh, the keeper got a hand to it, but it's gone in! Saltwood scores! Can you believe it! All square! Sudden death! If Thursday score, then that's it!" Alan said loudly.

The next Thursday player was walking nervously to the spot with his head down.

"His head is down. Has he chosen where he is going to put it? He takes a couple of strides back and... Oh! The keepers tipped it away! Advantage Wickside! I'm on the edge of my seat here! The Wickside team are going wild, but Bobby Gorman and Billy Thorpe down there are screaming at them to calm down! If Wickside score this, they are in the final. It looks like the attacking midfielder Jack Willis is next up. He's taking his time. The pressure really on this lad's shoulders for a chance in the final. The referee gives him the ball. The Thursday fans doing all they can to put him off. The Wickside fans are almost silent here. It's unbelievable... He's hit the bar... Oh it's gone in! Wickside are in the final. I've got a lump in my throat here. Wickside FC from the fifth or sixth tier of English football, I cannae remember, are in the AF cup final and

will face Artillery! The players staff and fans are going wild! "Alan shouted.

The fans were streaming onto the pitch. Some of them fighting with the Thursday fans who had also invaded the pitch.

Bobby, Billy and all the players are jumping around hugging each other and being picked up by fans. One Thursday fan grabbed Bobby, who duly right hooked the Thursday fan who then got kicked in the head on the volley by Billy Thorpe on his way down to the grass which sent the fan sprawling.

"Boys! Let's get the fuck off the pitch... Livo!" Bobby said with a nervous smile.

Jack Willis was held aloft by Wickside fans who were singing his name at the top of their voices.

ASTON PARK EXECUTIVE BOX

Vicky, Anabel, Albert, Liz, Jimmy, Ali, Connie, Rhouska, Jean, Ginger Pat and Little Pat and all the family were going mad with joy. Albert had tears streaming down his eyes but was not moving too well in his wheelchair after being partially paralysed by his heart attack. Bobby looked up toward the director's box, pointing and blowing kisses, just as he did when he scored his first goal for Portham.

Liz leant down and hugged Albert.

WICKSIDE FC CLUBHOUSE

All the players and management were lined up together. Bobby was standing on a stool. A tailor and his assistant were stood in front of Bobby.

"Ok sir, I reckon you're about a thirty-eight leg. Let's have a look..."

The tailor placed his tape measure at the top of Bobby's leg, just under his crotch.

"Easy tiger!" chuckled Bobby.

"He can be a bit of a tiger when he wants to be, can't you boss!" Sniggered the tailor's assistant.

Everybody laughed.

"I bet! I dress to the right in case you were wondering!" Bobby said giggling.

Everyone laughed again. The tailor blushed and laughed.

"Do you want your suits or not? I've a lot to get through" The tailor's assistant laughed forcefully but really meant them to shut up and let him get on with his job. His assistant was also his partner. He had begun to regret asking him to help on this job.

"I bet you'd both like to get through us all quick, eh?" Billy Thorpe guffawed.

They all laughed again.

"You should be so lucky!" The tailor's assistant looked Billy up and down with a frown.

"Ok calm down girls! We'll get the measurements done and your suits will be ready for the final fitting next week." Assured the tailor.

Bobby looked concerned.

"Next week? That's when the final is. Its Thursday today so next week is cutting it fine... What if we need any alterations?" Bobby was not happy with this news.

"I thought the final was the week after? It's a bit early for an AF cup final, isn't it?" The tailor knew a bit about football but not too much. He had a confused and worried look on his face.

"It's because of the world cup. They've brought the final

forward. The top division will still have another game to play on the Thursday night, after the final." Bobby almost whined his words out like a young child. He was almost distraught at the possibility of not having the suits ready for the final.

"Nobody actually told me a date..." The tailor said trying to cover his arse.

Covering his arse was not something he would normally do at the clubs and parties that he and his assistant and partner often frequented. It was at one of these parties that they had first met and became more than acquainted.

"Well, you better hurry up and get measuring. After this, we're going to make the video for our AF cup song!" Billy was also pissed off at the communication breakdown but was staying upbeat.

"Ooh! Pop stars as well as footballers, eh?" Sniggered the tailor's assistant.

"We'll get it sorted don't you worry!" Shouted the tailor, waving his hands.

"Good. There's talk of our song being the unofficial world cup song as well you know. The World paper are sponsoring all this you know." Bobby said proudly of his little club, about to get some serious nationwide recognition for reaching the AF cup final.

Bobby gestured around the shop.

"I wouldn't know. I don't read that old tit rag!" Sniffed the tailor's assistant.

"I don't suppose you do, seeing that tits aren't your thing." Bobby said with a nudge and a wink.

They both laughed and the tailor nudged Bobby back with a side look and smile.

"And they're sponsoring our song." Bobby said proudly again.

"Ooh! What's it called?" The tailor's assistant asked enthusiastically.

"Come on Wickside Come on England. To the tune of Tom Hark by The Piranhas." Bobby said with a smile, as it was one of Bobby's favourite songs as a kid.

"The who?" asked the tailor's assistant, moving his head in mock expression as if he was hard of hearing.

"No not The Who, The Piranhas..." Bobby responded with an old joke that had been going around forever.

"He's only a young pup, before he was born... I remember though. I loved that song!" Butted in the much older tailor referring to his toyboy. He bobbed his head and shoulders, to the song he could hear in his mind.

"The original was an instrumental from the fifties by a band called Elias and his zig zag jive" Bobby had a vast knowledge of music.

"Well, I never!" Replied the tailor.

OUTSIDE ABBEY ROAD STUDIOS

The team were all having pictures done in various poses by The World photographers as they crossed the zebra crossing, made famous by The Beatles.

INSIDE ABBEY ROAD STUDIOS

The team were all together in front of microphones. The famous rock band The Know and an orchestra, were all set up.

"Now just so you know how it all works, these are the final scenes we will do. They will be mixed with all the stuff we did outside here, and at your club. The song is already recorded now. These scenes will be infill scenes between the other stuff. So, we'll get a few close ups and shoot you all together from different angles. Then we'll have a music video to edit together with the song. Right then! I will shout action, then you follow the conductors lead and sing the song. Right! Sound speed!" Shouted the music video director.

"Sound speed!" Shouted the Sound recordist.

"And... Action!" Shouted the music video director.

The conductor signalled the musicians and they all started to play. Then the players, coaches, management and all the other Wickside staff, including the tea lady, the bus driver, the canteen ladies, the groundsman, the office staff, the cleaners and the lead singer of The Know, started to sing the song.

DOES ANYBODY KNOW HOW LONG THE TRAIN WILL BE

I NEED TO GET TO WICKSIDE AND THE GAMES AT THREE

GOT MY WICKSIDE SHIRT ON LOVE THE SMELL OF THE GRASS.

THE TIN SOLDIERS ARE HERE ALL HAVING A LAUGH.

COME ON WICKSIDE YOU'RE OUR TEAM

COME ON WICKSIDE GIVE US THE DREAM

COME ON WICKSIDE WE'RE ON THE UP

COME ON WICKSIDE WIN US THE CUP.

A MUDDY FIELD A GRACEFUL TOUCH A HEAD OF THE BALL

IF WE WANT NO GOALS FROM THEM WE'LL HAVE TO GIVE IT OUR ALL

LET'S WIN THIS MATCH AND TAKE THE HEAT

NO EXTRA TIME NO PENALTIES.

COME ON WICKSIDE

YOU'RE OUR TEAM

COME ON WICKSIDE

GIVE US THE DREAM

COME ON WICKSIDE

WIN US THE CUP

COME ON WICKSIDE

WE LOVE YOU.

WHAT ABOUT ENGLAND THE WORLD CUPS HERE

WITH A TIN SOLDIER SPIRIT AND A BEER

THEY CAN BEAT THEM ALL AND BRING IT BACK HERE

AND THEN WELL ALL HAVE PLENTY TO CHEER

COME ON ENGLAND

YOU'RE OUR TEAM

COME ON ENGLAND

GIVE US THE DREAM

COME ON ENGLAND

WIN THE WORLD CUP

COME ON ENGLAND

WE LOVE YOU.

CHAPTER XVIII
THEY THINK IT'S ALL OVER

WEMBLEY STADIUM

The Wembley commentary gantry was full of commentators from around the world, all talking with gusto and in the common commentary tone of their respective languages.

"And here we are on a glorious sunny afternoon at Wembley to see what can only be described as an extraordinary game. This game being played in extraordinary circumstances. Division one Artillery Football Club, versus Wickside Football Club, who play five leagues below Artillery in non-league. This AF cup final is being played almost two weeks earlier than usual, due to the upcoming world cup. There is one more Division one game to play where Artillery could finish champions and gain a place in the European champions cup. It's been such a fantastic, unexpected season so far both clubs. You couldn't make this up. It's the stuff of dreams and this is why we love this beautiful game. The Football Game! It's back to the studio." Alan Bexhill said with an air of exuberance.

WEMBLEY HOME CHANGING ROOMS

The Artillery manager Davide Gramcer was addressing his

team.

"We must not underestimate them. We must not be complacent. We must respect them, but we must do our jobs. Go out there and win this game by playing our normal game. We will have to defend more. They play with the ball on the floor, much like us, but they interchange this frequently with long balls. So, bare this in mind. Our fans demand that we win this trophy. Forget the league today. I demand you win this trophy. This is the AF cup final so let's go and win the game!" Davide Gramcer encouraged his team in his heavy Belgian accent.

The Artillery players were pumped up and started to get up and walk out.

WEMBLEY AWAY CHANGING ROOMS

Bobby was standing addressing his players and staff.

"Well, here we are boys. Who would have thought it? We deserve to be here now. We have earned it. We have earned the right to be here. The sacrifices we have all made, to be professional footballers, have led us to this point. The AF cup final. Against Artillery. At Wembley. In front of the world. We have even filled our allocated capacity as people have flocked here to cheer us on, some of them aren't even Wickside fans. We've caught the imagination of the people. We have our family and friends here watching and even more people are watching at home or in the pub, and around the world. All I can say now is go out there and make them and yourselves proud. Forget anything else, you just go out there and give it your best shot. Attack and defend for your lives. Let's go!" Bobby clapped his hands three times.

Everybody rose as one.

"ATTACK!" Shouted the Wickside attack.

"DEFEND!" Responded the Wickside defence.

"ATTACK!" Shouted the Wickside attack, louder this time.

"DEFEND!" Responded the Wickside defence, even louder.

"Well done mate. I bet the gaffer's looking down at us now, eh?" Billy stared intently into Bobby's eyes. His own eyes slightly moist, at the memory of their old Manager, that had taught them everything that was needed to get them both to this point.

"Couldn't have done it without you Bill..." They embraced for a few short seconds then broke away and shook hands.

Bobby thought for a split second that he saw a ghost of their old manager Neil Glover, standing in the corner of the dressing room, smiling at them both. He looked again but Neil was gone.

"Let's do it for the boss!" Shouted Bobby, his eyes welling up with emotion.

WEMBLEY PITCH

The ground was full. The crowd were ecstatic as the two teams were about to walk out. The referee stopped the two managers by the AF cup where it was stood on a plinth. The band of the Coldstream Guards that had been playing, marched off of the pitch, past them all. Bobby Gorman and the Davide Gramcer embraced for a few seconds. The referee gave them the nod. They carried on leading their teams out. The teams lined up and were greeted by the Duke of Kent. They all shook hands with each other and so did the teams and referees and linesmen. The pitch cleared, leaving the players and referee. Everybody took their positions. The referee took a coin from his pocket. He asked who called heads or tails. Wickside won the toss. The referee placed the ball on the centre circle spot. The two captains took their positions. Then referee blew for kick off. There was split second of almost silence before the crowded roared. The Wickside captain kicked off.

00:01

"Come on Wickside!" Shouted Bobby.

"And here we go. Wickside kick off and immediately go on the attack and have taken Artillery by surprise! Oh! Wickside hit the bar! My word Artillery caught napping there. The ball comes back into play but is put clear and goes out for a throw in. We're in for some game here. Little Wickside taking no prisoners against the mighty Artillery. It's David versus Goliath here right now and the rock from the slingshot just misses!" Shouted Alan Bexhill.

00:10

Bobby and Billy both held their faces in disbelief. The Wickside crowd were roaring their team on, a small sea of black and red stripes, surrounded by an ocean of Red and white of Artillery fans. Lots of other fans of other teams were there enjoying the occasion and having banter with the real Wickside fans.

"Well done lads let's keep this up!" shouted Louis.

Dean took the throw and launched it long into the opposition area.

"I'm up!" Shouted Richard Jones.

The ball hit Richard's head and flew into the Artillery goal. The Wickside players mobbed and jumped all over him. The Artillery goalkeeper berated his defence. Billy Thorpe jumped high into the air then embraced Bobby and the rest of the bench, but they quickly calmed down as Bobby was almost on the pitch urging his players to calm down and get back in to position.

00:29

"Oh, Wickside have scored a fantastic goal! The Wickside defender Richard Jones rose majestically above everybody and directed the ball into the net. The Artillery manager is furious, but the Wickside players are ecstatic. The Wickside manager hardly celebrates and is shouting at his players to calm down. One nil Wickside with barely thirty seconds on the clock!" Alan Bexhill could hardly breathe with excitement.

"Come on lads! Let's calm down and keep it going! Screw your loaves now, screw your loaves! We have still got the whole game to play!" Louis shouted the phrase that he had picked up from Bobby, warrior like, with his hands firmly cupped to his mouth, to get as much amplification as possible.

Bobby's family and friends were in an executive box. They were all cheering. Pat and Albert embraced but Albert had to get back into his wheelchair. Pat and Liz helped him.

The players took their positions for the re-start.

WEMBLEY AWAY CHANGING ROOMS – HALF TIME

Bobby was addressing the players. Some players were getting rub downs, some were laying down and some were sitting.

"Right boys all I can say is well done! Half time and we're still one nil up. It's taking its toll though, I can see that. We need to try and conserve energy. Try not to chase too many lost causes. I know you're all so up for it and I don't want to change things just yet. "Bobby said as calmly as he could with the excitement that was running through his whole body.

"Keep it tight boys, don't sit too far back. Keep your eye out for their two wingers. They're bloody fast, as you've found out. Only forty-five minutes left now boys!" Billy said with a surprisingly amount of calmness.

"Johnny, I want you to sit in front of the defence this half and protect and sweep up. David, take your time with any goal kicks and the rest of you take your time with corners and throws while we're in front. You know what I mean!" Bobby demanded an answer.

"Yes boss." Everyone shouted. They did not need reminding to respond louder on this occasion.

"Right! Let's get out there and do this!" Shouted Bobby.

The Wickside players and staff were shouting and cajoling one another.

WEMBLEY PITCH

Both sets of players were in position. The referee blew his whistle and the game kicked off. The crowd erupted with cheers for their respective teams.

45:00

"*And as the referee blows the whistle the crowd has gone nuts here. The Artillery fans urging their team to perform better and the Wickside fans are just having a ball as their team are one nil up against a team in the top flight who are chasing the title. Artillery are on the attack here. They've bamboozled the Wickside defence and oh… A rocket in the top corner by the Belgian Henry Terriere to break Wickside 's hearts. One - one. Game on!*" Roared Alan Bexhill.

"They caught us asleep for fuck's sake. Wake up boys, for fuck's sake wake up." Screamed Louis who did not swear that much but he feared what Bobby and Billy would think.

"For fuck's sake Ellis! What were you doing?" Shouted Richard.

"I thought you were picking it up!" Shouted back Ellis, the young left sided centre half.

"I shouted for you to get it!" Shouted Richard, berating his young protégé

"I didn't fucking hear you! For fuck's sake!" Shouted Ellis, looking to the sky pondering the mix up.

"Oi! Stop fucking bitching and get on with it!" Bobby had his hands cupped to his mouth.

WEMBLEY DIRECTORS BOX

"I can't believe it!" Shouted Vicky.

"I bloody can! Them two fucked that right up. They were both still in the fucking changing room!" Albert said, admonishing the two centre halves at what he and the watching millions had clearly seen as a massive cock up between the two central defenders.

"They need to wake up, the lot of 'em!" Shouted Anabel.

WEMBLEY PITCH

69:00

"Right, that's it I'm gonna make the change and ..." Bobby saw something bad,

"Hang on what the fuck happened there?" Billy saw it too,

"Fuck! They both look hurt..." Bobby looked very concerned.

"Get on there! Now!" Shouted Billy towards Paul the Physio.

"On my way!" The physio ran onto the pitch towards the Wickside goal.

"It's OK boys. It does not look that bad." Louis said trying to keep his team calm.

"They'll have to get off the pitch lad." Said the referee.

Paul the physio arrived.

"Clash of heads physio. They're both knocked out. The goalies got a nasty gash, and the defenders nose looks broken. They can't play on..." The referee had spoken.

The physio reached into his bag and pulled out a small bottle of smelling salts. He unscrewed the cap off and held it under the nose of David. He woke up almost immediately. Paul held the bottle under Richard's nose. He woke groggily and pushed the bottle away.

"How you both feeling? David how many fingers am I holding up?" Asked Paul holding up his white, rubber gloved hand.

"Four. No three. No two..." Responded David, very incoherently

"You'll have to come off son. Sorry..." Paul said dejectedly.

"I'm alright!" Insisted David

David got up but couldn't stand straight. The physio got up and helped him off to the back of the goal.

"Sit down and stay there!" Paul said loudly.

Paul walked back to Richard.

"I think your nose is broke mate. How many fingers am I holding up?" Paul held up three fingers.

"Three, but it's a bit blurry. I need to stay on mate. Let me stay on please..."

He stood up straight.

"Let me see if I can run it off..." His nose started to bleed.

"Sorry son. I think you need to get them both off to the hospital..." Said the referee sadly.

The St Johns ambulance stretcher bearers arrived on the scene.

"Get the goalie off please lads. I'll deal with this one..." The physio said with authority.

"Right you are." Said the St johns ambulanceman, sternly.

Paul pulled out some cotton wool from his first aid kit and passed it to Richard.

"Get off the pitch, hold that under your nose and sit down and tilt your head forward." Paul said as he ushered Richard of the pitch.

"I thought it was backwards?" the referee remarked.

"No ref..." Paul gave the referee a knowing look.

Richard retched then a stream of vomit ejected from his mouth.

"He is definitely off." The referee said shaking his head.

"Yep!" Paul signalled to the bench. He held up two fingers up and signalled towards the bench to make a substitution.

"Bollocks! Get Liam and Darren on... Now! We'll go three at the back. Pull Dean across to form the three. Put Liam on the wing." Bobby's thoughts raced through a new formation to counter the loss of Richard.

"It's a risk mate..." Billy counselled Bobby, as was his responsibility, like a Consigliere to his Don.

"No choice mate... Let's do it. Talk to them and I'll pull Louis over to relay it." Bobby wasn't in the mood for being counselled

Billy ran back to the bench. The two young boys looked shocked as David was carried past on the stretcher and Richard walked slowly past. He threw up a mixture of vomit and blood. Both sets of fans were standing and applauding the injured players. The players from both teams looked shocked.

"Take your chance boys. Do those two proud!" Billy pointed towards the injured players.

Liam and Darren got their kit on quickly. Bobby was deep in conversation with his captain. They both nodded at each other. Louis jogged off. He stopped to talk to the referee then called the players over. The referee looked towards the bench.

"You ready then boys. This is your chance to shine. Go and enjoy it. Make it count for those two poor sods." Bobby was upset at the site of his two most trusted players whose names were always two of the first on the team sheet.

The two boys were ready. Bobby gave the thumbs up to the referee. The referee ran over.

"Ok boys no chains or earrings?" asked the referee.

The boys both shook their heads nervously.

"Let's check the bottoms of your boots and your studs then." The referee was having to cajole the two young players.

They both took turns in lifting the boots for the referee to check. The referee let them on to the pitch. Darren ran towards his goal and Liam took his position on the left wing. The whole crowd gave them both a round of applause. Both sets of fans were acknowledging their youth and the situation that they were in.

"The ball originally went out for a Wickside goal kick after that horrific clash of heads between the two Wickside players. I really feel for them to get injured and having to go off in such a momentous occasion. The goalie barely conscious and the defender with what I suspect to be a broken nose and concussion. This has given two of Wickside 's youngest players such an opportunity here now. So, the young goalie Darren Leech, nephew of Bobby Gorman and cousin of Liam, gets his first kick of the game already and sends it high up towards the opposing goal. There must be at least seven or eight minutes of extra time to come now. What a proud moment for the Gorman family here with the managers son Liam Gorman coming on too in such a momentous occasion. Gorman forced to bring in these two due to an exodus of players leaving for their rival Seaford Way in the summer when the new lottery winning owner took charge, offering over the top wages. I can't say too much as there is an ongoing investigation into the affairs of that club and chairman." Alan Bexhill informed the watching

millions all over the world.

95:46

"The referee takes a quick look at his watch as the corner is thrown in by the young Liam Gorman. Son of the manager Bobby Gorman. Such a proud day for both father and son whatever the outcome... What a long throw right into the mix and oh... The Belgian Artillery defender Didier Huit has brought down one of the Wickside players and it looks very much like a penalty. The Wickside fans are screaming for it... But no! The referee has awarded an indirect free kick just outside the box. Bobby Gorman and Billy Thorpe are raging down there! They believe it to be a penalty!" Alan Bexhill also believed it to be a penalty.

"Get up, get up." Bobby was shouting furiously at Darren to get up towards the opposing goal.

Wickside were squaring up to take the kick. Darren ran towards the other players. Tony floated the ball in from the left and Darren rose high to meet it. The ball made contact with his head and shot straight into the bar and cannoned back down into the throng of players. Liam got his foot under the ball as it landed. The ball bounced back up into the roof of the net. The Wickside players all celebrated ecstatically and tried to grab Liam, but he was off running towards his proud father on the touch line. They embraced hard.

"The two young substitutes combine to score what could be the winner as there must only be two minutes left! The young goalie almost scored but as it came back into play that young man Liam Gorman was there and quickest to react. What a lovely moment as the father and son embrace on the touchline. They are duly mobbed by the rest of the team! Father and Son now both legends in their own right at this club. Wonderful, wonderful Wickside! The Wickside fans are in heaven right now. And I have a lump in my throat again! Two one the score!" Alan Bexhill had never been

so emotional whilst commentating.

"I love you son!" Bobby squeezed his son so hard he could hardly breathe.

"I love you too dad..." Liam struggled to get his words out.

The rest of the team and the Wickside bench mobbed the embracing father and son.

"Come on ref the game needs to re-start." Shouted the normally cool, calm and collected Davide Gramcer.

"Right lads come on, were not finished yet!" The referee shouted at the melee of celebrating Wickside players and coaching staff as he came running over.

They all started to break away for the re-start.

"Come on lads we can do this!" Screamed Bobby.

"The Wickside players and Artillery players take their positions for the re-start. Artillery in possession. Jacquard Debend, one of the Belgian contingent is on the run and has gone through the Wickside midfield. Too many have gone to ground trying to take him out, but he is riding every challenge here and is through on goal, one on one with the young keeper who has rushed out from his goal and took Debend down. I'm sure he got his fingers to the ball... Oh... The referee has pointed to the spot! The young goalie furious! Signalling that he got the ball first but the ref's having none of it! The Wickside fans are furious... Booing the ref! I think he may have got this one wrong you know..." Alan Bexhill knew full well that the referee had got it wrong. But was trying to stay as much on the fence as he could, to remain in impartial.

The referee sent everyone away and pulled the yellow card from his pocket, showing it to a distraught Darren Leech.

"Yellow card. If he deems it to be a penalty it must be at least a yellow. Now the Artillery striker Henry Terriere lines up. The referee blows ... Bang! In the top left corner for the equaliser. This game can only have a minute left, maybe another minute for the

goals but it looks like we are heading for penalties!" Alan Bexhill sounded very despondent.

The Wickside players looked dejected.

"Come on lads it's not over yet! Get with it! Get with it! Attack attack" Fucking go for it now, go for it." Bobby eyes were bulging out of his head and veins were popping out of his temples.

"The gaffers saying go for it! So, let's fucking go for it. The kick off drill. You got it?" Screamed Louis

Tony nodded. Louis rolled the ball to Tony then made a run. Tony rolled the ball onto his foot then took a small chip then volleyed it towards Louis, who had run through towards the goal. The others saw what was going on and recognised the drill. Louis turned his back on goal and chested the ball down and put it through on goal. Liam blasted the ball, but it hit the bar so hard that it bounced straight towards the halfway line. The ball was picked up by Henry Terriere, who was on his own as most of the Wickside team were high up apart from Rory Maloney, who played Terriere on side. His Artillery teammate Trevor Parker was also running in on goal, wide to his right.

"And Terriere is onside with only the keeper to beat. The young keeper Leech holding his ground this time as he is on a yellow. Terriere passes the ball out wide to the right to the on running Parker... Parker smashes the ball high into the Wickside net! With surely the last kick of the game Parker has broken Wickside's hearts! An unselfish move on the part of Terriere who probably could have scored, but his move wrongfooted the keeper and left it on a plate for Parker" Alan Bexhill could not believe what he had just seen.

"Oh, fuckin hell!" Bobby's voice cracked with emotion. Tears welled up in his eyes. He looked to the sky for a split second and then looked back to the pitch.

The referee put the whistle to his lips and blew hard for full time.

"And that's it! It's all over! Wickside undone right at the end. Artillery's quality just shading it right at the end of an unbelievable fantasy football odyssey of an AF cup run for Wickside. Some of the Wickside players are in tears. Fair play to most of the Artillery players who are embracing the nearest Wickside player to them. Bobby Gorman and Billy Thorpe are on the pitch consoling their players too. Davide Gramcer is straight over to Bobby Gorman, and they embrace. Fair play to the Belgian Gramcer who since coming to the Artillery has brought a few Belgian players to the club and created a fantastic blend of Belgian youth and English experience. They both know how special today has been. Oh, what a day what a game. I feel privileged to have seen this today but commiserations to Wickside Football Club." Alan Bexhill knew that he and the millions of fans watching from around the world had just witnessed something special that day.

Bobby called over the team and got them into a huddle.

"You boys have done what I asked and made me so proud. Thank you all. We got here and we could not have done anymore. Listen to those fans. Even the Artillery fans are cheering us!"

"WICKSIDE! WICKSIDE! WICKSIDE! WICKSIDE!" Shouted the whole Wembley crowd in unison. Wickside and Artillery fans alike.

"Now let's get out there, dry our eyes and applaud them all!"

They broke from their huddle.

The Artillery captain Steve Adamson came running over to them all.

"I have asked if you could all come up with me to get the cup, but they won't allow it. They said I can take the captain and manager. What do you think Mr Gorman?" asked Steve

Adamson. He had never played in such an emotional game and knew how close the giants of the first division had come to losing to their non-league counterparts.

"I think that's a wonderful gesture. Thank you. I won't, but our captain will gladly take up your offer." Bobby could not face it but felt Louis should do.

"I don't know boss... No." Louis didn't feel comfortable going without his teammates.

"You get up there with them and represent us all. That's an order! We'll go and get our runners up medals together then you'll go up with them." Bobby was not taking no for an answer.

"Ok boss." Louis said looking to the floor.

"You are all winners. I love you all. This was an amazing day for us all and football! Are you sure you will not join us Mr Gorman?"

"No. It's not about me it's about all of you players."

"Go on boss!" Shouted Darren.

"No. I'll get more pleasure watching. Now that's the end of it. Let's go and thank our fans!" Bobby walked off waving and leading his players away.

"I think you have a few million more fans today!" Chuckled Steve Adamson.

THE WEMBLEY STEPS

The Wickside players walked up the thirty-nine steps and round to the presentation area. They shook hands with all the dignitaries and the queen's cousin, Viscount Lyons of Essex, presented them with the runners up medals to deafening cheers from the whole crowd. The queen's cousin leaned down towards Bobby and whispered in his ear as they shook hands.

"You have made the world a better place today. I feel like giving you the bloody cup! That was the best game of football I have ever seen... And I'm a Man Utd supporter!" chuckled the Viscount.

"That's a shame you're a United supporter. I'm sure Queen Liz, that's my mums name by the way, wasn't happy with you ending up that way but I'm sure she's happy today, as I know she's Artillery!" Bobby moved away, smiling at the Viscount who was cracking up with laughter.

The Viscount handed Bobby his runners up medal.

"Thank you, sir!" Bobby said through gritted teeth as he thought of it as a loser's medal.

Another picture that the press photographers captured that would immortalise yet another fine historical moment in football.

BELOW THE PRESENTATION AREA

The Artillery players were all shouting and celebrating. They stopped as the Wickside players started coming back down the stairs with their runners up medals in their hands. The Artillery players started shaking their hands and embracing them.

"You are all a credit to the game of football. I am proud to say I played this game against you today. You have made this a day that will never ever be forgotten. I will go at the back and you..." Davide Gramcer pointed to the Wickside captain Louis Ngunde.

"You will lead us all out with my captain. OK?" Davide was telling Louis, rather than asking him.

"Yes. Are you sure lads... Boss?" He looked to Bobby for approval.

Louis now loved Bobby like another father because he had shown so much faith in him when he took over, and when all the Seaford Way stuff was going on.

"Yes, go for it you Wally! Mr Gramcer, will you wait until I give you the nod from down there, please? I want us all to see this..." Bobby wanted to give himself and the team enough time to get back on to the pitch to watch the historical moment.

"Of course, Bobby. Please... Call me Davide." Davide felt embarrassed as he felt in awe of Bobby for so many reasons. Davide had been a lower league player in France and had clawed his way to the top of football having started his management career in non-league football too.

"I'll be by the dugout." Bobby walked over to Davide and hugged him and patted him on the back as Bobby had done his homework on Davide and knew that he had worked his way up to where he was right now. He had nothing but respect for his French counterpart.

"Ok. Well done, Bobby, you are a credit to the game, and I will forever be in debt to you for what I have learnt from you today. You have made history today and I have been lucky enough to have been part of it. What we do in life, echoes an eternity no?" Davide hoped that Bobby would know the line that he was referencing, from one of his all-time favourite films.

Bobby broke away and looked into Davide's eyes.

"Gladiator. One of my favourites. Thanks Davide. Let's stay in touch. I might try and loan a few off you for next season! "Chuckled Bobby.

Davide Gramcer laughed loudly. His players looked a bit surprised as he rarely laughed. He shook Bobby's hand. Bobby gave him one more hug and moved away and looked at his players.

"Right boys let's get down there!" Bobby shouted.

The Wickside players walked down. When they got to the dugout, the Artillery manager gave the nod to both captains. They began to walk up the steps to a roar of appreciation from the crowd. They all received their medals. Viscount Lyons handed the Artillery captain Steve Adamson the AF cup. He kissed it and held it by one of the handles so that Louis could hold the cup by the other handle.

"After three. One. Two. Three!" shouted Adamson.

They both lifted the cup. The crowd went wild, and fireworks started to go off. They passed the cup along to the rest of the players who were all going wild. Louis was subdued.

WEMBLEY PITCH

Bobby had tears in his eyes and was clapping hard.

EPILOGUE

ALBERT AND LIZ'S KITCHEN - ONE WEEK LATER

Albert was sitting at the kitchen table in his wheelchair. He was dressed in a pair of brown trousers and a white vest. He was reading The World newspaper. He drank some tea then took a bite of one of the slices of toast and marmalade that he had on his small plate. Both things that he should not have been having. At least the tea only had one sugar in it he thought. Liz was out, so his strict diet regime since his second heart attack could be forgotten briefly, for a few moments of bliss from one of his favourite breakfasts. His beaten-up old transistor radio, that was still working just about after all those years since he bought it just before Bobby was born, was on the table. The voice of Alan Bexhill crackled through the airwaves.

"And now for the sport. Artillery were crowned Division one champions last night, winning the league by only two points in one of the closest and unexpected title races ever seen, are double winners again after winning the AF cup last Saturday. Congratulations to the club and their fans. And with some breaking news just in there is an amazing and unprecedented situation after a joint press release by the AF and EUFA. The main points are that because Artillery have qualified for the Champions Cup after becoming league champions, a decision had to be made on what happened to the EUFA cup place that comes with winning the AF cup which Artillery now hold. It was widely expected that

the due to Wickside being a small club, the EUFA cup spot would go to seventh placed team in the league, which this year was Middleton after a great season after winning promotion from the second tier. But as confirmed in the press release just moments ago, valiant AF cup runners up, Wickside FC, The Tin Soldiers now find themselves in the EUFA cup next season. This amazing story just keeps on giving." Chuckled Jimmy Bullhill.

Albert chuckled to himself and pumped his fist slightly while he was still reading his newspaper.

"Yes!"

Liz came in through the front door, straight into the kitchen. Albert quickly stuffed the last slice of marmalade on toast into his mouth.

What you getting so excited about? I heard you thorough door. You know what the doctor said…"

"Our boys' team have only got into Europe!" Albert spoke with his mouth full.

"What did you say? Europe? How? Who they got?" Liz asked excitedly.

Albert swallowed hard and took a sip of his tea.

"I dunno…Europe away…" Albert looked out of the window wistfully with a smile and a tear in his eye.

Printed in Great Britain
by Amazon

40196969R00228